1866-1991

125th

ANNIVERSARY

MAKING
GOOD

MAKING GOOD

Loren Singer

Henry Holt and Company
New York

For their assistance with some of the historical and
technical aspects of this novel, I would like to thank
James W. and Barbara N. Johnson and Fred M. Kleeberg.

Copyright © 1991 by Loren Singer
All rights reserved, including the right to reproduce
this book or portions thereof in any form.
Published by Henry Holt and Company, Inc.,
115 West 18th Street, New York, New York 10011
Published in Canada by Fitzhenry and Whiteside Limited,
195 Allstate Parkway, Markham, Ontario L3R 4T8

Library of Congress Cataloging-in-Publication Data
Singer, Loren.
        Making good / Loren Singer. — 1st ed.
        p.   cm.
        I.   Title.
PS3569.I545M35   1991
813'.54—dc20   91-21080
                                                CIP

ISBN: 0-8050-1223-0

Henry Holt books are available at special discounts for bulk purchases for sales promotions, premiums, fund
raising, or educational use. Special editions or book excerpts can also be created to specification.
For details contact: Special Sales Director,
Henry Holt and Company, Inc., 115 West 18th Street,
New York, New York 10011

First Edition—1991

Book design by Claire Naylon Vaccaro

Printed in the United States of America
Recognizing the importance of preserving the written word, Henry Holt and Company, Inc.,
by policy, prints all of its first editions on acid-free paper.

1   3   5   7   9   10   8   6   4   2

In Memoriam
Sarah J. Rosenstadt
Ruth L. Singer

1.

November twelfth of this year is the Tenth year since 855th Service Company reported itself "all present or accounted for" at its first formation. This unique outfit has never held a Reunion except as a part of Seventh Army, as far as we know, and any of us there were ignored. "What the blankety-blank company was that, mess-kit repair?" (Smile) Never mind that, your correspondent perceives a general interest in a Reunion of our own. It isn't a craving, but It's There judging by the response so far. If there's any chance that You will join us, drop the enclosed card in the mail to your old company clerk,
      Wm. E. "Billy" Pattison

The 855th Service Company was first called to attention in November of 1945.

I do not remember good weather during that time in the army. There were fine days, but I associate the year with threatening skies, clouds lying low along the horizon, and a promise of damp and discomfort. On any day at all, there was a pall of black smoke within view.

Captain Alpheus Earley came out on the steps of the casern with two officers, First Lieutenants Abraham Berdichevsky and Len C. Proudfoot. First Sergeant Walter Pankow called the roll and shaped us into ragged ranks.

Earley introduced himself and the others.

Merolla, standing next to me, said in an undertone as he did so, "From out of my ass, the sun shines." I ignored the comment as pointedly as I could, setting my jaw and concentrating all of my attention upon Earley.

Twilight had settled upon this town, a town like so many others I had seen en route from Normandy. Of the sixteenth-century church that once had dominated its central square, three-quarters of the tower was intact; the rest was a heap of beveled stones beside it.

Earley could not have been more than thirty years old, but there was the sense of many more years about him. The dim light from the portico of the casern brought cheekbone and nose and the line of his jaw into dark relief and cast a shadow lengthier than his actual height before us.

"I don't know whether I should welcome you or sympathize," he said. "I know nobody volunteered for what will be a very dirty job."

There were scattered groans.

"Not in the usual sense," he went on. "You will be living a lot better than the people around you. You won't be cleaning latrines or pulling garbage detail. And you could say—I could say—that you have an opportunity to make some sense, to see some justification of what we took part in.

"I hope you will be interested in your assignment. I hope it will be more meaningful than any other experience you ever had, because what you are going to be doing is righting a wrong. A great many wrongs. You will all have a part to play, an important part. How well you do your job will show people one reason for fighting this war.

"We are the first company of this kind to be organized. Our mission is to restore to their owners the property and belongings taken from them by the government. There will be other companies like this one that will learn from what we do. They'll profit from our mistakes. That's always the way it is. But if we are honest and efficient and do our best, nobody will find any fault with us. If we aren't, nobody will have to. I'll be there first.

"I'm asking for your cooperation and your loyalty and a lot of hard and thankless work, not for me, but for your country and your comrades who are not here.

"End speech. Sergeant Pankow will assign you to your sections and your billets. Each one of you will meet with me in the course of the next few days to talk about whatever you want to, except shipping out. All of you are on duty here for the next six months. No exceptions no matter how many points you have."

There was a scattering of boos.

"Ain't that the shits," Merolla said. "Wherever I go I get fucked."

I had listened to Earley without extracting much meaning from his words. My hearing was selective. I understood that there would be no drudgery. That was satisfactory. The mention of wrongs and injustices and the dead was of little interest, except as I associated it with Earley's appearance and his character. A Humane Officer was easier to live with than a martinet.

"Ee-valuation Section," Walter Pankow bellowed. He read off a list of names that included mine. I picked up my duffel and joined the group. I was designated section leader.

There were six sections. Formed up, we straggled into the casern. In addition to Evaluation and Appraisal, there were Translation and Interpretation, Publication and Distribution, Documentation and Preliminary Adjudication, Security, and Transport.

Merolla, I was pleased to see, went to Transport.

There were five others with me in Evaluation. We made up our beds and exchanged background information. Tom Arquette had had an antique shop in New Orleans. Jerome Silberglitt had been a stone setter in a ring factory in New York. Charlie Scibetta had worked in a furniture store in Chicago. John Kowalski was a plating inspector at a silver company in Meriden, Connecticut. Ed Wersba had been an art student and a guide at the Museum of Art in Toledo, Ohio. I mentioned the pawnshop. I said that I had been the assistant manager. Had there been such a title for the job, it would have been mine.

My uncle had found the job for me. A great bit of good fortune in 1939 in that afflicted industrial town. When my great-aunt asked what kind of a business Garside and Kluckhohn was, he told her they did "short-term financing." A kind of private bank, she assumed.

Actually, of course, it was a pawnshop with the three traditional golden balls over the door, very scabrous ones, these, and the lettering on the two show windows, GARSIDE AND KLUCKHOHN, MONEY TO LOAN.

Kluckhohn had been dead for three years. Leo Garside made a point of showing me how well he had treated Kluckhohn's widow. I didn't understand the settlement he had made at all, but he took me over it point by point. He was a strange man, Garside. Odd.

When I think that, I immediately recall the tray of rings taken in pawn from members of fraternal societies. Odd Fellows, Masons, Redmen, Foresters, Elks. And the class rings, motto after motto that I tried to translate with my high school Latin. *Nisi dominus frustra; lux et veritas; vitam impendere vero.*

Then the rest of it. Medals, heirlooms, carpenters' and mechanics' tools, musical instruments, watches, books in fine bindings, meerschaum pipes, picture frames, luggage, all with a patina of importance upon them. Garside impressed on me the necessity of opening all suitcases and trunks. Once he had found a fetus inside. "Looked like a dried-out chicken," he said, watching me closely.

That inventory bred cynicism, misanthropy, contempt, impassiveness, and limited emotional response. I do feel emotion. I am occasionally sentimental. I can be touched, but there must be juxtaposition, say of loveliness and misery, physical beauty and a wretched state, if I am to respond. This in spite of Garside and Kluckhohn, although at the time I thought I was privileged to enter into the real world at such an age.

Our customers were service people by and large. Taxi drivers, hotel porters and bellhops, police and firemen, railroad brakemen, conductors or yard laborers, deckhands off the lake boats, waitresses, maids, bartenders, musicians. These last were not broken virtuosos, but merely fiddlers or horn players who drank and couldn't stay away from a dice game.

Some of our regulars must have lived in the middle class but they did not garden or get up at seven, or look at the child's report card and pat him on the head. Some had a place in a family structure; some of them were related to local powers or politicians. They had relatives who would lend money when they were in corners, jams, had problems, were up against it, in the middle or at the end of their ropes, but the relatives never satisfied their requirements. Also they did not escape without damage to their egos and to their bodies. They would get their fifty dollars, and a punch in the mouth to go with it after the family discussion. There was nothing much to be gained by either the lender or the borrower.

This was not true at Garside and Kluckhohn. The lender made money. The borrower retained his independence, if the pledge had any value. Also he had a future. He had a pawn ticket and could reclaim his possession, his heirloom, whenever his luck changed, or his ship came in, or he had a hot streak.

In the eighteen months I worked for Garside that happened twice: B. Wyczynski came for a silver frame with his mother's picture in it. The picture was a black-and-white cabinet photograph that had been tinted with cotton swabs by some dime-store artist. We did not have the picture. Actually, we did have it, but we had been using it on the pistol range as a target. There were a number of others in the back of the place where we took our practice. That was where I learned to shoot and how to handle all sorts of weapons, from little Colt revolvers to Mauser rifles.

B. Wyczynski was angry, but it would have been worse if I had given him the picture. That crossed my mind. He had the same brutish expression that the old woman had.

The other redeemer I could remember if I chose, but it's not important, unless one believes in man's ability to reform, change his habits, overcome his weaknesses, whatever.

So B. Wyczynski was very angry, but what is surprising is how quickly he calmed down when I showed him our record of the pledge with no mention of the picture itself. This showing of the record is, of course, preposterous but always accepted in the end. Garside was masterly at it. He could shout as loudly as any of his customers and swear endlessly before pausing for breath. He could be obscene in at least five languages besides English—Polish, Italian, German, Yiddish, and Russian—and, as I later learned, with a surprisingly accurate accent in all of them. He was a natural linguist with a very good ear, but without discrimination. He never knew anything about good speech in any language. For Garside, these rudimentary language skills were not knowledge gained for its own sake, but only instruments to help him in his business, to solve certain specific problems. Like the billy in his back pocket, the .38 with the two-inch barrel and no front sight in the holster behind his left hip, and the lamp with the complex lens and housing that he used to show diamonds.

There was a ritual when he switched it on. That included a lecture on the power of the bulb inside and how it refracted the facets of the stone he was showing so you could see how beautifully cut it was. This to a barge hand from Nebraska who was now engaged to a Swedish housemaid from the North Side who had met him on the Saturday night "Moonlight Cruise, 3 hrs 3." It departed from the foot of Canal Street at eight and returned, after all that dancing, at eleven.

We were open until midnight on Saturdays for just such a reason, to receive two enchanted lovers who had found each other as they stared at the moon shimmering on the oily waters of the bay.

One hundred points to the carat. This was a thirty-pointer in a "Tiffany" setting. He showed them the prongs holding the gem. Eighteen-karat gold with a platinum top. Garside made it sound like they could hold up a bridge. And the stone. Actually someone had been in that very day and said he'd be back to pay cash for it before midnight. That was why we were open.

I yawned and rubbed my eyes.

Blue-white in color. The finest quality, without a flaw. Through the loupe he was using. Look at the depth it has. She rubbed it on her sleeve. Garside shook his head.

"You clean it with ammonia and water and a toothbrush," he said, "that's all it needs, and don't make any marks on glass with it. With a gem like this you don't have to prove anything."

She looked at him and he looked at her, and they didn't withdraw for a conference. That was the sign. Usually it took the two of them supporting each other to stammer out their thank-yous and "it's more than we wanted to pay," or "we have to think it over," or "we have to wait until the bank opens." He had a money belt on.

Garside looked at his pocket watch, a flat gold one on a handsome chain. It never kept time. It was, however, very impressive, something a plenipotentiary might have carried.

"Why don't you just keep it over the weekend," he said. "I trust you. Have it appraised someplace—cost you twenty dollars to do that, but then you'll be sure it's what you want. They'll tell you what it's worth. Take it to Cornelissen's."

Cornelissen was the jeweler who sold to the town's elite. Sterling silver baby cups, little strings of matched pearls, ugly brooches. Solitaires. These two would never have the nerve to look in his window. Cornelissen had a mosaic in there that he changed every month. It was made up of loose stones, a hundred and forty diamonds, twenty-eight emeralds, thirty rubies, and a couple of chrysoberyls. He made storks and butterflies and bees and "vahses."

They would never have done it. A five-hundred-dollar diamond?

Taken in pawn for seventy-five dollars, taken out of pawn exactly on the day the interest payment was not made and placed in the window in a black velvet display box with a sign that read, in Garside's excellent calligraphy that I was trying to learn to duplicate: REDUCED TO $550.00!

She could not let go of it. Garside reached over and disengaged it from her fingers. He held it under the lamp and turned it this way and that. Reflections from the tiny facets flamed at them.

"Beautiful table," Garside said, pointing at the flat top of the stone with his little fingernail. "That flat spot there is called the table. You live here in town, don't you?" he asked her. She nodded.

He put the ring back in its display box and motioned me to take it back to the window. A waste of time, since anything of value came out of the window every night. I held out my hand.

Garside shook his head angrily.

"Take it," he said, shoving it at the deckhand. "Four seventy-five. I don't know why I do these things."

The man's hands went to his belt like a movie cowboy going for a gun. Her face lighted in the rays of the lamp. The money was out, twenties, tens, fives, finally ones. Garside did not deign to look at it. He was busy filling out the Registration Certificate and Guarantee, entering the weight and color of the stone, signing his name with a flourish at the bottom: "Certified by Leo Garside, Gemologist." Everything was on the certificate except the price paid.

No other ceremonial could ensure a closer union. Everybody shook hands with everybody else and they were ushered out by me plastered together. No power could put them asunder tonight.

"He ain't going to get much ass," Garside said dryly, "if he keeps paying four seventy-five a lay."

I took the paper carton from beneath the platform at the back of the display window and began to strip the window of its valuables for the night. Watches, rings, earrings, bracelets, necklaces, matched sets, compacts. Eighteen-karat gold-finished, gold-washed, gold-plated, gold-filled. All of these classifications were a mystery. I asked Garside about this once, so that I could talk about them to a customer.

"Never mind," he said. "It's a waste of time. It's all shit."

I put the carton in the huge safe that was set in the rear wall from the floor almost to the discolored tin ceiling. We kept the safe unlocked but closed all day, not for reasons of caution or privacy but because it was such a mess. Garside didn't want it cleaned up. He knew where everything was and it was up to me to learn the present disorganization rather than make him unlearn it. Whatever turned up of any real value, Garside kept with him or secreted someplace. A paper of loose stones in his vest pocket or inside the ball float in the toilet tank. Good watches, pendants, and larger items of value in old envelopes on the floor near his desk.

Every night I put the cashbox into the safe too, but there was nothing in it but a few singles and small bills, enough to change a twenty. The rest was in Garside's pocket. There were many ledgers and account books, all as full of holes as that safe itself.

The big circular door in front was impregnable; the back side could have been pushed in by a single blow from a hammer. It was a fake, as pointless as the grille mounted on the front door, and the wide silvered line around the windows, and the decal that stated that the premises were protected. That line and the rusted alarm box had not been connected in years.

The other sections that shared the second floor of the casern with us had also settled in for the night, before the truck-mounted generator in the courtyard was switched off. There was a dim lantern or two in the latrines, and that was the only light, but the quarters were warm enough. An engineer company had repaired the boiler and the heating system. Noblesse oblige; we were living better than any part of the society beyond the wall. Lying there, dwelling on my time in the pawnshop, that became reality in minute detail.

I saw myself standing in the middle of the store waiting for Garside to lock that cheesebox of a safe, having turned out all of the lights except one that shone on the massive door all night.

Garside gives the dial a random spin and throws his considerable weight on the handles to test the lock. He comes around the corner of the case and hands me my salary as I stand facing him. Twenty-four dollars for my sixty or so hours in the place. The transaction cannot be seen by anyone in the street. I need not count it. Not now.

Everything was a fake at Garside and Kluckhohn: emotion, family relationships, ethics in the conduct of business, accounting practices, talents and skills, appearances. It was rare for a day to pass without an encounter with a liar or a thief or a swindler.

There were police in and out of the store all the time, in every season and in all kinds of weather. Garside was their good friend. He equipped them with their weapons at less than his usual profit; he kept a coffeepot and a boiling teakettle on the hot plate near his desk during the bleak winter watches. There was always a bottle of rum and one of bourbon on hand to sharpen the taste and heighten the effect. He lent them money, advised them on purchases, department politics, family affairs, whatever. When they were seriously looking for someone, he helped. About such matters, he was very selective. He gave information so obliquely that the investigating officers could only mull it over, sift it, finally put a meaning on it, and make the arrest.

Garside behaved this way because he was a decent man. He had made a good living, even an impressive amount of money, from these people down here. Thus he did what he did unwillingly, but in the final analysis, he could be pressured. The information supplied was something he regarded as a distasteful but necessary service, not as simple as the whiskey bottles, and only a little bit worse than taking 10 percent off a .38-caliber Smith and Wesson. After all, his friends the police did watch over his goings and his comings and pocketfuls of cash.

For all their help and omnipresence, Garside was killed in his store at eight-thirty in the morning on a lovely spring day. The air was soft and pleasant, moist from the showers the night before. It was a Wednesday, the opening day of racing at the track across the river. I got there at nine. Lieutenant Marthia was there, and Ippolito, the beat patrolman, and Gorman and another detective. I did not think that it could have been I lying there.

Garside had a wife and two daughters, one slightly less homely than the other. Six weeks after I went to work for him, he had closed the store early and brought me home for dinner. Not bad for home cooking, I thought, surprised that his pretentious wife could do that well. She had not, of course, but that's all the experience I had of servants then.

Garside was silent throughout the evening. He let them take my measure, the three of them, and let me fend for myself, having utterly disapproved of the whole idea, I could see. Funny. They liked me even less than I liked them. I sometimes wonder what would have happened if the older one had shown the least interest in me, or been more kind. She did have a nice figure. She was a good swimmer, I understood.

When I telephoned, I got the maid. "Garside residence," she said. When Garside's wife came on and I told her, there was a good old-fashioned scream. A real peasant's scream, and then sobbing.

Probably because the first thing she thought was that she'd be running a pawnshop for the rest of her life.

"Serve her right," I muttered. I could see her behind the counter, terrified as the darkness descended outside, at the rear near the very spot where her husband had fallen.

"How'd she take it?" Lieutenant Marthia asked. "Bad?"

"Very," I answered.

He was sitting at Garside's desk, Gorman in a chair near the hot plate, drinking coffee. Garside's last pot.

"Best in town," Gorman said appreciatively. He pointed to a hole in the floor at the base of the safe.

"Looks like his own weapon."

I didn't say anything. That one *had* been made by Garside's own pistol. He had been showing it to someone a few weeks before; the man had been trying to sight it, and had fired it, missing Garside's foot by a hair. Just ticked the sole of his shoe. That hole was full of dust.

"Some thief must have grabbed it off him," Gorman said. "Put one into the floor to make him open the safe. Leo tells him to fuck himself and he put the other four into him."

"And ran out," Lieutenant Marthia said, "jumped on a boat, and took off for Duluth."

They stayed for another two hours taking fingerprints off the cases and the safe, the desk and the coffeepot and liquor bottles. There had been a robbery once, they told me, where the thief had poured himself a drink while going through the place. Then they all left except the lieutenant.

"What's missing?" he said. I liked Marthia.

I was very careful, very sensitive to the situation. It was quite complicated.

"I don't really know," I said. "There's nothing much in the safe."

He nodded. "There was nothing in his pocket except change."

"He was going to the races today," I said. Betting was Garside's passion. He did business along with it, thus making it less of a vice, but if he had to choose lending over betting or playing himself, the borrower could whistle. Marthia knew this better than I. He was patient with me. Even casual.

"How much did he have last night?"

I had seen Garside counting; I knew, give or take ten dollars, exactly.

"I don't know," I said. "I guess over a thousand."

"How much over?"

I shrugged. He had had two thousand two hundred and fifty or sixty dollars. Marthia wandered into the back room and switched on the lights, walking along pulling one string after another, two over the target range along the back wall, one in the toilet at the left, one at the back door. It was a dirty and depressing cavern. I should have made an effort to clean out the corners and sweep the floor, to improve it by some measure, however small.

Marthia looked at the back door, an old milled door, heavy with bars and reinforcement, inside and out. He kicked it hard. So hard that it shuddered. He put his hands in his pockets and stared at it while he spoke to me.

"Well," he said, "I wish this hadn't happened, not only because of Leo. He was a pretty good man, all things considered, and it could turn nasty. You see that, I guess."

I didn't answer.

"There's Gorman's idea of what happened, and that might be what did happen. There are a couple of others too. There could have been a former employee or an old customer, or even someone who was waiting inside and went out this here door and locked it again while we were here even."

"I didn't come back in here this morning," I said.

"Sure you did. You went to the toilet. Don't you remember?"

I didn't. I was sure that I hadn't. But it was a shock. Maybe I wouldn't remember that at all.

"If you say so," I said. "But I don't remember coming back here. Ippolito did. Gorman did. They know the place pretty well too."

Marthia nodded.

"A lot of us do. Too well. But that's another story, isn't it?"

He looked at me.

"I said, isn't it?"

I agreed. I followed him out to the front of the store. I was relieved to be out there.

"Where's his book?" Marthia asked.

I gestured at the safe.

"Not those. The little black one. The coded one."

"I don't know," I said. "I don't know where he kept it. I saw him use it, but I never knew what was in it."

Another lie inspired by fear. Garside had a personal memo book in which he kept the real records of the business. There was a word at the top of page 1, "ingodwetrix," and another jumble of letters where no vowels appeared at all. Next to that was a plus sign, the figure four, and a minus one. After no more than a few weeks, as I did the chores that had to be done with some regularity, I solved both of these rudimentary ciphers.

The first I understood while I was cleaning a tray of rings. Each had a celluloid tag, blue, buttoned around the shank of the ring. On one side was the price, on the other the letters, which were his cost. After I understood that, I had some satisfaction from cutting down on the chores if I had a good sale. I would calculate Garside's profit and knew I deserved that much of a reward. It didn't escape him, but he never let on that he had noticed. He was not going to instruct me or anyone else in conduct. In my case it was not necessary. I knew how to behave well, but I knew how little there was to be gained if I did.

It would have been like the room-service waiter that George Orwell described in the elegant hotel in Paris. He drops a roast chicken on the floor, picks it up, and serves it. What's important is swift and agreeable service of the guest. What's to be gained by returning to the kitchen for another bird? The fury of the chef, the cursing of the maître d' for room service, the impatience of the guest, the loss of the tip, and finally the contempt of the other waiters.

The attitude, the appearance, the demeanor of someone who

behaves properly, correctly, can be taken off and put on like a hat. One doesn't lose that ability through lack of practice.

As for the other code, plus four, minus two, and the first few notations I could glimpse, I solved that too.

I knew the cipher and I knew where the book was. I knew that KPSQ was Gorman and that the deciphered entries would add up to over four thousand dollars that he had borrowed. He liked horses too. There were other entries that I knew—Marthia's name was there: PSWL. An operation on his father, seven hundred and fifty dollars. He had returned over five hundred this year. Gorman's balance never showed a credit except once when a long shot came in. Two hundred dollars. He borrowed that again a month later.

I was lucky. If it had been Gorman and he suspected that I was lying, he would have walked me down to the lake and had a short conversation with me, just beyond the last piling on the pier. But Marthia was a gentler man, or perhaps he didn't like the thought of hurting a gawk like me, with my bony wrists hanging below the jacket sleeves of that 100 percent wool suit. The trousers were also too short; his thumb and middle finger would have easily met about my neck just above the ready-tied necktie I wore six days a week. That tie with its misbegotten combination of stripings, the worst kind of fustian. This probably did not affect Marthia. Probably what influenced him was the coffee I had poured for him, the errands I had run, the respect I showed him.

"Better find that book," he said to me finally. "You're going to have a lot of help from volunteers. Either find it or see that it disappears. Permanently."

I didn't go to the fuse box and pull out the whole thing and reach between the wall studs for Garside's book. I just swept up, wiped the wall and counter cases, and cleaned up generally after Marthia left.

That afternoon, Rose Garside's lawyer came in with her brother Aaron. First thing the lawyer said to me was, "Get the inventory and the books."

Immediately, I knew why Leo Garside didn't use him, and ten

minutes later I knew why Aaron wasn't working there. The lawyer left with the books, convinced that he had the whole picture. He was like Mr. Vinegar walking away with the door of the house on his back. Who could break in if there was no door?

Aaron sat down at Leo's desk and became an executive right on the minute.

I then had a future. Much has happened to me since, but I doubt whether I shall ever again have that sense that I had come to a threshold and could walk across into a more pleasant place.

I did not think of what I did after Leo died as stealing. I was taking a normal advantage of opportunity, which is what Leo Garside did in his business. It was not appropriation or sequestration or concealment of assets. Simply, no one knew about what I removed. It would not have gone to those it should have gone to in any case. I did not trust the lawyer, and Aaron was hopeless. The purchaser would have found the things eventually after he had made his bid, and I knew that they would begin to negotiate a sale of the place within hours, the transaction based only on what was in those records that the lawyer was going over.

I thought of turning over the lard can of gold scrap and findings to the widow. I could have gone to her home that night and dumped the spectacle frames, the tops of rings, the seals and chains from watches the size of small turnips, the fraternal pins with the stones missing, in her lap. That would have horrified the mourners. At such a time!

I took the contents of the can and a paper of loose stones. None was bigger than forty or fifty points. Perhaps ten carats in all. They were in the corner near his desk, in the box of thumbed-over envelopes marked "Will-call" in his own scrawl.

Six weeks later I resigned, if one can call it that. The prospective buyers had cruised the place, very knowingly, but neither of them asked me about the items mentioned. They credited everyone from the widow to her lawyer with the intelligence to burke such valuables as they kept in their own lard cans.

Two weeks after that I said good-bye to my great-aunt and my uncle and I left for Chicago. I told them I had been offered a job by a watch salesman who had taken a liking to me. They wished me well.

I said I would write.

In September of that year I enrolled at Bellefontaine University in Ohio. During the Thanksgiving break, a friend mailed a postcard to Alvin Marthia at police headquarters. The message told him where Leo Garside's notebook would be found.

I went to the college library to scan the newspapers that arrived from my home city. I did that for a week or so and never found any reference to the matter of new evidence in the unsolved murder of Leo Garside.

Still, I felt that I had satisfied a debt. Just as well, for I owed Garside more than I knew at the time. It was my experience with him that had qualified me for assignment to the 855th Service Company, Alpheus L. Earley commanding.

In a week, Earley had completed arrangements for our operations. The casern, a barracks big enough to accommodate a battalion, was to be both living quarters and work area. It had been built of stone in the previous century, three high-ceilinged stories around a small square, our parade ground, a few hundred yards from the center of the town. Our various sections were installed on the ground floor, and officers and men all lived in the wings of the building. Thus we had a base, competent personnel, equipment, and most important, Earley's determination to carry out his assignment. He was purposeful, resolute, and ingenious.

He ordered all the enlisted men to remove our insignia of rank before we made our first sortie. If stripes were still apparent on our sleeves, we drew new uniforms.

He had Transport maintain our jeeps, command cars, and trucks as though for a division inspection, and the Security escort vehicles were equipped with light machine guns. We were all to carry side arms.

"You will be correct and military," he told us, "you aren't out to win friends, so don't let me find you throwing cigarettes and candy around. And it's not a trade mission, so leave your coffee and soap in the billet. Wherever you go you have the authority, but that doesn't mean you have to kick any doors down. If you need it, you can get the cooperation of every unit in the area. I don't expect you to need it."

We never did. The routine established itself very quickly. We were an arm of a power structure that superseded the former—the one that no longer existed. It seemed that it never had existed.

We covered our sector, on the road each day at eight, back to our billet each evening. Then we would have a session with Earley to report on the day's work. It was rarely necessary to return to the same town more than twice until we came to Urbach.

We were there in forty minutes, checked in with the U.S. officer in the town, and he called in the mayor. He in turn conducted us to the custodian of properties of the town. Sometimes these were new appointees, but this man had held the post since 1920. He had lost his right arm at Sedan, he told Scharf, our interpreter, but in the previous war. Scharf said he made it sound as if that one had taken place on another planet.

He took us to his file room, the same golden-oak cabinets and furniture behind a high, narrow frosted-glass door. The files were orderly and complete. It is remarkable how tightly packed papers seem to be impervious to damage from bombardment or shelling— or even fire and water. Bodies, buildings, transport systems, utilities services, all are very susceptible to destruction, but file cards, forms, receipts, regulations, and instructions seem to remain unscathed. Almost everything remains legible. Too much so.

In Urbach, the Sequestered Properties file was not very long. At the most there were forty inventories. By lunchtime we were at the Rs. Riesner, Gideon, Cattle Dealer; Ruben, Joseph, Physician. Riesner's wife had owned two fur coats, one astrakhan, one broadtail, that had gone, properly invoiced and receipted, to the quartermaster depot in another province.

Dr. Ruben's possessions included "Salon Furnishings" that had been shipped to the section superintendent of railroads, and then to the district supervisor. That was five pieces of Biedermeier furniture made in Austria. His consulting room equipment, all set forth item by item, had gone to a veterinarian.

He had had an extensive silver service; we took that up in detail.

"Twenty-five a place setting," Arquette offered.

John Kowalski disagreed. "More," he said, "our plate was selling for eighteen when I was drafted, and that was just your basic pieces. This has oyster forks, fish knives, fruit spoons too."

"Hallmarked," Wersba said. "That means more if it's well known."

"Marquetry-fitted chest," Scharf droned.

"Fifty bucks for the chest," Scibetta said, hands folded behind his head.

I remembered some of those chests that Garside had taken in pawn.

"Never any market for them," I remarked.

"We ain't selling them," Silberglitt argued. "Just valuing them. Why should we screw the man? Make it a hundred."

That was as close as we came to philosophizing. There was too much to do. It was necessary to complete some of these valuations and come to an end of the beginning of the task.

We agreed upon a figure of forty-five hundred dollars for Dr. Ruben's possessions.

Then we came to the file of Hamplemann, Alexander. Not only was it out of place, it was thicker by far than the others. It had been typed, as though by an auditor or appraiser, on very good paper, and it seemed to have been kept intact. There were no receipts or invoices or distribution notices pinned to any of the sheets.

Ordinarily we did not go to the magazin, where property that had not been shipped remained, until after we had checked all of the inventory sheets. Not this time. We went immediately, animated and eager. The mission was no longer drudgery, counting teaspoons and dinner plates, pianos and fur coats, trying with our limited knowledge to place a value on ordinary householders' possessions. It would have made as much sense for the army to assign us to turn back all of the clocks in the sector.

The magazin was not so well organized as the file room. Even though the storage areas were sectioned off into cubicles with laths and chicken wire like the basement of an apartment building, the odds and ends deposited there had no common configuration, weight, or shape. Thus the various areas were only a disorder of goods in a cold and musty twilight.

We spent the whole afternoon on Hamplemann's inventory and barely got through a tenth of it, despite everyone's interest—even enthusiasm. Some of them were impressed—as though they had become acquainted with a personage.

Hesitantly, Arquette suggested to me on the way back that we should have left a guard on it. Almost everything he said was hesitant, as though he were unwilling to call attention to himself as existing. At thirty, he seemed to be drying out already, desiccating, withdrawing. Perhaps because he was thought to be a homosexual, covert and quite the opposite of Pattison, the company clerk. Pat did not go around soliciting, but he did draw the pointed remarks and vulgarities upon himself like a lightning rod, possibly to distract from others.

I didn't agree with Arquette. When I reported that night, I didn't mention the collection, mostly because I saw an advantage for myself in not doing so immediately. I wanted to make a contribution on my own, and not as part of a group.

Before I was ready, Earley paid us a surprise visit in Urbach on our third day there.

"What's holding things up?" he said to me.

We had opened the first of a number of cases, so carefully and even elegantly made that they looked like cabinetry. Scibetta had taken up a pry bar, but put it aside on the instant. Instead we dismantled it, that in itself no easy task. We had to remove numbers of wooden plugs glued over countersunk screwheads. When we lifted off the four-by-six side we had then to open a soldered tin liner; under that was a quilted cover, and beneath, it was compartmented.

In one space was a triptych, as Wersba called it. It was an Adoration. The most powerful figure was a gaunt shepherd who was not kneeling but standing by, withdrawn from the rest, and deep in doubt. There was also a very small painting of a cottage interior that Wersba said was Dutch. In the style of Vermeer. Wersba was twenty, and very opinionated and definite about such items and even the relative importance of artists in their own pantheon as well. But he did say "in the style of." Another space held several wood carvings, mentioned as such on the inventory sheet. Wersba argued that classification. Wood or not, they were true sculptures. They did have extraordinary strength, that much was obvious even to the unschooled assembled.

The remaining works were completely pedestrian: juiceless still lifes, garish alpine sunsets, patches of wildflowers, stags at bay, dead roe deer, trout laid out on a bed of grass with a rod and reel. Some were unfinished, like exercises assigned and never completed.

I returned to the file room with Earley.

"What's your evaluation of all you've seen so far?" he asked.

"Over a hundred thousand dollars, not including what's in the cases," I told him quietly, my back to the custodian.

I followed Earley out to his jeep. I had thought about what I wanted to tell him. I wanted to show interest and conscientiousness, not extraordinary intelligence or rare perception.

"I didn't want to say anything in front of the custodian," I said. "Sometimes he looks like he understands every word."

"Good move."

"I took Scharf with me to check on Hamplemann in the town records. He doesn't appear as a property owner or in the vital statistics. We looked in the cemetery too, and the parish register."

"Synagogue?"

"There wasn't any. There were only about twenty Jews in the town. I asked the custodian where Hamplemann lived. Where his house was. He said he didn't live here. Came from a city in the north."

"Then what's it doing here?"

"He said some men brought it in trucks in the spring of '45."

"Military men? Army trucks?"

"Right. Part of a convoy."

I told him what Arquette had suggested about putting a guard on the collection or turning it over to higher headquarters. He shook his head before I had finished speaking.

"No. But get it done. I want to include it in our first public notice. It's been all right for this long, it will be for a while longer. Bring the inventory to me when you come back tonight. We'll talk about it then."

He was becoming impatient. His days were full, no doubt, and he could see other Hamplemanns in other sectors, and their goods and possessions, most of them with a stain of blood on them somewhere. He wanted to get at them.

I stepped back a pace and saluted to close the encounter properly. The driver stared straight ahead through the windshield. Merolla. His lips moved. "Brownnose," I read. That didn't matter to me. I thought I had accomplished what I wanted, to find a better place in a vast and powerful structure, where I might even prosper.

That night when I took the inventory to Earley in his quarters, Berdichevsky and Proudfoot were there too. All of them in wool shirts, sweaters, and field jackets. The boiler had failed for good and the army had not filled our requisition for coal stoves.

Berdichevsky was in charge of the Documentation and Adjudication Section, a short, rotund man who had been an instructor in German history at a midwestern college. He would have very little to do until our first notices of unclaimed property were published. Presently, to fill in the time, he was making his way slowly through the town archives, noting ideas for monographs. Sometimes he wrote preambles to them. In the evening he was teaching Proudfoot to play chess.

Shotgun Proudfoot was security officer. He had received a number of decorations, and eventually a battlefield commission. He was turning his platoon into an elite unit. They wore white scarves, varnished helmet liners, pressed trousers, and gleaming boots.

Earley handed them the Hamplemann inventory and turned back to me.

"I wanted to speak to you before this. You didn't file a demobilization request when the others did. Why not?"

I said I wanted to stay in awhile.

"Pankow's asked to transfer back to his old outfit in Japan, the First Cavalry. Would you want his job?"

Shotgun grinned.

"Ain't that always the way. Can take the man out of the horseshit, but you can't take the horseshit out of the man."

I couldn't see myself as first sergeant. It was too far removed from the primary sphere of company activity.

"I'd rather continue with what I'm doing," I said thoughtfully. I did not embroider.

He told me about a directive that had come through recently about commissions for specialized personnel who wanted to remain in the service.

"Fill these in," he said, handing me a sheaf of forms. "I'll approve them."

"What's a Manlicker?" Shotgun asked.

"Mann," Berdichevsky said, "licher, *c-h*. Touch your tongue to the roof of your mouth. Mannlicher. It's a sporting rifle. Very powerful and accurate.

"Did you actually see all of this? All of these things?" Berdichevsky asked. I told him I had seen most of them.

"He thinks it's a cache," Earley said. Berdichevsky disagreed.

"That's because you don't know the country. It probably belongs to some provincial museum, or one of the little principalities. Even an old family."

His tone was professorial; he seemed to be preparing to lecture, clearing his throat, raising his hands to describe a shape.

"I don't know," I said, "the section felt that he was a real individual. Rich. Powerful. With a lot of taste."

Berdichevsky was a good-humored man. He smiled often and did so now.

"I know. I like your section. They're interesting. Maybe one of them will become a connoisseur. But what background do they have? What experience? A plating technician. A private who worked in a furniture store. And you are out of a pawnshop. Right? I don't mean to insult anyone, you understand."

"You aren't," I said steadily, but I could feel myself flushing. "That's one of the reasons I think Hamplemann is not a museum. Or a nobleman. I think he went around appropriating for himself. For the future. Some things are rare and exceptional, sure, but others are just amusements. Hobbies."

I mentioned the operatic record collection stored in matched mahogany boxes. Some of the disks were one-sided, recorded when the artist sang into a horn. It began with Battistini in 1907 and Caruso in 1910 and Leo Slezak, went on through the twenties with Tito Schipa and Rosa Ponselle and Hina Spani. None were later than 1933.

I mentioned the Schuco toy automobiles and the Märklin trains. The canvas bags of coinage from banks of another era; the stamp albums, the doll heads from Dresden; the Swiss music boxes; the regiment of hand-painted lead soldiers, and the sheet music that was as common as any found in a middle-class household's piano bench.

"Sure," I said, "there are enameled medallions, and first editions in fine bindings, and paintings and drawings that I don't know anything about except what Ed Wersba tells me, but—"

"Those are for his declining years," Earley said. "He didn't grab them out of a love of beauty, Berdie."

"No sir, Berdie, not him," Shotgun put in, "he grabbed them because he was a thief. Like all of them. Except you and me, and I have my doubts about you."

"When we draw up our list for publication," Earley ordered, "I want his name included just as you found it—misplaced. Understand?"

"Why send him a message?" Berdichevsky asked. "If he's what you think he is, he will know enough to stay away, certainly."

Earley shook his head.

"It will give him a case of nerves. He will have to check up on it. Send an observer or come himself."

"Then we'll grab him and hang him right in the square like the Russkies do," Shotgun said. "You got to admit they don't fuck around."

He glanced at the papers having to do with my commission.

"Don't put in, man. Don't sign it. You're better off as a buck-ass private in the rear rank. Nothing to do but lie on your ass and wait for orders. Look what they made out of me. A bush-league Patton."

"I don't want any more talk about hanging," Earley said. "It has no place in our thinking. If we find criminals, we see that they are punished. That's the end of it. We don't take them out and hang them, where I come from."

"What's that mean!" Shotgun demanded. Tone and manner had changed.

"Nothing," Berdichevsky said quickly. "Not a thing."

"If you hang a thief one time, you don't have to do it twice. Remember that where you come from."

"You're both right. I can't tell who I agree with," Berdichevsky said. He reached up to slap Proudfoot on the back. "Come on. Tonight we're working on pawns—little, limited creatures like us who are clumsy and don't move around much but have a surprising strength together."

When I passed Berdichevsky's door, the two of them were sitting over the chessboard under a pale circle of light from a lantern. The chessmen were metal—silver or pewter. The knights wore medieval Teutonic helmets.

Next morning the Evaluation Section met in Earley's office for a lecture. Earley introduced us to Cyril Faulds, who I thought was a British officer. There was an RAF moustache, the demeanor, even the accent and intonation, with numbers of *g*s dropped. He sounded like a voice on the BBC. I never did discover what his antecedents were, but I did learn that he was an art dealer in New York. He was one of a group of appraisers, antiquarians, and/or experts who had been dragooned, inveigled, or impressed into the service of justice and the right. On a per diem basis. Earley sat in with us.

"Got everything but the pips, hasn't he?" he muttered.

Faulds had indeed, and it did not take him long to show us what a gulf there was between us. Much of what he had to say was over our heads; a number of esoteric references emphasized that. Even those of us who had some knowledge of porcelain, plate, or pictures were slighted or disparaged by an inclination of the head or a covert glance at his watch, as though every query were meant to absorb part of our working day.

"When speaking to me," he said to Wersba, "I would ask you not to use the word 'paintings.' You will simply not be working on that level. You will not be discovering old masters or new ones. All such have been recovered or the whereabouts is known. You will be seeing pictures. Like the ones that hung over your 'davenport' at home."

It fell to me to escort him, and he made no difficulties. He was on time for transport, punctual at mess, and made no unreasonable demands.

There was something of the ferret about him, however. When he surveyed any kind of collection, he missed nothing—type of crate or box, method of packing, even the proportion of content to container; and always the tare, if given. That was the background of either a customs officer or a smuggler.

He did not seem to have any broad or detailed knowledge of any specific field, either. He said that could always be picked up out of various reference works. What interested him more was the market. That was what established real value. He referred to it as "intrinsic worth."

We heard from other formations that his arrival always caused a stir. Officials billeted in the more opulent residences would invite him to lunch or to dinner and seek his opinion on "their" chattels. Wherever he went, he took his Leica and a notebook in which he entered the details of what he had seen and thought enough of to photograph. That did not include the surroundings or any of us.

He overheard references to the Hamplemann inventory and that did interest him. Earley had told me not to show it to him, and that roused the only emotion I had seen in him. He protested, and they met to discuss the matter.

Earley explained why he thought it important that it not be publicized. Rumors would spread, swiftly, in times like these; there would be exaggerated accounts of its value, speculation about it belonging to one of the more notorious criminals would increase, and no claimant would come within reach.

Faulds agreed that these were all sound and sufficient reasons that he could understand and appreciate. Still, his interests were professional and impersonal, and thus far in his travels he had seen very little that was worth attention. Also, on this level, this echelon he was working on, he had no contact with the press and would never seek it. He was above that self-serving behavior.

However, if he did see it, it might improve the company function and help it to make rational assessments of the value of the properties they were surveying.

Earley mulled that over for a bit and finally gave his permission. But he took me aside and told me to spend no more than an hour with him in the magazin.

"The copy of the inventory stays with you. And don't leave him alone in there, either."

Faulds scanned the sheets quickly and passed over most of what we had checked with hardly a pause. The furniture, silver, bric-a-brac, coinage, all of it, he simply glanced at before we went on to the "pictures" in the case we had opened. He looked closely at the one Wersba had said was in the style of Vermeer, and did not even deign to bring it out into a better light. He spent a few moments on the triptych—more on the back of it than the front—and put it down without comment. He paid considerably more attention to the group of still lifes. Despite instructions, I had to leave him there for a time; there was some bellowing outside by a detail from the constabulary. They wanted to see the authorization for the use of the jeep.

When I returned, Faulds was closing a small clasp knife and returning it to his pocket. The pictures were all back in the case.

On the way back he said little except to ask for our total evaluation. When I gave it, he smiled sourly and shook his head.

"Reduce that by eighty percent and you won't be too far off," he said. "And the precautions were not at all necessary. If I wanted to steal anything, it wouldn't be from that clutter.

"If that's the most important collection you've seen, you're wasting time and money. I suppose the army's got plenty of both."

He left the first thing in the morning and Earley wanted a report.

"You would think the supercilious bastard would have had the courtesy to give me his comments even if I did think they were worthless. Who the hell is he to sit in judgment? A man organizes a convoy at a time when the country's falling apart all around him to preserve and conceal this collection, and he says it's trash. From his great height, he disposes of it.

"We may not know the price of a sixteenth-century chamber pot, but we've got some common sense. And some sincerity."

With that acuity that he displayed so often, he questioned me in more detail.

"Didn't have any interest in anything? Not one flicker? The piano? Tapestry? The icons? The marquetry work? You're sure, goddam it! And you were with him every minute as ordered. Right?"

Temporizing opened the way for him, as usual. And also as was usual, he put aside intensity and listened. I passed along the details. My brief absence; the case of still lifes; the knife into the pocket.

"Let's go," he said. We picked up Arquette and Wersba and returned to the magazin. When we removed the pictures that Faulds had seen, Arquette scrutinized them. In three he had cut tiny flaps in the lower left- and right-hand corners. When Tom raised the bits of canvas another canvas appeared. Two were signed, one with a carefully executed little triangle like an embossment with a capital *K* inside it. The other bore a legible name. "Klee."

"Knew where to look, didn't he?" Earley said. "Are they important?"

Wersba nodded. "One's Kandinsky. The other is Paul Klee.

They're both in museum collections, I know. I guess we should have taken more time with these."

"Starting now," Earley said, "we will."

The three of us, and Silberglitt added. Having been a stone setter, he had the necessary skills. Each nail was removed from the stretchers and the top canvas lifted. Then all of the assorted fasteners were replaced in the original holes—some had been set irregularly with the heads bent and flattened, as though the artist who had prepared the surface originally had been in great haste to begin the work. All of that sometimes unskilled preliminary work we duplicated exactly.

We finished a number of them by Saturday, and the custodian having left, we propped them up in his office for Earley's inspection. That was the first time we had looked at them as one might see them in a gallery. Heretofore we had been bowed over them with watchmaker's pliers or tack and nail pullers, separating the canvases at the back of the frames with scalpels from the company first-aid kit a centimeter at a time. No young anatomy student would have been more cautious than Wersba. From the start he had considered it a weighty responsibility. That increased as he progressed.

Set out then was an associative presentation of great power and perception. The works were for the most part dissimilar, yet there was a unity, an interconnection among the makers. The Kandinsky and Klee canvases were now displayed with others—Kokoschka, Otto Dix, Corinth, Franz Marc, George Grosz.

However much or little we knew of the history of the three or four preceding decades, we now learned a great deal more. Not only of specific details, but of how those times of disquiet, turbulence, and fear of an apocalyptic future had affected these observers. That is what I felt, although none of us exchanged informed opinions on its relevance. We accepted what little Wersba could tell us about these artists, and the bits of biography registered to a degree, but they were not really pertinent. They were overwhelmed by the actual accomplishment.

"I don't know how they rate as artists," Earley said. "They're more accusers. Of everyone."

We opened the remaining cases and went over every picture in the inventory. In the interim Earley wrote a report describing the discovery. It attempted objectivity, but did not do so successfully. He filed this with higher headquarters. A Signal Corps photographer appeared and made two sets of Kodachrome slides, in itself a rare occurrence. One was forwarded to the top echelon, the other remained in the company.

Finally, Earley, ingenuously, I thought, mustered the whole company—"No one is excused"—to see a showing on their own time. This was inspired, no doubt, by the general order that all personnel visit a concentration camp. It was not well received, but no weekend passes were issued until every man had gone through the mess hall where the paintings were propped up on tables.

Not all of our company were impressed.

"Jesus Christ, anything you want for the taking and this asshole steals these! Let me out!"

"Would you let this bastard paint a latrine!"

Some of them were responsive. I was checking them off the roster as they left. Several glanced over their shoulders as though a powerful presence followed them on.

Shotgun spent more time than Berdichevsky there, particularly on the works that dealt with aspects of World War I. *Trench Warfare* and *The Wounded* by Otto Dix. Berdichevsky hurried along, nodding his head angrily as he passed, as though confirming some strongly held opinion.

Then the miscreants caught in the previous week for various punishable transgressions returned them to their cases and took them back to the magazin. The effect remained with me. It was an encounter, a joining of revelation and trauma—too long after the fact. Much too long.

Two weeks later, after a number of delays for requisitions with a higher priority, a mobile printing unit delivered one thousand notices of certain property held for return to the list of persons set forth below.

These were duly posted in the public squares of our sector, in town offices, and in the camps for displaced persons operated by various relief organizations. They were also included in the weekly publications issued by the military governments of all sectors, English, French, and Russian, in four languages. There was wide interest in these flimsy sheets. They were utilitarian as well as informative and instructive.

Some of our posters were defaced, some turned up with pleas for information or offerings printed by hand on the back. Earley dictated a warning to be included in subsequent printings. "It is forbidden to deface or remove these notices. Severe penalties will be exacted for defacement or removal of these notices!"

When the posters first went out we felt some sense of accomplishment. It meant that there would be results from what we had done. There was a common feeling of altruism. We waited benignly for claimants as though we had opened a soup kitchen in this land of the famished.

Our central gate was manned by Shotgun's guardsmen on a twenty-four-hour basis, and a number of holding areas were sectioned off by plank-and-sawhorse barriers so that there would be some control over the crowds that Earley expected to descend on us. He wanted no mob scenes.

He need not have concerned himself. It was February and the land was locked in winter cold and bleak. It was a land upon which the sun itself seemed unwilling to shine. For consecutive days it appeared only briefly, yielding no warmth and hardly a shadow. It was a pale orb, seldom unobscured, drifting for a brief hour and vanishing without effect. There was snow, quickly discolored by engine exhausts and brick and mortar dust, snow that never did disguise but only limned and accented irregular, patternless devastation.

Almost all of the motor traffic was military. Drab vehicles humped over with canvas passed through on missions at a distance from the country and its people.

The business of the town itself was at a standstill, as though the last reserves of human energy and ability had been spent, and the smallest effort to meet, to barter and exchange, to find coal or kerosene or what there was of foodstuffs could barely be managed today.

Sometimes there were groups of people on the roads between towns. I do not remember them as walking, but rather shuffling, attached to each other by some tenuous bond—direction, birthplace, a possibility of assistance. All of them were muffled in odds and ends of dark clothing with never a glint of color or brightness about any of them, man, woman, child.

There were the dead not properly interred on both sides. There were the thousands unaccounted for to any authority. There were all the others, ill and threatened with deprivation if not starvation. At this point only a comparative few had any interest in the new right of replevin. There were some, but few of them behaved as we had thought they would.

Even in translation by Scharf or Berdichevsky and the other interpreters, if they were stirred out of a projection of despair, they were as hostile as though we were the ones who had seized their possessions.

I suppose it was the officiality of the operation. The questioning, the waiting in the queue, our uniforms, the lack of expression, the face of power and the face of indifference. We knew nothing of the hierarchy of suffering, or of individual status in times past. That was evident to them.

Some were aggressive and impatient, demanding and insolent. Only a comparative few could bear any longer the structure of polite civility. They knew how ephemeral that was. But Berdichevsky maintained it and demanded it from everyone in his section.

"If there's an argument," he told them excitedly, "you lose! Every time, they are the winners! They are right! If you won't accept that, get out of the section! I don't give a goddam if I have to see every one of them myself!"

With every claimant he behaved like an old relative. He listened and nodded and clucked over the chickens and the cows, the soup tureens, the 1928 Opel. He looked at pictures and documents and letters that proved cases. He bent close to listen to what could only be whispered.

When the end of the working day neared, he would be apprehensive, concerned that he could not finish, and unable to allot as much time as his claimant wanted—nay, required. Time to sit back and nod after a particularly remarkable statement, to wait for Berdichevsky's reaction.

Shotgun's guards took care of the decision. At 1630 hours the official day ended, but Berdichevsky issued passes, numbered and signed, to be presented next day. It troubled him when they went out into the lowering afternoon. Worse, he could not keep their tales at any distance from himself. In a few weeks he aged, and he lost the mordant edge he had acquired in the sometimes bloody passage across Normandy and into Belgium.

He, derided by Shotgun at their chess games for the tiny thimblefuls of cognac he took, began to drink. That was one of the comforts we could acquire easily. There wasn't much beer, and what we had was bad; thin and sour with a head like old soapsuds and full of gas. Scheissmacher or Old Pipi. But there was brandy in bottles with gold-foil labels, liqueurs of all kinds, sherrys from Spain, and Polish and Russian vodka available. That trade sprang up and flourished before the firing stopped.

So he and Shotgun would go to the inn just off the market square every evening. My promotion had come through very quickly, considering the numbers of papers the army was now moving all over the continent. Earley swore me in at a ceremony in his office and gave me an old set of his gold bars. I went back to work half an hour later, having sprinkled the insignia with a cup of instant coffee and a package of Nabs. That was Earley's manner.

But that evening, Shotgun and Berdichevsky took me with them and poured out.

"Got any problems being a mustang?" Shotgun asked me. I shook my head. None of us had ever paid much attention to rank in this company and now, with demobilization moving more rapidly, no one would have cared if they had made me a general.

"I sure did. I was platoon sergeant and platoon leader all in one day when we come out of the line, and they all took to calling me 'chicken shit.' Me. As if I went looking for it."

Berdichevsky gestured to the innkeeper for another round. The innkeeper was a tall man and must have been quite heavy in better days. Now his whole body seemed to be in mourning like his face.

"Every time I look at that son-of-a-bitch," Shotgun said, "I think about them counterattacking. That'd straighten him up and make him smile again. You s'pose he's poisoning us?"

"It's too soon," Berdichevsky said moodily. "When it finally penetrates that they lost, *then* drink from a sealed bottle."

"Time for chow, Berdie, ain't it?"

Berdichevsky shook his head firmly.

"Listen," Shotgun told him, leaning forward, "may seem funny coming from me, but you are taking on too much. Your goddam eyes are turning yellow and you got a complexion like wallpaper paste. And you ain't chubby anymore either."

"Never be chubby again," Berdichevsky said. "That's how I show my kinship."

"Makes as much sense as hanging yourself."

"I thought about that too."

"Just like you now that I'm catching up. As of last night it was a hundred and twenty-three to twelve. Of course, you were so pissed you didn't know which man was yours."

"I don't like the pieces, either," Berdie said. "I'm going to the USO and get one of my own. Wood. Made in Vermont, and a board made of paper with Parcheesi on the back."

Shotgun was an alien. Despite his concern, he could not follow his friend for seven hours and more every day into the new land that he was hearing about. He did not realize that Berdichevsky demanded of himself that he enter that land each day, carrying a haversack or a flimsy suitcase or a parcel wrapped in creased brown paper, to walk in company with the rest.

In Berdichevsky's own mind he boarded their train and disembarked at the railhead. He waited for his name to be called off the bill of lading, to assemble again and walk with them down a dusty, flint-surfaced road, without his carbine, without his uniform, without his insignia.

"Whatever you say, Berdie, as long as we get some goddam food. See if he's got something that you don't eat with a spoon. And no turnips."

Tonight it was rabbit with dumplings and carrots.

"It ain't rabbit, it's cat," Shotgun said. "As long as he took the hair off."

Berdie held up his glass.

"Fire one more for effect."

If I had been commanding the company, I would have switched Berdichevsky to my section and given me his. In mine he would have been dealing with possessions, things that have no personality and don't speak. They might inspire momentary pity or some sadness, but they don't deliver histories. And I, since I didn't know the language, would be listening to Scharf or one of the others translating in a monotone, concentrating on the actual tumble of speech and not on catches in the voice, whispers, nuances of fear and amazement at what had occurred, at what had happened to them.

Berdichevsky's wider knowledge would have made my section into a seminar; all of them would have been the better for it. Arquette and Wersba would have had a proper intellectual to work with, and Kowalski and Silberglitt and Scibetta would have acquired discrimination. Their lives would have been changed as mine was.

But Earley was commanding, and even in a unit as small as the 855th, many things that are important are overlooked. Earley had put an organization together that functioned. It would be expanded and improved and would complete its assignment. It was a satisfaction to him as it was. And in the atmosphere that prevailed all around us—no sewage facilities, limited water supply, shortages of soap and deodorizers—it was impossible to detect the smell of one or two soaks.

The thought precipitated the nausea. Also, I had been rolling my eyes, the better to see the bars on my shoulders. With so much of the plating worn away they made me look like a real veteran.

I stood up, my teeth locked together, and mumbled something about air.

"Sure, get rid of it," Shotgun said, "make some room for that cat fricassee."

I walked out, erect, and not until I was outside did I reach for the wall. It moved disconcertingly, as though swung on pivots. Then the whole market square began to heave as though bracketed by artillery. I made it to the gutter, and the matter became involuntary. Finally I sat up, waiting for the muscles of my stomach and abdomen to halt their contractions. Now I was uncomfortably warm, almost in a sweat. The temperature had risen twenty degrees. There had been snow flurries when we came from our casern, then a rattle of hail against the windows of the inn, and then a downpour. Now there was a thick warm mist pressing upon the remaining roofs of the town. It was as though the weather system itself had become part of this transitional time, unstable, precarious, unpredictable.

A truck rumbled into the square and halted, a cast of pale yellow before its headlights, a red efflorescence behind it.

A man dismounted over the tailgate and waved, a gesture that was more dismissal than thanks to the driver. The first thing I noticed was the black and white wing-tip shoes that he wore—the white suede portions now darkly gray, and too big for him obviously, from the way the toes turned up.

The rest of his costume was equally bizarre—this when most of the civilian population, men, women, and children, wore strange combinations of clothing, some from the military discard heaps, some from the bins of the relief organizations, some from the peddlers who stocked carts with odds and ends rooted from the rubble and ruins of abandoned houses.

This man preferred panache to serviceability. His hat was Italian velour with a wide brim, worn up on one side, down on the other, a checked mackintosh caped at the shoulders, a double-breasted chalk-striped suit, a frayed silk shirt, and a heavy and well-stained brocaded tie, so hard used that the broad end could no longer meet the lapels of the suit. He pulled out a large wallet, took the torn half of one of our notices from it, and pointed out our address with a very dirty and uncared-for index finger.

"Where?" he said.

I pointed toward the casern and he went off at once as though marching to a cadence, shoulders squared, back straight. He was a presence in the town, an exception. As he disappeared, the clacking of the metal plates on his dandy's shoes was disturbing, as if I were hearing the footsteps of a leader separated only momentarily from an army of followers.

I thought that I had been away from the table a long time, but when I returned they had not yet been served, and were sitting in silence, Berdichevsky in an almost catatonic state.

"Everything come out all right?" Proudfoot asked me, grinning.

"What happened to him?"

"Don't know. Seems to be listening to voices. Every so often he turns his head like an antenna."

"Maybe he picked up Hamplemann outside," I said. "In the square."

Berdichevsky returned as though I had spoken his name.

"An elderly gentleman. Tall, thin, well bred. A fine, distinguished-looking man. Marked by suffering like the others."

I shook my head.

"It might not be him at all. He didn't say he was."

"But that's the name that came to mind the moment you saw him."

I nodded.

"Out of the shadows and the mist," Berdichevsky said, peering out of the window. "Hamplemann. How appropriate."

2.

Your Committee wants Your Reunion to be everything you want it to be, so we are giving you a chance to "Sound Off" about that by means of the enclosed questionnaire, or Fragebogen. *Do you remember how many of them we processed in the old days? (Smile) Fill them out and send them back Immediately if not sooner so we can get as many of the things you want to do into the Schedule before we freeze the plans for Entertainment!*
Billy Pattison, AUS (Retired)

H amplemann must have felt that he had reached a goal when he arrived at our headquarters. He had overcome many difficulties—transport, shelter, food. He had had to elude well-meaning relief organizations, the military patrols of six nations, and captious intelligence personnel along his way. With success within reach, he did not do what Berdichevsky expected him to do: line up outside our door at dawn.

I saw him several times during the day making a reconnaissance. At least twice I saw him in arm-waving conversation with departing claimants, familiarizing himself with our procedures.

Berdichevsky lost his concentration. His attention wandered from those who appeared at his desk. More than once I heard voices raised in anger at what people thought was his indifference to them.

Finally, at 1600 hours, he came in and his name was entered in the log.

"Hamplemann, Alexander," he said, speaking into a sudden silence—this engendered by his outlandish costume. He handed Scharf the torn half of the notice that he had shown to me the night before, and spelled it out for Scharf loudly.

"That," he said assuredly, "is me."

Scharf nodded to a chair and began the engorging process. As did all of the others without exception, Hamplemann rummaged out his cache of papers and placed it before him, as though it were a relic of a kind that had magical powers.

Just so did the others produce their passes, permits, proofs. Sometimes these were bundles wrapped in a scrap of canvas or oil-skin or butcher paper tied with cord or string or even a bit of wire, to deposit between themselves and officialdom. Scharf and the rest of us had learned that no interrogator could reach for the packet himself. If this were done, and the order disturbed or a single leaf be torn along a crease, the whole sequence of the claimant's history would suffer distortion. Worse, a part of his identity would be lost, and the subject transmogrified.

Hamplemann conned through his with a forefinger as though verifying the count.

Scharf glanced at them and put them aside.

"Too late for all this. You will have to come back tomorrow."

"I come from a long way," Hamplemann said. "I could not come earlier."

Everything he said fell into a silence around him. In the large room surrounded by a balcony and a narrow corridor at the second-story level, the desultory conversations died.

"I will speak to the lieutenant," Scharf told him. "He decides."

Like most of the others, the lieutenant—Berdichevsky—had fixed on Hamplemann's presence. But Berdichevsky had riveted his eyes on what lay before him, taking up this form and that, scanning each, consigning it to one basket or another. I could not believe, myself, that this plump officer type could "decide" anything of importance.

The circumstances—Scharf leaning casually over Berdichevsky's desk, his careless jerk of his thumb at Hamplemann, the impatient shaking of Berdichevsky's head—did establish what Berdichevsky particularly wanted: to impress upon Hamplemann the fact that there was nothing to fear.

Finally, when Berdichevsky agreed to examine his claim, Hamplemann came forward and seated himself with utter confidence, and this inspired a curious response from the rest of us, much like that when some action had been expected—an attack or a report of troops in strength before us.

Hamplemann seemed to arouse this sense of dry-mouthed foreboding; his presence gave an emphasis to our isolation, our transience, ourselves as a separated cohort, away from the masses of men and matériel that fortified confidence. More, he seemed to be ascendant in here, no matter how ridiculous his clothing was.

It was Proudfoot who dispelled that; Hamplemann was aware of him, even though he did not turn his head.

"Straighten that belt," Proudfoot told Elrod, the door guard. "Who are you, Gary Cooper? And why wasn't this place cleared of all nonmilitary personnel at sixteen-thirty? As ordered?"

"It's my fault," Berdichevsky told him. "We have this final claimant. He says he has a job in the north and has to leave in a hurry. Tonight."

"Then let me in on it," Proudfoot said. "I don't give a goddam if I have time to fix the guard roster. As it happens, we'll just give Private Elrod the overtime. The gunfighter. You search him?"

Elrod shook his head.

As he spoke, Proudfoot glanced at Hamplemann and motioned him to his feet, Proudfoot positioning himself so closely to his chair that Hamplemann could only straddle it, knees bent. Then Proudfoot searched him quickly, removing from somewhere in the back of the mackintosh a Walther pistol and several ammunition clips.

The clips he scattered carelessly upon Berdichevsky's desk among the papers and documents. The pistol he waved under Hamplemann's nose.

"Tell him," he said to Scharf, "to take off his hat. We do not wear hats inside unless we are soldiers armed."

"Understood," Hamplemann said.

"Why do you have this weapon?"

"For safety. The country is not safe. Protection."

There was some truth to that. Almost every night between curfew and dawn there were scattered shots heard; not all of them were from our weapons.

"You look like a damn night rider yourself," Shotgun said, turning away. He nodded to Berdichevsky. "He's all yours, Lieutenant, thank you kindly."

Berdichevsky stacked up the pistol clips. His fingers trembled slightly, his face was flushed.

"The pistol should not be held against me," Hamplemann said loudly. "It was as I said."

"Never mind. I want to see your questionnaire. *Fragebogen.* It is not here."

"I gave it," Hamplemann said, "to this numbered police and they gave me him in return." He pointed out a paper and Berdichevsky took it up and frowned over it.

I have come to know the expression that Berdichevsky assumed. Customs officials wear it habitually, passport control people put it on for tour groups so that they will be sure to understand that they have been out of their country, or that this one is not so easy to enter as all that.

"Where is the 432nd Military Police Battalion?" Berdichevsky called out to the room at large. No one answered. Berdichevsky shook his head.

"Unsatisfactory," he said. "You will have to do another."

He reached into his desk and drew out a form six pages long. This was the questionnaire devised by the Psychological Warfare Branch to separate the wolves from the sheep, the *Fragebogen.* It was the first step in processing citizens of the country back toward normalcy.

Prisoners of war, displaced persons, persons who wished to retain government jobs at any level had to provide a proper *Fragebogen.* They were processed at higher headquarters and placed in a central file there, where information or individuals could be correlated and checked, one bit against another.

It was also designed to enmesh the wicked and to establish innocence without dependence on whim. Its weakness was that only two types of persons could manage a *Fragebogen* successfully, one a complete innocent and the other a liar stained with guilt.

Hamplemann objected strenuously, so much so that he lapsed into his own language. Querulous at first, he then became furious; the sound of his voice seemed to arouse echoes from these walls, the noise of past argument.

He prodded his pile of documents: baptismal certificate, food ration card, transit pass from the displaced-persons camp, passport from the Weimar Republic, choral group membership, shooting society identity card, so much like the documentation all of the other claimants carried, yellowed, foxed, brown-stained bits, each with a seal and a stamp and scrawl, eagles with spread wings, pine trees, runes of one sort or another.

One man had shown a paper from the *mohel* who had circumcised him. A woman had handed us her instructions from the local elementary school about the materials the parent must supply to each child during the fall term in 1934—two clean white handkerchiefs and a pen wiper among other items.

"Silence!" Berdichevsky shouted suddenly. "Shut up! Already you received special treatment, now you want more! No! Fill it out or get out!"

He threw the forms at him. Hamplemann fell silent on the instant, lips compressed into a slash, jaws tight. He nodded, as though to remind himself of an obligation overlooked, and bent to gather the scattered sheets.

"I have no pen and ink for him," he said when he straightened, "and no place to write." Berdichevsky pointed to the guard desk near the door. Scharf brought him pen and ink. He doffed the mackintosh and bent to the task, scratching diligently away.

Perhaps Berdichevsky could recall his maternal grandmother's maiden name and his grandfather's birthplace. I could not have, but then I had very little interest in antecedents. There were no remarkable individuals there. This is not to say that I was sympathetic to Hamplemann. If he were eventually going to be formally or informally obliterated, it did not matter. That was the temper of the times, a conditioning to indifference. I wonder if Hamplemann thought that bizarre dress and a grotesque appearance would help his chances to file his claim and leave unhindered.

He worked away at his *Fragebogen*, dates of entry and departure from the gymnasium, the year his degree was awarded, his military service, his work record, his political affiliations, date of his marriage, birthdates and present residence of his children, all followed by "(if any)," five personal references not including relatives, his religious education and practices.

All of these queries, honestly answered, could conceivably create a cartoon of a man, a stick figure, a profile cut from a sheet of tin. These images could be further detailed, fattened with the comments and testimonies of others. But the method does not turn a jackal into an old dog eating table scraps.

Berdichevsky called me over to him. He put a hand on my shoulder and walked me to the rear of the room. There he smiled and gesticulated. I thought he had suddenly cracked.

"Take a driver and a couple of men," he grinned, "and withdraw these things from Herr Hamplemann's collection." He tucked a paper into my hip pocket. "When you read the list, you'll know what to do with them. Bring them to the inn. I'm going to take him with us to eat."

I didn't think there was any need to conspire about the matter. The man was a threat, no doubt about that. He inspired fear that all of us masked, and that was certainly common. There was a way to dispel that, and among us were one or two who could work themselves to such a pitch that they would obliterate him and never regard it as anything but an act of courage in an isolated, static scene that faced adversary against adversary, they having only a small advantage.

I would have taken part in that. I could see the sense in it. Berdichevsky's planned exercise—ensnarement, confutation, and conviction—had no value.

If Hamplemann turned out to be as much a villain as he seemed, none of the credit would filter down. It would be Earley who would be given the Legion of Merit some Wednesday afternoon at army headquarters. He who would be photographed and interviewed by *Stars and Stripes*. But all the big ones, the ones that symbolized the government, had been taken or were suicides already. The panoply and the power were gone. These quick were even now scheduled to stand on a hinged platform with their scragging a measure of time away.

Hamplemann's confession, if and when Berdichevsky could extract it, was of no importance. That was for God and his priests to hear, not for an audience of the imperfect. Once the details are offered and those have been taken down, complete with coughs and pauses, what then? Every time it is reread something is lost. Agony and malevolence pale. All that remains is a snippet of the history of a strange society somewhat similar to others, except that it was intended not for mutual protection but for destruction.

"Don't be obvious about it," Berdichevsky added, "drift out."

I drifted out with Merolla and Silberglitt and Scibetta while Hamplemann plowed on spelling out his past.

Merolla drove as though the weapons carrier were under attack. If the other two had not been with us, I would have sat silent, teeth closed, jaws locked, until the moment it whipped up into the air and turned on its back. I told him to cut it out.

"Tactical maneuver," he answered. "The captain says the less time on the road, less danger."

"War's over, you fuckhead," Scibetta choked out, "but it's starting for you again the minute I get out."

I picked up the keys to the magazin. When we arrived there it was full dark. Only one of our three flashlights worked. Merolla parked so that the headlights fell high upon the facade and cast a brown glow upon the clutter inside. They carried out the things we had come for and I remained behind to lock up. The light from outside vanished as the vehicle turned, ready to move in the direction we had come from. Now there was only a pale sienna circle on the floor before my boots. I could not force myself to stay longer. The shapes of shadow were a frieze along the upper portions of the magazin walls—soft, silent, dark shapes of figures, surrendering to the dark. I had to wait for several minutes outside the door before I could fumble out the right key and manage the locking up. When I had to sign my name to the receipt I gave to the one-armed custodian, my hands were still trembling. It was as though they belonged to some aged, palsied man. The custodian looked at me sympathetically.

"This place is full of ghosts," he said.

It took forever to return. Scibetta's threat, or the night itself, had had an effect on Merolla. He picked his way with care; again I was angry with him. He had a talent to annoy in small ways.

Berdichevsky was at the inn arranging details according to a figure that he saw in his mind, a design as weighty and simple as a pyramid with an area at the top big enough to accommodate a gallows.

There was an old plush drape strung on a heavy rod that divided the room into two sections. There were two tables in the smaller one, for officers, and a long one in the other, for the enlisted men. The drape ended about five or six feet before the center of the bar.

Kowalski and another man struggled down a narrow staircase that led from the second floor carrying a massive record player. It was an old Bosch machine with fretwork muses over the speaker cloth.

The patron suffered visibly as they inched along.

"There," Berdichevsky said, "next to the piano. Hurry up," he told me, "unload. Everything you brought goes back there too."

Eventually, on the officers' side, a table was set for four with a gleaming white cloth on it, service plates, two wineglasses at each place, and a lot of massive silver. The enlisted men had a long bare trestle so scarred with pits and pocks that it looked as if a generation had danced on it in hobnailed boots.

But the schnapps was there and a cluster of other bottles as well, and pitchers of beer for those who didn't feel comfortable with anything else. Berdichevsky had been lavish. Wonderful odors came from the pass-through wicket, smells so hearty and promising that the place assumed a glow.

The effect on Hamplemann could not have been more pleasing to Berdichevsky. The guest was smiling when he crossed the threshold as Proudfoot escorted him in, rubbed his hands with anticipation, and held them out in a curious gesture as he approached the table, as though to grasp perfection, like a traveler returning home.

Berdie asked him his pleasure and poured out, gestured to the cigarettes in a large salver before us, and sat him between Shotgun and me.

The innkeeper set out half a dozen bowls; pigs' feet and knuckles, boiled and soused in brine or vinegar. Even the ears and cheeks were there, as if to prove he had held nothing back. There were also Norwegian herring and sprats, and smoked oysters. All of this was wasted on me and on Proudfoot. Berdichevsky clung to his alcohol.

Hamplemann fell to alone, from bowl to bowl, herrings, sprats, oysters, together with a bit of freshly baked dark bread and small sips of vodka, taken delicately with the little finger extended. That was the only observance of gentility; hands, jaws, eyes were never still. He followed the content of each dish, computing the capacity of his stomach relative to what remained.

"Goddam," Shotgun muttered, "the wrong animal got cooked."

Hamplemann hooked the last pig's foot out of the jelly with his forefinger, probed and sucked away at it, and swallowed like a constrictor. He sat back, tossed down the remainder of his vodka, and clipped a cigarette into the corner of his mouth. In the same motion four or five more disappeared into his breast pocket.

Berdichevsky lit it for him with his Zippo.

"A good machine," Hamplemann said, picking it up. He snapped it again and again and blew at the flame. Finally he succeeded in putting it out. "But not perfect."

Someone sat at the piano and made his way through the sheet music I had brought from Hamplemann's collection. He showed not a glimmer of interest. Wersba appeared at the corner of the drape, glass in hand, and stared at our party. Berdichevsky glared at him and he withdrew.

"What do you celebrate?" Hamplemann asked.

"Lincoln's Birthday," I said. "He freed the slaves."

"Such a good man. And dead so young. Too bad."

"Everybody didn't think so," Shotgun told him.

Hamplemann understood.

"Politics. There should be an end to that." He raised his glass in the hope.

Scharf was instructing them in a lyric, loudly.

"I had a comrade, it says." He hummed in a strong baritone.

Hamplemann did too.

"You don't know the words?" Berdichevsky said.

"Too sentimental."

"I will change the program," Berdichevsky said. "What do you like, concertos, symphonies, opera?"

"Anything. I am happy to be here."

In the middle of a chorus, Berdie set the gramophone going at the highest volume. There were mutters of discontent for they had gotten into their stride back there, the alcohol dominating for better or worse, and the thin, scratchy recordings with each exceptional voice projecting in unique personal emotion had a disquieting effect. They mocked Caruso singing *Pagliacci*, and howled down Leo Slezak doing "Land so Wunderbar." That seemed to change Hamplemann's mood.

"That's a favorite of yours?" Berdichevsky asked, leaning forward.

"For Boers," Hamplemann said.

The innkeeper served a fresh ham with pickled cabbage, turnips, and roast potatoes. He carved slice after slice and heaped up the plates.

There were three bottles of Alsatian Riesling before us. I could not finish my ham; Hamplemann was pleased to do so. Then, after a torpid five minutes, we had a jar of rum cakes and a pot of coffee.

Hamplemann picked his teeth, regarded each morsel as he dislodged it, and consigned it below.

"Enough?" Berdie asked.

"Replete. Finally replete. I will have the shits, but it was worth it. Not in years did I see such meals. It is an occasion."

Shotgun shook his head. He had passed up the preliminary delicacies but had matched Hamplemann fork for fork through the main course. It was another contesting.

"Tomorrow'll be roast turkey with pan gravy," Proudfoot told him, "and next day roast beef. Then I suppose we'll be back to the pork again. Army gives you a lot of it. Especially in winter. I get damn tired of it by spring. Especially having sausage and bacon and ham every morning with my eggs."

"Of course," Hamplemann agreed. "It is very rich. Puts fat on the liver."

"Well, we get a lot of exercise," Shotgun said, leaning back at his ease, "chasing thieves, murderers, cutthroats. Werewolves even. This is good country for werewolves. You ever see any?"

"In my dreams. Only in my dreams."

"I mean real ones. The ones that the MPs say stretch wires across the roads at night. Or put out shoe mines just to say they're still here."

"I would never know such people."

"Why not?" Berdichevsky asked him.

"I was away from them always. They persecuted me."

"How did they do that?"

"Many ways. Terrible ways. I couldn't speak of it. Painful."

The innkeeper was clearing; Lucrezia Bori accompanied him shrilly. There was a whirring along the floor and out from behind the drape three small model automobiles ran swiftly past the bar. Even the innkeeper smiled faintly as they whizzed past his feet; a Bugatti, a Daimler, a Mercedes touring car. There were cheers.

"Pay off, you bastards," Merolla shouted. "I win."

"Which one hit first, sir?" Kowalski asked. Berdie got up and retrieved them.

"This one," he told them. "The Mercedes." He showed it to us. "Look, it has a little gearshift. Four speeds and reverse."

Shotgun was more and more impatient.

"Yeah," he said, "wonderful. Wonderful music, wonderful plates. You ever get to North Africa?"

"No."

"I did. We heard they had a lot of funny customs there. Like robbing the dead after an action. Never saw that, but people told me it happened. They'd take watches or shoes if they could find 'em. Whatever. But they were most of them starving themselves. Now here I am in a country full of churches and schools and civilization and people did the same thing. How do you figure that?"

"I did not do it."

"Then all this shit we been showing you all night long ain't yours, right? The cars, the phonograph records, this here crockery you ate off? Them glasses you drink out of? It's all somebody else's. And you are trying to steal it. That it? Say so. I won't shoot you. Not allowed no more. Unless you attack me. You want to attack me?"

"I have no reason to."

"This officer here, Lieutenant Berdichevsky, set this up so's he could prove to you that you're a thief or either that or that you're working for one. What do you say to that?"

"I also deny that."

"You're just a millionaire who got so much he can't remember half of it. But in your case, you don't remember any of it. Do you?"

"You see," Berdichevsky broke in, "you're an outrage. These things, all these things you saw here, you're claiming. But you don't recognize one of them. You're just remembering what's on the list. The inventory. Where's your copy of that?"

"I have none. I remember."

Behind us a postprandial drinking bout began. First they sang the bawdy songs at the top of their lungs. Later they would try harmonies and sentimental ballads.

"I want to know from you," Hamplemann said, as though deeply insulted, "how you can say so. I say to you this: if I came to your country. To your rooms or apartments to drink a coffee some night. As we sit, I compliment you on your table and chair and your pictures on the walls. I might say with politeness, 'Oh, sir, what a beautiful picture of apples and pears and grapes. Where did he come from and who presented it? And your dishes—' "

A visit from Hamplemann to his friends in America, to see our backgrounds. I shook my head.

"See," Hamplemann said, "he understands."

"I fed you," Berdichevsky told him, staring at him intently, "listened to you lie. I am giving you an opportunity to show some decency and remorse. You hide behind a pile of false papers and pretend to be an innocent. You are making a mistake. I tell you this. This place belongs to no one now but us. Tell me about the collection, how it came to be and who owns it, and you can leave for the north in the morning. If not, I'll bury you, hat, cape, and shoes."

"Some cognac for the nerves," Hamplemann said. Each of us had a glass with him. I thought Berdie needed it more than he did. Berdichevsky had a very strange coloration then. Around the eyes, nose, and mouth he was pale, almost gray; the rest of his face, neck, and throat was reddened.

"What is true," Hamplemann said quietly, "is that many things were given to me to keep for people who were worried about them, losing them, you see. So I said I would even though I could be in trouble. Now I come and prove they are mine and look for the people to give them back and you want to kill me. And you are democrats, republicans, officers too. But all right, now you know I don't lie. The things aren't mine, but I have to return them."

"I'll help you," Berdichevsky said. "Give me the names and we will do it together. Starting tomorrow."

"Impossible. Maybe they are all dead. Or in another country. Maybe to China even they went, they were so frightened. To Archangel."

He looked at me and nodded agreement to his own statement.

"We will do it better and faster," Berdie said. "We have more resources than you."

"I know. Armies and governments and soldiers. What do they care about such things as these? They have bigger worries. Mines and piano wires on the roads. Snipers. Werewolves. Looters. You say so."

Shotgun took his pistol from its holster and placed it on the table before him. He clasped his fingers on top of his head and leaned back in his chair.

"Chasing you is like running down a damn greased pig. But you know what happens finally. It winds up meat."

"I had business in an official place," Hamplemann said, "and some people were brought in with a radio. A radio suitable for long distances to listen in to. One of them did not move when instructed to go forward. Ha! A fellow took out a pistol also. But he hit the listener right on top of the head like that and he fell down on his hands and knees and started to bleed so they left him for a minute and then the man raised his pistol again and the other one jumped up so fast like an acrobat and went exactly where he was told. You see?"

"Berdie," Shotgun said quietly, "you ain't going to get anything out of him but a lot more bullshit. You can keep feeding him and pouring liquor into him, but what you got to do if you got the stomach for it is take him to a quiet place and kick the crap out of him. Show him what the radio listener felt like. If you want me to,

I'll come along and take turns with you. For Christ's sake make up your mind."

"I can't. I thought I could, but I can't."

Shotgun snorted.

"Why? Because you watched him eat and heard his gut rumble? That's all that's fucking human about him. You know where you'd be if he was sitting where you are?"

Hamplemann smiled broadly and poured himself another. If he had ever doubted his safety, he did not any longer. Behind him there was a bellowing of bawdy lyrics.

> Cats on the rooftops, cats on the tiles
> Cats with syphilis, cats with piles,
> Cats with their asses all wreathed in smiles
> As they revel in the joys of copulation!

At the end of the next verse, he joined in on the last line.

Berdichevsky stared at him with revulsion, his principles like a weight on his back, his arms on the table extended toward Hamplemann, hands down, fingers splayed out, not flexed but rather enervated, as Adam's were before the life was given him.

He was no factor now, and Shotgun was not either. Hamplemann understood that. Proudfoot did not originate actions but responded to them, ably, effectively, directly, with the concentration of a rifle barrel. But here he was not concerned or troubled, and shared nothing of Berdichevsky's emotions.

As for me, I was dismissed. Strangely, I thought he had measured me, also perceptively, and in this one area understood me and what I was and am better than anyone else there. He sensed absence of morality, knew my shallowness and self-interest, and ceased to consider my importance in this embroilment. For Hamplemann, this struggle was no more than a skirmish. He had not won, but he had lost nothing, yielded nothing, suffered no injury but insults.

As though he had read my mind, he glanced at me and said in a parody of a British accent: "A lack of breeding, don't you know."

Then he settled down to enjoy what remained of the evening, taking up the bottle as he pleased, helping himself to the fresh coffee the innkeeper had brought, smoking as he wished.

That set off a drinking bout, another field of battle between him and Proudfoot, who would have been on firmer ground if they had had whiskey on the table. Berdichevsky dropped out early on, but not before he tried to make a case.

"Nothing says you are as vile a creature as can be brought forth," he stated. "You have the evidence to prove the opposite. It's only the way you look and the way you behave. Your whole demeanor. There's the proof. Nobody has to march you into a courtroom and bring witnesses. The next man to pass by in the street can tell. I knew when I saw you come in with your stack of papers."

"I saw a picture of Rembrandt once," Hamplemann said with a grin.

"In Amsterdam? Amsterdam, the Rijksmuseum."

"On a postcard. It was on a postcard. He looked like a pig a little, don't you think?"

"If so, a pig with a human expression! Not noisome like you."

Berdichevsky spoke about philistines and the wrecking of civilization, not by destroying works of art and churches but the relationships between men, giving a whole generation the knowledge that none of their fellows could be trusted not to destroy them.

"Them!" he repeated hoarsely, shaking his finger. Pedagogue's gesture.

Hamplemann rolled his eyes wildly in his head.

"I surrender to you," he told Proudfoot. "But only because of my food. It took too much blood from my liver. I go now."

Behind us they were now singing songs that dripped with sentiment, howling for the loves back home, shrilling, whispering, trying to find the soft round notes of the vocalists they remembered.

Hamplemann pillowed his head on his hands and snuffled into his suit sleeves.

"Party's over," Proudfoot said. We dragged our guest to his feet. He smiled beatifically, bestowing a terrible breath on each of us in turn.

"Could a dragon smell worse?" Berdie grunted. We maneuvered him across the street and on through the gateway of our casern.

The guard corporal got to his feet and nodded sleepily.

"Put him in and lock him up," Proudfoot said. We leaned Hamplemann against the wall. Berdichevsky clapped his velour hat down on his head. We left him there. The guard corporal unlocked the door of a tiny room beneath the stair and swung the door wide. The guard, Elrod, his rifle at a casual port arms, approached Hamplemann in an odd movement, as though he intended to sweep him along the wall with the butt.

Hamplemann seized it from him and slammed the steel-shod stock to the side of his head, just beneath the varnished helmet liner. He aimed the weapon first at the guard corporal and then at us. I could see his finger, white at the joint, squeeze the trigger as Elrod collapsed on his back. I heard nothing but the sound of the helmet liner as it bounced twice on the floor. Hamplemann's face froze in a grimace. For seconds he worried at the trigger guard trying to release the safety, then he fled, rifle in hand, down the stairs to the entry in two bounds and out into the night.

Proudfoot followed on the instant. The guard corporal, Berdie, and I bent over Elrod.

Outside there was the sudden snap of a single rifle shot, and then silence, as quickly broken again by a kind of dirge as we looked down at the guard. Music it was, but as if a male chorus were bewailing the outbreak of another war.

The words began to come through; the party at the inn had ended and the enlisted men were returning, howling the last lyric. "Roll out the barrel, we'll have a barrel of fun—"

Then Proudfoot was in their midst, bitterly angry. He silenced them swiftly, ordered out the remainder of his guard platoon from their beds, and called the noncoms to Berdie's desk to explain the pursuit.

"First," he told the guard corporal, "get a jeep and a stretcher and get Elrod over to the MP barracks. There's a doctor on duty there all night. Try not to kill him before you get him there."

He put Scharf in charge of the casern. Not because there was any danger foreseen, but because he did not want "ten drunk bastards running around the area with weapons."

Most of the village lay along a crescent formed by a steep riverbank. The river was a hundred feet wide and swift.

"If he can get across, we lost the son-of-a-bitch for now," Shotgun said. "Then we'll get him tomorrow or a week from Tuesday."

A mile or so to the north a canal joined the river, but there was only a footbridge that spanned it now. The engineers had closed it as unsafe. To the east there was a pontoon bridge. He dispatched another jeep and four men to set a roadblock there, and two more detachments to patrol the road to the west and the south of the town.

He took a Browning automatic rifle. Berdie and I had our carbines and a flashlight each. We followed him out into the night.

As a military operation, it was negligible—the movement of a few vehicles and a handful of men—but I felt a vast difference between what was now occurring and the patrols I had taken part in. This was no cautious probing, no purblind fumbling across a hump of ground. Proudfoot was master of his engagement as though he had fixed the very motions of Hamplemann's feet, the indecisions he would feel when he arrived at a divergence of two lanes or a rubble-strewn intersection.

"Stay one on each side of me," he said. "Give me the light when I say. Hold the light away from you at the end of your arm. I don't know if he can hit a cow in the ass with a bull fiddle, but if you do that it'll be a mistake if he kills you."

We set off along the riverbank. The last chinks of light from the casern and then the inn vanished behind us into a dark that metamorphosed as the minutes passed into values—from impenetrable black shapes at ground level to paler and paler grays tinted with reds of brick or purple of stone heaped in piles.

Proudfoot moved ahead by five or six paces, his concentration unaffected by Berdichevsky's movements or mine, whether we stumbled or grunted aloud at a misstep. He went along as though across meters laid out upon a chart, as if he were looking down at so many squares set upon a chessboard: no presence here upon the bluff; none in the district of ruined storehouses; no one above the quay at the point where the canal·joined the river. Here a sullen whirlpool lay just outside the main current of the stream, and a dark foam appeared and vanished, appeared and vanished with the flow.

He halted for a moment.

"I thought I saw the hat," he said. But if he had, it had not floated long. Berdie cast his light's beam upon that point and played it there fitfully. Nothing. We went on. To our right, up along the canal toward the ruined footbridge.

Proudfoot pointed at it; I held the flashlight away from my body and arced it at the length of my arm, across the approach to the footbridge. The notice the engineers had posted there leaped out at us in four warnings: DANGER! PÉRILLEUX! ACHTUNG! OPASNO!

I aimed the light again, pass and repass, and from the corner of my eye, behind and to the right, there were three flashes. Berdichevsky and I went down on our faces. Proudfoot swung about to respond as though hunting quail in a field, knowing the very copse from which they would fly.

There did Hamplemann appear, bounding along, coattails streaming, the rifle up. I could see him timing his steps to hurdle the barrier. My light had struck a rock and wouldn't work, but Berdie, kneeling, caught him just as he went up, mouth open, eyes wide.

The automatic rifle rattled at him, one short burst. He seemed to pause in midair, then he came down scrambling, outward and away, almost to the other shore before the last section of the bridge gave way and he was carried with it down into the canal.

Proudfoot advanced to the abutment, knelt to sweep the water, and opened fire again. This time there was only one round, a lesser, muffled explosion, and he dropped the rifle and remained there on hands and knees.

Berdichevsky and I moved forward, he shining his light upon the dark water. I emptied a whole clip along the bulkhead and lower pilings.

Proudfoot stood behind us, left hand over his eye.

"Blowback," he told us.

There were deep powder burns on his cheek and both eyelids and a wound on the cheekbone. He carried the rifle back with him, and sat stoically in the casern while he was bandaged. We waited for transport once more. Already there were more casualties this night than I had seen in the last days of hostilities.

The two of them, Berdichevsky and Proudfoot, sat opposite each other on straight-backed chairs, arms folded on their chests as though to mark and emphasize the comradeship.

I left them alone and did what was necessary, recalling the jeeps and men we had sent out, drafting a preliminary report on the action, returning the weapons to the rifle racks.

"It was my goddamned obsession that caused it," Berdichevsky said. "A confusion of the mind. Doing justice with other people's strength."

"You're doing me a lot of good," Shotgun said. "Giving me a pain in the ass besides the one in the face. Shut up about it. I ain't dead, he is. Got him somewhere between his collarbones and his ears."

That was as much emotion as he would demonstrate. Proudfoot did not accept pity.

Earley returned at eleven the next morning. The weather had worsened. The trip that usually took two hours had required five. He also had been given no indication that the 855th was not in the same shape this day that it had been when he left. Until he saw the Morning Report—the daily accounting of the status of all of the company personnel.

For months it had not varied except to report cases of influenza or pneumonia or venereal disease. Today, there was an officer injured, line of duty, a private injured, line of duty, both transferred to hospital. Under "Remarks," there was a civilian presumed dead. Nothing could be altered on this document.

He came to the door of his office and shouted.

"What the Christ happened here!"

Someone should have warned him. All he had encountered was impassivity, and now submissiveness. Berdichevsky and I standing in front of his desk, I remaining silent and Berdie waiting to make a confession and take the responsibility.

"What happens here is my responsibility," Earley told him angrily. "All you have to do is what you're told! When you were in the goddam artillery, who told you where to fire and how many rounds? Did you have the responsibility? I can't even give it to you, and I would sure like to, like two tons of shit."

We then settled down to transform the events of the night before into inevitable consequences, carefully eliminating any trace of emotion or thought from our actions. None of us had acted. We had reacted:

"While carrying out duties assigned to this unit the military personnel listed sustained injuries in the line of duty when attacked by a civilian claiming certain properties held under procedures stated in orders issued by the Judge Advocate General's Department, Seventh Army, dtd 11/11/45 . . ."

In the same official tone—there was an indication of hurt pride together with the confession that contributed to its integrity—the report noted that "the said civilian, Hamplemann, Alexander, after disarming a guard, took his weapon and disappeared from the company's headquarters. A search was ordered by the Acting Company Commander. At approximately 0045 hours, the search party under the command of Lt. Proudfoot came under heavy fire, which was returned."

"Heavy fire," Earley said. "I wonder about that."

"It seemed heavy to me," I ventured. "Maybe just 'fire' would be better. More accurate."

He left it in.

"Immediately after the action was joined, said civilian attempted to cross a footbridge over the canal at the western boundary of the town and was seen to fall from it into the canal."

There were some final insertions and eliminations and Earley gave it to Pattison to type.

"Did you secure the collection?"

Berdichevsky shook his head.

"Then we have to take precautions with it. That will help the report too. If we take steps to safeguard it."

He ordered a truck and a five-man detail. When he left at 1500 hours, the guard had already had to clear the snow from the portico to the casern gate twice.

Berdichevsky reported Earley's detachment overdue to the Military Police at 1900 hours, but they were not patrolling that night and did not find the truck until the next afternoon. There were many snow-mantled six-by-sixes about then, some hulks, some more recently disabled.

A Military Police sergeant brought us the news. Five dead. One survivor, Merolla, in the same hospital as Shotgun and Elrod.

"Hit a mine," the sergeant said. "Probably two mines. We had to get a detector and sweep the area before we could take them out. Probably missed a turn because of the weather. Was it an official movement?"

Berdichevsky nodded slowly.

"What was so fucking important? Wasn't no cargo in the vehicle. Just them."

He handed Berdichevsky a sheaf of scorched papers, forms attesting to the total loss of the truck, and three dog tags strung on a paper clip.

"There's the trip ticket for the truck and the registration and maintenance sheet. Couldn't get a final mileage reading. You better put in a figure yourself and save a lot of bullshit. Won't accept the loss unless there's a mileage reading."

Berdichevsky took almost no part in handling that and the other loose ends. I traced Earley's signature on the report of Hamplemann's disappearance. I wrote the one on the accident and gave it to him to sign. Pattison helped with the forms for the loss of the truck and the handling of the possessions of the other casualties.

All Berdichevsky did was write letters to Earley's wife and to the families of the enlisted men. There was a lot of understated emotion in them.

I told him that I liked the letter to Earley's wife very much, particularly the part that read "every one of the officers and men who served under him have asked me to offer their deepest sympathies."

He did not answer.

Eventually a black-bordered card came back and was posted on the casern bulletin board: "The family of the late Alpheus L. Earley thanks you for your kind expression of sympathy."

The new commanding officer, Captain Daniel Estes, had it removed on his arrival. He instituted close-order drill for all personnel every morning at eight, and held what he called permanent boot inspection each day. All boots were painted under the insteps, one pair blue, the other orange. Blue was worn Tuesday, Thursday, and Saturday; orange on Monday, Wednesday, and Friday. His father owned a shoe store in Iowa.

He had no interest in the claims we processed or the business of the company. So far as I know, he never spoke to a single claimant even through an interpreter.

"If they want to talk to me," he said, "let 'em learn English." He also remarked that he didn't "give a goddam about any bunch of clip-cocks that were damn lucky to be alive anyhow," and that since they had cheated their way into their possessions, they had no right to squawk when they were taken away.

Berdichevsky applied for and received his discharge a month after Estes arrived. He took a job with a Quaker relief organization.

We had a series of replacements for him and for Proudfoot, none of whom remained very long. I took over the claims-processing activity. I had all the precedents, and I knew how it was done. As it had been done.

We moved our headquarters twice; the second time to a very badly damaged but sizable town. In late March of 1946, the grip of winter began to fail, almost imperceptibly. One morning there was an aura of green upon the hills—not yet a true color, but there was a common feeling that spring was near—the season of promise.

My situation did improve, but not without some disquiet, all of it inflicted by Captain Estes. He left the company's mission to me, and he administered it, having instructed me that the only measure of my efficiency was an increase in the number of claims handled each month. I was to see that the figure was a rising curve. No excuses.

I complied, with an ever-increasing volume of regulations to guide me. Estes never read these, but there was a confrontation if any one of them bypassed his In-Box. At 0802 next morning, we would face each other, I at attention, he sitting behind his carved walnut desk. He would uncap his lighter, made from a .50-caliber cartridge, and puff on his first Wings of the day. That triggered a bowel movement that occurred between 0825 and 0845. He would hold up the official envelope.

"Read the address." I leaned forward and peered at it and nodded.

"I mean read it! Loud and clear! Every fuckin' comma and period that's on there!"

So far as I knew, the address was all he ever read, but he was careful to initial every single sheet during the months that he had the company. This procedure finished him finally, just before the wife and kiddies came to join him. The nine-hole golf course the engineers had been working on was ready; the villa he had quartered himself in was freshly painted, furnished, decorated, and staffed with two hardworking maids.

Then he had the bad luck to run into his alter ego, a lieutenant colonel from our headquarters in Frankfurt. I was all set for his surprise inspection, having known about it for weeks. Estes, however, was as isolated as a shepherd on an alp.

I escaped with nothing but some complaints about the quality of our typing—some carbons had been inserted the wrong way: "ass-end to"—so that the information was on the reverse of the original sheet. Nevertheless I survived. As for Estes, he did not go down in flames; he was simply backed into one of his own corners. Justice was served.

"You," the colonel said to him abruptly, "do not follow orders." He gestured at the six chairs ranged opposite us. All were occupied by people with bags, bundles, cartons, and old ammo boxes. Ten or twelve more were leaning against the wall or sitting on the floor. It looked like a drawing by Goya. *Homecoming* or *Return*.

The colonel stuck his index finger into the middle of the thick blue binder on my desk. Every single directive was in it in the right order and all were initialed "DME." He flipped it open to the page.

"Read it," he told Estes, "so's I can hear it."

It was a pleasure to listen to that reading, given in the same dry tone that I had used: "'All Service Companies will provide adequate seating and sanitary conveniences for claimants awaiting processing of their claims.'"

As soon as Estes reached the period and closed the volume, he had another difficulty.

"Further," the colonel said, "what is classified information doing out here in the open like this?" The cover of the binder was stamped CONFIDENTIAL.

There were, of course, other inefficiencies and oversights, and none of his achievements were redemptive. Neither the upward curve in claims processed nor evenly worn boot soles could save his situation.

After Estes left, the company came to me, but without an advance in rank. That did not influence me to improve efficiency, but I could not have accomplished that if they had made me a brigadier. There were simply too many difficulties to overcome.

Take interpreters, for example. All of the best-qualified men were subject to transfer to Nuremberg for the culmination of this great drama. They lived there like dukes' bastards. There was an excellent mess; there was a constant stream of important people coming through to stare at the benighted figures in the dock as if that were an animate Madame Tussaud's. Joe Scharf, our top man, returned over a weekend and told me about it.

He said Goering was hardly recognizable—that star of the newsreels for over a decade.

"He looks like a claimant," Joe said. "Like a bag of old clothes. A permanent latrine orderly." And Hess. A Russian was asking him one of those questions that went on for twenty minutes or so. After that had been rendered, Scharfie would try to translate a lot of unintelligible mumbling from Hess, who was rolling his eyes, nodding, or simply staring into space. Then the Russian would get up and bellow at him again at length, and Goering would laugh and mimic Hess's response.

Scharf thought that the atmosphere in the courtroom was grotesque. The accused couldn't stand each other, the members of the tribunal, the witnesses, the prosecutors, or the translators.

The prosecuting staffs taking part in the proceedings were each running along in a different pattern, as though four legal systems were in some kind of competition.

Scharf laughed. "They insult each other politely all day long. 'My learned English colleague,' or '—with all due respect to the esteemed Russian procurator.' The Russkies never say 'United Kingdom,' so the Limeys don't use 'Soviet Union,' like the tsar is still alive."

Scharf stayed on there, and Rutkowski and Szalay, and they could speak Polish and Hungarian besides German. The ones who knew Yiddish were in very short supply too.

I tried to replace them with locals. I went to the Military Government officer who sat next to the Bürgermeister in his office, to request residents who had some knowledge of English and European languages and who had been or could be denazified quickly. But our assignment had no priority. All I got were weather specialists: "Hot"; "Not nice today"; "Bad." And they would sit frowning for an hour over even a neatly printed *Fragebogen*. Hopeless.

There were all the other responsibilities. I had to enforce the nonfraternization policy that lasted all of ten months. I submitted reports on our compliance with the anti–venereal disease program—we were not as bad as some units: our company never went over 50 percent of our strength. I was supposed to certify that all personnel had visited a concentration camp on their own time. I had to try to prevent the company's share of the black market from overwhelming our official duties.

Those suffered. Most of the enlisted personnel were even less qualified than the ones first assigned. The Evaluation and Appraisal Section made no sense at all. Publications was in the charge of a recent graduate of a vocational high school who had never before seen a lithographic press; Documentation and Adjudication was only a mail transfer that shipped material onward to the next echelon. Security and Transport were separate subsidiaries; the former dealt in rations, tobacco, liquor, and other luxuries; the latter in gas, oil, lubricants, tires, radios, small appliances, tools, and spare parts, like a tiny Sears Roebuck.

As a unit we were slowly disintegrating. We had no standing in the military at all. We did not have the fixed structure of an infantry or artillery or signal company with a prescribed strength in vehicles, weapons, personnel, and equipment. Almost anything assigned to us could be commandeered by any other component.

All we had was our exposed position in the casern. We were an official installation, and that was enough for us to be plagued, hectored, and visited by any group of passing migrators, west to east, east to west. They halted here for milk for a child, a spare ration, a ride to some unknown village in Czechoslovakia, Lithuania, Bulgaria.

The strength of the company had dwindled from almost three hundred on our original roster to sixty men and two officers. Me and my second-in-command, Charlie Probst, who simply arrived late one morning, still unnerved from his encounter with the commanding general at division headquarters.

I had had no contact at all with the general; in fact, I had seen him only once, at a division review. My company did not participate; both its mission and its unmilitary appearance were better left ignored, for the general was utterly unpredictable and quite unstable. But he was colorful and dynamic, like an ammunition dump exploding.

The review was eye filling and absolutely symmetrical. There were precisely measured intervals between the infantry companies, the tank battalions, and the artillery regiments, all with gun barrels raised and pointed east. Had there been a breeze to stir the banners and guidons, the effect would have been better. But they were limp and unstirred even by the lashing rhetoric and the music: "The Thunderer."

Nobody had warned Charlie Probst about the general before Charlie reported to take command of the six-man Counter-Intelligence Corps detachment that worked out of division headquarters. It was the general's order that every subordinate unit commander appear for interview. Actually, most simply passed before his desk while he cocked a snook at them from one permanently baleful eye and sniffed to detect any of the odors that he most detested—disloyalty, benevolence, intelligence, or empathy.

Charlie had completed the Counter-Intelligence Corps officer candidate course just two weeks before he came to this station. Trained operatives were then in great demand in the field.

On top of everything else he had learned at Camp Holabird, Charlie's instructors had deposited, together with his purple-enameled gold badge, a lump of rhetoric, adding it like the last item in a clothing issue. This was a sense of his stature and importance, and included a vague statement that when he was on official business, his rank was the equivalent of major.

As it happened, the general had conceived of a two-pronged mission for Charlie's detachment, so he did not dismiss him after ninety seconds but detailed what he wanted done. He said that he knew that the division was honeycombed with "Red cells" in which the techniques of subversion and revolution were being taught to the troops. These had to be discovered right away. At the same time, their effectiveness had to be calculated. So the CIC team was to be infiltrated into every unit, to listen and to report; to clear or condemn.

"Clear?" said the general.

"I'll put all my men on it immediately," Probst said. "Sir."

"You too," said the general. "Dismiss."

After he dismissed someone, you were literally gone, as though vaporized by the word. Size, weight, or rank made no difference.

But what Charlie had been taught by his own branch mattered to him. He stammered out a statement that someone with the rank of major wasn't properly employed eavesdropping on the babble of enlisted men.

All that the general heard, of course, was that Charlie was a major. So he put down a copy of *Stars and Stripes* that he was about to tear into with a red pencil and disemboweled Charlie instead.

All of this was reported with embellishment throughout the area: How the general had begun quietly so that there was a base to build upon—"You are either a goddam idiot or a lunatic." And then how he had seized Charlie's uniform blouse at the shoulder and twisted the cloth until that base-gold bar was an inch from Charlie's nose and bellowed, "What does that mean! Answer me! What does that say about your rank! What!"

I got Charlie the same morning, still in shock when he appeared with his freshly cut order assigning him to me and his Smith and Wesson .38 bulging under his arm.

"I'm supposed to turn this in someplace," he said, gesturing at the pistol. His hands didn't seem to be working very well. He was quite uncoordinated, as though all of the tendons had been suddenly slacked.

After a time, when he had calmed down, he was a very efficient second-in-command for me. He took over Estes's position administering the company. I got him a safe to keep directives in. I had a key; he had a key. His work was impeccable, and no detail ever escaped him. If he had a fault, and I did not think of it as one, it was that he would never do anything without authorization.

If there was a name or a signature or an initial that was not his upon any and all papers, there was serenity. So I had rubber stamps made up—the country was full of rubber stamp makers— and I got him a kind of Lazy Susan for them and hung it with stamps made up for any happenstance, some quite arcane. There was my signature or someone else's, properly illegible, and above that things like ON LEAVE TO DATE STATED; ABSENT, OFFICIAL DUTIES; IN COMPLIANCE WITH STATED REGULATIONS; and so on. These inkings insulated him, and he operated with efficiency behind the palisade.

All of the difficulties that I had in commanding the company could have been solved if I myself had had Berdichevsky's intensity or Earley's sense of dedication and obligation, or Shotgun's presence. Then again they may not have, because the whole postwar circumstance was in a state of flux. Even though the makeshift operation of the company had taken on some shape, and its skeletal structure rattled down into a process with a sense of order about it, the mission—which was eventually to be called "Making Good"—was impossible to perform. Our activity did disguise the fact: We were a unit in being, created to carry out an assignment. If the unit is there, it is being done. First the statement of reality; then reality is there.

Admittedly, I was behindhand in noticing the changes that were occurring under my own eye. I was not anticipating but only following, unlike historians, sages, managers, old servants, and experienced businessmen, who are better prepared for today and tomorrow.

We were still interviewing cigar makers, carpenters, machinists, small retailers. We were listening, sympathizing occasionally during their disquisitions—all horrifying but usually very similar in detail— when suddenly I realized that what heretofore had been only a sprinkling of men with briefcases appearing in the queue was fast approaching a majority. Third parties were arriving in force.

The briefcases were not elegant ones covered in pigskin or elephant hide and fitted with shining brass locks and corner guards. These were satchels girded with the kind of straps and buckles that might have harnessed a Clydesdale. As I saw, they were portable offices with niches for ink bottles, foolscap, pencils, rulers, oddly shaped paper fasteners, and with some space reserved for whatever foodstuffs the owner had brought along to sustain himself during the long hours in the line: a piece of salami, a chunk of cheese, even a C-ration can or two, depending on his connections.

These representatives were not as patient or as tractable as the claimants. They were here to conduct business with Authority; under the new system there was little to fear. Actually, they were far more privileged than I.

They were perceptive enough to learn very quickly that I knew nothing of the law, or indeed, of any legal system.

My great advantage was that I knew how the program functioned. If they had ever been able to familiarize themselves with my compendium, The Regulations, I would have been as powerless as the gate guard. Still, I could not bludgeon them indiscriminately with real or imagined directives. Those I had to husband and quote only in the most difficult of confrontations. That was my law, The Regulations, and from Moses to Justinian, from Prince John to Blackstone, in the time, it was the only code that mattered.

They regarded this as something to be circumvented by any means. Upon their arrival in numbers, the Making Good cauldron in my sector simmered, bubbled, and sometimes boiled over. It was as though I were living inside a portfolio of Daumier sketches.

I sat out in the open as Berdichevsky had, so that the whole process could be carried on under the eyes of the claimants. Nothing was done outside the public view—not even filing. Everything went into or came out of the gray steel cabinets that lined the walls of the central section of the casern. All of these, temporarily detached from another service, were stenciled PROPERTY OF THE U.S. NAVY. They should have been painted yellow to signify the dawn of a new day. I had only my nameplate and my desk and a single clerk to separate me from the onslaught. All was intenseness. I had no domain; rather it was a butt for their arrows.

The regulations stated that claimants present had priority. The third parties commonly agreed that this was discriminatory. They presented proof that some of their clients were injured, wounded, bedridden, or poverty-stricken. Some suffered from typhus, malnutrition, rickets, retardation, senility, schizophrenia, paranoia, depression, or catalepsy. Some were infants, children, or simply dead. But they had rights also! That must be established. Today! Now!

The regulations did not cover the matter of the time frame either. Obviously, those suffering the earliest tribulation should be permitted to have their cases taken up first. In fairness and decency, how could there be any other arrangement? How could Making Good ever become the orderly and responsible system it was meant to be if those whose sufferings were already more than a decade old must wait for their vague day of justice?

This procedure, they felt, made the program "a mockery"; "another betrayal"; "preposterous"; and most frequently, "unrealistic": "I protest." "We must protest."

They did, ad hoc and officially, while presenting me with their cards. All of them had leather card cases, much worn. The cards themselves, while quite yellow at the edges, were engraved with the most graceful scripts. Most were announced as "Doctor"; the least was "Counselor." I don't recall one simple "Herr." Despite that much uniformity, there still existed among them a kind of caste system. Certain of them did inspire deference, it seemed to me, but I couldn't see why. National origins had weight. Westerners, the fewest in number, were granted some precedence. There was thus no pushing ahead of Englishmen, Belgians, French, Dutch, or Scandinavians. Below that plateau was a common level shared by Germans, Austrians, Czechs, Italians, Poles, Hungarians, Rumanians, Bulgarians. Lastly there was a sprinkling of the less well oriented: Latvians, Lithuanians, Ukrainians, and a very few Russians. None of the latter group held Soviet citizenship.

This company of litigators worked a transformation in the

functioning of all my subordinate sections. We dealt less and less with objects that had mass, weight, and substance, and more and more with sheaves of papers. We ground them out and copied them endlessly. Our single purpose was to become only a way station in a long process of litigation. No one, least of all I, could know how far into the future this would extend. Oddly, this fact was a comfort. It led to changes in the emotional climate around me. As the professional representatives began to outnumber the claimants, there was some levity, some occupational and personal joking, lively exchanges of anecdote, and less lugubriousness generally.

My staff and I were not a part of this. We might as well have been a segment, a tentacle, of the old regime. Since we had the power and were thought to control the mechanics, we were simply the natural antagonist, as policeman and criminal, leftist and rightist, insider and outsider.

Also, since some of them were bold, knowledgeable, and enterprising, all qualities that would have been required for their survival in hectic and unsettled times, we began to receive various offers. They came directed at every level, from the guard at the door to the *"Herr Leutnant,"* with delicacy, with circumspection, and without any pretext at all. Most blatantly: When Dr. Schlicher presented me with his card, there was a tightly folded note with it. I let it fall to the desk, looked down at it, and smoothed it out. It was a handsome bill, a twenty-dollar U.S. yellowback, most carefully preserved. Both of us stared at it. I folded it up and handed it back to him. He tucked it, without any show of embarrassment, into his waistcoat pocket. And smiled.

"You ought to know," I said, "that it is no longer currency. Hasn't been since 1932 when the country went off the gold standard."

"So. Then perhaps you would like it as a memento?" He felt in his pocket for it. I shook my head and called for the next man.

Then there were women. Numbers of them, some with the most exotic backgrounds, were available somewhere in the vicinity. "A Parisienne, formerly with the Folies Bergère," for one; a Polish

girl, granddaughter of a count, no less; even a genuine Russian bal-
lerina.

On a higher moral level, there was much information that
could be given to me about miscreants, murderers, high officials who
were living "right under your nose."

In responding to these offers, I cranked up my field telephone
and called loudly for the "headquarters, War Crimes Investigating
Commission," waited a moment or two, and offered the handset to
the would-be informant. I didn't even have to wave them away; they
left quickly.

When I parried these overtures, it was not only out of principle. There was some satisfaction in showing them that they should
recognize the difference between this and previous times. Still, I was
no moralist, nor was I incorruptible. They had the awareness of that.

They formed a committee, ad hoc, no doubt, and probably in
the queue. Four of them constituted this body, and it approached
me at the close of the day to suggest a meeting with me on other
than official territory. That meant Willy Korn's establishment.

Wilhelmshof was the neutral ground where residents, occupiers,
and those now at hand in such numbers—third parties, entrepre-
neurs, and prospectors of all types—could meet. For the whole
country was a new dominion. If an undeveloped wilderness is not at
hand, a tract like this one is full of opportunity. In many ways this
is the better one, for the natives have suddenly learned to value
"civilization" and all of its appurtenances very highly. After the first
traumas dissipate there is a general desire to establish it at least one
more time.

Willy Korn, the proprietor, was one of those men who is at
his best in adversity, like Crusoe or the Admirable Crichton. He was
the kind of man who would have begun, after surviving Pompeii, to
saw cooled lava into building blocks, select a safer ground, and start
again. He had his hands, great energy, optimism, and faith—and very
little competition. There was no one else at hand with his self-
reliance and perseverance.

By the time my company had moved into the town, he was

already in operation, first as a central point in the town square where information could be sought and exchanged. His wife took charge of a rectangle roofed over with rusted corrugated sheet metal that had a gap in the center where a wrecked chimney passed through. That was the first coffee bar. Willy scrounged enough coal and peat to keep a fire going, and that, at the least, gave a jog to the recollection of more pleasant coffeehouses. Behind this he put up an extensive lean-to, within the crumbled walls of what had been a guesthouse for centuries.

Actually, Willy was a squatter, but that was no deterrent; he went his indefatigable way, gleaning from any source pile, and always with an end use in view. In little more than a year he had an establishment.

In the early days of Wilhelmshof, Korn had run a common table for those who had any sort of skill or experience that he could use—carpenters, masons, ironworkers, electricians, plumbers, and some very dedicated laborers. Theirs was a quiet table. There was a sense of relief about it—that there was food before them, and a day's work beyond.

The constabulary stopped in often, and the workers all had their papers examined—minutely. None, to my knowledge, was ever picked up. It may have been that Willy Korn had run his own denazification proceedings too, although he was no altruist. After he had made all his improvements he wound up with the only decently restored inn for fifty miles around, and he settled down to run it. He did not branch out into contracting and building, which he might have done with this nucleus, nor did he become a local leader. Politics were over for him. Whatever they might have been.

Wilhelmshof was operating eighteen hours a day. Before dawn a baker and his helper arrived with a handcart loaded with baskets of dough, mixed and raised the evening before. They started a fire on the circular hearth and heated the great ovens that flanked it, producing bread, rolls, doughnuts, and pastries for the house and a long line of purchasers. When they had finished, Korn's wife took up the preparation of the bill of fare for the day. There was always a thick and nourishing soup, and toward evening, roasts appeared, turned on a spit powered by an antiquated but reliable clock mechanism.

Pangenesis. The outer walls were of stone, set with care so that the mortar between them was scarcely noticeable. Hand-hewn beams were notched out to support the ceiling, all interior walls were smoothly plastered and whitewashed. There were casement windows, new-leaded and with *oeil-de-boeuf* centers, sturdy hand-pegged chairs and tables in the Tyrolean style, and wide board pine floors, freshly sanded every day.

When I arrived the committee was already in session at a choice table in a window embrasure, assuring us privacy although the room was already crowded. Now there were fewer service uniforms at Wilhelmshof. Most of those worn this night seemed to have been designed by the wearer, for in the time, it was important to have at least the appearance of official connection.

That may not have been by choice, for I had read that there was a shortage of civilian suits in the United States, and if that were so, other nationals had no choice at all. Nonetheless, there were strange shoulder patches, embroidered acronyms that mystified: UNRRA I knew, but UNECORG, USCR, and others I never did catch up with. And their insignia of rank were equally murky—gold or silver disks, doubled or tripled or in combination; bronze tildes; buttons bearing the profiles of classic figures; fourragères for all.

In my group, the Chair was a gaunt and aged German, Doctor of Jurisprudence Ferdinand Tyroler, the only committeeman who did not rise when I approached their table. The others more than made up for this default. They exuded bonhomie like sweat, and Dr. Tyroler, it was entirely possible, had exhausted almost all of his day's energy ration.

Counselor Dirk Bos, a "Dutch citizen of Rotterdam," introduced himself and his fellows, although we had all met previously. Each grasped my fingertips formally and smiled his pleasure widely: Joseph Voord of Ghent; Thomas Lauer of Cologne.

We settled in, first discussing what I would have to drink.

Counselor Bos suggested Dutch gin—*jenever*. He had discovered that it was without doubt "the real thing." It had passed the test; when he held his hand just above the glass, a green spot had formed on his palm. "I cannot even find it at home," he added. Lauer ignored this gaffe, this whiff of the recent past, and it did not appear that Dr. Tyroler had even noticed the remark. He was drinking white wine from a graceful iridescent flute. Wilhelmshof's bar glass, like the china, silver, and napery, came from many different sources. My shot glass of bourbon, supposedly Old Grandad, bore the seal of Yale.

All about us there was enterprise in various stages of development. Contractors, engineers, buyers and sellers of goods and services were at work spinning the first filaments of acquaintance into cables strong enough to bear the strains of a long and fruitful association. I sensed that opportunity was everywhere, knocking at such a tempo and so high a decibel level that quiet conversation was difficult. And all of the members of the committee had no desire to raise their voices. Neither did I. Instinct.

"Firstly," Bos said, "there is no reason to think that we are any better or more important than the rest. But such being the case, it is decided that we will represent all."

Dr. Tyroler glared at him; unused, no doubt, to denying his own probity.

"In some cases," Bos added quickly. "However, there are certain procedural matters that if discussed would be of help to all. Those who must deal with the problems. That is to say, you and your company, and we who represent—"

"—claimants with the same rights as those who come to you," Lauer added. They all nodded agreement.

I considered that for a few moments. Another drink arrived. For me. Then I nodded also.

"You can discuss anything you want to," I said, "with the understanding that all decisions will have to be made by my superiors."

I tried to think of the name of he who sat at the top of

our obscure pyramid. A colonel? A brigadier general? Certainly no one of higher rank would be concerned with this febrile exercise in humanitarianism. The claimants well knew that no force and no philanthropy could ever be a palliative. That past was the reality.

"So," I continued, "you should put your ideas about the procedural matters on paper and I will forward them. Through official channels."

They considered that very briefly. Dr. Tyroler poured out another glass of white wine and moistened his lips, staring at me, the while impassive, as though taking the measure of a defendant-to-be.

"As I have said," Voord remarked, "nothing ever changes." He nodded confirmation. Lauer agreed. Bos did not. He hunched himself toward me.

"Sir," he said, "we were all right in our own habitat. We knew how to survive there. Here." He tapped the table before him. "But the habitat is no longer ours and may never be again. That is obvious. We need a guide."

"Not so much a guide," I said, "as guidance."

He agreed immediately. "Of course. I did not mean someone to take a blind man across a square."

Of course not. There was then fifteen or twenty minutes of circumspect conversation. This yielded the terms of a broad agreement. An agreement in principle, it was, although much of it sounded like a colloquy among lower primates. Grunts, hummings, glottal stops.

The original purpose of the meeting—procedural arrangements for the representatives of claimants—fell from the top to the bottom of our agenda. What appeared instead was an agreement that included preferential treatment for certain of their clients, and the transfer to them of background information on claimants who had suffered the most substantial losses. According to my records.

There was mention of an "honorarium" to be paid to me. It was a sticking point. They were so sensitive to my reactions that

Lauer halted in midphrase when I sat back in my chair and took a moment to consider this.

Together they consolidated the position. It seemed that the honorarium would cost no one anything out of his own pocket. Neither the claimants nor they themselves would pay the percentage that was to reward me for my assistance. It would simply be added to the claim and paid by the unidentified authority that would eventually settle. At the time, none of us, including the guide, knew where the checks were to be issued or when. Nothing certain about that; nothing concrete about it. But the agreement did have an effect on me.

It was corrupt, and I knew it, although nothing went down on paper. No one made a note or even scribbled on the back of an envelope.

"But we have an agreement, then," Bos said, smiling.

"Unwritten," I answered.

"In your best interest! For a layman to write a contract like this with four like us is an error in judgment. Better this way. We have no reason to jeopardize the arrangement. None at all. And money is no issue for you just now, of course."

True. I could buy more with my PX privileges than with my pay. There is nothing like a barter economy when one has access to what is most valued. Hershey, Maxwell House, Gillette, Campbell, Palmolive, Armour, Camel, were not just brand names. They were introductions, cooperation, status, height advantage, love. They were commodities that inched ever higher in price, vastly more attractive than glass beads and brass wire had been in the Far Islands. That was fact and it was demonstrated almost immediately.

The sun had not yet set, but Frau Korn, anticipating, moved from table to table in the darkening room bringing candles in pewter holders to each. Outside in the square a band of brothers was debarking from a slab-sided bus made in Detroit. These vehicles were appearing in numbers everywhere; they operated under every flag, moving casuals of all kinds.

This one had been repainted over its original olive drab, but not enough pale blue had been available, it seemed, for the front fenders, the roof, and most of the stern quarter were still an uneven sienna. A greyhound, beautifully executed in white, belly to the ground, was painted on the side, and beneath it in translation, "Grauhund."

At first glance these passengers did not have much in common. Some were emaciated, some barely ambulatory. A very few were sunburned and looked quite fit, neatly dressed in U.S. Army chinos. There were perhaps thirty in all. Dismounting, they gathered as though ordered to assemble, outside the windows of Wilhelmshof. They crowded themselves together without jostling to peer inside.

They did not speak or gesture; they simply stared as at some rare and beautiful stage performance, following glasses raised, lips pursed for sipping, the smoke curling from cigars and cigarettes, the forks and knives in satisfying motion from plates to mouths. As one man they smelled, tasted, chewed, and drank.

One of our fellow patrons rapped his knuckles sharply on his table and gestured to Frau Korn.

"Draw the curtains, madame," he said peremptorily. "No need to sit here on display."

"It is not possible," she told him. "It is late to be given to us the curtains."

He went to the door and called out.

"Who's in charge here?" There was no answer, only a shuffling of feet and some little movement. Then a man brushed past our diner and entered. Berdichevsky. I had not seen him in a year.

Oblivious to both the customer and to me—I had risen to wave to him—he made his way to Frau Korn, set the cardboard carton he carried on the floor, and launched a persuasive and voluble speech. She demurring from the first syllable. Then our diner took a hand in the matter, and the others in the room suddenly quieted to listen.

"If those are your men out there, we order you to move them along. Somewhere else!"

Berdichevsky ignored him.

"Half a canteen of soup for each man," he said to Frau Korn. "Twenty-eight of them."

She could not take the responsibility. That much soup would cause an immediate shortage inside. Undelivered curtains were one thing, but soup was another matter. Tonight, broad bean with bacon. Not possible.

I picked up my musette, went over, and shoved it at him. He looked inside it, grinned with pleasure, and shook my hand.

"I did not mean that you should donate this soup. I mean to pay for it. And not in scrip. Here are three cartons of Chesterfields. Not Chelseas, madame. Ches-ter-fields!"

Typically Berdichevskyan to overturn the whole local price structure. Frau Korn's eyes widened. Although matters of trade and barter were her husband's province, this price was extraordinary. Three more pristine cartons still wrapped in waxed barrier paper to add to their inventory.

Our fellow was outraged. Undermining a satisfactory economy, particularly so soon after a devastating war when some measure of stability is just reappearing, is mindless at the least.

"Who in the hell are you," he snapped, "who are you to come in here making deals! If you and your scum aren't out of here in two minutes you can explain it to the constabulary!" He pointed to one of his tablemates. "Go down to the police post. Get somebody in authority up here!"

He had enough rancor for me as well.

"And what the Christ kind of officer are you to finance him? Maybe there's an excuse for a goddam DP to be chiseling around the country, but you ought to know better."

"He's a humanitarian," Berdie told him in English with a good wide smile. "And we'll all be gone soon. It's just that the detachment hasn't had anything to eat since yesterday. And this is where they scatter. From here they walk. For some a long way."

Our fellow gave him a curt nod, finally. "See that they do." He returned to his table and took up his cutlery.

It was not Berdie who organized matters at the kitchen entrance. Frau Korn did. She and a waitress carried out two great round metal trays with the soup servings in bowls, and a generous supply of the fresh Wilhelmshof loaves. Berdie's passengers gathered around a tarp at the rear of *Grauhund* and fell to in the soft twilight.

I concluded my first meeting with the committee. Each of them presented his certification that he had fulfilled our rigorous requirements for representatives of claimants. None had had any association, as member or official, with any of the proscribed organizations. All had proof of citizenship in their various countries, and of their professional qualifications to practice.

I agreed to open a file for a few of the claimants they were acting for—families who had removed to Rotterdam, or Buenos Aires or Brussels in the early thirties, had disappeared or remained uncontacted, and who had been listed in our circulars issued on such and such dates. They had not yet established whether they were representing heirs or survivors or those actually listed. But they felt that claims should be entered while they pressed the search for Handmacher, Weisbond, Kavaler, et cetera, et cetera.

It was all very reasonable, and no misdemeanor, just a small infringement of an order that I sometimes followed scrupulously if I wanted to put an obstruction in the path of one of the more obnoxious ones I dealt with. A file was not usually opened until information submitted by claimant or representative had been given at least a cursory check by our Documents Section. These days it was only an incompetency that might not respond for days, weeks, or even months.

"One more suggestion I would make," Bos said. I was, I told them, going to renew my acquaintance with Berdichevsky out in the square. I paused to listen—out of courtesy, nothing more.

"It may be that you have records of sizable properties still unclaimed. And we have sources to trace them with. If you would feel that we could be of service in that direction, you have only to inform us. It is not impossible that something could come of that, and all of us being of some service, that too could be part of your honorarium. In addition to assisting these parties in receiving rightful compensation. Eh?"

"I'll see," I said impatiently. Every time I agreed to a request, there was another, like a grasp on my sleeve.

He smiled widely.

"Not only in your own company, but others as well. Eh?"

I nodded, pumped each hand in turn once, downward, in the style they all favored, and departed much happier to be out in the clear air of the square.

I sat down next to Berdie, he squatting on his heels like some peasant veteran of an earlier war, smoking and smiling beatifically as he watched the dispatching of the refreshment. They all dined in a more mannerly fashion than those inside Wilhelmshof. There was a tone of appreciation undissembled.

In the twelve months there had been changes in Berdichevsky. He was haggard and his face and forehead were lined. Now, when those who had survived their time in combat were straightening up from their premature aging, reentering an era that would be vastly less threatening, and able to calculate a future in something more than days, he looked more than ever burdened down.

I told him so. He handed me an oversized business card.

"You think it's easy to be a capitalist?"

GRAUHUND BUSGESELLSCHAFT. I.A.B. BERDICHEVSKY, GENERAL-DIREKTOR.

"You'd be surprised what an impression it makes. Even some of the Russians know the name. And everybody takes a director general seriously."

"Who do you hear from these days? Shotgun? Anybody?"

"I had a letter asking about you. He's in Japan."

His passengers had finished. A two-man detail, self-appointed, stacked the bowls and spoons on the trays and carried them back to the kitchen. What remained of the bread was carefully divided and stowed in pockets or packs. In twos and threes they nodded to him and drifted away; a couple of them paused to shake his hand and mumble a thank-you.

"Last stop?" I asked.

"For the moment. Probably the clutch." He nodded at the front bumper, where the last of them was wiping his bowl clean with the heel of a loaf. "The water pump. Maybe even the transmission. I am amazed at how much I know these days about engines. No repairman will ever screw me again. If I ever should happen to own a car someday.

"That's our mechanic, Hermann Fincke. My instructor. He said he drove for General von Witzleben. A hundred thousand k's."

The last I had heard of Berdie was that he had been working for a Quaker relief organization.

"Very good people," he said. "Their program made sense and they try not to be political. They want to support farm production so that the innocent don't spend another winter starving. But I didn't know anything about that, and the results aren't soon enough for me. I helped to plan the supply and distribution system. It was like working in any other headquarters. Then one day the bus broke down—for good, it was said—and I took it over. Here I am."

The mechanic drifted over and waited politely to be recognized. Berdie listened. From what I could understand there was no absolute diagnosis yet for *Grauhund*. But steps could be taken.

Fincke had heard of a tank wrecker, "*Amerikanische*," that was operable in the vicinity, and he thought he could have the use of an abandoned military vehicle maintenance facility for a day or two. Berdichevsky commended his perseverance and his enterprise. Fincke raised a finger to his cap and left us.

"And so," Berdie said, "I'm stuck. You want somebody to reminisce with?"

"The billet is five minutes' walk," I told him, "and I'm giving you bathroom privileges. There's hot water for two hours every evening, and I'll waive mine."

He grinned. "That's just self-preservation."

3.

Your Organizing Committee can now report that a solid cadre of the old 855th will be on hand next November. We are finalizing plans and expect to cut orders and send them to you no later than 1 September! SPECIAL NOTE: *The Committee wants to be sure nobody is left out because of lack of funds. We know about Mortgage and Car payments. Funds are available through the generosity of certain Committeemen so that any member can be present on a Completely Confidential basis. (Smile) Whether you're short a twenty or the whole six hundred and fifty bucks (estimated cost), which includes a three-day Spree in Gay Paree, check the box enclosed and say what you need. No sweat! Those who have it are requested to put up half as soon as possible. $325.00.*

Billy "The Clam" Pattison

My billet on Lutheranallee had been turned down by a number of other officers. They had taken a look at what remained of the street and had never gone further. The house did look like a habitat for vandals—one exterior wall had been sheared off from roof to street level and a comb of emptied spaces gaped. But beyond that the interior was still sound, and my rooms were not only comfortable, they were snug. This was due to the abilities of some of the other tenants, half a dozen familial groups I had never sorted out.

They did have an organized approach to the problem of existence. The old or infirm left as early as I did each morning to barter or trade or forage for whatever foodstuffs appeared in the central square—still something of a shambles. Later I would see their children, with sacks or baskets or pails, sifting the ashes from the heaps behind our casern for bits of usable coal.

Most of the others applied themselves to the only regular employment open to them while they awaited the clearance of their official histories.

This was rubble removal, the major industry in an era that recalled the sense of man as builder and as destroyer. The task had opportunities and openings for all, whatever the sex, age, physical condition, capacities, or disabilities. A man without a leg could sit beside an irregular cairn and separate mortar from stones. A wraith of a woman could use a besom.

Since there could be no specific date assigned for the completion of the work—that could only be considered in terms of era or epoch—the pace was measured and even. If there were problems shifting large timbers or twisted I beams or blocks of masonry, enough workers gathered at the point of effort to deal with them. Similar difficulties had been solved by the work force that had labored on the Pyramids.

Only the most rudimentary equipment was at hand—shovels, picks, pinch bars, sledgehammers, and whatever else they could fashion for themselves for mechanical assistance: levers, rope slings, wooden hoists, gin poles, stoneboats.

Enclave by enclave, corner by corner, there was accomplishment. Paths were cleared and widened, bricks and stone were sorted and stacked. Lumber, after nails and fittings were salvaged, was yarded by size. So was sash, glazed and unglazed, and so also were staircases, piping, wire and cable, plumbing fixtures, and sinks, tubs, and bowls, some from the time of the last emperor.

We passed along, Berdichevsky and I, our faces expressionless, like two visitors from another planet who had descended very recently from above. We spoke in half sentences, phrases that made a point between ourselves only. I mentioned other reclamation I had seen. I pointed out a half-timbered, stuccoed facade nearby. There, one morning, they had turned up a grandfather clock. When that was pried up, they found a corpse beneath it, white with plaster dust, and with a grimace of pain or rage plain upon the mummified face.

"Schwert," one of them said. They lifted him to a barrow, his name chalked on a bit of shingle on his chest. One of them trundled him away toward the town cemetery. They bore the clock off on its own litter.

At this time, Lutheranallee was the only street in town with a rail line. This was a very narrow-gauge affair, and not for public use. Its rolling stock had come from an amusement park—the scaled-down model locomotive now hauled a dozen rubble bins mounted on the trucks of what had once been brightly painted carriages bearing children and parents on momentous ten-minute rail journeys. We watched it pass. The tarnished brass bell clanged; the steam whistle piped up; the tiny smokestack puffed importantly.

"Very enterprising," Berdie said, grinning.

At the end of the day, there was always a gathering outside my billet. This was a kind of picket line of tenants squatting before the entry to prevent others from installing themselves inside. There were many who would have been pleased to establish yet another household in a corner of the cellar or up on the roof. When we arrived, they made way, silently.

My three rooms were a vast improvement over a room in the BOQ, all that I was entitled to otherwise in terms of my rank and assignment. Here there were no beaverboard cells and endless drunken bellowing after the month's liquor ration was shared out.

"Bath is one floor down," I told him. "You have fifteen minutes, portal to portal. Scrupulously observed by all."

"Let me have your allowance. I can't get to the skin in fifteen minutes."

I agreed to forgo mine. He held out a blue denim barracks bag that could not have been issued after 1940.

"Is there a laundress in the vicinity?"

"Several hundred."

"I'll pay double for this batch. And tell her not to open it until it's underwater."

Noisome as it might be, it was received with thanks by the woman I delivered it to. For together with it I handed her a bar of GI soap worth more than its weight in any kind of marks.

And when he returned, a shade or two lighter and smelling that much better of Lifebuoy, I had rustled out enough of my own clothing to fit him out. Badly. But even in his days on active duty no one would have mistaken him for a French officer.

He put away a can of Spam fried with eggs, half a loaf of Willy Korn's bread with butter, and most of a pot of coffee. Then he settled down on the formal, horsehair-stuffed leather sofa with his feet up and a tot of cognac on the floor ready to hand, very well at his ease, and stared at the cracked ceiling.

"A time of galvanic change," he said. "War into peace, peace into plenty, plenty into pocket. You found a home."

I supposed so.

"Wasn't easy, either." I told him about Estes and what had happened to the company since. This was an enjoyable interlude for a time, while I held out my own cleverness for admiration, remembering to understate, including a leaven of self-depreciation. He listened appreciatively for half an hour, sipping, smiling. But then he began to fiddle with the ammunition box at his feet, and finally he put an end to my survey.

"What was your meeting about? With the pillars of the community," he asked. "What are they, a committee?"

"Sort of. Chosen by their peers. They're lawyers. Represent claimants outside the sector. Argentina, Vladivostok, Mexico. You know."

"Sure. Some are even farther away. At a vast distance."

He had another swallow and smiled beatifically.

"They're Gogol's people," he continued. "Dead Souls. But there's something praiseworthy about that too. They deserve representation, certainly. Is there a directive on that procedure now?"

"It's not very clear. They wanted some clarification on that also."

"What kind of clarification?"

I had the sense that he had assigned me a different allegiance that placed me at some slight distance from acquaintanceship, comradeship, friendship. We still sat together, but we had parted. The concerned and the unconcerned. In his view.

"The program's been changed," I said. "It's different than it was even six months ago. A year is a decade. More. All they wanted was for me to help put our operation into an understandable order for them. They had questions that somebody ought to answer."

My voice rang like tin coinage in my own ears.

"A whole structure," he said. "A whole staff of men with more rank, more power, and more influence. In Bonn, Frankfurt, Munich, Berlin. But they come here. To meet with you. Okay. That's reasonable."

He set his ammunition box down on my table, unlocked the padlock through its hasp, and opened it.

"My most valued possession." He unpacked it, removing papers in batches and bundles: yellow foolscap, loose-leaf pages, message blanks, sheets of stationery, part of a stenographic pad, foxed official forms from the German military and four occupation forces. He set out his collection, laying it out according to some scheme known to him. To me it was incunabula.

"This is an epiphany," he said. "You're familiar with this part. It's a copy of the Hamplemann inventory. I copied it out after your group found it. I worked on it at night, sometimes until two or three in the morning. Shotgun rigged me up a lamp from a dry cell battery and a truck headlight."

He walked to my window; some of the panes were glass once more. On this night, there was no moon, and in this time, there were few gleams of light when darkness came, no glare cast up above to indicate that a few miles in any direction lay a village, a town, or any small city. All that was visible below the building was one more of the many concentrations of matériel to be disposed of one day—

as scrap, or as merchandise. These artificers' works were mostly close support weapons, small-caliber antitank or dismounted twenty-millimeter antiaircraft guns, mortar tubes. In the gloom beneath, they clustered forlornly, the once-deadly muzzles raised at the empty skies or at darker eminences in the distance, as though threatened from every direction. The barrels of some had been blown apart by ordnance detachments, and these had flowered almost symmetrically.

"I had problems after I joined the company," Berdichevsky said. "You knew that, I guess. And they stayed with me when I left it, too. Severe ones. But I don't think pathological. Do you?"

I didn't think so. But I shrugged. There was strange behavior, irrational thinking, odd habits within my view certainly. My own included.

"What the cause was, I thought," Berdie said, "was the people I was dealing with, you know, physically. The emotions that they aroused. All day long, and I could never put them in order. The claimants inside, the DPs outside. The dead. The destruction. The hatred, the villainy.

"Our kindness, even if it was ordered from above somewhere. Earley's decency. That bastard's infamy. Hamplemann or whoever he was. Malignancy. Shotgun's reaction. Simple. Direct. As though he were putting a group in a target.

"After that, actually after Earley died, I left the company and went with the Quakers because I thought I needed an antidote that would counteract the sense of outrage that this place cast on me. Me. Not the others in the headquarters I worked in. Not anybody else, just me.

"It didn't have much effect. I told you. It was too far removed. That's why I took *Grauhund* out on the road. So that being with the others, hundreds of them, I could find some sense of humanness—in me and in them. I wanted to be among them just as I had been among our own.

"So I took over the bus and trundled it along. Load after load of crushed and exhausted *Übermenschen.* The stink was extraordinary.

Still is. I'd watch them in the mirror to see if I could catch them mulling and musing and wondering how they had come to this. Didn't. At least it wasn't apparent.

"Wasn't surprising either, I suppose. What wounds, what treatments. What experiences. For some. From others, silence. Just the grinding of the gears and the noise of the engine. You could put your fingers through the muffler.

"We were driving along together on this journey to somewhere, near the Austrian border—Dornbirn. It's the lesser Alps. Lesser, greater, it makes no difference. One alp being much like another, just degrees of beauty, I found, and now I had no interest in that either. Just hazardous in various ways. We are moving slowly, just below the summit, crawling behind a large farm cart and a starving horse. I took it into my head to pass there.

"And I could not make it with the accelerator right on the floor, and nowhere to go as the horse was now himself lugging out to the edge of the road, poor spavined creature. The engine was roaring, the whole chassis shaking. I think. I don't recall hearing it or feeling it. I remember looking in the mirror. My passengers were all utterly indifferent to the situation, staring straight ahead as though they were on a roller coaster waiting for the plunge downward. As though the danger were an invention, an amusement.

"Thinking I would try a lower gear, I tried to downshift quickly. Of the four possibles, I couldn't engage one. I looked up in the mirror again. Now I think I was looking to see who I was going to die with. We had no more movement upward to the top— maybe a hundred yards more, but this was our zenith. No doubt. And we were about to begin the course down, backward.

"Then a hand closes over mine on the gearshift, takes my wrist as gently as a nurse, and removes it, nudges my foot off the accelerator, and stands beside me. 'Steer and clutch,' he says as calmly as though he were giving a lesson. And, one eye on my foot and the other on the road, he slips the goddam thing finally into second. How I don't know. Just a grind, grind, grind, and finally the gear engages. We crawl up to the crest and over, and I pull over and *Grauhund* just leaned against the rock wall like another exhausted warrior.

"That was Hermann Fincke, the driver, mechanic, and maintenance division of *Grauhund.* The two of us got out and he opened the hood and shows me the clutch cable, almost chewed through, and grins.

"We sat down together and had a smoke; he stares upward at the sky, listening to the progress of the horse already three or four switchbacks below us. The rest of them stayed in their seats with expressions on their faces like train passengers accepting a delay. Philosophically.

"So he found some 'seizing vire' in the toolbox and repaired the clutch cable. Got us down into the valley all right. And from that time on things changed on board."

"How?"

Berdichevsky sat back, hands in pockets, and stared at his ammo box.

"Subtly. I don't know. But afterward some of them began to pitch in. Contribute, at least, you'd say. I'd say. They made most of the improvements. According to their abilities. The baggage rack on the roof. Shock absorbers. The spare-wheel carriers. Even that whimsical dog on the sides. And I began to distinguish one from another even though none of them was on board very long. Just Fincke stayed on with me. But there began to be exchanges. Talk. Personalities appeared. You know how it is."

"I suppose so. Doesn't matter so much to me."

"You have a different scene. You have other responsibilities. Probably even a social life."

"You could call it that. Mostly it's a blank."

"Anyway," he said, impatiently, "I began to differentiate. And from time to time, I'd ask after our friend Hamplemann. You know, of course, that politics is taboo. Instant silence. And individuals by name also. Usually.

"But once in a while there'd be a flicker of reaction. And a couple of times an answer."

He shrugged, sat down again on my sofa, and stared down at what looked like the raw material of a planned collage. There was Hamplemann's inventory, and the other ill-assorted sheaves.

"One of those was from a *Volksturmer*. Looked to be about sixty. More. He had been a guard in a museum. The Hall of Decadent Art. A permanent exhibition of what would no longer be tolerated in the state in the way of sculpture and painting. But people lined up to see those things, work by some remarkable artists. Otto Dix, Klee, Kokoschka, Corinth, Käthe Kollwitz. More went to the hall than to the collections the party approved of. Anyhow, the decadents were all confiscated, and the pictures went to Lucerne to be sold, and the *Volksturmer* went along. Five were brought back in a crate labeled 'A. Hamplemann.' "

"The ones we found in the inventory."

"No doubt at all. I think they were the first acquisitions."

"Did you get a description, or an address?"

He shook his head. "That doesn't matter. It's a start. Actually it's more important."

He gestured at his appanage with his Parker fountain pen—a parting gift from his classes when he entered the army. His signature was engraved on the barrel. He gestured with it as he lectured on his topic.

"The *Volksturmer* pointed the way. Look. All of the entries are numbered, right? For Christ's sake pay attention!"

"Do I have to look at your teeth to prove I am!"

"They are pretty green. Is there a dentist in the vicinity? An American one?"

"I'll call him tomorrow. But he'll want to do it on his own time, after hours. Everybody in the country has something going for him. He'll want payment."

"How?"

"Cigarettes, probably. Or coffee. He's a randy bastard."

"Fuck him. I'll do it myself with pumice. Never mind, just look at the number of the entry on the inventory: lot number 1829. The first two are the day of the month, then the month, then the year. Confirmed by the next entry, 'Mobilieren, 12118, sofa; armchairs, matching, 2; tables; lamps.' These lot numbers are also dates. It's like a provenance almost. Happen to know what that date was, twelve, eleven, eight?"

"Armistice day, World War I."

"You're twenty years away. We are on Hamplemann's personal record of achievement. That was Kristallnacht, so called. A week or ten days of riot and disorder. A pogrom for schizophrenics— patriotic looters.

"Now, I know that it's difficult for you to visualize this, but make an effort. Say you lived in Paris or New York or London, and there you are in the center of the city. The stores you never even had the confidence to walk into are smashed wide open, and jammed with people helping themselves to whatever they wanted to take. There was everything you needed and everything you didn't but thought you did. After a couple of days, these people began to discriminate, like shoppers. They looked for their own sizes, tried things on, or held them up to themselves for fit. Chose colors, fabrics. Others were still more selective, and they had some power— enough so they could organize a living room full of furniture. This was from Kaufmann and Broidy, a fine store, it is said. Are fine stores a part of your past?"

I reminded him of my experience.

"Not germane. These places, establishments, were great temples of possessions. What they stocked and offered to the public—in every country, not just here—made them the museums of the present and the future. They glittered and glowed like theaters. They were the palaces of the common or uncommon shopper.

"Whoever bought there leaped up into any class he could afford. He could come in a peasant and leave a princeling. Eat off porcelain, drink out of crystal, lounge on brocade, sleep under satin and goose down, dress in broadcloth!"

I had another cognac. This induced clarity of thought: Berdichevsky was a skilled actor—a "thespian" appearing before an audience of one. He was performing a drama of his own fabrication.
Nothing about this was either simple or direct; still the speeches and
the vignettes fitted into a form and a pattern. He had an overview
of place, time, era. I was driven like a gear; he functioned like a
finely tuned apparatus.

"The point," I said, a bit thickly, "the point."

"Differentiation," he said. "Selectivity. The sense of Hamplemann as a person of some influence and ability.

"He didn't simply walk in and pick up leavings. He didn't grab
an armful of shoes or stagger out with a dining table on his back.
Not him."

He smiled, considering.

"He watched. Surveyed the possibilities. After the first fury
subsided, the first waves washed into and through and out, he entered. Went round the back, I would say, to the loading docks.
Backstage. Then inside to the receiving office. He had this understanding of operations—like this one or others. That much I know
about him already.

"He poked about in there for a while, and from there he went
to the freight elevators. Huge, no doubt. A whole bank of them
with a capacity of tons.

"Up he rose in silence, past clothing, notions, glassware,
and china, to furniture. *Meubles, Möbel.* It's up there so that the
unwashed won't be testing the mattresses and putting their dirty
hands all over the polished surfaces. There he wanders from one
luxurious salon to another. Until he sees one that's just right for
him.

"Checks the price tickets. He trusts himself to know what's
the best, but why take the chance? He makes his choice, takes out
a notebook and jots down the stock numbers, descends to the warehouse area, and locates 'his.'

"Already, at this time, he has enough authority to organize
help and a truck—or maybe it's done out of friendship by comrades.

A favor. No matter. He acquires it. And what is important is not the furniture, but the way it marks out this path. See!"

"I see. You can have my bed."

"Listen to me," he said. "This is a very valuable document. It can bring us to the brink of a great understanding of what happened in this country."

"You. Only you."

"Goddam! I have no one else to tell this to. Just you. You have the experience of it. You sit here and watch one society try to deal with the destruction brought about by another. Surely the first time this ever happened! You write down volumes of misery, losses, injustice. And all of them together only a minuscule part of the whole history of the time.

"So too this creature!" He jabbed his pen at his trail of foolscap. "He has significance! Not because I say it and want you to agree. By way of his own history that he wrote down as he came along in the wake of upheaval and disaster.

"First he gleaned as if picking up some tithe that the Bible ordered left in the fields as the right of the poor. If we want to be 'just,' grant him that.

"From that point he set out on a journey. He set himself on some path that he never considered. As we all must consider. Good. Bad. Right. Wrong. And on his way, look and see what he became, this man."

I could see and understand. I had from the beginning, but there was no reason for me to walk Berdichevsky's path. Anyone could see that it was rubble-blocked, ill-defined, tortuous. With no promise of a journey to be completed, a height conquered, or a satisfaction found. Expedience was a better route for me. I thought I had done well by following it this far.

I appealed to his sympathies.

"Berdie," I said, "I have to get up at 0500. There's an inspection at 0800. Joint. Americans, Brits, Russkies, even the local Gauleiter. I can concentrate better tomorrow. After that's over with."

Immediately he retreated into himself. He glanced at me narrowly, as though truth or falseness were to be seen on my forehead. Then he gathered up his materials and replaced them carefully in his ammunition box, padlocked it, and sat down on the couch.

"In that case," he said, "you take the bed. This is fine for me." He fitted it better than I, certainly.

The inspection did not take place at 0800, but at 1015. There were no members of any occupation force, merely a nondescript group of German provincial politicians, all of whom represented one of the two or three approved parties that were meant to establish a democratic state in what was intended to be a new nation.

Claimants, counselors, and hangers-on alike regarded the politicians with either utter indifference or outright hostility when the staff shifted its attentions away from matters at hand. The representatives behaved with absolute humility and deference, asked no questions, received no information, and bowed themselves out after an hour of watching files opened and listening to pens scratch.

My committee waylaid me on the way to lunch to ask about the delegation. All of them sensed something of advantages to come, it seemed.

"So," Counselor Bos said, "is it that there will be local participation in this program? Under the Military Gouvernement, of course."

"Assuredly," Lauer added, "supervised by you. At least at first." I shrugged.

"Possibly. Eventually. But don't plan on it. Not for some time."

"Who would know better than you?" Bos asked.

"Nobody," I said. That was truth, at any rate. In less than two years no one could trace the initiative that had begun our operation. And what would spur any authority to do so? And in the new state-in-conception, wasted and pollarded, Making Good would have a priority lower than the revival of oboe manufacture.

"It's a long, long way away. Anything else on your minds?"

"The investigator for whom you purchased soup yesterday," Counselor Lauer said, "is not an intelligence agent, is he?"

"An old comrade. We served in this company together. Now he is director general of a bus company. He's in transportation. It's not very profitable yet."

"He's well known in a number of districts," Bos said. "For him there are no borders, it seems."

"He has a winning personality. And his service is in great demand."

Lauer nodded and smiled. "Why not! It's free. But how does he exist? And purchase gasoline alone?"

"The generosity of people like me, I suppose. I never asked him. Why does it concern you?"

"Please do not misunderstand. But an arrangement like ours—between you and us—is subject to be misunderstood. And there are so many agents busy with enforcing so many new laws and regulations and pursuing transgressions. Even if they are not transgressions one must be very careful. Also alert."

"Sure. Why do you call him an investigator?"

"It is rumored. His freedom of movement. He is permitted to go all the way to the East. As far as Cracow, I heard. We heard."

"Impossible. Not in that bus."

"Perhaps there is more than one vehicle."

"It is unique. Like him. There ain't no more."

"What is peculiar," Counselor Bos said, "is that he should have an interest in someone we have been asked to represent."

"Who would that be?"

"One Hamplemann. Alexander Hamplemann. Of whom I know nothing save that he is said to have been deprived of an estate of great value. In this country, of course. No doubt in yours it would be trifling. Seen to be trifling."

"Who asked you to represent him?"

"His estate only. Not him. He has not been located as yet."

"Wife, mother, sister, cousin? How did you come to it?"

"A letter from one who claims to be his trustee. Executor."

"How do you know whether the estate is large or small?"

"Only by the content of the letter. It said 'in excess of one million marks.'"

The others nodded soberly. Serious business, this was. They emphasized it.

"It should be pointed out," Counselor Voord said, "that much of our task is not well compensated. You have seen that from your many interviews, I am sure. Livestock. Sticks of furniture. Pots and pans. Pitiful. But we must work as hard to recover pennies as pounds."

"Dollars," Dr. Tyroler corrected, sepulchrally.

Voord nodded impatiently.

"So if," Bos said, "if we have the good fortune to represent at least a few of the claimants who suffered major loss, it is an advantage not only to us, but to those many who cannot afford to pay. Even the expense to us."

He tapped his swollen briefcase: "Here alone are forty-six."

The partners added theirs to the total; among the four, the figure came to almost three hundred cases.

That number, the suggestion that Berdie was some sort of undercover man, and the reference to Hamplemann were all that remained with me when I left this alfresco conference. The speciousness of the rest of it made less of an impression. Everywhere, altruism was in the air, so much of it as to displace some of the oxygen.

No cynicism diluted that substance in the upper levels of operations. Where I lived, closer to the furrowings, it inhibited no schemer, influenced no one, and impeded nothing. These four were as adaptable as varying hares. By corrupting me, they had already raised themselves above their competitors, and even above the claimants, who were supposed to be placed at the center of the sphere. And above me as well. They were on their way.

Anyone who has spent time in service falls quickly into a routine, wherever he happens to be. So Berdichevsky was outside Willy Korn's that evening, and we returned to my billet together in a murky twilight. Then it was bath time, ten minutes for each. Then a drink before and as we cooked our dinner companionably, he setting up and clearing, but not as neatly as I did, and I made a mental note as to additional scouring and the storing of various implements. After he left.

But there was someone to share the ham and fried potatoes with. And coffee and brandy. And again I sat back while he went at his ammunition box and the trail of depredations.

The sun was moments from its setting, its last rays red as blood at the base of a vast cloud of cumulus that lay over almost all of the western horizon.

This night he was pedagogue historian, master of the past, prophet and seer. He did not immediately launch into his exposition, however, nor did he pay as much attention to his documentation. When he finally began, there was a sense of the past that had coherence, a kind of unity and wholeness that I had not seen or heard from any source previously. And I had read, listened, and to an extent been involved as both bystander and participant.

"You know," he said, "that we aren't yet at the midpoint, and this is the bloodiest century in the history of man. Already. It must, therefore, be significant. It is a negative Renaissance. Devivescence.

"Here we sit in the locus of all its development. All of its energies settled in this place. And that's not true of the former. That age called forth response throughout the western part of the continent. Each nation had its own contribution to make to it. Its glories are everywhere.

"Here—or between here and certain boundaries, two, three, five hundred miles apart—this century approached its own unique stature. Here the world learned how to absorb, to accept the death of multitudes. Not out of the Apocrypha, or Xenophon, but of their own contemporaries. Brothers, fathers, sons, comrades. You see that, right?

"And then other thousands upon thousands, maimed, wounded, injured. And there was adjustment: banners, glory, poetics, heroics, tinny songs, poppies, memorials. Memorials everywhere. Cenotaphs in every marketplace. Now this was also a conditioning to accept that abattoirs and killing grounds have a part in every era.

"All of that sense can be, and right here it was, transformed into a theory that bloodbaths purify, strengthen, and ennoble a people. Then there's only the necessity, once that's known to be a sound hypothesis, to set all this into a political framework. So that then all was ready, after certain developmental and organizational steps, to charge ahead into the future."

He went to the window and looked down upon the military junk heap in the deep swale behind Lutheranallee, then up and across the unbroken blackness beyond, toward the approaching occlusion. This was no limitless front that meant a sweeping weather change at an end to a season. Rather it was a large local castellation in halting movement. Even its heavy electrical charge seemed to be turned inward, for the lightning bolts that flickered within its mass did not strike downward, but flared like narrow and irregular red paths along its base as though directing its energies against itself. Berdichevsky pointed this out.

"Nature becomes one with the national character. But that was unthinkable at first. All went well. A kind of order, however barbarous in places, ensued under the Son of Chaos himself. This continued. Unopposed, politically, morally, economically, intellectually. Whoever saw it or observed it as an outsider knew very little about it.

"But now, ah now, it will be spread out like the remains of some ancient civilization for pathological examination. Professionals in every discipline will come in to help with the dissection. So I haven't much time to waste. I must be up and doing in my own little operating room that you and I came upon by chance.

"It's for me to study the motivations and achievements and the character of the Hamplemanns. And I want you to help."

"I don't have the temperament," I said. "Or the interest. In fact I'm probably worth studying myself for some of the same reasons. You know that."

He certainly suspected it. His expression indicated it.

"That would increase your value. You have some abilities that are beyond me. Maybe you were born with them. Maybe you acquired them along the way. Maybe you were conditioned to use them by what you're experiencing here. That's all to the good."

I shook my head.

"You might be too much of an influence on me," I told him. I gestured at the room, at all of its necessities and the few luxuries as well. "I'd lose that edge and all those advantages I have now. And besides, I expect things will continue to improve for me."

This was not false pride; there was a basis for the statement. I had already begun to make calculations on what could be passed along to my new partners. Even without Hamplemann, there was an impressive list hidden away in the files that would be credited to me eventually. A base to build on. Cash. But there was no need to mention that just now.

"A very promising career is how you see it? Having survived, you're entitled to it, I suppose."

He returned to his seat on the sofa, picked up the brandy bottle and held it to the light, then poured himself a generous measure.

"Since there will absolutely always be enough," he said, and raised his glass to me. "Your future."

I acknowledged it and took his place at the window, soured by the evening, the day's work, the denigration of my character. I deserved better from him.

The storm was almost upon us. Now in the fitful gleams of the red-orange bolts, I could see rain tails, sudden sheets poured out from base to shattered land.

I heard a high-pitched, recently familiar whine pierce its rumblings. He came out of his place, I thought in sudden confusion, as though he had suddenly run amok and was set to kill. He seized the collar of my shirt and dragged me down and away from the window, and there the two of us lay on the floor, our faces inches apart, jaws set and eyes staring. In seconds, there was the explosion, up on the roof.

"Mortar," he said. "Over." Then there were two more in rapid succession, one short round that fell below at the base of the building, and the accurate third one that exploded on the coping above my window, blowing out the glass that remained, an isinglass car curtain that sealed one corner, and all of the other patched panes.

We waited, rigid, for minutes it seemed, in the dark, for the lights had failed—they were wont to do that on their own at any time—and then I rooted out my lanterns.

As it happened, there were no casualties; the shell that landed on the roof had blown numbers of holes in our makeshift cistern; the one that struck the base had fallen into a cellar entry that was unused and stoutly planked against squatters.

There was no reaction either inside the building from the tenantry or outside from any security agency. No force that did not hurl the former from their pallets into the street would rouse them, and the latter forces concentrated their attentions in areas where higher authorities lived. Too, the three mortar shells might have been taken for thunderbolts from the storm. That passed. The smell of cordite dissipated with it. The breeze fell and all was still in Lutheranallee.

Having made our brief survey of the damage, we sat down again in my living room. He was silent, his ammo box of paper scraps between his worn, scuffed boots.

So it is that I see him, rumpled and disheveled, the look of the bumbler about him, his thinking so full of clarity to him, so muddled in the transference of it to someone else. He was some kind of mental outlander living a life apart. He lived in a child's world where Nemesis still existed and tracked Evil apparent, disguised, or dissembled. He was an unpractical, plodding nonentity of a presence. A vast distance separated him from me. But he was a powerful influence.

"Well," he said finally, "I'm off tomorrow. I seem to be some kind of lightning rod. Or did anything like this ever happen here before? It's not usual, is it?"

"Never. No decapitation wires on the roads. No booby traps.

All the fighting is between the occupiers. Have you seen anything like this?"

"It's as I told you. Passiveness and impassive faces. Still, to zero in three mortar rounds like that is no sudden impulse. Took some planning. Never mind."

He flapped his hand and brushed away the consideration.

He was gone before I awoke the next morning. At ten he appeared at the back of the queue. My ad hoc committee members were not present this morning, and it occurred to me that there was no longer any reason for their daily attendance. Under our new arrangement, their clients past, present, and future would have their interests and their claims well secured. By me. Restoration of the true, the civilized, bureaucratic structure was the note of the time.

There was still a good turnout, even if the numbers did not approach those of the recent past. This day all went smoothly. The refinements that Charlie Probst had added—a little pathway of signs in four languages, charmingly illustrated by a girl he knew who taught art at a Red Cross center—made known all of our services, conveniences, and refreshment areas, instructed claimants in the details of processing, and moved them along in a most orderly way. Men have been given a Legion of Merit for less.

There was only one contretemps, having to do with a farmer who wanted compensation for a herd of cows, remarkably productive they were, that had been bombed and also strafed in early May of 1945. He had a cartload of tanned hides with him—full of .30-caliber holes. In vain did one of our people try to tell him that none of our aircraft mounted .30s in 1945. He shouted, pleaded, and waved testimonials from his minister, his neighbors, and a corporal in the Military Government. Charlie handled that well. He drew up a document severally and suitably stamped and signed—addressed to the adjutant general in Frankfurt.

That impressed Berdie when we sat over coffee during the ten o'clock break for all present. That was my innovation, though the offices sometimes looked like a soup kitchen afterward. But it eased the formal tone and damped any sense of adversarial proceedings.

"That Probst is a treasure," Berdie said. "That must be the type they mean when they talk about good administrators. If you ever wanted to leave, the work wouldn't suffer. If that's a concern."

"You know damn well it's not. There's a basic difference between us. You think you're involved somehow in a choice between good and evil. You're not. The choice is between good and indifferent, which sums me up. I'm indifferent like the rest of the known world—or most of it. I've seen it and I know."

"You sit here day in and day out, and you see, but you don't have any awareness," he told me quietly. He waved at the nearby tables, at an aged woman—Frau Raup was her name, and this was at least her tenth appearance here. I knew little more about her—how she had survived over the past years. Her clothes were threadbare but neat, clean, and as we watched, she brushed a few crumbs from the breast of her blue coat to the top of the plank table, gathered them in her hand, and sprinkled them on our doorstep for the little flock of stunted sparrows that forgathered there.

"She has an inventory too," I told Berdichevsky. "It's the stock of a hardware store she and her husband—he was a deaf mute—had in a village near here. Cook pots and hand tools, mostly. Blue enamelware roasters, saucepans, kettles the size of vats. Pliers, wrenches, saws, screwdrivers, all with a pedigree. I would like to help her—there's no one else and the husband died in a home, she said, in 1936. I thought she might be someone for Bos. Maybe that's the way. If I remember to do it. And if he agrees. And if he does anything beyond assuring me that he will. But she is skewed in the head. She thinks that if she keeps coming here every day, one day this will all be restored to her. And probably that Raup will be too. There's nothing to be done."

"In that case, yes. Perhaps. But something should be done. But Hamplemann is very different. Those things that he collected," Berdichevsky said, "are not simply property. They aren't inanimate. What he took had the sense of the former owners upon it. The silver has a patina from their hands. The music from the piano sounded in their ears when they sat and listened. They are not phantoms!"

I stood up to return to my desk.

"All right then," he said. "One more favor. I am turning *Grau-hund* over to Fincke, but he has to have a costume for day-to-day wear. Something between U.S. official and unofficial but with an air of having connections about it, you know. Maybe a noncom's blouse and shirt, pants, and a decent pair of boots if your people can spare them."

That was my supply sergeant's trust. He, Kennelly, had his own establishment. But he was prudent, very sound, and never shorted our own people for immediate black-market gain. Instead he worked our Reports of Survey imaginatively. So, although we replaced clothing at a rate that would have made a regiment suspect, he had never had a problem. Our enlisted men's uniforms, towels, socks, sheets, blankets, mattress covers were damaged by fire or smoke, exposed to contagion, or attested to be louse infested, and bales were forwarded for exchange. But he never moved anything to his own clientele before we were properly supplied.

In a land that boasted so many gifted tailors and sempstresses his stocks were wonderfully profitable—so much so that he had signed on for another hitch—remaining in grade.

Thus half an hour after Fincke appeared, he was outfitted from head to toe and needed only an American-style haircut to transform him into a reasonable replica of a U.S. serviceman.

I saw him and Berdichevsky to the gate. He handed Fincke the key to *Grauhund*'s ignition, a key so worn that it was little more than a brass splinter. Still, it was a little ceremony, and for a moment both were quite solemn.

"I'm going to Paris first," Berdichevsky said. "Fincke will take me down the Dutch coast, maybe to Brussels and on to Calais, and I'll drop off there. If you should change your mind, write me Poste Restante, Paris."

"Poste Restante, Paris." It conjured up images of American expatriates in the years between the wars, stopping at the post office to pick up a check that would keep them drunk and happy among the Left Bank chimney pots for two more months. Berdichevsky's mission seemed considerably less attractive. Still, he looked quite youthful and dynamic as he turned and waved. Shining anticipation at the beginning of the quest.

I passed into the casern. The guard—only a doorkeeper these days, and a slovenly one at that—nodded familiarly. The whole installation was nothing but a slickered-over clerical backwater, moving papers, destinies, and lives at a snail's pace.

That made me suddenly and unreasonably angry. I snapped at him as Proudfoot would have. The guard's embroidered version of my bellowing yielded some small improvement for a few days. When a month had passed, that vanished. By then, it was no longer a concern of mine.

The inspector general received a communication that detailed all of the forbidden activities the personnel of the 855th were involved in. This covered not only the illegal but the unethical. The IG turned the information over to the Criminal Investigation Division. They filtered four or five "replacements" into the company, and in ten days, knowing where to look—at Security, Transport, Supply, and the company commander himself—they had a case.

The event arrived at a pace I had not thought possible out of the clanking official machine. I had never imagined that this indifferent engine could process any concern so swiftly.

I should have considered that public knowledge of malfeasance in so sensitive an area as the restoration of sequestered properties confiscated by a totalitarian state would have to be suppressed. I should have known that the assignment of a diffident and maundering captain from the judge advocate's office to the affair was a planned attempt to show me how indifferent Authority was to the matter. The captain tittered and shook his head, and mumbled over his brief.

"Your indictment starts with 'Conduct Unbecoming to an Officer,' but that's always there, so that's not so bad. But it gets worse, because you transferred military information during hostilities—there's no peace treaty now, of course, and if they want to go hard on you, they could charge you with treason, espionage, all of that. And that's the kind of mood they're in these days. Do you want to read it?"

I didn't.

"So they said I could offer you an alternative. You resign your commission and be reduced in rank—"

"To what?"

"Private. Then you wouldn't face trial, and you might even get a white discharge. The only other one you'd get, if you didn't get a dishonorable and time in Leavenworth, would be a blue one. That's not for you. Not at your age. I would go along with them. I'm just here to explain the situation. Not to try you or threaten you."

"I'm not going to testify about the rest of them," I said.

He noted my courageous stance. Every miscreant has to come away with some sop for himself.

"It's not necessary. They have more evidence than they need."

"What will they get? Kennelly and the rest."

"They're lucky it's so common. What they've done. Down one grade for some. Six months and two-thirds for some. They're not in bad shape."

He gathered up his papers and stood up.

"Well, that's that. You did the right thing. Believe me."

With that, everything had changed and nothing had changed. Fifty feet away were the rest of the day's claimants in the sector served by the 855th.

The line of the wronged, it occurred to me, extended a great distance, and now I was standing in it. On the instant, my uniform and my insignia had no substance. I was shadow, even though still unprocessed. So I sensed a need for haste. I left immediately, returned to the billet, and set about packing. Two footlockers and a barracks bag were enough.

Two days later notice that I had been relieved of command arrived and was posted prominently on the bulletin board at the entry. Charlie Probst succeeded me immediately as acting company commander. The responsibility weighed heavily.

"I don't think I can handle it," he said. I didn't offer any assurance that he could. It may well have been he who turned over this little black kettle of corruption to the inspector general.

Despite the lack of mail or telephone service for civilians, my committee knew of my relief very quickly. They were waiting in front of the billet the day the matter became public knowledge. Dr. Tyroler was not present.

"A quinsy," Bos said. "Of the throat. Impossible to speak."

I offered my sympathies and led the way to my rooms, already swept and cleaned for the next occupant. My maid was just leaving, dragging a bundle of odds and ends. She took everything—C-ration lemonade and candy packets, socks that needed darning, half-empty tubes of Burma Shave, Kolynos, and cakes of Bon Ami.

"Generous," Lauer remarked, as she smiled her way past. "Perhaps we should not have come here to cause you more problems."

I waved that away as of no consequence. The disgrace did not weigh very heavily.

"Well," Bos said, "one door closes, another opens. But it is very harsh and unnecessary. You did nothing very wrong here. Perhaps if we wrote a letter to your superiors, you would find reinstatement."

"Wouldn't help," I told him. "Don't do it."

"You are returning to your home?" Lauer asked.

"I think to New York. The city of New York."

There were nods of approval.

"Then," Bos said expansively, "we must by all means continue our arrangement with you. It is our understanding that there are many persons who have had losses quartered in that city. And if some were located by you as our correspondent and directed their claims to us for representation, we would be pleased to continue to pay our honorarium. On the same terms, of course."

The others seemed a little pained by his last remark. He ignored this.

"I wish to establish a relationship also with advocates of similar interests. We have done so in Zurich already. You will write to us there so that we can forward funds that may be due, and instructions."

He gave me two cards with the address in Zurich handsomely imposed. With these and Poste Restante, Paris, to correspond with, there was a future.

Our farewells were formal and without sentiment.

I got my discharge, white after all, signifying honorable, at Headquarters, Seventh Army. I rode there in a truck with a dozen others, also enlisted men. None of them looked to be miscreants; in fact they seemed to be extraordinarily bright and well spoken, and well satisfied with their lot. Then I learned that they were all taking their discharge in Europe to go to universities—Bologna, Oxford, the Sorbonne. There were even two entering Heidelberg to study modern history, one of them told me, grinning.

"Some joke, huh?" Assuredly.

The two bound for Paris gave me the name of a hotel on rue Soufflot where they had spent some time on furlough. Not much in the way of luxury, but there were many other advantages. Frenchwomen.

One was separated from the army of the United States as simply as one was absorbed into that body. Physical examination, including a free tetanus booster, service records brought up to date— my most recent assignment was given as "Private, Clerk-Typist, 855th Service Company"—and a certain amount of unnecessary bellowing.

"Wounds or disabilities!" a Medical Corps technician shouted, holding up a printed form, "service connected or not service connected, should be reported right here and now. If you fell off a fucking truck and hurt your head or your back or your elbow picking your nose or scratching your ass, write it down now! So's twenty years from now when you can't walk or hear or see across a table, your Uncle will pay your bills. Your grateful fellow citizens owe it to you for defending them with your life. It's not charity! If you have a ten-, twenty-, or ninety-percent disability, there'll be a record of it. Do it now!"

Then there were cartons of decorations and other distinctions for distribution—wound stripes, service stripes, medals for conduct, courage, marksmanship, battle participation, theaters of operation, and pamphlets and applications for membership in three veterans' organizations; and at long last, appearance before the finance officer for separation pay and travel allowances.

I drew the back pay due me as a commissioned officer, three more weeks as a private on overseas duty, and an additional sum in lieu of transportation and per diem maintenance between here and the army post in Ohio where I had been sworn in.

It came to more than eight hundred dollars, most of which I stowed away in a money belt I had never had occasion to use before. Then the times seemed sunny. A few hours later, I managed to board a train carrying a tank battalion to Antwerp and my spirits rose again. Then on to Lille, Lille to Paris, Gare du Nord. A total of two days in transit, but that too was fortunate. I arrived on a soft May morning, just after dawn, a magical hour.

It seemed to me that I had passed from an uncongruent land where the aftermath of destruction lay everywhere, disfiguring, deranging land and lives. But as I walked, drawn in the direction of the Seine as if there were no other to follow, and the great panorama along the banks presented itself in the silent morning, there was another side of man and his works. Remarked, remarkable.

Later I found the rue Soufflot, and the hotel recommended. I spent two very pleasant weeks in Paris, but I never had thought of this as anything but leave time. Through a casual acquaintance who had friends at the Red Cross headquarters in Paris, I got a seat on a C-54 to the United States; one of those reserved for "family emergencies or other compassionate reasons." Forty dollars to him.

Twenty-two hours of roaring and bucketing later, with stops in Iceland and Maine, I was "home."

4.

Attention! Some of you people are as hard to find now as you were when there was work to be done! (Smile) We need your help! To insure a good turnout, low prices on Air tickets and Hotel rooms we have to invite Every man who served in the unit, especially in the First days. So if you are in touch with any of our buddies, even if it's only at Xmas, Call or Write him and find out if he has received our mail. Or better yet, send his address and we will do the rest. Help us to help you! Call or write him today!

 W. Pattison

*T*ransition time had not ended when I arrived in New York, but there was only a sprinkling of men wearing uniforms or one or another of the components. Boots, field jackets, chino shirts or fatigue trousers or faded navy jeans were in evidence, but they were worn more for utility than necessity. There was color and purpose all about, movement and intent, and nothing of the grim, dull common effort to restore a national social structure.

The Travelers Aid recommended the Vanderbilt YMCA to me, and I moved in for an extended stay, since I had neither place nor position and limited resources. These, being a child of the thirties, I husbanded. Until I could enroll for unemployment benefits, the fifty-two twenty club, I cast up the balance in my money belt three or four times a day.

This was an orientation of a sort in itself, an indication of the cost of living in omphalos. Actually, I was not unemployed, since once a month or so the Bos affiliate in Zurich forwarded a letter of instruction to me, care of General Delivery. Pinned to each was a little sheaf of bank notes of various kinds. Sometimes there were English pounds, sometimes Swiss or French francs, Danish kroner; once even some ten-thousand-lira notes. Even the most impressive did not yield very much when I exchanged them in an office in Rockefeller Center, and the amounts were always rounded to the lower dollar.

"No breakage," the clerk told me impatiently, "take it or leave it."

I took it. The largest came to thirty-six dollars. Still, it was income. As for the correspondence, it made very little sense, simply names for me to contact. It also demonstrated almost complete ignorance of the geography of the United States.

"You should make every effort to encounter M. Mendelowitz of Springfield in Illinois State, and J. Mendelowitz of Miami in Florida State. Investigation of their landed property is said to occur shortly."

Nevertheless, I made out an index card for each and put them in alphabetical order as I had done with the original group that I had brought back with me. My approach to the problem of locating those living in the immediate area was preposterous, but it took some time to realize this; thus weeks passed before my brain overtook my legs. This even though on my very first sortie, I spent five hours on various subways and streetcars searching out M. Abeloff or Ablof who lived off Pitkin Avenue in Brooklyn, and J. Abarbanel on Fordham Road in the Bronx. That did not include the time lost in wandering about, map in hand, asking directions. These were rarely correct even if the response was not merely a wave of the arm. Frankel on Essex Street, Franks on Arthur Avenue. Handel on 229th Street, Handler on Nostrand Avenue.

Of the few I thought I had located, not one permitted me to enter, nor would any one of them admit to being, or even knowing the name of, the person I mentioned. I spoke to an eye in a crevice between door and doorpost, explaining my mission in the simplest English as quickly as possible. All ended as quickly. No eye; no crevice.

I did come to have some appreciation of the life of the city. In June, some sunny streets were pleasant early in the day. Here there were geraniums being watered above on a windowsill, there stoops swept and washed down. Some sections were enclaves— almost distinct little villages in East Harlem, Queens, and Brooklyn.

The days wore on in frustration, heat, and humidity. The breeze faded to an occasional flutter, exhaust fumes lay in strata at every intersection. To and fro I rode in isolation, rattling along on pointless journeys. If I had had the whole of the 855th Service Company to order out, there would have been no progress or profit realized in this enterprise.

The names in my files would have to be brought to me, just as they had been on the other shore where they had had to supervene many more difficulties. That was exactly what the army had understood. Its endeavor had had form, structure, and organization, and it had presented itself as knowledgeable, efficient, reliable, and active. Little of this was true, but it appeared to be so; it convinced.

I counted up my capital yet again, and set down what I thought that I would need. I addressed a letter to Zurich giving the details of the new plan together with an overstatement of the costs involved. I did not wait for a reply, but took some steps to establish myself in a more stable position.

In this I had a stroke of luck. I happened upon a storefront restaurant that was in fact considerably more than this. Reisenberg's was similar to Willy Korn's place except that here the problems for address were not the result of Armageddon but rather those that had arisen in an economy that pulsed with energy, competitive spirit, and the need to supply an infinite number of wants, all within reach if not grasp, and all to be acquired at a better price. Whatever that was, one could have done better.

Through the advice of some of the patrons I found a small

office near the Flatiron Building, a two-room apartment over an automobile repair shop four blocks away, and wholesalers of everything from suits and haberdashery to stationery, office furnishings, appliances, and even cigarettes. In the circumstance I heard numerous and various opinions on my choices. I had settled on conservative single-breasted suits, disparaged like button-down shirts as offering no opportunity for a tailor or cutter to demonstrate real talent. One man indicated the detail on his own white-on-white; it had fleur-de-lis shadowed into the material, a three-initial monogram on the pocket and the right sleeve, and french cuffs heavy as manacles. He had a dozen in what was close to my size that had not been called for. I could have them for next to nothing.

In a brief time I had the benefit of decades of experience in the labyrinthine ways of living in this city. The municipal government and all of its functions were of no importance. All had contacts with some member or other of that bureaucracy through acquaintance with each other or family connections. Thus influence was always available to fix parking tickets, void violations of building or maintenance codes, halt legal proceedings, or circumvent ordinances. Generally, city government was only to be tolerated; it was in no sense a domineering force, thus it was neither unmoral nor unethical to contravene it for the betterment of the individual.

The federal government was another matter. This was seen as having some vestige of high moral purpose about it, a residue associated with the Roosevelt administrations; that had ended there. It did not extend to Harry Truman, for his failure in a clothing store proved him inadequate. No head: "If he can't make a success of a fucking retail business, what kind of a president could he be?"

If the clientele could be characterized in its general attitudes, two prevailed, cynicism and fervor. Much of this was byplay, amusement, mental exercise. The prime interest was business.

This was not economic theory. It was buying, selling, moving goods, lines, items, making, starting up, picking up, unloading, getting in and getting out. All of this activity in this one small sector stemmed from an astonishing number and variety of businesses.

Thread, findings, paper, padding, horsehair, felt, furs, flowers, flags, shook, shavings, cartons, hangers, favors, novelties and notions, soaps, solvents, goods and services. Many of them I had never known existed and never imagined where they were found, or where, how, and even why they were traded.

For some of the proprietors and their associates the war had brought prosperity. The smallest businesses and manufactories became in some measure suppliers to a market larger than any of them had ever thought existed: the government shopped with a price list that had no end and a purse that had no bottom. Now it seemed that this was a continuum, and if one or another wished to leave it, there was another vast bazaar being constituted, a civilian population primed to satisfy the needs frustrated by the imposed austerity of the immediate past, and the desires some never knew they had.

I heard of a number of very successful men who lunched at Reisenberg's counters. This was made known to me by the regulars, for I was almost as ingenuous an arrival as any turn-of-the-century immigrant, and presumably ready for induction into a society that had so many paths leading upward. They spoke of Stiller, the toy man with sales in the millions; Eisner, the girdle manufacturer who was even now setting up factories in Atlanta, Dallas, and even Puerto Rico and shipping an astronomical number of dozens; his business was so important that his son-in-law, a "graduate ophthalmologist," had left his practice to put his intelligence to work in the family enterprise. And he had a "lot of good ideas too!" There was Bach, the world-famed importer of coffee and tea who had branched out into real estate and small coffeeshops—these were not at all like Reisenberg's, they served "gahbage," but they were all money-makers, and besides they were a built-in outlet for his imports. If he wanted to, Bach could charge them ninety cents a pound for his coffee, since they couldn't buy anywhere else and keep lease and name. There was Mitschnick, the heavy-machinery trader who was now exporting whole steel factories to South America, Europe, even Asia. "What's the postage alone on that? That alone I'd like to have!"

When—and it was infrequently—one or another of these supremely successful men was present, there was some change in the air of the place, but no actual deference was given, or for that matter expected. No one truckled on either side of the counter, and no one gave up his place in their favor. But the discussions were livelier, there were better attempts at witticisms than usual, and some demonstrations of weighty thinking and opinion were heard. To be condemned later: "Keep it up, Moe. Next time maybe you'll get close enough to kiss his ass."

I think myself that they were dropping in occasionally to make comparisons, to survey how far they had come, if they had changed greatly, if they still understood what they were as men. Probably they had once shared the same fantasies that the lesser entities now had, that one day all of the greats would become the permanent backers of all the others, and march along into the brightest of futures.

Some of my fellow patrons could and did instruct and inform, but they could not educate. That was beyond their capability or their area of interest and concern. They might convert, in one of their extended and loud political or economic dialogues, but those were sectors far removed from their private and personal situations. Those they seldom or never mentioned. Perhaps they might have, if closely questioned by some companionable sociologist or listener. But who would care to know how or why they had come to be thread or embroidery or coat-front salesmen or what travails they had overcome before they could set their feet down with some firmness in the middle class? Most pertinent, to me, was that although any number could state how this could be achieved, none could say why such a multitude of small elevations had to be scaled. I could not see why so much effort had to be expended to mount what was hardly a vantage point. From it, all that most of them would ever view was a number of backs and shoulders, all pushing on. Pushing on.

Reisenberg's regulars also included a group that had been pushed out for one reason or another. This was a squad that had first come there for the leftovers. Nothing was saved over there.

Whatever was not sold the same day went home with the staff or was given away, most of it to these raffish reformed and unreformed alcoholics or semivagrants, some of whom had a lingering and occasional desire to earn a few dollars. One or two evinced traces of a past in which they had been able to organize and administer an operation. These delivered the takeout orders, and some even had enough ambition to work up routes for themselves on a floor of 200 Fifth, or 100 Madison. It was a business within a business. No capital necessary. They too were an object lesson. One could always begin again, however humbly.

Absorption of so much, and the organization of this new existence, took time, but there was still the awareness that I had had no response to my commitment from my correspondents abroad. So I marshaled another installment of my dwindling resources and took the subway to Radio City. In the arcade near the cutlery and souvenir shops there was a manned telephone exchange with a dozen or so partially soundproofed booths. I organized my notes and the outline of my new plan and placed a call to D. Bos, Advokaat, of 9 Prinsengracht, Rotterdam. Some three hours later we were connected, and the purest parody of a business association it was. He sounded as though he were speaking from Neptune's home; his voice came and went in burbling waves, and mine sounded like that of Hamlet's ghost with an occasional screeching treble.

"Howoo, howoo," I heard. "Vovely soomer."

"I am going to advertise in the newspapers," I said, repeating the words again and again, more loudly with each repetition, just as my neighbors were in their own cubicles.

"The *Zeitung*," I shouted. "But I will need more money! To reach more claimants. Hundreds need the services! Thousands!"

Afterward, I understood what had happened. Obviously, he had thought that was the sum I was demanding. That was why he had become so angry; I had heard his rage. That was almost the only thing I could hear. For the rest, I would have done just as well to have held a shell to my ear. When it was over, and I was the poorer by forty-four dollars—he never did reimburse me for the call—only his last word came through, in a hollow basso profundo rumble like the last notes from a hand-wound Victrola: "Impossible."

No matter. I returned to my office and drew up the first Notice to Owners of Confiscated Properties to appear on these shores. I followed the format that we had used at the 855th. Briefly I was an impresario with unlimited financial backing, sitting at my battered secondhand desk and considering which of a dozen or more newspapers best suited the circumstance. *Times, Mirror, News, Tribune, Post, Sun, Telegram, Journal-American, Eagle,* and others, all claiming a readership of many thousands. I would take a quarter page in one or two for a formal, authoritarian, official proclamation. I quickly learned that all that I could afford was a column inch somewhere near the lost and found. That, well condensed, and possibly legible, would accommodate half a dozen names. With the hundreds already in my files for contact, I might as well return to the door-to-door approach.

A single alternative occurred to me, the foreign-language press that served the splintered ethnic brigades that had migrated. I called at three of them, and paid cash as required in each of the dingy offices that were hard by the decrepit linotypes and the presses. They looked old enough to have set the story of the Diaspora. In due time I picked up tear sheets of the names I had listed. No one had spent much time in proofreading, but both the telephone number and my address were correct. For days there was no more of a response than there had been after we had published our first notices in Germany. This similarity I considered to be a good sign. I was quite mistaken.

When I arrived at my usual time, eight-thirty, on a bright soft morning, there was a large group entering, and more waiting before the two aged elevators, these creaking upward as though the weight within were too much to bear. I waited my turn, edging forward into the elevator with the rest, as the lobby filled again. We left all in a mass on my floor, the third, the wide corridor jammed and the center of the group before room 308. Mine.

"Coming through," I called out, holding the keys above my head. They divided quietly enough, taking my measure as I moved among them, face to feet. Then there was sudden, ominous silence as I entered. Before I could turn toward them, the door slammed suddenly and sharply against the wall, and as many as could force themselves inside did so. I found myself behind my heavy golden-oak desk, and thankful that the previous tenant had left it; it made a formidable barrier. The whole mass flowed around it, like ambulant figures from a photograph of a multitude. Short, tall, fat, thin, they crowded together, swirling about me, ranged themselves along the two tall windows streaked with dirt that gave on the air shaft, co-alesced in every foot of the space, and commonly voiced anger, annoyance, frustration, and impatience.

In the center of the irregular first rank was a man in a fusty blue summer suit so old that it had changed color at the shoulders to a brownish iridescent hue. He wore a misshapen varnished straw hat and, chewing on a toothpick, stared at me unblinkingly while he spread both arms to hold back the others, he now giving ground, the toothpick passing beneath my nose, then heaving himself back on his heels while shouting loudly for quiet. As he did so he never took his eyes off me. To and fro, forward and back, the bellow, a fleck of spittle, the toothpick thrust out and drawn back, the stare. It was a fixing, a probe into my nature and my character; no accurate vernier, but a measurement nonetheless.

Quiet never came, but there was subsidence, a tone that some-times rumbled upward and threatened. I could speak over it but only to be challenged at every pause to unkink or correct the phrases I had used during those years in the army—subject, predicate, and a spate of subordinate instructions that would address objections on any grounds. This did not serve at all.

When they finally got the point—that I had no power or ordainment to return property, but only a wish to represent claim-ants—actually even that was not valid since I was acting on behalf of another—there was a renewed outburst of anger and I was dis-paraged and demeaned in several languages. The translations were almost instantaneous: "A corpse rat!" someone shouted. That, and "shit eater," "flyblow," and even "scab."

Once they had grasped my purpose they began to depart, in groups as they had come, mutually supportive and protected, until only a handful remained; and they were in command.

Perhaps it was the air of the West, the atmosphere in the republic, that transformed swiftly—both them and me. They had become hard as flint, the issue of luck, queues, mercilessness, hardship, and the certainty or uncertainty of imminent death. And my urbanity, so recently acquired, was only a transparent coat of glaze on a common clay pot.

My feeble concept, the advertisement, was appropriate only when backed by infinite official power on a ground where evidence of that power was everywhere apparent. Each heap of rubble, each devastated factory, each cordite-stained crater bore example. That penetrated. Without that, in my one-room office suite, unidentified and supported only by my hesitant and indefinite speech, I was simply a low factotum for a suspect intermediary.

The toothpick chewer became the spokesman; he sat down in my only other chair, rested his hands on his knees, and leaned toward me. His constituency, half a dozen elderly men, two aged women in youthful sundresses with frilly shoulder straps, and a scattering of younger men, no doubt ordered to appear, watched and listened.

"So who appointed you what?" he asked. I told him about Bos and his efforts, and even attempted a phrase or two about his concern for the claimants. The reaction was palpable: snorts, gestures, derision.

"I came on account of my uncle, and a good thing for you too. He's a butcher with arms bigger than your thighs. He would have made chop meat out of you. But I made the trip, so I give his name. Abraham Kuhl from Leipzig."

He wasn't in my file. Nor were any of the others. None gave a first name, only surnames: Mrs. Fleichsel, Mr. Kavaler, Mr. Zvirin. The spokesman spat his toothpick on the floor before my desk and held the door for the others. Leaving, he slammed it hard, and to ensure a result delivered a resounding kick; the glass cracked, and most of it fell inside. I heard their voices raised in continuing indignation until at last the elevator doors closed; they were gone like some migrant flock.

I sat down at my desk, not so much shaken by the exchange as I was at the damage to my immediate future. The prospect of an increased income—I had applied several multiples, stopping conservatively at ten times what I was receiving—had not only vanished, unforeseen expenses had been added. I glanced once more at the door.

Framed in it was Berdichevsky, smiling ironically. He had gained some weight in the months since our last meeting, or perhaps it was his clothing. No one had ever worn a uniform less smartly, and he had carried that propensity into civilian life. He wore a shapeless seersucker suit widely striped in light green. Differently styled, it might well have been issued in a concentration camp.

The telephone rang loudly and insistently as he entered. When I did not pick it up, he did, listened for a moment, and replied.

"Niemand ist hier. Hier sind nur Hühnchen."

"So," he said to me, "you seem to have lost another command. Come on, I'll take you to lunch. Last time you fed me."

He led, chatting all the way across town like a guide on a tour bus, pausing now and again for the view, whether memorable or no, toward the victory arch at the foot of Fifth, at Gramercy Park, at the tiny old Jewish cemetery on Sixteenth, he peering through the rusted iron gate at a few clumps of myrtle and some straggling pachysandra, at the brownstone where Theodore Roosevelt had been born, paint peeling from its front windows, and the carriage block before it cracked through to its base.

"Nobody gives a damn unless they own something," he said. "Heard from Shotgun a couple of months ago. He's in Korea. Got a battalion. He's regular army now. Sent him a pocket chess set. I may send him a hand-knitted helmet liner this winter. What do you think?"

"Better than a cake."

"I paid a condolence call on Earley's wife. She lives in Connecticut. Beautiful woman. She ought to marry again. Looked like the other part of the classic American romance."

I wondered about that.

"Well, you'd have to see her to agree, I suppose. But he had a fine character. It's just too bad that he died that way. I mean it's just not properly arranged. There should have been another ending."

We had arrived at the Café Royal, a hybrid transplant that had flourished for a time in New World soil, a few blocks north of the Lower East Side, that way station for masses of immigrants.

Now it was anachronic; to some extent, its patrons were patronizing the place when they came there for the taste and smell of the food they had known in their youth. Few thought of a dinner there as any sort of celebration of success, as they might have once when they had come up from Hester Street or Allen or Grand.

Still there were remnants of past grandeur: tall etched and beveled mirrors set in the paneled walls, deeply fluted pillars, service stations with marble tops, chandeliers, bentwood chairs, and tables of a generous size. There was also something of the coffeehouse atmosphere, racks of newspapers in the window bays, some weedy ferns and rubber plants in gigantic brass planters.

The waiters were a separate breed; they wore fusty tuxedos, and at this hour were armed with fresh white napkins. They stood in small groups sorting heavy table silver, some of it engraved with the crests of long-gone competitors or hotels that time and midtown developments had overwhelmed, and they skewered each other noisily and familiarly as they prepared for the coming of the custom.

So it took time before we had two well-thumbed menus thrust at us, and more before we could even try to place our order. Now I was impatient, almost seething to return to the office and renew the engagement, to force acceptance of my disparaged services.

"How's the liver?" Berdie asked. A shrug.

"Calves'?"

"It's possible."

"The stuffed cabbage?"

"Not so special."

"Breast of lamb?"

"Not ready yet."

"Sweet and sour fish, then." A knowing smile from him. An insider's smile.

Thus the third association with Berdichevsky began. First as superior officer, second as practicing altruist and a kind of almoner, now here in some other guise, demonstrating a sociologist's or historian's knowledge of Jewish-colonial New York. Still, I ordered the calves' liver. The odds were in favor of its genuineness. At the time, lights did not sell at a premium in the meat industry. I drank beer, he had iced tea.

"You don't have any talent for that business," he told me. "Get out of it and go into something else if you want money. This city is full of better opportunities. If you stay with this, you're going to have even more problems than this one this morning."

"Like what?"

"Oh, dependence, dishonor, maybe death."

I did not feel any chill of fear or any twinge of conscience either. I had seen enough of the one and had awareness of so much of the other that there was little effect.

"What makes you think so?"

"For one thing, the attack on your billet. That was planned."

"How do you know it wasn't aimed at you?"

"It was coincidence that I was even there."

"You were getting to be well known then. People asked me about you. How you were able to move from zone to zone, in and out, whenever you wanted to."

"Nobody knew that I had Hamplemann on my mind."

"You told me you were asking about him. If any of your passengers had ever heard of him. And you got a few answers finally."

"Never anything definite. No description. Certainly nothing that bore any resemblance to the creature who tried to file the claim with us. All he is to this day is an amorphous presence, this gleaner that one day will have weight and shape."

"If you can find him."

He sat back in his chair, stared out at the traffic on Second Avenue, and turned back to gaze at me.

"That won't be denied to me. What's more, he'll bring himself to me in the end. It's preordained. I'm the instrument."

"You sound like a mystic."

We were served, and he lectured me as he ate, boning his fish, waving his fork for emphasis, while doing full justice to his heavily laden plate.

"Matter of fact, I was born with a caul. But this situation has nothing to do with mysticism. Hamplemann and I have a kind of association in the mind. We have reached an understanding. Correction. I have. But he has the sense of it too. There's a certain anxiety that he must bear, and it weighs on him.

"He never had any concern at all about our operations in the 855th. He took a chance, but not much of one. And he himself had nothing to lose. He simply picked the wrong representative. That one projected the wrong signals in the wrong outfit at the wrong time.

"Because of me, being so strongly affected for one thing. Because Earley was so committed to Making Good. Because we were not simply going through motions, doing only enough to appear to be carrying out an assignment. Now I will go ahead with this. It's the sort of thing I am fitted for, called to, you could say, like a priest. It's my vocation."

It was certainly not mine, and as I finished my second beer and called for another, I saw how completely different we were. He is a variant who lives in a different milieu. Native, yet alien; observant, aware, but one who would not make his way into the center of his time. And here I was, this short-term émigré, already charged up to make an entry.

He continued, accurately, perceptively.

"It was a mistake to talk about death and dishonor. You might consider it, but it was overstatement. I knew that would have no effect as soon as I said it.

"You're already at home here. You'll make a place for yourself quickly. You fit in, you're intelligent, you listen well. You just don't have the right situation. You'd be better off selling moustache wax. What I want you to do is leave it. I'll take over your office, do whatever is wanted by your overseas connections—I won't give that a priority, but that's no problem. If they're successful, they'll replace me, just as they would have you, since you're only an expedient anyhow. And if they aren't successful, they'll turn to something more profitable like rebuilding their country with American money."

There was no reason not to agree. My only motivation in the whole affair was as complex as leaping from one tussock in a swamp to another that might be firmer.

"And you can go on about your business. Any business that appeals to you. I know some people here. You'll widen your perspective. Some of them have daughters too, you know, that they'd like to see married, and—"

"Living happily ever after? What the hell are you, some crazy old matchmaker? In some ways you make very good sense by some lights—not mine, necessarily. Then you come up with this. What are you doing, settling my future for me? You go first, and I'll see how you make out."

He grinned. "I had my chance. Nobody else would have me. I have nothing to offer of any value. No more youthful appeal. Not well favored. Outside all the proper channels. So my wife told me when we parted a few months ago. I have to admit she's right, too. When I went into the army, she bloomed like a rose. In four years without me, but based on my allotment, she developed her own real personality, authority, money. She even got better looking. It's amazing what can be sucked out of a dress shop on Park Avenue.

" 'Irene Berdichevsky, Couture.' The name did wonders for her. That even she will admit." He drew the name in midair with a flourish. "She's a White Russian refugee. Possibly a princess from an émigré family on the run since 1917. In fact, she's from Marion, Ohio. Her father was a window washer, and her mother was a dressmaker. But I admit it was all her own doing. All she ever got from me was a trace of a Continental accent and a little vocabulary. And that monthly government check. That's what she built on. At our last meeting she agreed to return it out of profits. So we part on good terms.

"She's outrageously candid now. When she was telling me about the struggle in the first year, suppliers pressing for payment, a tiny payroll that had to be met, the store rent—she slept in the back of the place—she said she thought more than once about how much my GI insurance would do for her. That ten thousand would have secured the future. And we hadn't seen each other for years, of course. I was one of the first draftees. My number was the second one drawn by Newton D. Baker, the relic from World War I."

"You're thinking of a different kind of relationship for me, though."

"Certainly." He finished his fish and probed his back teeth for small bones, reflectively. There was not much assurance in the comment. Not that it mattered. Marriage was not much in my mind. I didn't feel the need for a consort or partner. I lived in a different mode, the one that I had followed with varying degrees of enjoyment or frustration for the last three years: a pacing around any square, Times Square two nights before, Washington the week before. A certain number of circuits before notice ripened into acquaintance and acquaintance into groping, occasionally into coupling. If there was a strong attraction, we went to my apartment, still incompletely furnished with items from the Volunteers of America.

Only after dinner and drinks, my caricature of myself as man-about-town, thin-pursed *bon vivant*, but I felt that it raised the relationship to a better plane. I was convinced that most of these four- or five-hour affairs were conducted with amateurs. That may have been true. There was no reason to think that young women were any less driven than I. Or even any less predatory. Romance was no accurate description, of course, but I could enjoy *Madame Bovary* nevertheless, and even *Women in Love*, and other works that analyzed relationships that differed so vastly from mine. I had no interest in searching them out. Perhaps one day some remarkable association would appear, and I would have the conviction that it would be unique. At the time, I didn't even hope so.

"Never mind," he said. "If you won't let me replace you, take me in as a partner. If it suits you better. Irene will pay my way. Or maybe you'd rather I buy you out. I'll do it as long as you don't price it as though it's a growth industry. Over time, it's going to shrink."

"I'll think about it."

I did actually, on the way back. But I made the decision when I saw the superintendent nailing a piece of plywood over the smashed glass in the office door.

"The glazier'll be here tomorrow. That's on you," he said. "He gets cash."

The phone rang insistently, halted, and rang again, as though the call were pulsing endlessly in the line. I did not speak, but merely lifted the receiver and held it to my ear.

"My name is Hamplemann," the caller said. "I think we have some business to discuss."

"Hold on," I told him. I handed the phone to Berdichevsky. "For you. Hamplemann."

He took the receiver with both hands, his face pale, his eyes gleaming, and tried to keep his voice steady. The conversation ended quickly. He made a note on my calendar pad.

"Better spoken than Hamplemann One. We meet tomorrow afternoon in front of the building at four. Will you join me?"

"A pleasure," I said, and handed him my duplicate key.

Berdichevsky did not appear the next morning. I had arrived at seven and posted a hand-lettered sign, CLOSED, on the plywood that had replaced the glass. I turned on no lights, and did not pick up the phone when the calls began to come in. There was endless movement outside, and incessant knocking, pounding, and thumping upon the doorframe; by ten, there were no more respondents.

An hour later Berdichevsky arrived, eyed the space critically, and nodded his satisfaction.

"I thought I might have overbought. But it will fit." His office furnishings came half an hour later, and he bustled about instructing two deliverymen. Unlike me, he had needed no advice on how to save money.

"Ninety-five bucks for the lot. The whole shooting match."

This mismatched suite included an enormous rolltop desk, two massive oak filing cabinets, a typewriter with a number of its keys at permanently different levels and a table for it mounted on wooden casters. This could not be moved unless he squared off against it like a football lineman. There was also an eight-foot-long imitation mahogany dining table and two side chairs, all layered with a patina that no solvent could penetrate, and a pair of lamps with bases meant to resemble snare drums and shades that were fringed all round like tarnished eighteenth-century epaulets.

To express either his goodwill or his relief, the dealer had thrown in a desk ornament two feet wide and equally tall made of some base metal from which most of the thin silvering had flaked away. This had various holes and indentations for inkpots, pencils, and paper clips and a clock set in a ship's wheel; the whole was surmounted by a green glass shade that was wired for four bulbs. Lastly they rolled in a high-backed swivel chair. He handed over a dollar for coffee money and prepared for business.

The contents of the ammunition box that I remembered went into the only file drawer that could be locked, and he then set about unpacking and sorting numbers of other files of less importance, evidently. There were also a carton or two of stationery and envelopes, a fruit crate full of books, a large suitcase of laundry, and a bulky Hallicrafters shortwave radio. At that point there was little remaining of my own, undemarcated space. That didn't disturb me, for this was only a temporary accommodation. As of the previous night, I was only abiding; Berdie worked away, concentration could overcome speculation. But he checked his watch often, the hours passed too slowly, and ten minutes early he looked at me and nodded at the door.

At three minutes before four, a handsome black limousine, an old Pierce-Arrow, left the right-lane traffic and eased to a stop, the rear door inches from my hand. The driver did not go with the equipage. Instead of whipcord and leather puttees, he wore a rayon shirt and his pants legs were rolled up to the knees. The twelve cylinders must have thrown a lot of heat.

"Hop in," he said, and as we took our places, he wheeled into a sweeping U-turn, the traffic on both sides of Fifth Avenue halting magically, without a curse from truck or taxi.

"Noblesse oblige," Berdie said, and we settled in, hastening smoothly up the avenue, ticking off the blocks steadily. I admired our reflection in the windows at B. Altman, Saks, Bonwit Teller. We turned left without hesitation before a double-decker bus at Fifty-ninth, rolled west, and executed another flourish to halt before Rumpelmayer's.

If the Café Royal was a way station for those who lived on the Lower East Side, Rumpelmayer's served another group, more recently arrived. Those who frequented it were more émigré than emigrant, some dressed in style, however unmodish, with some dated elegance.

Our respondent crooked a finger at us from a table outside; he did not rise to meet us despite Berdichevsky's wide and ingratiating smile. That smile was, in fact, as expressive of the prospect of a pleasing encounter as the rictus of a corpse struck down during a paroxysm of laughter. For an obvious reason: to the astonishment of both of us, this Hamplemann had some aura of the predecessor, whom we had last heard of falling into a canal with, according to Shotgun, four or five rounds of .30-caliber slugs in him.

This version was taller, fleshier, but he projected the same self-possession, the same confidence, the certainty that the meeting would be managed by him. Also, his clothes were as much a costume—if not quite so outlandish and better cared for. He wore a pongee suit, a beige silk shirt, a yellow tie with a marquise-cut diamond stickpin rising from it, and a high-crowned white panama hat worn with the brim turned down on one side. It was the style of our own man remembered; Hamplemann vivified and subsidized, come to New York for the summer season.

He sipped an iced chocolate. Lately he had finished several

pastries, the frilled papers they were served in so thoroughly cleaned that not a crumb of icing remained. His voice was a rumble, accented, but his English was more fluent than my German would ever be.

"Already you have my acquaintance," he said. "Begin with who you are."

"Formerly," Berdie began, "we served in the United States Army in a property-restoration unit."

A nod.

"So now you have no official position. True?"

"True."

"And no power, no influence, and no authority to return such properties as were removed."

"Not true."

"Where is the proof of that?"

"In what we did. We were the first to work on these matters. We organized it. We were in charge of it. We found the possessions, we stored them, valued them, and sought the people who had lost them. We interviewed many of them and forwarded their claims. My comrade here has only recently resigned his post. What was it, six months ago?"

Close enough. The circumstances need not be mentioned.

Hamplemann leaned across the table confidentially, grinning at us with a mouthful of fine porcelain teeth.

"But only a very small number could you find, eh, of the people who had lost these things. Is that not so? Hey? Unless you have the most modern equipment, very modern equipment so as to cross the river."

We stared at him blankly. We had been thinking of a canal and a river near it.

"The Styx," he said, triumphantly. "Most of those who suffered the losses, that's where they went. Eh?"

"As far as I'm concerned he can enjoy himself some other way," Berdichevsky said angrily. He touched my arm. "Let's go."

"You have a thin skin," Hamplemann said. "Take a coffee and

we will talk seriously." He snapped his fingers, and a waiter materialized. "A pastry? Very good here. The baker is from Vienna." He stared across Fifty-ninth Street as though gazing upon Schwarzenberg Garten. The three of us were all dwelling in times past, but his locus was farthest and the least serene.

"Three brothers," he said, musing, "Hermann, Ludwig, and Alexander, the junior by some years, but far senior in matters of importance—money, the management of assets, influence, and survival. Hermann was a physician. Ludwig, Ludy, a lawyer. A very im—"

"—pressive," I suggested. He glared at me.

"Imposing. An imposing trio by late-nineteenth-century standards and even part of the twentieth. Two with beards. One clean-shaven. Two with medals from the Great War, during which they looked like Ludendorff and Hindenburg at thirty. The other performed valuable economic services. Two with handsome wives and one son and one daughter each. One with no wife and no child. Mistresses instead.

"Which one am I? In our town after 1937 we all had the same name. Isaac. The women Sarah. All of us were issued new papers. The whole community. It did not strengthen our bonds. I then made ready to leave. I was ready long before that, but I remained like a fascinated spectator.

"For me it would have been as simple as leaving a room. Open a door. Close a door. To outwit clerks and petty officials was never a problem for me. For them it was impossible. They had a position to maintain as good and worthwhile citizens. It was a duty, like tax payment and military service."

"In those times," Berdie said. "Made a lot of sense. Like the divine right of kings."

"I will criticize. Not you!" Hamplemann said loudly. "What did you suffer. Eh?"

All around us the tables were occupied. The conversations were a babble—French, German, Hungarian. There was hardly a word of Yiddish.

"So," he continued, "these three Isaacs remained in place. Two with dignity, the third scraping his feet with impatience to be away. Every time they met there was the same argument as long as the physician and *Advokat* would listen. Then they would part.

"First one privilege gone. Then another. Then the rights. Then the justice. Then a pause. Then humiliation. Everyplace and everywhere a difference, however. Sometimes a kindness here to sweeten, a little decency to call back to them the better times.

"Still, one could see. Not far, but one could see!

"Ha! Physician Isaac said that this was simply an infection that would run its course. *Advokat* Isaac said that it was simply a trial. Evidence would be taken and a just verdict—or some kind of verdict—handed down. The verdict was not stated publicly. But it was not so closely held either."

He ordered another pot of coffee, lighted a large cigar, and dwelled upon what he had told us.

"Have you ever filed a claim for reparations, confiscated properties, anything?"

"I had no reason to. I lost nothing. Clothing. Furnishings."

"Then why did you call us?"

"It is my duty. To Isaacs One and Two. There is a debt owed to them. That I will collect with interest."

"What did they lose? Is there a record of any kind? That you have?"

"I brought it with me when I came here. I have already forwarded a duplicate to the department of the Military Government in charge of such affairs. Can you or he do more?

"I have resources of my own as well. I came here a man of property. I transferred assets worth thousands out of there under the noses not only of thieves, but of those honorable ones who served any kind of government with the same faithfulness. I can make my way without your help or his or ten more like you. Understood?"

Berdichevsky nodded impatiently.

"Let us make an agreement then. I have a list of my own of the possessions of a man with your name. The same name."

"Where did you get it?"

"In the town of Urbach."

"Never. I was never there. And neither were my brothers, to my knowledge."

"Nevertheless that is where we found it. It is pages long."

"And what is on it? Our silk hats worn on special occasions? Furs? Jewelry? Our father's paper mill? Dresden dolls with real hair a hundred years old? Treasures? Trifles?"

He gestured as if to make memory vanish.

"No more. This drains me."

We did not commiserate. He had made his own judgment that other members of the Hamplemann family were more deserving of a place here than he.

"Since you have already filed your claim," Berdie said quietly, "I would appreciate it if you would let me know when you receive a response. And from who, and if anything out of the ordinary happens. Any communication that is unofficial."

"Why?"

"Because of your competitor. He filed his claim earlier than you."

"Then he is a liar, and also a thief."

"Perhaps. Small sins, all things considered. He might be a murderer even. But in these times that's not important."

Hamplemann's face paled.

"Everything you say puts more distance between us," Hamplemann said. "That's enough."

"I didn't say that to be brutal. Or even unkind, but to make you see that this is no personal matter. It's not a clumsy legalistic affair to be settled by exchanges of records and processing documents that when over there is a pile of papers and a check to cash.

"Is that enough for you? Payment for eight lives. Where is the satisfaction then? Or even afterward? Even if you take the money and do something noble with it. Whatever that would be. It's beyond you or anyone else."

"Noble, eh? You think I am a monument builder? I am. The monuments are a special kind, thousands of them of lead and brass.

If there is enough money, hundreds of thousands. Not candles. Not tablets. Not mumbled prayers. Monuments with a purpose and a use."

"That's irrational. Ammunition is impersonal. Unrelated to the matter at hand."

"Not to me," Hamplemann said. He took out a notecase and fumbled in it. "What is your fee for this consultation?"

"No charge. Gratis."

"Also worthless." He put down a five-dollar bill and left us, walking westward. Berdichevsky fingered the money and beckoned to the waiter.

"I'll have a glass of slivovitz. You?" I shook my head.

"We don't stock it," the waiter told him. "Martell, Remy Martin, Hennessy, Metaxa—" He continued. It was an impressive list.

"The first one." Berdichevsky turned to me. "Curious. No Pierce-Arrow."

"After all that, maybe he needed some exercise. Or he had to walk off his anger."

"Maybe. Did you believe him?"

"Why not. Sure."

The welter of tales, histories, eyewitness accounts I had listened to in the past had required neither judgment nor sympathy. Merely an absence of rejection, obvious disbelief, or rebuttal.

They were simply a text relating experiences, and every spoonful of comfort, every slight betterment in existence, displaced some weight or reduced some of the impact from the recounting. It was distance, however small in space or in time too, that did this. This man's recollection was, for me, much vitiated by the pongee suit on his back and the rich pastry in his stomach.

Berdichevsky put Hamplemann's five dollars on the check. The waiter looked at it and sighed.

"Be another fifteen cents with the cognac." Berdie added a quarter. The waiter made off with it but paused briefly at a nearby table to pass a moment with another patron.

"Serving all kinds of cheese," we heard him say, "Swiss cheese, Roquefort cheese, and refucheese. I recognize them no matter how good they talk English."

"Don't forget my change," Berdichevsky called. He returned with a dime on his plated salver. Berdie put it absently in his pocket and stared away into some distance, beyond the monument to the crew of the battleship *Maine.*

We walked eastward.

"He's an improvement, but not an advance. Over Hamplemann One. Too bad. I had high hopes for him. Would have been very satisfying to find an absolutely legitimate claimant. Justice would be done comparatively quickly."

He sighed, but then brightened somewhat.

"Still, what else would I do with my life if he had been the heir? Or at least parcener."

"What the hell is a parcener?"

"A coheir. To an estate. The man simply has no significance. He's representational. That's all he is. Neither he nor his brothers had any distinctive qualities in their lives that would have led them to pile up what's in that inventory.

"They picked up as most people do—on impulse, perceived need, remembered wish that was never fulfilled. Gifts for others. That kind of decision. The before-Christmas urge."

"Chanukah."

"He made the point that they weren't even religionists. They were assimilated to their shoe soles. Our inventory wasn't an assemblage made by a Jew. This was a deliberate chain linked to placement and circumstance. First it was to satisfy deprivation, frustration, real or imagined. Then it became something more. Conceit, the emergence of a new and more powerful individual, with the personality of success. It was character change. Elevation to another plane."

Before Van Cleef and Arpels's window, passersby had formed a little knot, a single mass crowding shoulder to shoulder. We joined them. And had our glimpse of a heavy crown with an enormous pear-shaped diamond set in its center. The whole of the tiny window blazed with sprayed yellow, blue, brown gleams from the rest of the circlet. The Empress Josephine's tiara, according to a card beneath.

"What I'd like to do is go in and find out if it's genuine or a copy. Think they'd tell me?"

"You wouldn't impress them as a serious buyer."

We walked on down Fifth. So unmistakably New York. Behind us the great white cliffs of buildings looking out upon the park. The concentration of superficially splendid hotels, half-elegant, half-dowdy restaurants, and subdivided bars furbished up in a mélange of modes and periods. Georgian, Regency, baroque, 1930s moderne. On past store after store, collection after collection of furnishings far in advance of this summer season, this time, these people. Some were displayed with pretentious sophistication, a promise of a highly styled life in the postwar abundance. This was not implication, it was guarantee.

When we passed Thirty-fourth the retailers gave way to wholesalers who dealt with the rest of the country. These were importers of lamps, bric-a-brac, china, glassware, dealers in silver, curtains, yard goods, brasses, toys, clothing, suitings, fabrics, furs, hats, scarves, robes, and underwear to fit or disguise every shape and size. In the district at this hour there was far less activity. The showrooms were almost deserted, and yet there was a sense of movement, of orders taken and orders shipped, of vast supplies in transit from and to the corners of the earth.

"Volume," Berdichevsky commented knowledgeably, "money on the move. The farther downtown you go, the more to be made and the quieter it gets. Nothing but the rustle of papers."

That annoyed me. As though this outlander could make any worthwhile assessment of the place. Ever since I had come to this city, I had had an awareness of what he was addressing now, and of how far away I was from any significant part in it. My poor savings, my tenuous arrangement with Bos, my scabrous office and living quarters, were simple stopgaps that implied increasing apprehension. I was clerk-at-a-distance, buffer, seine in a scheme that offered no rewards. In it there was not even the excitement of the gamble, of a truly resounding failure or an utter disaster that might at least arouse the determination to overcome and flap upward like the phoenix. All about me, I was sure, just such struggles were occurring.

I knew that there was opportunity everywhere to become a part of this new army, to sniff about for crevices that could be enlarged through applied energy or a twist of fortune, and on through toward a life in a more pleasing land. The land of plenty.

Berdichevsky seemed more than able to do another four or five miles over the pavement, but I was suddenly very tired. That lumpy mattress I slept upon, or the weight of decision, possibly. I crossed Fifth at Twenty-fourth and sat down on a bench in Madison Park. He joined me, of course, but at a little distance; close enough to converse, but far enough away to indicate that there were differences between us.

Finally, after some minutes, he nodded at the cenotaph on the island opposite that stood on a base of polished granite.

"Did you know that that's the valve control station for the water supply that comes down from the Catskills? The reservoirs up there."

I glared at him. "Fascinating."

A shrug. "Worth knowing."

"Thank you. And behind us is the Appellate Court, and next to you is Lincoln's secretary of war."

"Why so pissed off? Did I do something?"

"Nothing you can help. Because we were close once, and we won't be anymore. We are going to part company, and I don't have so much companionship that I won't miss you. That will bother me, but not as much."

He nodded comfortably, as though relieved. Any subjectiveness that he could worry at was satisfying to some extent. It was grist for him, the theorist working to find sound principles of behavior in an area that no one could understand.

A young man hurried past us, one of so many of my contemporary *velites*. He wore a neat suntan summer suit, and there was a sense of the military experience in his pace and his carriage. More, there was a sense of purpose and concentration. He was bound for a meeting, no doubt, with someone of means to pattern himself after, to adapt himself to and to learn from: how to speak, gesture, maneuver, work.

"He's going to advance himself," I said. "He has direction and a goal. I envy him."

"You should. But you're just as good. Better. You learn fast. You adjust well. Why, you even used that misbegotten company of the mismatched to your advantage. I was impressed. But I really appreciated your buying the soup for my passengers.

"Sure, the world needs men like you and the one who just went by. But it needs others too who don't just move from country to country and unpack their goods and do business the same old way. If you do that, you become a part of the past, and some of the past was a horror. We know that. Don't we?"

I didn't answer until he pressed me.

"Has nothing to do with me. It's an alley I blundered into on orders. A passage I walked through for a couple of years."

"True. But whoever you are, whatever you are, and however you got there, you were a witness to evil. You're marked by it.

"It's true also that there is more to your life than that. But for a time you have an obligation. No great jousting, no capering about in heroic poses. That was no alley you blundered into, it was a path, and some of it is swept clean of footprints already. No matter. Everything we know is eroded by time and changed outlook, but these pictographs are unique.

"Come and go as you please, but don't let us lose track of each other. Neither of us has so many partisans that we can afford the loss."

This was affecting, certainly, and gently spoken. I knew enough about him to be aware of his faults, but they were trifling compared to his distinctions. I did not, however, want to be concerned with high purpose or moral judgments. They have too little importance to me and nothing to do with the way I want to live my life.

Semblance is enough. I learned its utility early. I have no reason to doubt its value.

He returned to our office alone. I went to Times Square and sought out other companionship. As it turned out, there was little satisfaction for either of us. She had reason to be quarrelsome, I suppose, but I did not insult her deliberately. It was only that I had carried that Zippo lighter of mine for five years, and when I excused myself and went to the men's room I picked it up and took it with me out of habit.

"Did you think I was going to steal it?" she said. "I don't give a damn about it, or you either for that matter."

She took out her billfold.

"I'm paying for mine."

Two brandy Alexanders. I tried to apologize. It was too late in the evening for another attempt and too early to go home. From the Astor Bar we went to Toffenetti and sat in the window on the second floor. Having established her independence, she ate well, defiantly well: Our Tender Black Angus T-Bone Steak, a Baked Idaho with High-Score Butter, Old-Fashioned Strawberry Shortcake with Genuine Whipped Cream.

Between them, the two establishments combined extravagance and purported sophistication with surfeit and thrift. That had brought about a reasonable amount of success. Not tonight. Resentment lingered; the penultimate scene ended in frustration on the staircase a floor below her family's apartment on upper Broadway. Even after I had returned her money.

Still, this had not been a completely wasted day. It had set me to thinking of a longer view of my future. In time, Berdichevsky's pursuit would be only a shadowy interlude, a remembered obsession. There would be some vivid glimpses of him animated—on the night the first Hamplemann had died; of him clutching the wooden steering wheel of *Grauhund* as it careened downward; of him listening, head bent toward some fearful claimant—but our association was already dissolving.

5.

Over the next weeks, I set about changing the arrangement with the Bos group. Subtly, I hoped, arranging my departure in a way that would give it at least the appearance of a decision reached out of common agreement. I wanted to be done with it by early fall when the pace even in New York quickens measurably, and a new business year mushrooms out of the end of the summer. So my reports to Bos in Rotterdam indicated very little hope for the future.

I described the pool of claimants that I had tried to meet or contact as not only difficult to enroll, but threatening, and militant as well. That pained me somewhat, for when we had entered into our agreement, I was the ascendant partner who commanded direct and impeccable sources; without me he would have faced the same obstacles as his numerous competitors. Now I was emphasizing my own shortcomings and the inability to sustain my position. Postconflict, there was a return to the proper order, and he and his partners were the ones to manage it. They understood how to take advantage of the opportunities that recent history presented to them.

They knew what sort of claimants to look for, what businesses and professional practices were most easily assessed, which corporations' earnings could be most firmly posited and projected. They had passed scatheless through the political maelstrom and the physical fire storm and settled themselves in the new times, respected and possibly even revered by their contemporaries.

Since we had never had any sort of personal relationship, but only a semiofficial one, I could only surmise Bos's reaction to this projected divorcement. The only outburst had taken place during my overseas phone call. There had been some carping about delays in responding to queries and instructions, and a few critical comments, but the tone had always been quite mild, and usually prefaced by some meaningless phrase supplying an excuse or an out for me. All I had to do was repeat it: family business; finding a place to live; traveling vast distances to New Jersey or the far reaches of Pennsylvania; renewing old acquaintances. These passed back and forth as commonly as the salutations. So at first there was only reassurance from him on my competence and my past contributions. Their settlements in the Ostrov and Etkin claims were due to my referrals—I had no memory of that—and there was no reason to be pessimistic about the future. He even hinted that there would be more income as the caseload of claims grew and more government personnel were assigned to settle them.

But then I wrote him in detail of our meeting with Hamplemann, and that roused a surprising reaction. He had been writing to me on a flimsy blue sheet that folded in upon itself and sealed—somewhat like the V-mail forms that the military had distributed during the war to save weight on the correspondence from the home front that had had such an important effect upon morale in the services. So his letters had to be cut open with care, for he habitually added his afterthoughts in a tiny penscript near the edges. And an important instruction might be overlooked by me, or worse, some gnome lost forever.

Unfortunately his reply about the Hamplemann encounter was included in five of these sheets, and all of them were not delivered at the same time, so when I slit the first and began to read, I found myself in the center of a storm; there was no pleasant preliminary.

> ... so I find the association worthless in that you expend big sums of our money that is hard to compile to have chats in fancy coffeehouses with clients already represented by us and who you have no reason to pursue. This is the result of posting costly notices in journals no one reads. Through certain information we have I can tell you that this man is an impostor and needs no more attention from you or from us. I thus call upon you to reply posthaste and explain why you pay no attention to our agreements that we made and proceed according to that plan to locate and offer our services of a legal nature to those in need of such services to process their claims hurriedly as is proper. Having full knowledge of the undersigned's ability to do so!

Other sheets dwelled on the difficulties the organization had to overcome, the necessary researches from records that were incomplete or missing, the inefficiencies of the newly installed government officials, the unreliability of the transportation systems that made travel endless and exhausting, the spiraling costs of continuing the operation, even the shortages of office supplies; and always apparent the ingratitude of the claimants.

> ... so it may be that the parties concerned may wish to consider other possibilities in the way they spend their capital and their energies. Or to restrict their clients to those who have a better understanding of how these affairs should be conducted.

I read through the screeds twice and sent a brief letter telling him that I too was considering other opportunities, and that our association could be ended whenever he wished. A week later a bulky envelope arrived. Berdichevsky, who was now carrying on an international correspondence of his own, thought it was for him and came over to peer at it.

I went through it quickly. Despite what he had said when we had first concluded our agreement, Bos had filed papers of incorporation in the Netherlands. The Citizens Adjustment Agency of Rotterdam, N.V., listed the names of all of his partners as known to me together with others I had never met. I was listed as secretary. The papers dissolved this corporate structure, retired the stock, and distributed all assets according to the balance sheets enclosed. There had been some good times, but latterly, increased expenses had swallowed up undivided surpluses until there was almost nothing left. My end was a check pinned to the accounting for eight hundred guilders. Acceptance indicated satisfactory settlement in full of any present or future claims against the corporation.

I handed this hagiography to Berdichevsky. He leafed through it smiling.

"And all because of your spendthrift ways. A sound business combining an honorable and necessary service with a decent return on invested capital is finished. Too bad.

"Tell me, did you pad your expenses very much?"

"Of course. But that was because they were so slow to reimburse. I was always three months behind. More." Actually I had been tacking on 30 percent recently, but I had begun at 10, so it averaged out.

"You know," he said, "this could do you a lot of good. It'd look fine on your résumé that you were a principal of a corporation engaged in international trade. Especially these days what with all the interest in overseas markets. Experienced people are hard to come by."

His concern for my welfare I found cloying and unacceptable. I thought it should have been reserved for his own situation. Besides, it was inhibiting, it weakened my self-confidence, and it was much too soothing.

"Anyhow, you don't have to worry about the office rent. As I told you, I'll take it over. Won't be any hardship for me."

"Shit," I said, graciously, "I can manage my half for a while, and when I connect someplace you'll have to do it anyway. And you've got a long way to go."

I took the check uptown to cash it. This, I learned, would take the better part of a month, there was a charge for the transaction, and a loss on the conversion.

It should have triggered some depression, this new low in my affairs, but it did not. Instead, euphoria; I set out like a tourist to see some of the sights I had denied myself until I had secured a niche in the city. I went out to the Statue of Liberty and climbed to the torch; I went back uptown to the top of the Empire State Building and gaped there.

When I returned to the office at four-thirty I found Berdichevsky with a visitor, a large man in blue serge sitting at my desk with his feet propped up. He nodded to me pleasantly enough and introduced himself to me.

"Starkey, Homicide Division, Brooklyn. Your partner here tells me you're the one started this operation, correct?"

Ever since the events at Garside's, I had not faced any sort of encounter with the police with equanimity. At such times all sins of omission as well as commission flooded in upon me. And standing in front of him before my own desk in my own office while he questioned me didn't ease matters this time. Noting this, Berdichevsky intervened.

"I just told you all there is to know about the business," he said calmly. And to me: "They found a body in a canal in Brooklyn two days ago. No identification, but a scrap of paper with our telephone number on it. He wants us to go out and look at him. I don't see the point in it. How do we know he ever came here?"

"It's your duty as good citizens," Starkey said. He bit at a hangnail on his forefinger and spat it on the floor. "Like it's mine to investigate it. For a couple days anyhow. So let's get going."

"How'd he die?" I asked.

"I'll give you the details after you take your look. If you can't tell us anything, you just file it away and forget it. You get a lot of calls in this business?"

"Nobody's knocking down the door," Berdie told him, and winked at me.

"Lately," Starkey said, dryly, nodding at the plywood panel. "Let's get going."

We took the subway during the first wave of the evening rush, Berdichevsky and I depositing our nickels in the turnstile, Starkey passing through the wooden gate, his shield held high. On the Utica Avenue train we stood in silence, Starkey reading from one or another of the newspapers within his purview. At Kings Highway on our way out he picked up a discarded copy of the *Sun.*

"They never miss a murder, and they really go for the rapes," he said. "This exit."

We followed him, falling into step automatically. The hospital loomed on the right, a great gray encompassing pile of masonry at the service of a population larger than most cities, scaled for it, and with an entry to match. Massive columns three stories high and a portico that reduced those who entered this temple of healing to dimensions most easily managed. We passed this and walked instead a lengthy path of unleveled concrete slabs beyond the emergency room, where several ambulances had halted, doors open and gaping, on an apron of asphalt wide enough for the casualties of a hard-pressed infantry battalion, and entered the morgue. There were two sets of viewing rooms opposite each other. Now completely disoriented, I sat down in a steel chair, one of several drawn up around a long table. Three sides of the room were lined with windows all hung with closed venetian blinds.

Starkey picked up a wall telephone, listened and blew into it, took out a notebook, and prepared to read. Finally there was a response.

"I.D. for your case number H-aught-aught-four-six-eight-one.

"Want some coffee or a Coke? There's a machine out in the hall."

Neither of us did. Berdichevsky sat composed and silent, but I was oddly tense, and even chilled. The blood had drained from my face, I knew, and my fingers trembled and twitched, although I had no expectation that this unnamed cadaver had anything at all to do with me. And I had seen, I was sure, more dead than Starkey ever had. We waited, I to be shocked. There was a sudden glare behind the blind in one of the windows. In one motion, Starkey raised it and stood aside, his massive head bowed, as though sorrowing.

Hamplemann Two, as we had referred to him. Naked to his chest on his seven-foot-long tray, gray and waxy, his sparse hair neatly parted and brushed just so, frozen beyond the temperature inside there, but still animate to me and to Berdichevsky at my shoulder as well. In these bleak minutes in which we stared at him, there were other disjointed gleams experienced—the pongee suit, the limousine, the rich pastries, his tale told.

"That him?" Starkey asked.

Even as I nodded, Berdichevsky spoke.

"I really can't be sure," he said. "We had that one meeting with him, and to tell you the truth his clothes made more of an impression on me than he did."

"His clothes! What the hell difference do his clothes make? Is that the guy or isn't it? Your partner here thinks it is. Get together. You were both with him, weren't you?"

"His mouth looks different somehow."

"What are you telling me?" Starkey said, exasperated. "Do I have to put his dentures back in?" He picked up the telephone once more.

"Yeah, me. They're not positive, for some goddam reason. Let me have his clothes and his bridgework, will you? I know. It's suppertime for me too. Bring 'em out."

We sat down to wait, as at some impersonal wake, until finally an attendant appeared with a large cardboard carton and a small one, each numbered on a strip of adhesive tape. Starkey took a complete set of upper and lower teeth from the one and set it on the box lid.

"What're you going to tell me about that?" he said. "Could be George Washington's."

"They're distinctive," Berdie replied. "So were his clothes."

"Help yourself," Starkey said, and Berdichevsky did so. The pongee suit, stained and discolored, a pair of gaudy flowered suspenders attached to the trousers, the double-breasted jacket, a satin tie, and then suddenly he turned away. At the bottom beneath the white leather shoes was a caped mackintosh. There was a smell of the sea, bilge oil, and salt incrustation upon it all.

"The name he gave us was Hamplemann," Berdie said. "Alexander Hamplemann. He said he was from Austria. A small town there. I don't recall the name. You?"

Neither did I.

"Spell it." Starkey took it down in his notebook. "Okay. That does it for here. We'll go back to the precinct and fill out the forms."

We had little more to contribute there. The room was empty and silent, as though evildoers and antagonists were mutually observing a quiet time through the dinner hour. Together we made our way through Starkey's forms, and when we had finished, there were hardly fewer blank spaces than there had been when we began. We left our addresses, signed at his instruction, and rose to leave.

"How did he die?" Berdie asked. "Drowned?"

"Uh-uh. Wouldn't look that good if he had, between the crabs and the gulls. They found him half on the canal bank. If he'd been all the way in I'd never of got the case. Would have wound up near the Con Ed intake on Fortieth Street and been a Manhattan problem. Or if the tide was right, out around Sandy Hook and been nobody's problem. Wouldn't have been enough left. He was shot. Three or four times and it was a good group, according to the coroner."

He held up a sheet with two line drawings of the human figure on it. The group was noted in red pencil on the rear view.

"Must've been an automatic weapon, thirty-caliber. You could cover it with a half a dollar. Either of you experts?"

He grinned. "Gotta start somewheres. If anything else turns up in the next few days, I'll get in touch with you."

"One thing," Berdichevsky said, "isn't it unusual that there wasn't anything on him but that scrap of paper?"

"In that neighborhood it's amazing they didn't take his teeth and his shoes. Nope."

"What are the chances you'll find out who did it?"

"A little less than zero."

We went out together into the soft July twilight. He waved us toward the nearest subway station, but Berdichevsky flagged a cruising cab and sank wearily into the seat, hands in his pockets, chin on his chest, his nose barely above the level of the window.

"You did see that mackintosh, didn't you?"

"Of course."

"And what did you make of that?"

"I can't make anything of it." It was true; even allowing for my unwillingness to be drawn into the past, I could find no meaning in the sight of it that I could accept. He could, and did. The occurrence arranged itself just so, and could be fitted into the scheme of his hypothesis. So the rational vanished and was now replaced by a concept designed to accommodate it. There was no need to argue this. He went on alone like an obsessed explorer. His moonscape.

"He left his mark. He wanted this to be seen by me. By us. We left him behind us separated by years and distance and death. To the point that I came back here and organized a search, piling up detail after detail, concentrating all of my energy on finding him. And he makes his own plan and strikes.

"This isn't frightening, you know, so much as infuriating. I can see the son-of-a-bitch or his brother with the gall to continue the same revolting way of life that was supposed to have been uprooted and destroyed—erased! And telling me so. That it's here with all the same methodism.

"Worst of it is that Hamplemann Two was a true believer, poor bastard. He thought that world was gone too, and that all he had to deal with presently were a lot of faceless people who were under orders to accommodate him."

He brooded for a time in his corner.

"Well," he went on finally, "at least I know he's still alive. I'd hate to find him laid away in some pleasant cemetery with a little obelisk over him and a framed photo and evergreen boughs on top of the mound.

"What is striking also are the changes taking place here. Under our noses. All of that uprooting and the movement of thousands back and forth across borders and continents and oceans by people who lived for generations in one place and never left.

"Now nothing and no place is too far, even for an action as wretched as this one."

In the weeks following I pursued my own ends cyclically— days of job interviews, nights drafting letters according to the examples that appeared in books on career building that I borrowed from the library. Some I wrote were wonderfully Olympian. The very occasional response that I received inspired delightful daydreams.

In less than half of this office—for Berdichevsky quickly overran the early demarcation line and processed a depressing amount of wastepaper and trash that threatened to overwhelm both of us—I sought a rewarding place while he tried to apply some systematic approach to his search. Selfishness and selflessness accommodated, but there was no room to exclude one from the other. He sometimes had to answer telephone calls for me from various employment agencies that had nothing to offer but low-level drudgery, and I had to listen to him harrying Detective Starkey, sometimes losing his temper in the process.

"Yes," I heard him shout into the phone, "I am a goddam relative. Brothers. We are all brothers! In this country the individual is important. And this one was shot down in a city street. If that's not enough to interest you, then I'll go higher. To the goddam mayor if I have to."

I thought myself that it was a matter of Starkey working his way through a sluggish official correspondence that caused delay, but Berdichevsky found that unacceptable. In such circumstances he could be as intransigent as any general officer.

"You saw the way he works," he said, "he could never even have made it in the 855th, where incompetence was king."

Finally Starkey called him with a progress report. Hamplemann had a social security number, a chauffeur's license, and now even an address.

"About time," Berdie told him. "I want to go with you when you go through his place. Or just give me permission to go in myself."

The latter was impossible. Evidence had to be handled by trained people. Berdichevsky was amused.

Without any prospects on the appointed day, I went along to East Sixteenth Street, one of a number of what had been handsome town houses well before the turn of the century. It had been neglected for an equally long time in the present one.

Hamplemann's room was on the fourth floor up a narrow staircase that leaned precariously outward at some landings. It had been a gracious space in other days; there was a carved marble mantel, much stained and chipped, and the ceiling and cornices had been molded with festoon, swag, and medallion; what had once been a pair of french windows was reduced to one and a trifle, for the room was halved with a flimsy beaverboard partition that bulged as if resisting pressure from beyond it to be restored to its original dimensions.

Within this space, Hamplemann Two evidently had lived two separate lives, or perhaps more. In an alcove, curtained off by a limp length of flowered chintz, was his wardrobe—three or four expensive suits and several pairs of shoes, and two whipcord chauffeur's uniforms, a pair of black boots, well shined, and matching leather puttees. In a battered chest of drawers were two differing collections of shirts, underwear, and socks, some for service, some for the man of higher station.

At his desk, a plywood rectangle supported by two flimsy file cabinets, there was another furcation: one branch in which he had kept his correspondence with official agencies here and abroad, the other crammed with documents concerning a bewildering number of business operations; a number of these included contracts, agreements, financial reports, loan applications, and duns.

Berdichevsky leafed through this mass with care; Starkey paid it no attention. He had found what he had come for—in a flat drawer under the telephone, the instrument itself an eccentricity here, was an index much emended. Berdichevsky peered into it also. Left to my own devices, I glanced at the books stored in an orange crate near the bed. It was a curious collection: half a dozen library books in German, and all of them long overdue. Most were novels from between the wars. Mann, Zweig, Remarque; in English there were biographies of Ford, Edison, Morse, and some lesser lights. There were several stacks of *Fortune* magazine, and some issues of *Business Week.*

Photographs of the families that he had described to us Berdichevsky turned up in an ornate little coffer on the chest where he had also kept his toilet kit, a small cut-glass decanter, and four tiny matching liqueur glasses. "Kümmel," Berdie said, sniffing. Starkey was ready to leave, and now he had no objection to leaving us there.

"Got all I want," he told us. "Tell the super that somebody's coming around to seal the place, and to leave everything where it is or else. That if a shoelace is missing I'll put him in jail."

After he left, Berdichevsky waited for a time at the door.

"Walks very quietly for so big a man," he said. Then he went to the rude desk and opened the first of the file drawers.

"Too much information makes for more complications, I imagine."

I sat down on the bed, took up *Buddenbrooks,* and quite suddenly fell asleep. When I woke it was late afternoon, and Berdichevsky was closing the last drawer; a sound of finality.

"Find anything?"

He nodded his head slowly. "Too much. Depressing, like this place itself. Like a condemned man's cell after the sentence is carried out. There's nothing left but the sense of what occupied him, and in this case it demeans.

"Seems to have spent most of his time on one scheme or another, trying to claw his way upward. There's a checkbook, a register actually, big enough for U.S. Steel, with a balance of thirty-six dollars and forty cents. The AHAM Company. Business cards and stationery for same. This address."

"Did you find the inventory he was talking about?"

"That I did. He was compiling it himself. Four or five different versions of it. Every time he remembered a possible inclusion, he tacked it on."

"Ah, Jesus. There's never so terrible an occurrence that someone won't see it worsened. Cheapened, dishonored in some way by some means. A small fraud conceived by a small mind."

"Clues too. Clues. To a personality I don't want to deal with. He was naturalized two years ago. Got a passport six months ago. He had an airline ticket sent to him. Round trip to Vienna, eleven hundred dollars, marked as paid. But he cashed it in. That was his last sizable deposit except for his salary checks."

He sighed heavily and rose to his feet.

"How would you like a weekend in the Adirondacks? Ought to be good for us both. What do you say?"

"An urge to travel?"

"I want to talk to his employer. Mr. Herman Gruenbaum. The owner of the Pierce-Arrow, who is spending the month at Saranac Lake. Ruhig in the Pines."

"When?"

"Now."

We left at six-thirty, he having rented the only car that was still available over the weekend. Shortly I knew why. It was an oversized Chrysler convertible with wooden sides fastened to the body with chrome-plated rivets as big as half-dollars. This machine volatilized every fluid poured into it within a hundred miles, and Berdichevsky's lead foot reinforced its inefficiency. We stopped at Hawthorne Circle for service, and twice more on the Taconic; when we reached Albany, I prevailed on him to stop for the night. That was difficult, for he was full of anticipation and the thing did hum at eighty-five or ninety. He wondered aloud if it would run at the limit on the instrument panel—one-twenty.

In the morning we were away early; at seven along the Hudson a heavy mist had risen, dissipating below the gray cut-stone buildings of state on our route north. Then we were in the foothills of the Adirondacks. Berdichevsky thought it looked much like the country along the Austrian border, lakes everywhere, and endless stands of pine and spruce.

Ruhig was not easy to find. We drove almost completely around Saranac Lake before we were directed to it by a trucker about to pull out of a narrow side road with a load of logs behind his tractor. Then we found a small sign framed in birch branch, and followed a narrow corduroyed and grass-grown way to a random grouping of outbuildings. Beyond this was an enormous rambling structure set in a clearing high above the lake. This, and others flanking it on both sides, were built of great peeled logs, stained dark brown, roofed with heavy shingles, and further anchored to the plateau with a series of native stone chimneys. Each section was fronted by a weathered porch, where at this hour in the late morning a rank of green rocking chairs creaked companionably to one another.

This rusticity was insistently reinforced by representations, parts, or sometimes whole preserved specimens of fauna hunted, trapped, or caught not only here in the north woods, but on other continents as well, and displayed everywhere in the great public rooms. There were snakes coiled along branches, bats framed with their wings spread and hung like pictures, bears standing upright and holding out brass cups like so many fur-coated beggars or clutching receptacles for umbrellas or canes or fishing rods, families of woodcock, grouse, or pheasant under bell jars, elephant feet holding this or that door open to the breeze, lions and tigers skinned out but still with their mouths angrily agape and fastened tails up or tails down to various walls; on the ceiling beams were plaques mounted with the heads of oryx, rams, boars, and the horns of deer, moose, caribou, elk, and even a rhinoceros. Fishes—trout, pike, shark, salmon, sailfish, and alligator gar—were also a part of this decor.

What we saw of the guests indicated that they had had little to do with this predatory achievement. The youngest we encountered was Mrs. Gruenbaum; she was at least fifty, and her husband twenty years older. He was paddling about with a number of others in a kind of swimming crib at the foot of a two-passenger funicular that led from the lawn to the lake. At his wife's shrill call he halted in his archaic but forceful sidestroke and stood up in water waist deep, surprised at the interruption of the regimen.

"What is it, what?" he was saying even before the funicular had reached its terminus.

"He's dead, Herman. They say that Alex is dead."

"What happened to the car?"

"It didn't happen in the car. It's fine," Berdichevsky said. "I'm sorry to say he was shot."

Mrs. Gruenbaum covered her lips with her fingers. "Burglars," she said, "but what could they get from him, poor man?"

Gruenbaum agreed. "He didn't have a quarter. Are you the police?" Berdichevsky passed on that.

"Didn't seem so to me," he said. "When we met him he sent a car and chauffeur to pick us up and bring us to Rumpelmayer's."

Gruenbaum was outraged.

"He! He sent a car! He sent a chauffeur!" Mrs. Gruenbaum handed her husband a robe. "He went to Rumpelmayer's!"

"Put it on and don't get so excited. Please."

We sat down in lawn chairs, the Gruenbaums staring at each other in utter disbelief in either circumstance or event.

"How long had he worked for you?" Berdichevsky asked.

"I brought him over myself in 1938," Gruenbaum said quietly. "He came with the clothes he stood up in. And whatever I did for him it wasn't enough. I took him into the business—he was my shipping clerk finally, before he left. But that wasn't good enough for him. Ten times he left and came back like a bad penny. Always with another idea to get rich. Secondhand sewing machines, pallets and skids, plastic remnants, a diaper laundry."

Mrs. Gruenbaum wrinkled her nose and shuddered.

"For that I lent him three thousand dollars. Lent." He smiled bitterly. "That ended it. That was that. I told him there wouldn't be a next time, and that if he came back, he could put on a uniform and drive the car. I'll be goddamned if he didn't do it."

"It was a refuge for him," Mrs. Gruenbaum said. "He could have some peace."

"Sure. Between schemes."

"How did you happen to bring him over?"

Gruenbaum shrugged, and looked off into the distance across the lake; as the sun passed the meridian, the whole stand of pines seemed to advance and cast a timeless image of themselves upon the still water. When he spoke, he conjured up a kind of impressionist's picture that had presented itself to him a decade ago. There were at that time no photographs, no documents, no absolute proofs of the existence of a great evil, but only, and only now and then, a few feet of newsreel footage, some talk, some rumor, some reportage that gave substance to fear; often, that was dormant, overcome by other preoccupations and considerations.

"It's in the blood," Gruenbaum said with a gesture of impatience and self-disparagement. Dislike.

"The men's club at the temple we belong to had a drive to find sponsors for our 'fellow religionists'—that's the way they talked then—like Jews were a sect like Presbyterians or Episcopalians. And if it could be guaranteed that people who came here wouldn't go on welfare, they could come. Under the quota.

"As I say, it's in the blood. Wasn't even Hitler. He was still a nothing compared to the ones before him that terrified my father and his father. Little local slaughterers. That's what I saw. Or felt. Atmans, hetmans, tsarist police, cossacks, Polish peasants.

"So I took one because he was from the same place my father came from. Myself, I was born here." He rummaged in the pocket of his robe for cigarettes, lit one, and tapped the package upon the broad arm of the chair, musing on that past too.

"What did he tell you about his family?" Berdichevsky asked. There was a rapport between the two of them now. And Mrs. Gruenbaum bent her attention toward me.

"Beautiful here, isn't it?"

I agreed that it was. And for a time she questioned me so that there was an obbligato under the theme of the visit, a gentle probing into my life and situation that had nothing at all to do with the corpse in the morgue that had brought the four of us into association.

"I knew him all these years," Gruenbaum said, "and I have no idea what he said was true and what wasn't. Not that I cared after a while. It was a philanthropy. Whatever I expected, I don't know, but I didn't get anything, if you understand. No emotion. No friendship. No feeling. I think he liked Rosalie, but he never said so.

"He had two brothers. One was a doctor and one a lawyer, according to him. That could be. He was a 'financier,' according to himself. That he was not. Believe me. In the first place, he didn't even know the language."

"His English was good, I thought."

"Figures! Money! Yield! When he looked at a balance sheet it came out exactly as whoever told him it did. Or as he was sure it did. And believe me, the deals he got into weren't using big-time accountants to prepare the statements. Every one of them had holes you could drive my car through.

"When I pointed them out—and I took the trouble to a couple times—he had to convince me I was wrong. Me with a net worth in seven figures. The worst thing about that was I couldn't agree too fast. He had to convince me. Take me by the lapels, put his face into mine, and convince me."

Gruenbaum paced the lawn, expostulating.

"I live in a duplex on Park. He had half a room on Sixteenth

Street. I own a Pierce-Arrow. He rode the subway. I spend a month here every summer and a month in Havana in the winter. He went to Far Rockaway on Sunday. But he convinced me finally, every time. The fool."

"Did he ever talk about filing a claim for confiscated property? His or his family's?"

Gruenbaum snorted.

"That was our last business meeting. I had a glimmer of hope then." He smiled sourly, remembering.

"The minute he started to talk, I started to calculate. His airfare, something to keep him while he was over there. Something for a lawyer. Is that what you two are? Are you representing him?"

"Others," Berdie said. "Not him."

"Well, so when I began to get the drift about the estate he was going to claim, that was my first thought. I'd at last be rid of him. But I tell you I pitied the poor bastard more then than I do now that he's dead. All it was was another goddam delusion. I know what those people owned. It's the same crap they own today or brought with them yesterday. Go to any apartment where they live and take a look. What are you going to see? Polish splendor, Russian magnificence, French elegance.

"I know what was in his mind. The rich American going back to claim his birthright. In my suits that we had cut down to fit him. Pathetic.

"So"—he looked at his wife and shrugged—"the limpet is no more. The end of the Hamplemanns."

"Not yet," Mrs. Gruenbaum said quietly. "Who is going to bury him?"

Berdichevsky shook his head. "The city, I guess."

"Never. No potter's field, Herman. You brought him this far, you'll take him the rest of the way."

He nodded agreement.

"Who do I get in touch with?"

Berdichevsky wrote out Starkey's name and telephone number.

We did not accept Mrs. Gruenbaum's invitation to stay for

dinner and the night if we wished. We sat on for a time, and they left us there; she slipped her arm about his waist, and they walked away slowly toward the main house. The stillness of the summer day was ending. In the shallows along the shore, a fish leaped, a tiny silver bar. From under the eaves of the lodge a swallow took flight, and then another.

Berdichevsky drove more conservatively in the fading light. The descent of evening was lovely. The car top was down, the air soft, the lowering rays of the sun fell full upon the heights all around us—Marcy, Nipple Top, Colden, Big Slide.

"Good people," he said. "The damnedest thing is, he's finally made it. He'll be buried out of the Riverside on Madison Avenue. The Gruenbaums' rabbi will preside, leaving them under still another obligation to the synagogue—no, 'temple,' he said. Proper obsequies. A few mourners from the company even. Ancient prayer and modern efficiency. Affluence at last.

"I wonder where that airplane ticket came from, though. Gruenbaum hadn't given him any money yet. That was to come."

I had nothing to suggest, and no plan beyond severing our connection in the next few days. It seemed appropriate in the circumstances. I didn't intend to live any longer in the atmosphere that Berdichevsky had chosen. That was a circle of darkness, and I intended to separate myself from it.

I have never had any difficulty accepting a parting. That is probably due to self-concern or a lack of interest or emotional involvement. Many people seize upon abstractions and serve them—friendship, comradeship, associations in one area or another. Work, school, neighborhood, military service. To me they were simply passages in which one finds oneself companionable for a time, but these all open out eventually and the distance between presences widens. I made the same protestations others chose to make, but rarely the commitment.

This is a failing, no doubt. It can be a handicap, and most certainly a shortcoming. Still, presuming on an acquaintanceship has its own drawbacks. It hinders one's personal development and impairs the self-reliance that may mean survival one day. That's another of those apothegms that are absorbed into the mind and stay there. Encrusted but recalled instinctively, and not purposeful at all. Just baggage like an overload of poetic quotations. Those one can sprinkle about readily, however. They have utility and can brighten a conversation and may even mark an intellectual.

Typically, I received the recollection, overrode it, and wrote a final draft of a letter to Cyril Faulds, our onetime lecturer on valuations and appraisals. It was his improbity that had brought that singular part of the Hamplemann inventory to our attention. I had not forgotten the gleam of his pocketknife, and there was the tacit understanding that I had seen him commit that offense. It need not be mentioned but I thought it an advantage.

There were other factors that set me to the effort. I preferred a small operation like the only one I had known, in which one was aware of profit and loss instanter, a business in which knowledge and method could be acquired comparatively quickly. One that could be set up almost anywhere in pleasant surroundings, and required a minimum of capital. I thought I had some understanding of this traffic in treasures and also in trash. I had willy-nilly been associated with it on high and low levels. Somewhere between the two I was sure that I could find a niche.

Thus the letter to C. Faulds & Company, Successors to Faulds & Sons, Ltd., London 1746. When I thought I had eliminated all gaucheries I put it in the mail. In a week he replied, three lines setting date and time. I was there an hour early. In a coffeeshop diagonally across Lexington Avenue I waited, carefully dressed and recently barbered, with clean fingernails and well-shined shoes, determined to put my hand to the shining brass knob on Faulds's beautifully varnished milled door on the appointed minute.

What set the place quite apart from the many others in the neighborhood and along the other side streets was the sparseness of its stock. Understatement, obvious understatement, was one of the specialties of the house. There was neither a disorderly scattering of objects, as if the proprietor were hoping that one or another might catch a buyer's eye, nor an imposing collection of furnishings that implied exorbitant cost. Rather the place was a comfortably sized presentation as though in a proscenium, as an anteroom to a life of luxury and tastefulness. The foyer of elegance, Cyril Faulds presiding.

He did not rise from behind his table but merely granted me a nod that indicated also that I was to take one of the armchairs opposite him. He glanced at my letter, the only piece of paper to be seen, as though to refresh memory.

"I would think you would be better off in one of the larger department stores," he said, without preliminary. "B. Altman's has always had a good reputation. They have a training program that is very sound, I understand. Perhaps I could recommend you to their buyer."

I said that I knew I was better suited to a smaller place where I would not have to compete from day one with people who probably had more experience and more knowledge. I added that I wanted to work for someone whose abilities and judgment I respected. Someone with a longer view of the field and more specialized interests. That was the only reference to the scene in the magazin that I made. But he was as sensitive to nuance as a chef is to seasoning, even though he seemed to take no notice.

"Fake ingenuousness butters no parsnips with me," he said. "Might do in some quarters but not here. I deal with fakes and fakers all the time. This is a one-man business. That's that."

He crumpled my letter and let it fall into his brass-mounted wastebasket.

"If you want to trade on something you think you saw, let's look for common ground. What was in the rest of those cases? The ones I didn't get to see. That would be of some interest as a first step. Indication of good faith, you know."

He permitted himself a tiny smile, no more than a suspected wrinkling of the lips beneath his luxuriant moustache, and leaned toward me confidentially, in fellowship.

"Your letter was no surprise, though it was a bit late in arriving. Of that whole company there were so few that seemed at all enterprising. Company commander incorruptible. Absolutely. And the mountaineer and the aging red-poll who smelled of brandy. Hopeless. An odd assortment in every rank, right down to the preposterous clerk—Pitts?"

"Pattison."

"Mmm. He wanted to make common cause. Made some assumptions, no doubt because of my profession. I couldn't bear to disillusion him.

"And the one with a couple of courses in art history, the museum assistant. He and the antique shop proprietor were your best-qualified authorities. Bumblers and innocents far beyond their depth.

"And you circling about with a great air of efficiency. Ever so helpful. Mindful of the future too, no doubt. Well and good, here you are. Let's get on with it.

"If we can strike a proper bargain, you may advance rapidly. To a partnership or even sole proprietorship. Very possible. I don't intend to drag along forever selling the odd rummer. Even if one can grow old peacefully like my neighbor across the way there."

The shopwindows opposite were streaked with grime, and in them was a jumble of oddity and curiosity—lamps made of conch shells, a stand of rusted rifles and muskets, a harmonium, a drooping wicker hallstand.

"Just lately he seems to be turning into parchment. Sits in the rear like a gargoyle and don't rise when the bell over his door tinkles. Not for me. Let's get to business."

He flipped a notebook open, drew one of the gold-nibbed pens from the onyx block before him, and suddenly halted this preparation. He seemed to have been transported to another place and was directing his whole attention to it. Slowly, reluctantly, he returned. When he spoke, it was soliloquy.

"In all those months there surveying all those tons of goods and possessions, there was only that one collection that had substance. I knew it on the instant."

He sat back in his graceful armchair and hunched in it, dwelling on that with such an air of covetousness that he salivated and paused to dab at his lips with his handkerchief.

"All right," he said, finally, "where is it? What was the disposition?"

I told him the cases had disappeared. There was a cynical smile and a nod.

"Of course. Bound to. Many other things have disappeared. And some remarkably reappeared. Some of the very things I saw during my time with your unit. Some of it flowed back home to Nebraska or Texas, duty-free and uninspected. I'm not referring to Lugers and P-38s.

"I have got in my cellar a complete dining room. Eighteenth-century and rare. Table, twelve chairs, gilt-bronze mounted buffet. The lot. Even the wall hangings. The French would be pleased to have it back. It's valuable and it will be profitable. Eventually. One don't hawk it in the street. But in due time some thousands will be forwarded."

He continued to convince me of his attributes as ally. He was not only knowledgeable, but utterly trustworthy.

As he spoke, I saw the pattern I had imposed upon my life at this point, some of it by design, some merely adjustment—a sidling, rarely long considered or reflected upon, and all meant to achieve a vague and misty objective. Here it was again. I had come here to use his trifling misfeasance to serve my own ends. What he had concluded was something quite different. He was candid.

"Who else is involved? How many? Is it a group? Are you the intermediary?"

"No."

"Well and good. Then it's share and share alike. It will take time, but what we come down to is proper organization and management."

He went on putting up this structure of his that was so similar to others'. Hamplemann's, Bos's, even Berdichevsky's: Have a goal and keep that in view; turn it over in the mind and embellish it with practical method. These are visions of accomplishment, something before one, whether the gold piece nailed to the *Pequod*'s mast or the serving out of a just punishment.

Faulds rattled on and was suddenly interrupted by the bell over his own door. It hung on a large open coil spring and looked as though it had come from a Victorian kitchen, as dissonant in this shop as the harsh jangle itself.

A tiny aged woman, all in black, entered most hesitantly. He rose to his feet as though he himself were attached to the bell spring.

"I don't want to interrupt," she said, "but I wonder if you would help me. May I wait?"

"No need to," he told her politely, this prospect momentarily displacing those that lay ahead.

"I am looking for a container for my husband's ashes. His remains."

Faulds mulled this over, pulling at his lower lip.

"Well," he said, considering, "there are funerary jars, Canopic vases, that sort of thing. Even amphoras. But the motifs on some of those would not be suitable. Unsuitable I should think. Definitely."

"Oh, he wasn't a religious man at all," she told him. "But he was a big man, and there are some large bits of bone. Orange colored.

"I didn't like what I saw at the crematorium. Too much the feeling of a headstone, and I will be keeping this at home. May I see some of the things you mentioned?"

"Just now I have nothing at hand. But if you will leave me your name and address and some idea of what you wish to spend, I shall be pleased to see what can be done. Would that be helpful?"

It would indeed. All of the information was exchanged for one of his handsomely engraved business cards. She mentioned Sutton Place, the oil business since 1910, and fifty-six years together. Price was not a consideration, simply what was appropriate. He escorted her to the door and watched her progress down Lexington, as though calculating longevity.

There was evidently a lesson in the incident.

"That is the sort of thing to be prepared for, you see. As well as the type. A moneyed eccentric. Never know what it may lead to. Contents of the house to be disposed of. Putting together a little shrine. All from the bones of an oilman in a jar on Sutton Place.

"Now let's get on with it."

Her visit had refreshed him. He had demonstrated his cleverness. That swiftly, he could seize a trifling opportunity and turn it to advantage. He opened a drawer in his table, moistened his finger, and drew out a sheet of his heavy stationery, dated it, and set to calculation.

"Let's see what we might expect. Very roughly, of course. As I recall there were eight of those cases. What, perhaps ten to the case, plus?"

I supposed so. That annoyed.

"Strike an average then. Nine. I had the time to check only the two items. Klee, and the Pole, Kandinsky. Did your people identify the others?

"Why are you holding back?" he said angrily. "We aren't making a bloody auction-house catalog. Give the names you remember."

I did, hesitantly, and at once aware that I was betraying a trust in the doing. Nevertheless I recited.

"Marc. Corinth. Nolde. Dix. Müller. Beckmann. Grosz—"

As I spoke, he glowed. Fervid appreciation: a portion for those names, more for his own good fortune, however unfulfilled at this point. Values, numbers, were racing through his head.

I stopped.

"That's it," I told him. "That's all." Like a suddenly willful donkey who halts halfway to the marketplace. The balk was almost inadvertent, but I went no further.

In past episodes—after Garside's death, the arrangement with Bos and his partners—I had not considered myself dishonored or dishonorable. Nor was I very troubled after I had been removed from command of the 855th. I did not rivet my attention on it for long or dwell on implications—that perhaps I was growing a tail of transgressions. If any of these events had been highly publicized, if I had had to give some explanation to relatives or friends, I might have offered a defense—injustice, ignorance, youth. I never felt the need to do so. If such actions were a part of my character, so be it. No one's perfect.

Faulds stared at me, baffled and frustrated. What I had meant to be a well-weighted job interview was something vastly different to him. He thought of it as a takeoff point. A leap over the heads of the many, and an end to the traffic in funerary urns and to his patient treatings with the unlearned, leavened with an amalgam of charm and hauteur. This was rapidly decomposing. His pen nib raced over the paper, but it could not keep pace with thought and persuasion.

"Hear me out! Hear me out!" he said loudly. "You must understand what an opportunity you have here. These works together are a collection. They represent a whole movement in art. Don't you see that? It would be like holding the same number of French impressionists in one era. It would yield much more than if they were dispersed. That is exactly how I will offer it.

"It will take time. Capital. Patience. But no matter the expense, the profit would be enormous. You're not stupid! You can see that! I can prove it to you."

He had already. His argument registered in every detail. But even if his assumption were fact—that I could send him directly to a pickup point—I would not do it. Not out of my respect for the character of Earley or because of my discomfiting role as confidant to Berdichevsky as he slogged away toward his goal.

It was because of that disparate group of iconoclasts who had made them. The power of their visions and their statements of the truths they had seen elevated them to a place far above Faulds and his cozening. I knew that there would be no association between us, and that I would do nothing to help him put his hands on any of these works. Their value was no part of my attitude, whatever it was, whatever his projections of it were.

I, myself, could not pronounce them either failed or successful; I did not know if the works we had uncovered in the company would ever be seen again. Thus I did not sit opposite Faulds trembling with a desire to do right, like some zealot. I was only very sure that I would not commit the wrong.

"There's no way I can help you," I said quietly. "I wouldn't if I could."

"You are behaving like a bloody idiot! An idiot! You're turning a tidy affair into a free-for-all for thieves. These will turn up one day. Too many people know of it. A cache like this stays in the mind. The mind! With every year that passes it takes on more importance, more value."

The other thieves would have the same handicaps, I thought. They would do as well to wander the sector of Earley's last mission with divining rods. Even if they could and did locate his departure point.

"All right," he said, rising as I did, "just think about it. Don't close your mind. We can come to an accommodation. It's money, man. Money!"

I walked to Fifth after I left him and took the bus downtown. There was a copy of the *New York Times* on the seat next to me, neatly folded to the editorial page. There was a lofty discussion of two competing economic systems. It was impenetrable, for I had little real knowledge of the one and problems finding a place for myself in the other. The encounter with Faulds demonstrated that.

Already the reasons I had distanced myself from him were becoming indistinct. The chain of impulse remained, so too some of his arguments and even his phrases. I did not feel myself much the better for the decision taken. It was the kind of situation only a masticator like Berdichevsky could worry at until it was pulped enough to be digested into nourishment for the spirit or the psyche.

6.

The vote of Your Committee was Unanimous! Wivies, mothers, and friends (Smile) will not attend our First Reunion. Instead we are offering a package for them for the five days apart. This includes a room at the Luxurious Hotel McAlpin (right opposite Macy's). Plus: Admittance to the wholesale showrooms of dress, suit, blouse, and lingerie manufacturers! A fashion show at Russek's exclusive fur salon. A five-course dinner at Mama Leone's and a seat at the year's top musical, Damn Yankees. *An evening at the Copacabana, world's most famous nightclub. Tour of Radio City and NBC studios and tickets to a popular quiz show (to be announced)! All for Half the cost of our own trip (Smile)! And everybody speaks English. (Mit an accent)*
     B. Pattison, Arranger

*A*t nine the next morning I took the elevator to the employment office at B. Altman. I sat down in a broad-armed wooden chair and filled out the application rapidly. I had had so much recent experience with these forms that I had standardized the replies. I extended my military service by a few months, gave the highest rank reached as corporal, and transformed Garside's pawnshop into a jewelry store. The ten lines set aside for an essay on my interests and my goal in life took a bit more time. I did not put down my desire to serve mankind by way of a career in retailing. Even if I didn't want to work in yard goods or trimmings, like Kipps before his inheritance arrived, I did not list my preferences as fine furniture, antiques, or rare books and autographs, lest Altman's place more value on a hardworking ex-serviceman than on an unpolished aesthete.

I turned in the finished work and received the pleasant but noncommittal smile when I handed it over. This was not based on content, but only in appreciation of the fact that I had left no blanks and had the date right. Still, I felt encouraged, as though there would be accommodation here for me. I left with a sense that I had taken a step forward. The place had a sense of stability about it.

In sharp contrast to our office. It had not taken very long for the traces of my presence to be dissipated. What remained of it was in distinct contrast to Berdichevsky's. My card files of claimants were neatly boxed; my records of job interviews, Bos's communications, bills, and expenses were all in labeled folders. Even my pencil sharpener was empty of shavings. Now that little area of orderliness was only an outcrop. The next surge from him would overwhelm it.

At the moment, there was no suggestion that there would be one. Eyes closed, he was lying back in his chair almost horizontal, with his feet up on his decrepit typewriter.

"How'd you make out with Faulds? Progress?"

"Doubt it."

"Common occurrence. Some days I come in confident that I have a life with purpose. That I'm committed to something worthwhile that I haven't found anywhere else. Then I look back and see all these blunders and false steps and presumptions. And on top of that how poorly organized I am. Busy all the time and pretending I'm progressing when I know damn well I'm not. Compared to me Diogenes had it easy. I'm looking for a specific thief out of thousands."

He brushed it away with a gesture.

"Shit. No one forced me into this. What didn't the esteemed

expert Faulds like about you? You looked fine. Your breath? It's a fact that Sen-Sen has helped more people get jobs than nepotism. True, you know."

"Turned out to be a misunderstanding. He thought I was there to talk about the pictures in the inventory."

"Goddam!"

I told him what had passed between us. Listening, he rose and paced the worn linoleum. I thought of a toy grenadier with a large key between the shoulders, off on an eighteen-inch march, a halt, a buzz, and an about-face. As the key moved there was advance, all in the same plane.

What troubled him most was Faulds's certainty that the collection of pictures in the inventory was significant and important. That this had not been simply a grab by a looter, but an act of a higher nature.

"Why, that could make that bastard a completely different man! Not what I know him to be at all. He might be extraordinary. That he took risks to preserve the works for the future."

"Scratch a thief," I said, "and find a museum curator. Maybe an art dealer."

"Be as honest as you can be," he said. "Would you, knowing all you know, believe that was his motive? Tell me exactly what you think."

It was not a plea but a weighty demand, although I did not think that my opinion or any other would turn him from his course. Still, if I would not be his auxiliary, I would not be an adversary.

"He's a thief," I told him. "Sure you could make this a defense. But how do you reconcile it with everything else he took away over the years? And everything he laid hands on that isn't still in that inventory. Disposed of along his way so he could get himself laid or eat a good meal, or find some transport.

"You want to deal with every complexity. I don't. I sat opposite Faulds and I saw the effect on him when I was reciting the names of the artists. The whole Faulds presence that he'd put together cracked like an old flowerpot. All you could see was greed.

"It's only an accident that Faulds isn't Hamplemann or he Faulds. If anything, it strengthens your hypothesis. People like him support any kind of political movement if they think they can better themselves. In any way at anybody's expense and to any extreme. You're no prosecutor making a case. You have evidence and your own convictions. Abide by them. It's right."

This was not very deep, but it was forceful. And who can weigh sincerity? A couple of ounces can pass for a ton if you want it to.

He took my hand in both of his.

"I'm grateful, and not just for what you said. Or because you have listened to me and helped me. For things you did by accident or design. Even if they were only coincidence they were invaluable to me. I think of them as people will think of epiphanies. When you paid the woman for the soup for my passengers, it was the loaves and fishes to me.

"You placed the advertisement that brought Hamplemann Two. Now there's this meeting with Faulds. It's a revelation. It takes me out of this preoccupation with the claimants."

He picked up a sheaf of that correspondence and shook it at me.

"Sure it's important to help them along. To show them how to proceed. What avenues are open. Whatever they can retrieve, well and good. But who am I to deal with this? I have no resources. I can keep this cell until I'm senile or committed or wind up in one of Gruenbaum's philanthropies. A professional guest at other men's tables.

"But now there's an avenue of approach. It will take study and planning, but the course is clear. Hamplemann did not have an oversupply of studies of dead fish and ripe fruit. He was a connoisseur of the masters of twentieth-century painting. Then he had guidance from knowledgeable persons, specialists. All I need to do is work back from the paintings themselves. They were well known— some, at least. There was interest in them from collectors."

He went to the corkboard beyond his desk. There he had

posted the original inventory and the variations he had built upon it in the past. He had charted some acquisitions, associating them as closely as he was able to from a scant store of information. Some of it, he well knew, was the merest guesswork.

He had placed pins on a *National Geographic* map of Europe to represent the points of origin of particular items—the Steinweg piano, the Biedermeier dining table and chairs, the boxes of delft tiles, the yards of Belgian carpet, the lace, the barrels of glassware from Bohemia, the silver flatware from Denmark, the kitchen and children's bedroom furniture from Norway.

This was simplification, a kind of adjunctive military campaign map to show flank movements toward a tile factory or a raid on a carpet mill. Still, it was a jog to his theorizing. It had its effect. It presented a picture.

"This is a warrior who marched with a shopping list instead of a weapon."

Of the cases of paintings, only the single one had a confirmed source—the one delivered to Hamplemann after the contents had not been sold at the auction in Lucerne in 1939. There on the map was the *K* for *Kunst*, meaning "art," and the same coding method used to identify other items. The next *K* was dated September 1940, another in March of 1941. Hiatus until December 1943, when two more cases were dated. The last of the *K* entries were annotated in May of 1944. Only three more acquisitions after that date—wall hangings, tapestries that had been ignored by us, and a consignment of copper pots and odds and ends of kitchenware.

He faced me, arms folded before his situation map, as though about to conduct a staff briefing.

"What we have to know now is the content of each case. You and Wersba and Arquette unpacked them and removed the overlays. So you made and kept your own record on that."

"Wersba did. Some of them, we—they couldn't identify. They weren't all that familiar with them, and I remember you didn't give a damn at all. You barely looked at them."

"It was painful to look at them. Now I could admire them. From this distance."

"Some of the attribution, if you can call it that, was guesswork. Some of them scrawled, some used symbols, which I suppose is to be expected with a group like that. Some used an oversized initial to go with the size of the ego.

"We listed all that we could and assigned a number if we couldn't be positive. We did put down which case they came out of and went back into. That was our master list and went to Earley. He kept it. Maybe Wersba and Arquette know more."

"What about the photographer? The one Earley got to take the pictures."

"No idea who he was. He came from some press office. I saw them, and most were lousy. The reflections from the flashbulbs were right in the pictures themselves. I think he made three sets. Earley kept one with the master list and he forwarded another to some fuckup at Marburg. We never had an acknowledgment, just the messenger's receipt. The photographer kept one set."

"So they all exist. Pictures, list, and duplicates."

I agreed. Certainly they existed. Pictures, photographs, lists, receipts. All filed carefully away somewhere according to procedures laid down in some other era. Like the quartermaster general's records of rations issued to the troops at Gettysburg.

Whatever circumvallation Berdichevsky faced seemed to reinforce his determination.

"You should have transferred to the CID," I told him. "You could be doing the same thing on Uncle's money."

He grinned. "With my name? I wouldn't get clearance until Lenin's corpse dissolved. I can live with my own incompetence but nobody else's.

"Never mind. At least I can move along. Eventually I'll extract what I have to know. It isn't insuperable."

We left it at that. I declined his offer to buy a celebratory lunch. I thought that was premature and maybe even bad luck. It was simply incautious to walk under a ladder when a step or two to the side forestalls harm.

Knowing him so well, I knew it was unnecessary to offer further help. He moved as so many do, in spurts and lapses, by turns galvanic and quiescent. Now he was ready to frame actions as they occurred to him. He left next day for Washington; he had a friend there, a military historian who could open doors for him.

I was happy to have the beveled-glass doors at Altman's between us even if I were not making a long-term commitment or making a sensible move toward a secure future. I could not look that far ahead.

Still, the training program there was suitable and not very taxing. I paid close attention to the instructor, but I had none of the competitive spirit that animated many of the other trainees. I thought it was wasted on what I believed would be a moderately paced movement toward oblivion for most. I did master all of the ironbound rules spelled out in the personnel guide I was issued that covered all aspects of store policy. Arrival routes, departure inspections, staff lavatories, stairwells, department locations, methods of receiving and dispatching merchandise, size and shape of numerals and letters on sales slips, cash register operation, and the functions of the rigid chain of command. I did well enough that I was offered two assignments at the end of the six-week training program: furniture, and stationery and writing instruments. The former seemed to promise more activity and I chose it.

I had a brief interview with the department manager, Mr. Mullaney, an older man, brusque and dismissive, who turned me over after five minutes to a younger and more intense and energetic one, Ronald Scott, who was the department's top producer. He wanted a personal assistant and was so well regarded that store policy had been adjusted to meet this demand. It was part of an internecine power struggle, and I was the single visible result.

"On the floor," he told me, "I'm Mr. Scott. Anyplace else,

Scotty. Keep it in mind that you are working for me, but try not to rub anybody's nose in it."

It was my nose that was rubbed in it. More changes were brewing, and Scott was the catalyst. It had been his idea to install a decorating department on this floor to offer advice and show samples of fabric, carpets, lamps, china, glass, silver, and even linens and other accessories. At that point, he had arrayed against him and his plan seven or eight other managers and buyers, each defending his own space and sphere. The sales figures he had shown from the first day, however, made argument irrelevant and even threatening to an incumbent's twenty or thirty years of hard-won advancement.

Now Scott was engaged in another project; he was arranging a whole series of rooms in period styles, all decorated by him, and once more bringing together the merchandise from the realms of the opposition. The contretemps had gone all the way "upstairs" for settlement. There had been two resignations and a firing. Scott had presented a variation on his original argument. Now a customer need only choose one of his basics—Early American, Empire, Queen Anne—and the room would be delivered *in toto* to those who chose to live in another era. The total sale would be a staggering sum and benefit all involved.

His success came at a high cost. To both of us. He was loathed for uprooting and overturning time-honored and timeworn systems. He had made enemies who opposed him and tried to frustrate his plans in any way that occurred to them. As his messenger and factotum, I bore much of the brunt of the resistance. It fell to me to organize the delivery within the store of all of the myriad items he had requisitioned to complete his presentation.

At his instruction I made out the endless forms that detailed transfers of merchandise, all properly signed and countersigned. Once that was done it took hours to locate the responsible parties, find what was wanted, borrow a hand truck to transport it, load it, maneuver it through dark, narrow, and crowded corridors, and bump my way to the freight elevators.

There was hindrance at every point in every assignment; but the elevators, with their operators, were the most trying. They were twenty feet wide and entered through heavy steel doors like great toothless jaws that closed at waist level. Seldom did I see an empty one, and even when I did, mere yards away, I saw the doors clash together. If I were second or third in line with my truck, a large hand was thrust out before I could move in. "Overload," and I could only wait. I never did board one that was properly leveled for me. After one painful attempt to shove the truck over a six-inch threshold, and the thing rebounded and hit me just above the groin, I was careful to back in. Whenever I debarked, the wheels landed with a thud to announce my return.

When I went to the carpentry or electrical shop to expedite the building of Scott's sets, some message from underground had already arrived, and I could only leave my properly executed forms under the telephone receiver or spitted on a spindle. These were never even acknowledged for days. Pursued by schedules and other furies, Scott himself ran, mouth agape, to yet another confrontation.

One busy Saturday afternoon when the carpet department had been unable to locate a five-thousand-dollar Sarouk rug he wanted, he took matters into his own hands once more. The stock clerk in charge of this well-guarded inventory turned up the volume on the intercom that communicated with the shopping floor, held the speak button down, and shared Scott's remarks with a wider audience.

"You lazy bastard," he shouted, "you son-of-a-bitch lying on your ass all day reading comic books, get me that fucking rug!"

Hours later he had still not unwound. I sat with him in a bar near Kip's Bay. His hand was clenched tight and trembling around his martini glass as he raised it to his lips, and he swallowed the half of it as though it were medicament. For minutes he was silent, reviewing the affair and his situation, and eventually mine. Even in the brief time at Altman's, I knew that I would not remain for long—perhaps a year that might yield some sort of reference. If not, so be it. I did not have far to fall, and I had known from the first that I was completely unsuited to the place. I was far more of an entrepreneur than a loyal, diffident, and disciplined employee. That much had crystallized as a sense of what I wanted for the future. Actually, the only excitement and satisfaction I had had in the months there were in dealing with the obstacles ten categories of personnel had placed in my path. And his.

"Nobody can get along with this crowd of cretins," Scott said. "And I won't be for long either. I'm going to complete this project, get it done. Every fucking corner and every fucking display, and I'll collect on it too. And after that I'll make more out of it than they ever would pay me, the goddam misers."

He looked at me appraisingly, as though to measure loyalty, and unfolded his plan to start his own decorating business. He had backing from a number of manufacturers and importers. He had a customer list lifted almost daily from Altman's.

"Every day," he said, tapping his forehead, "I store half a dozen of the best right up here. And type 'em out at home.

"I want you to come with me. I'll start you at a hundred and go on from there. And you won't have to wait a year for a two-buck raise."

We went out, euphoric and anticipatory, into the icy November night, I with the conviction that I had entry into one of those little realms that I had learned about at Reisenberg's counter. Small, profitable, well placed, and directed by somebody able and forceful. He was foresighted and fortunate, and by the standards of the time, daring.

Scott was a gifted promoter of himself and he had a wide and varied acquaintanceship in his field. He took every advantage of it. When his suites at Altman's were finally completed—in January, a month behind schedule—he staged an opening for the press and favored customers. As though paid for, reports of his achievement, his approach, and his impeccable taste appeared in the daily newspapers and illustrated in magazines. His Chinese Chippendale dining room and his Brittany kitchen sold in the very first hour right down to the service plates, the wooden spatulas, and the tiny copper pots used as measuring cups. In that lowest of months, after excessive

Christmas expenditures, his sales amounted to over a hundred thousand dollars. Six weeks later, having made a series of completely unreasonable demands, he left. He leased a deteriorating town house on Fifty-sixth Street off Third Avenue, where I joined him. There was no farewell party for either of us.

He opened for business in October, by which time the basement and three lower floors were agreeably furnished in an assortment of styles and periods that his instincts for the market dictated. He had been booking orders and designing for a number of privileged and affluent clients through the summer. I did the follow-throughs, expediting, checking shipments, flying in aged DC-3s to North Carolina, Buffalo, Grand Rapids, or Chicago, dealing with a more cooperative group of artisans and service people on floors, walls, and windows, and working closely with his fearfully efficient sister, Leah Schottenheimer, on the management and the office work.

From the first day I was deeply involved, as were all of the others he had brought in, from the designers who assisted him to the porters and maintenance men. We all understood that he was a man of integrity. Nothing shoddy or poorly executed was acceptable, no matter who had shipped it; no backer ever had advantage over a supplier who made better frames or paid more scrupulous attention to detailing and finish.

The approach paid its own dividends; there were few complaints and fewer returns. He also, for all his borrowings to finance the business, was careful to reduce his risks to the minimum. He explained fees and charges at the first meeting with a client, collected a sizable deposit on the spot, and shipped only on receipt of the balance due. There were protests from a number of wealthy patrons accustomed to running up thousands of dollars in bills, but the rule remained the same for all. Pay now.

To celebrate netting over thirty thousand dollars in less than a year, he gave his first annual gala the evening after Christmas in his fourth-floor apartment above the showrooms. The whole staff attended together with friends, clients, suppliers, and press people.

There were personal gifts for all and a bounteous buffet. He presided like a slim Fezziwig.

When it was over, and the caterer's staff was finishing the cleanup, and he had got over his annoyance at mars, cigarette burns, holes in some rugs, and some broken crystal, he sat down with Leah and me over a brandy.

"Hell with it," he said. "We'll take care of it tomorrow."

He contemplated the immediate past and the future. He was negotiating for the two town houses on each side, and he described the reasons for expansion. This was the beginning of a new era of home building and furnishing. There was an avant-garde of old money and nouveau riche to be guided, many of them by him, and a broad market for his good taste, his knowledge, his appreciation for expert workmanship, and the balance he had struck between ostentation, comfort, and attractiveness.

"One suite suits all," he said, grinning. "What's really strange, Lee," he told his sister, "is that with all the fancy embellishments, I wind up living the same kind of life my father did. Papa's revenge.

"My father had a secondhand furniture store down near the Bowery. We lived over the store. Schottenheimer's. Only the best borax. His distinction was that in that neighborhood, and with his clientele, he stayed open on Saturday.

"Here I am with a degree from Carnegie Tech and I keep the same hours and have the same immigrant's feel for the business. I didn't like law or medicine, so Papa cursed me and put me in a furniture store."

He made no effort to escape this fate, and neither did I. Over the years the opportunities arose. I mentioned them to him from time to time: a distributor in Chicago wanted me to manage operations there; a manufacturer in Durham offered me a lucrative sales territory on the West Coast; an Italian designer asked me to organize and operate his planned showrooms in New York.

When I told Scott about them, he countered with a raise and insisted that the offers had nothing to do with it. He said it was the only way he had to calculate what I was worth to him. I had no intention to accept, ever. Far better to accompany him in his climb. I logged the many hours and concentrated on the details. Eventually I began to spend some of the rewards on an apartment off Gramercy Park, on a social life further away from Times Square, and on relationships with women that had a little more stability. One lasted eighteen months. There were difficulties, most of them of my own making and so encapsulated in my past that no woman, however attractive and well endowed, could dissolve them. Eventually resignation overtook determination. Word came to me that I was thought "cheap," "only out for one thing," and a "waste of time. Unmarriageable."

I thought I was just conservative, practical, and somewhat skeptical, particularly about Romance. I was also immersed in the unique American postwar world. Limited casualties, however deeply affecting, to the comparative few. A land untouched by any devastation or destruction. For all of the pretense and posturing by its leaders, who brevetted it the new center of power and of civilization, it was almost as parochial as it had been in 1890. It may have banked for, brokered to, supported, and exported to its coexistents, but the gulf between grew and broadened. All of that only improved my situation and had its own influence on the way I lived.

I lost the very limited associations I had had in the past with one or two members of the company. Berdichevsky stayed in touch, although he had moved to Washington and came to town less and less frequently.

When he did, I took him to lunch at successively less expensive restaurants, since none pleased him. Admittedly, I had overridden parsimony in order to establish position. Not to be achieved with this gadfly. After he bitched about the prices at the Italian Pavilion and L'Argenteuil, where he nonetheless dispatched everything to the last crumb, I took him to P. J. Clarke's. There again he lectured.

"Why does a place like this exist? A sloppy saloon patronized by people who try to duplicate their fathers' habits. The shot glasses are half the size they are anyplace else and they get twice as much money.

"How can they call this a table? The size of a coaster.

"Is its charm because of ten pounds of ice cubes in the urinals? The bellowing of the cooks? A hamburger shrine is what it is."

I told him we could go to the White Rose if he chose. "Forty cents a shot for your favorite. Golden Wedding."

"It's a quarter in Washington. Right in Georgetown."

He didn't like my apartment either. It was far and away the most attractive place I had ever lived in. Everything had been chosen by Scott and billed to me at his cost. The four rooms were bright and airy, the furniture the best of reproductions. Windsor chairs, traditional sofa, handsome desk, mahogany pieces in both bedrooms.

"When you want to sell it," Scott said, "it's better if it all matches."

I was quite proud of it. I had accomplished something and the place demonstrated that. Berdichevsky recalled my past accurately.

"Come a long way from Lutheranallee and the two rooms over the car repair shop, haven't you? Good for you," he added hollowly.

Not he. There weren't many changes in his presence or his dress. He still wore his officer's trench coat, raveled at the cuffs and with one shoulder tab missing a button.

I poured him a large cognac for old time's sake, and to give him time to adjust I gave him a survey of Scott's successes and, only incidentally, mine. For orientation I mentioned the names of some of "our" clients and their standing—"one of Ford's original investors," "married to a Du Pont," and so on. Even one such reference was a surfeit.

This recital together with the seizure of the dinner check, the apartment, even my self-depreciatory remarks, did much to emphasize the gulf that lay between us. That could only be spanned by some honest emotion. I didn't overlook that, but I didn't stop talking either. Until he held up his hand.

"Neither of us knows how to behave just now. So why don't

we just shut up and get drunk. Or go out and see if we can get laid. We could bring them back here and clean them and me up a little first, of course. What do you say?"

There was not much capacity left at this point. Also it was not a good hour to go shopping.

"It's okay," he said, "I'll take the ugly one. In fact, the uglier the better. It's rarer than great beauty."

"You have some exceptional tastes."

"In all things, my boy. In all things."

I offered to recommend him to the bartender at the Cornish Arms, where he might find exactly what he was looking for. If I remembered correctly, she looked like the portrait of Famine in an editorial-page cartoon.

He waved that off.

"Never mind. It won't be critical—the need, I mean—for another two or three months. We'll talk instead. But not about your fucking business. No more triumphs. Agreed?"

"Sure. Just thought you'd be interested," I said airily. My glass was empty, one of four cut-crystal snifters a supplier had sent me. I poured a little more than I had intended to.

"We'll talk about you, instead." That disturbed, but did not deter.

"There's more than a little of Hamplemann in you," he said. "A bit more legitimate, but the instinct's there. Which is not all bad, of course. One gets hospitality, courtesy. All of that comes in its own good time. So I will criticize no more."

I didn't like the comparison. I thought of it as only another measure of the distance between sometime comrades. The selfless and the selfish.

"Me either. You're on a higher plane, but I have more money."

"Half true, anyhow." He raised his glass to that and spoke about his time in Washington. He was making progress. Slowly, but it was encouraging. Tantalizing. His contact, Maurice Miller, was invaluable.

"He's got a doctorate in history from City College. Taxi driver in 1940 when he graduated until he was drafted. Wrote a worm's-eye view of the taking of the bridge at Remagen that worked its way upward through channels to army headquarters and found so much favor there that they made him a master sergeant and assigned him full-time to work on its history. Discharged and went to work for the Department of Military History.

"He's still overwhelmed by his good fortune and so am I. If there's anyone I envy in this world it's him. Roam where you will and look into any part of the monumental struggle. It's all open to him, the whole mountain. Bales of details on all levels from the stratosphere to the foxhole. Some bloodstained. Literally. A treasure trove."

I nodded. "What's he going to do with it?"

He reacted as I had hoped he would.

"What the fuck kind of question is that! You don't have to be a goddam philistine to make money, do you? What he will do with it is separate fact from fiction. Pursue truth. Make a contribution to his time. It's something that honors a man in the doing, if you can understand that. It's transcendent, that's all."

He withdrew into himself, as I had seen him do before. Rebuffed in his rare enthusiasms, denied agreement with his views, he would chivy himself along into silence, one facet of his personality angered by another.

"I'm sorry," I said. "Slipped out. I never should have said it. Work like that, his, yours, is further and further away from me. I see them from a different place."

Finally he went on, though scarified, forgiving again according to his nature. There was only the one area where that was not forthcoming. Now he was restrained, and he went on to satisfy his need for understanding and approval.

"You know the 855th and the other units were hybrids. They were part of the strength, so called, of the Seventh Army when they were first formed. Then they were incorporated into the U.S. Army of Occupation. That's where the personnel and unit records remained. I saw all movement orders, morning reports, and requisitions, from inception to deactivation of the company. It's still listed as a reserve component.

"But the actual operations—what was done and how we did it—are not included. All of that went first to the staff of the Military Government. Then, believe it or not, it went to UNRRA for whatever use they could make of it. As of last year that was shipped to the United Nations Colloquium on Reparations. I followed that out to Flushing Meadows. They had no room there for that and a lot of other material. But they did send me to a warehouse on the East River, and that's where I found them. Damp and disordered, but there they were."

He rummaged in his kit bag for several large manila envelopes and tossed them on the coffee table between us.

"This was very satisfying, going through those files. I don't know what the other units were like, but with ours I had a sense of high purpose. I did. You could review those records and see that we had gotten somewhere. Accomplished a task. Clumsily, inefficiently, you could see that, and ignorance and sometimes indifference too. But the concept overcame all that. There was a change when your friend Estes took over. You could see it falling apart."

"And when I did too."

"Not really. There was a revival. A noticeable reorienting. It shows. There was the accident report when Earley's detachment hit the mine. The odometer reading on the truck. The men's personal effects."

"How? You sent Earley's back yourself."

"Not so. What I shipped was in his office and his quarters. What was on him they took charge of. Pocket diary, ordnance map, keys, Elgin watch that stopped at 1848 hours. Wedding ring. That's one path to follow.

"Here's another." He picked up one of the manila envelopes and slid a stack of black-and-white prints out upon the table.

"The photocopies I made of the color shots the photographer took. I've got the original slides in a safe-deposit box."

"How'd you get them?"

"I took 'em. Who cares? Nobody knows they were there, and nobody ever will. At least I'll make use of them."

I picked up the topmost.

"These are the ones from Lucerne. From the degenerate-art auction. Hamplemann collection. Lot One."

It was a work by Max Beckmann, a familial scene. Six weighty figures crowded into a small room lit by two overhead oil lamps. The door is ajar, and hangs askew. Outside the night is pitch black. Three generations are represented, all of them much foreshortened here.

At a small round table are three women. One, elderly, has an open Bible before her; she covers her face with a large hand. At her left a handsome woman seems to be dwelling on her own presence here. In the light of a candelabrum, a third woman concentrates on her newspaper, *Al Anzeiger*. A young boy lies full length on the floor reading. A fourth woman, half-dressed, primps before a hand mirror; the candle that lights her reflection has just gone out in a puff of smoke. A man lies on a piano bench, his feet in wooden shoes propped up before him; he rests with the mouthpiece of an oddly shaped horn at his chin, his hand cupped beneath it. A cat sits on the keyboard of a grand piano. A priestly figure wearing a crown appears at the corner of the wall. There is a scatter of other items all about—a kite, a large, limp-leaved plant in a crock, a hat, a dish, a pot. Within the cramped space all are intent on pursuits far removed from it and from each other. If there is a bond, it is only the space itself. All are alone. A gathering of savants.

Even in this poor copy with its indefinite black and gray tones, this family study made a powerful and unpleasing statement. One that could arouse anger and disquiet among those who believed in the strength and cohesiveness of a family, a people, a state.

I put the print back on the stack. There was no need to look at the other batches that he pushed toward me.

"They all correspond with the dates in the inventory. Here, from Brussels, late 1940, and Amsterdam or Rotterdam in '41. In '43 the next two, France, and also the last, 1944. Winter of '44.

The tide was setting toward the ebb, and sensitive as he was Herr Hamplemann suspended collecting in favor of preserving and protecting.

"And I have to call a halt too, for a time." He rubbed thumb and forefinger together.

"But it's not only that. I'm tired. I said I envied Maury Miller and I do, but I don't have the temperament for his kind of winnowing anymore. If I ever did. Things are changing vastly. The war brought an enormous bureaucracy, and that's the pattern now. Bigness, staffs, records, standard procedures, analysis of detail. That's everywhere.

"Just in the one little area I was interested in and I had an experienced guide, the days passed by in a rush with no perception of progress. Then you move to another paper citadel and begin once more with step one."

He leaned back in his chair and closed his eyes. I had my own experience with form, method, structure. Once in place, even if laid down yesterday, they hardened circumstance, immobilized people, limited thought.

"What are you going to do? Take a job, or a sabbatical?"

"I could. Miller says he can bring me in with him. But he's pretty perceptive. He knows I'd only be pursuing my own ends.

"No. I'm going to try to raise some money. I don't need a lot. I spoke with Herman Gruenbaum. He was interested enough to arrange a meeting for me with the men's club at his temple. I don't expect to convert anyone, but it won't take much to support the work. The staff of one. Maybe I have unsuspected talents as a fund-raiser."

"Right now I've got more than I need," I said. "I can spare something. But do me a favor before you start and get some decent clothes. What you'll say is persuasive, so's your commitment. But you have to pay some attention to appearances."

"Ha!"

"It helps, damn it. Tells people you aren't some obsessed derelict. I know these groups better than you do. What you have to say will interest them. They'll see themselves maybe, or their relatives, when you show them the inventory and the copies of the pictures. The past isn't that obscure yet. They'd be making another contribution to the cause of justice."

"I am not going to bullshit them. That's not for me. And my appearance has nothing to do with anything. I'm not begging and I'm not selling. All I want is enough to keep going. To Belgium and Holland and France to find out how a collection like this found its way into those boxes. Whether they were sold or seized. These things have a history that goes back two decades and more. They were known to a lot of people, and I'll find out who traded in them. I'm going back to the magazin too, to see what remains of it. It's time-consuming and it's necessary, and it's important. A hell of a lot more important than what I look like."

Purpose, but never malleability. Perhaps that would advance his cause better. He had managed to pick apart some strands from the skein of concealment and accident that had balked him for so long. I was, after all, no authority.

I put him in the second bedroom. A four-poster, high and narrow with a mattress at the level of his chest.

"Looks like a catafalque," he said, and undressed. His underwear was khaki, his socks matched. "Don't look so surprised. They're new. Bought 'em on Houston Street. Surplus. I guess nobody wants to wear it anymore."

He stayed on for ten days. The meeting at Gruenbaum's men's club went well. They raised over eight hundred dollars for him, and arranged meetings with other congregations. Gruenbaum's wife handled the auxiliaries, and for a time, he shuttled back and forth from Washington.

He called a halt to this activity in late February and booked passage for Le Havre on the *Liberté*, née the *Bremen*. I took the morning off and went with him to the boat. He sent all of his baggage to his tiny cabin over the protest of his steward, who was trying to demonstrate that he had not always served in third class.

"What they have instead of steerage these days," Berdie said. I could understand the objections. The accommodation looked like a holding pen for mutineers. The attractive decor and the bright Bemelmans touches on French Line vessels ended three or four decks above. We waited for his half-dozen sturdy cartons, well secured with twine and tape, and his battered B-4 bag. Having arrived early, he had his choice and, taking the lower berth, crammed his consignment under it. Then we removed to the light and air in the little bar outside the third-class dining salon.

I had brought a bottle of champagne, having been instructed by so many movie sailings. I handed it to the steward who had glumly accompanied us, together with a five-dollar bill. This was possibly the last cash he would see from this voyager. It brightened matters; he returned with a paperboard bucket of ice and glasses. I toasted quest and future.

"I don't like to waste six days," he said, "but it's two hundred bucks cheaper than a plane ticket, and all found."

"How much did you raise?"

"Twenty-four hundred altogether. And Gruenbaum gave me a letter of credit for emergencies for another five hundred. Very nice man. But I don't like the feeling I have. The responsibility to them. I wonder how much satisfaction there will be at best for them. Or me, for that matter. Even if all goes well.

"Won't be much if it all ends in a mass of judicial blether."

A number of fellow passengers appeared, mostly family groups, it seemed, and a scattering of men and women who might be students, brighter and more cheerful as befitted the beginning of an adventure. The rest looked like emigrants.

"Well, cheer up," I said. "Stay with the younger set. Make it a voyage of discovery."

We finished the bottle and went out on deck into the slate-gray day. Even at this hour there was a grudging mist low upon the Hudson. The gulls were motionless, assembled in groups on the corrugated metal roof over the pier; the misanthropes among them took station singly on bollard and piling. The ashore call sounded and we walked together to the gangway. I shook his cold hand and left him, descended to the pier and out to the right to watch the departure, the singling up of the hawsers, the coordinated maneuverings of the tugs fore and aft. There were others out there too, a few, huddling in their coats on the windswept concrete. An elderly woman wept ceaselessly and silently; an emotional farewell. To whom?

The vast hull eased away almost imperceptibly, the wrack of the port swirled against its side, and it slid out into the roadstead, turned to straighten itself out against the current and the north wind. Then it gained speed rapidly, sounded progress and intent, and moved down the bay to a mournful chorus of foghorns along the way.

I had done what I could for him, even leaving an envelope with two hundred and fifty dollars in it under his pillow. That was safe enough. No one would be turning down his bed.

Before the ship's wake had vanished, there was a sense of depression that could not have been caused simply by the aftereffect of gulping half a bottle of lukewarm champagne. The fascination of the voyage, whatever its promise of fulfillment or failure. No matter the "mission," if one could even call it that; it was far more desirable than returning to R. C. Scott and Company, now incorporated.

There were important conferrings going on there, and downtown on Wall Street also. Several of Scott's clients were much impressed with his farsightedness and his approach to his business. He was selling the good life as a philosophy, and he thought he could market it to thousands instead of tens. If he could raise the capital, branch out, expand, he could sell to the legions who were buying the new houses that were being built with such speed and efficiency all over the country.

He projected a sense of the oracular, like an aura that may have surrounded some tribal leader whose hunts and chases always ended in success and plenty. There was a plan for a stock issue, and charts and projections were being drawn up, all of which proved that Scott's business was poised to become a corporation, a vertical and horizontal combination with infinite possibilities for profit. Most important, there was going to be participation for me in a sure thing.

I would have a chance to buy as large a block of stock as I could afford at the offering price. That would be a large melon, and I could specify the size of my cut.

After the next eighteen months—a year to pile up record sales to demonstrate the annual improvement in the business, another six months to publicize our history and promote our bright future—I would have a place among made men.

Fulfillment. A notable accomplishment for one like me, one who had expected and truly deserved smaller rewards. This was accident, not enterprise and careful management on my part. I didn't offer any opinions when Scott briefed me on these events. I had no understanding of the complexities involved in turning profits into certificates of participation in a business, and I did not enthuse, or at any rate, not at the right pitch. There was plenty of that about, even if never enough.

I regretted the plan. I never voiced it to Scott in any other way, but I was very certain that it was not for the best. The close association between us would be diminished by a new and larger staff bred to replace action and activity with the theory of management, and to substitute meetings and reports for personal responsibility. I could see how he intended to resolve the situation in my case. He left it to me, knowing that I would do my utmost to help him succeed. In the aftermath, the least I could come away with was an ample reward, and that repaid past effort and present exertions. It was the end in view that I found depressing, not the labor or the details. I was used to those, immersed in them, and had been for years. I found it satisfying to solve difficulties and differences for him. That would not be so in the years ahead when I would be dealing with a hundred hollow images of Scott pretending to have his talents.

I actually hoped that some obstacle would appear, some complication that the law firm could not solve, or even that some revered officer in the underwriting group, renowned for his success in raising capital for industrial emperors, would laugh this project into the discard bin. It didn't happen, and the future didn't glow, another quirk. When I anticipated, there were shadowy places that threatened, that I might have to pass swiftly; here they were again.

That, I thought, was why Berdichevsky's departure was so depressing. It was in distinct contrast to my own situation. Whatever difficulties he would encounter, they were of his own making, no impersonal force would have any impact on him, and the end of his seekings and searchings was far along in the distance. So I believed. It proved not to be so.

I could subordinate and ignore our association, but I could never dismiss it completely. There were times, just before sleep, when a moment of memory produced a vivid presence. Mazed and meshed with this were related flickerings in swift succession, a kind of sharp reprising of closely held occurrences never shared with anyone: moments of cowardice, malignant intention, wretched behavior, and as if in balance some few acts of benevolence, kindness, and courage. All of the latter rose up like well-burnished tokens, and usually there were enough to bring an uneasy peace, if never satisfaction. I didn't imagine that Berdichevsky had such morbidities to deal with; his books were better balanced, his past the more wholesome.

There were other reminders of him, these from Cyril Faulds, who had mounted a campaign of persuasion, and persisted with the same doggedness and tendentiousness. There was a series of letters in his own hand, a kind of layman's history of the depredations in art acquisitions. Of how common it had been over centuries. He sent me a couple of books—handsomely illustrated volumes. One dealt with the Louvre, the other with the Berlin Museum. With these he enclosed notes calling my attention to the statements he had underscored in each. These emphasized how numerous "masterpieces" had arrived by some machination in the hands of their present possessors.

In his last communication, he repeated his earlier argument, as florid as any opera libretto, ending it with a threat:

> I ask you once more and finally to collaborate with me on any reasonable basis, even, after the works are recovered,

to apply for a cash settlement from the legitimate owners of the property (if such can be found), instead of selling them ourselves. This should put an end to the issue of morality that you think has so much importance here.

If you continue to ignore my efforts to cooperate with you, I will pursue other alternatives that exist. Some are known to me, some I can find. My success will leave you wrapped in your own shroud of virtue and that won't provide much warmth for someone with your past. I hope you will change your mind. I am ready to meet with you at any time.

He underlined "Sincerely" three times.

I heard no more from him. I forwarded the letters to Berdichevsky, now in France, and put the books on my shelves. When I passed his shop three or four months later, C. Faulds & Company was no longer there. His competitor from across Lexington had installed his own disarray there. The varnish on the milled door was cracked and starred, detailed in black grime. Save for the bell that jangled over the door, all else had changed as well. No hint of elegance or painstaking presentation remained. Even the beautifully painted walls and the wainscot were hidden by an ill-matched amassment that looked as though it might have been picked up as cast out in any slum. Far in the rear of what was now the same cavern he had inhabited opposite was a sallow, spidery old man at a desk, reading in deep concentration beneath a forty-watt bare bulb.

"Well," he said finally.

"I'm looking for Mr. Faulds. Cyril Faulds."

"Removed."

"Any idea where?"

"Deceased."

"Was he sick?"

"Accident. Belgium."

"Is there anyone to contact?"

"Wife in California. Mail's forwarded."

I didn't write for details. I did wonder for a time what other avenues he had followed, and if they had led him to Belgium.

I put the information into a note to Berdichevsky, and simply to include a snippet of more consequence than the rest of it, I enclosed the series of Pattison's postcards announcing the proposed reunion of the 855th. I thought he would be amused, for I had laughed out loud when I received my first. When I was in command, everyone who had managed to transfer shouted with joy when the notice was posted on our bulletin board. None lingered over farewells. No field hand would have been happier to leave a plantation.

Notifying him of Faulds's death was only filler material. It did not inspire any speculation. His connection to the company and its only dramatic scenes were merely tangential. So too Pattison's communiqués. He persisted, building on a foundation that was all sand, as though anyone could believe that we had been members of some severely tried combat unit, depending on each other for survival, suffering tribulations until the final triumph. Grotesquerie.

It was Berdichevsky who chose to weld both affairs together. It may have been that he had more insight from that distance. Either that or, as I imagined it, he was muddling about in his own subjective maze, taking up curious and confounding incidents and setting a matrix. These he seemed to have locked into a chase, for he telephoned me at three in the morning, my time, from Brussels. There were no preliminaries from him; he began before the overseas operator had confirmed that it was my ear at the receiver.

"I want you to sign up for this reunion," he said, "and tell Pattison that I will be there. Put up whatever money he wants and I'll settle up with you. Hear? This is important!"

"That's ridiculous," I told him. "It's all right for you, you're there. But I can't just go. That's our busiest time, and Scott's working on a stock issue. Even if I gave a shit about seeing them again, which I don't."

There was a momentary crackle of interference, and a mention from the operator about obscene remarks. Berdie broke in immediately with a gabble of French and English about privacy.

"Okay, fuck it," he said quickly, "we are cleaning it up as of now. Get off!"

There was a protracted silence then, as intense as anything he might have expressed.

"You're still on, aren't you?" I asked.

"No one can walk so far alone," he said, quietly and clearly. "It's perilous. My own obsession is threatening my stability. My sense of myself as an outlander in my own time. All of those armored conquests will have come to nothing. The star-crowned success and the square miles of catastrophe. And I am sifting through this for what? To satisfy my sense of what is right?

"I'm succeeding. Faulds was shot and dumped into Antwerp harbor. That's a fact. That's what the procurator's office told me. The avenues he said he'd follow are the same as mine.

"Which means that inventory has as firm a grip now as it did ten years ago. A stronger one. And the way to pursue its whereabouts is by way of this reunion. This grass-roots longing to meet again as a unit.

"It isn't only preposterous, you are right about that. It's also a fusion of venality and contempt for all of us who were in that company. There's also a willingness to go to any lengths to fulfill his accomplishment. Even if and when he finally lays hands on these pictures they are only transferred from one cave to another. But that would be his. Hamplemann's own."

"He's dead."

"There are always successors. Successors, inheritors of the talent and the instinct. This reunion is an arrangement with a reason for being that is not ours. I need an ally. Will you come?"

I said that I would.

"I'm scheduled to go to Italy in December anyhow. Maybe I can move it up a couple of weeks." I had meant to leaven the bleak seriousness of what he had said. To put the matter in a different light and dimension. As being, in my case, simply an extra leg on a business trip. He ignored this.

"Thank you," he said, and there was silence.

Rhetoricians and rhetoric. What they can conjure up. Sometimes they are so capable that one follows them into an enclave far different from our own surroundings, and finds in there the world they want us to see exactly as they do.

Next day I called at the office of ETO Tours. It was not as well known as Thomas Cook. In fact, at the address given on Eighth Street, the sandal maker who worked cross-legged in the store window on the street level did not know of it. Perhaps it was up above somewhere. It turned out to be the third floor, and it shared that with the headquarters of a personnel service that specialized in restaurant help. Cooks, waiters, dishwashers, and porters.

Inside there was a chest-high counter that restricted the movements of the patrons. Beyond was a pair of windows that looked out upon what had once been a garden, now a disposal area for whatever trash the tenants on four sides chose to toss out. Two dusty plane trees barely surviving there were stultified in the unseasonable October heat.

Two yellow pine desks faced each other, Pattison at one and at the other a younger man collating sheets from several stacks of paper and stapling them together. Pattison recognized me immediately. I hadn't changed all that much in that decade between twenty and thirty. He was familiar only on account of his communications. If I had passed him on the street, there might have been no more than a second glance as toward a barely remembered high school classmate. He had lost some years. His premature baldness was disguised beneath a lustrous, streaked-blond hairpiece, and when he grinned widely, as though he had practiced a recent superciliousness, there was a line of shining white teeth, carefully squared. He was twenty pounds heavier, expensively dressed in a tan shantung suit, a striped shirt with a dazzling white collar, and a violet satin tie; he was also wrapped in a secure superiority.

"We may have a cash customer, Robbie," he said. "I shall give him my personal attention."

"How are you, Pat?" I said.

"Prosperous, thank you. You too? What will it be, a bedroom

for two on Canadian Pacific to Banff and Lake Louise? Our special honeymoon package to Bermuda or Nassau?"

"Not just yet. I'm joining you at the reunion."

"What a wonderful surprise. But wouldn't you like to think it over? You'll be the only officer attending. None of the others even deigned to reply. Neither did most of the noncoms. This seems to be only for paddlefeet. Gravel crushers. You'd be out of place."

"I'm a hybrid," I said patiently. "I remember my years in the ranks."

"Of course," he said, warmly. "You were one of us for a time. But you went up like a rocket, and came down just as fast." He concentrated. "Conduct unbecoming an officer. Some of us thought you should have fought that. After all, everybody else was stealing."

"I wasn't."

He giggled. "Isn't that what they all say?"

"What I want to say is that you can cut the bullshit. Just give me the price and I'll write you a check for me and for Berdichevsky. He's in Europe, so leave out the airfare for him. Just the land arrangements."

"Him too. That will raise the tone. He and our departed leader, whom we will be honoring with a commemorative plaque, made us conscious that we were all on the side of right and justice, didn't they! We were so much the better for that.

"Still, former Lieutenant Berdichevsky must pay for the package. No exceptions. Unless of course he wants to plead poverty. In which case I would have to refer him to the committee, and they may have already exhausted the contingency fund for deadbeats. I was surprised there are so many. So few of us have done well. You. Me. One or two others."

"No problem. Give me the figure for two."

He raised his finger; Robbie began to punch the keys on an aged adding machine and handed him the tape.

"Six hundred and ninety-six fifty each. Head tax at Idlewild and Orly included."

I made out a check and handed it to him. He scanned it and

stowed it in his wallet. "Fifth Avenue Bank and Trust, eh? I thought that was only for old farts."

"What about a receipt."

"We'll mail it to you when your check clears. Plus agenda, hotel vouchers, and air ticket. And a complete roster."

"The check's good. I'll take the receipt now. Signed."

"Would your old buddy screw you? After all we've been through together?"

"It crossed my mind."

It was the amalgam of venality and vindictiveness that roused the thought. It rankled since it was undeserved. We had not been friends, but I had not been among the persecutors. I had once moved between him and a couple of tormentors who were whiling away some time baiting him. He may have remembered that too, but now he was demonstrating that I had always been lumped with the others, and that he needed no help these days. An independent. He wrote out the receipt swiftly and with his practiced neatness. He could have and should have served in a higher echelon than ours.

· I left. Two wide and sunny smiles lighted the departure, and the reunion now became something of a preoccupation, edging and inching its way into my thinking along the channel that Berdichevsky had dredged.

Those pictures. That laborious, purposeful assembling of these works, begun in coincidence. Now they were a lodestone that generated a hesitant tracking and trailing, and afterward a more extreme pursuing. Toward their recovery. No conscious effort to deny had any effect. ETO Tours and its arrangements fitted the scheme like a keystone in a Roman arch. There had been a decade with only the three separated instances of violence.

There had been the dispersion of and disinterest from all of those who had known something of Hamplemann's success, seen his acquisitions, reacted to his character. Except for one, Berdichevsky, the subjective sociologist of no independent means, a theorist in history who would not seek a place among his fellows. Not even to support himself or to seek allies who might agree with his conjecturing, or by opposing them to bring them into sharper focus. I considered this as I wrote to him that night; the unwilling and impatient acolyte had become a convert, straying away from the commonalty where living a clean, pleasant, and ordinary life was the priority.

When I told Scott that I wanted to take time off during the last week in November, he was furious. It was, after all, the holiday season, when ingatherings took place and sometimes a toll. When hearth and home shone, when families and selected friends reinforced their belief that they lived in the best of all possible worlds.

For Scott, our leader, and the rest of us, it was a harrowing time when all of the orders for ornament and embellishment that had been agonized over for months past and agreed upon, now had to be delivered. To dwellings on the East Side of Manhattan, to a Georgian mansion in Beverly Hills, to a Newport-style cottage in Southampton, and to a couple of hundred others near and far.

When he learned why I wanted the time, he objected the more. Why would I consider damaging not only my future but his for the sake of a drunken get-together with a bunch of nonentities I hadn't seen for ten years and wouldn't see for another ten? Where was the sense of it?

By early November, after I had worked myself into the loss of ten pounds and a lather of frustrations, I had organized most of our responsibilities into charts for follow-up by the rest of the staff. I took them through the methods and contacts to be used in every conceivable mishap that I thought might occur. Previously, I had held those bits of information and experience very closely, as most insecure people do. It's supposed to make one's position impregnable; this is the indispensable man, the majordomo who holds the house together and keeps it functioning. That mattered less just then.

Scott hadn't missed the performance. He came into my office and handed me an envelope.

"An advance on your bonus. I see we can stumble along without you for a while. Thanks."

I converted it into traveler's checks, and went home to pack.

7.

All personnel should have received the following in Your ETO Tours Flight Bag: Air Ticket, Idlewild, New York—Orly, Paris via TWA or Air France. Payment Vouchers for Your Hotel, Meals, and Entertainment (Smile). Agenda that gives you date, time, and location for all scheduled events. City Map of Paris, courtesy of Galeries Lafayette. This store offers discounts of 20–50% on perfumes, Swiss watches, jewelry, and other luxury goods. Do Not Forget Your Valid Passport and your Sense of Humor (Smile). Direct requests for help or complaints (God Forbid) to me or R. Castellano, AA (Always Available). One Snafu: Return tickets Paris—New York will not be issued until two hours before departure on account of a special price for group travel. Look out Paris, Here comes the 855th!

Monsieur W. Pattison, Contrôleur

My impulse was to remove ticket, vouchers, and agenda and drop my ETO Tours flight bag in a trash bin. Doing so would reflect good taste and travel experience, no matter how recently acquired. There was, however, an obligation to the group, and not wishing to set myself apart, I carried the thing along like a gift from a pinched but thoughtful relative. As recognition signal it was unnecessary. I didn't see another in the boarding area and no old pals approached me.

There was to be a delay. On the tarmac below a group of

mechanics in hooded yellow rain suits had removed the cowling from one of the engines. A gust of wind strong enough to move the three rudders threw a spat of rain against the lounge windows before me. The plane itself looked tired, but that may have been simply its conformation. It was a Constellation and the fuselage was a lengthy and dramatic ogee that drooped low over the nosewheel.

We boarded two hours after our scheduled departure time, and remained in front of the terminal for another hour. The plane was hardly half-full even with a large group under the banner of an upstate medical society. My neighbor across the aisle uncapped a quart of duty-free scotch and fortified himself with a paper cupful. He was an engineer on the way to Italy to work on a hydroelectric project, and he did not like scenes like this one or much else about air travel. He had spent eighteen months flying the Hump into China during the war.

"Not one goddam thing went wrong. Ever. It was miraculous. Not a blown fuse or a fouled plug. And that made it all the worse, and it's carried over to this day. Even if I'm half-smashed, I'm on the edge of my seat. I've got ears like a bat."

I was a great admirer of machines and those who understood them. I told him so.

"Less you know the better." The cup was losing its shape but he managed to refill it. There was a confident roar from one engine after another, and a great hurry to rev them up, as though the aircraft itself were impatient to be away. For me, never a thought of fragility or incompetence. I was one with the intrepid spirits of the past. When I flew the Atlantic it was with the gallants, as a son of the Lafayette Escadrille.

Having assisted the takeoff and completed the steep climbing turn and bank to the northeast, my neighbor closed his eyes in quiet relief. His flexors eased, and he settled back and stowed his bottle.

"Won't need it for a while," he said, checking his watch. "Seven hours before I have to start booting it home."

I passed the time in reading and reflection, beginning with the Pattison agenda. It seemed to state that the whole affair was intended to satisfy the shallow desires of a company of oafs. He had certainly convinced himself that this was true. As one of us—and that he had never been—he spelled out the difference between a *capot* and a *chapeau*, and suggested some precautions so that no one would bring back a gift of the buboes.

At last, after the disdain and insolence, there was the discussion of the only formation that was obligatory, the commemoration of our honored dead on the Saturday before departure. That was only mawkish.

Still, in the circumstance, traveling at this great speed, twenty thousand feet above the sea, with the stars to mark the passage, I thought of the affair as a cosmic event.

Here were the vast distances I was covering, like the rest of the unknowns, to arrive upon a path that led to the center of our common past. That part of it, at least, deserved attention. A meaningful ceremonial was our obligation. So few lives were ever touched by high purpose, fine sentiment, noble example. With morning that judgment receded.

My companion across the aisle measured the level that remained in his bottle.

"Enough to get us down?"

"If I'm careful. It can be tricky."

He managed it but it wasn't easy; he agonized through the wide sweeping turns and the loss of air speed. For me, this tippler, the gaggle of doctors and their wives, and my agenda over the next four days completed the severance from life in New York. I was transported like a traveler in time to a place in which concerns and activities were handed down from an authority above. Not a higher order, simply a different echelon that presides over Everyman's affairs.

So instructed, I went along in the proper direction on this fine autumn afternoon. There was more of a smell of charcoal smoke in the air than aviation fuel. The plane had accomplished its purpose, and the French national presence established itself on the instant.

I took a taxi from the Invalides to the Hôtel Marinier, a high and narrow building down a few doors from the Place de l'Odéon.

I presented my passport and the ETO Tours voucher to a young woman behind a counter. The passport merited hardly a glance, but the voucher required close scrutiny from the young woman and the *patron*, a bulky man wearing a heavy woolen shirt, a sweater, and a shiny gray suit. Having concluded that the paper was genuine, he handed me a steel pen and a registration card, and I took possession of the ordinary skeleton key to *"cinquante-huit,"* this linked to a leaf of bronze that weighed at least a pound.

A number of the Marinier's charms were not readily discovered. Fifty-eight was one. It was at the very top of the house, a winding flight of stairs beyond the elevator's limit, and turned out to be a suite that looked out upon the square. The beds were swaybacked, the furniture ill-used, the inner chamber windowless, and the bathroom obsolescent, but with the french windows opened there was immediate acquaintance with life on the plaza below. I sat down to enter into it as the afternoon sunlight slowly diminished; there was a random increase in movement. Workers in blue smocks turned homeward; schoolchildren scattered on the dead run past the theater. There was a familiar figure there half-obscured by the last column of the portico. Hamplemann, and not a specter, for there was a long shadow behind him that detailed that outlandish costume I had always associated with him since my first glimpse ten years before.

There was a sudden thumping on the door, and I opened it reluctant to leave this sighting. Berdichevsky in the highest of spirits dumped an assortment of baggage inside, and seized my hand.

"Come on," he said, "that's Paris outside. Let's go."

I told him what I had seen, and he followed me to the window. Nothing but the swirl of the caped mackintosh, the back of the hat brim, the manifestation of a strong and viable presence.

"Gave me a turn also the first time I saw him." He stowed his B-4 bag in the armoire and tossed a net bag of books and journals and his old ammo box in with it. Downstairs he piloted me across the *place* and up to a scabrous bar near the Luxembourg Gardens.

"Outside's best," he said, weaving his way to a rusting steel-topped table against the facade. "Inside it's depressing."

He waved his hand impatiently for a waiter and settled in. There was a chill in the air with the coming of evening, but those reading their newspapers or books did not seem to mind nor did the couples deep in conversation or gazing raptly upon each other. We ordered marcs and coffee and clinked glasses ceremoniously when it arrived.

"First time I saw him, actually realized who it was, was outside the post office on Vaugirard. That was a couple of weeks after I phoned you about this reunion. I walked back here and had a drink and he passed by on the other side of the street. Couldn't see his face clearly, but the same clothes. Different shoes. These are boots. Hard-toed boots. I didn't feel menaced or threatened at all. But I was curious. I would have liked to call him in and share a table with him."

"And ask how he was making out as a civilian?"

"To find out what kind of a deal he made with Pattison. That's how he knows where we are staying. Our schedule."

"Any of us could have given it to him."

"Impossible. We're assigned to separate hotels, and we won't know where the others are until we have our first meeting. Tonight.

"Hamplemann had his information earlier. From the source. The only informed source. There isn't any other. I think the relationship goes back quite a long way. And it is very logical, of course.

"Hamplemann has a twentieth-century mind. He's a creature of his time. He sees life as an organized process that fits into tables and boxes in which most people carry out the functions assigned to them. They are managed by orders or past experience, or threat or promise. States, nations to him are designed like military hierarchies, highest to lowest, each member having a defined role or responsibility. All nations. No exceptions.

"And there's the corollary that he learned about. Once you're familiar with how these hierarchies work, you can use them. Within limits, of course. You obey, you cooperate, you fulfill every quota placed on every product or service, and that done, having proved your loyalty, and allegiance to system and superiors, you have room for your own maneuverings.

"Does that seem familiar to you? It is to me. Makes the whole world simpler to move around in."

I ordered another round for us, recalling my own similar method of operations. Everything in order, all instructions carried out, all directives read and followed; then all that latitude to serve other interests or merely my own.

Berdichevsky in the ascendant. He tossed off the marc, and pushed his coffee cup aside.

"Having this understanding of the ways of the world, his own, the British, certainly the French and Dutch and Belgians where he was stationed, we know, and finally ours, he reconnoiters, probes gently, and sees exactly what he knew he would see. The same kind of structure, same inefficiency and indifference intended to be and pretended to be quite the opposite.

"So having made some basic preparation, he marches boldly in and files his claim. He has nothing to lose by it, certainly."

"Come on, for Christ's sake, Berdie. He knew goddam well we weren't going to roll out a truck and load it up for him. And look what he looked like. The impression he made. He had fat on his ribs, he wasn't any goddam DP."

He waved his hand impatiently.

"Didn't matter at all. He was filing a claim. Pushing himself into the record-keeping system. One day, in the normal course of such events, it would be processed. He only had to wait. If it worked, well and good. If not by way of the 855th operations, then eventually by another authority.

"What he didn't realize was that this company of bumblers actually meant to carry out its assignment as directed. That it was commanded by what was to him the worst of all possible individuals. An idealist. And he was assisted by an obsessive—me—and a very able and intuitive security officer. Proudfoot.

"All of us were outsiders, not very closely connected to the military and its methods. Except superficially, the military had very little to do with the company's function as we saw it.

"So his planning and his papers and his investigation before he came in didn't matter a damn. What did was what we saw when he finally came in. A wolf wearing a lamb's fleece. I never forgot what Shotgun called him that day. 'A damn night rider.' A resourceful one too. Confident. Even brazen. With a goal in mind. So he fenced with us until he got his chance. He knew he was headed for a PW cage and that it wouldn't bother Shotgun too much if he didn't get there alive.

"In any case, he survived. I don't know how. When Shotgun fired at him I had my face in the ground and so did you. Maybe he did hit him. Maybe he's one of the ones that survive. Marked for survival in the center of worse firestorms. Happens.

"What matters now is that he's still involved, and was all along. He had a go at eliminating both of us. He was informed about the claim Hamplemann Two filed with the government and ended that competition. That means that he had help. I think of it as direction, not assistance."

"Who?"

He shrugged.

"There are all sorts of candidates. I thought it was Faulds at first. But he's dead too. I know Pat is associated with the present effort. All participants on both sides have some scruples of knowledge, parts of the whole. I suppose I have the most. But I am only speculating. I have a sense of what I am about to witness, but there is really nothing to do but go on with what's before us. Off to the *Fest.*"

They had all arrived at Wagenende and assembled in a private dining room on the second floor. The restaurant itself was an odd choice. The mounted heads of deer peered out between bunches of pine boughs from the dark wainscot; on the shelving were beer steins in pewter, ceramic, and carved horn. The chandelier was a rustic cartwheel. It looked like an inn in the Black Forest.

Only a handful of comrades were there, some clustered around a small bar, a few others at one end of a long table where places had been set for double the number.

All of them were immediately identifiable, as though we had moved that very night into our casern together. Beards and moustaches, eyeglasses, gray hair, added weight were evident, but to me almost imperceptible. All of us were presences preserved.

Only Pattison had removed to a distance. When he came forward to greet Berdichevsky and me, he had further transformed himself into what I presumed was a Parisian gentleman of fashion. He wore a chalk-striped double-breasted suit, the jacket pinched in just beneath his armpits. There were furbelows as well; when he raised his hand to pat the crest of his hairpiece, there was the gleam of an intricate signet ring, a large gold wristwatch with a massive bracelet, and a cuff link with his initials closely entwined. Identity.

"Is this our Pat?" asked Berdichevsky in wonder.

"None other," he said with a pleased smile. "And the same old Berdie. Don't mind the informality, do you?"

"Not in the least. It's the tone we want now that we're a little band of brothers."

"Orphaned these ten years, but still full of the old piss and vinegar."

Berdichevsky moved off to shake hands and chat; I did not join him. There was enough insincerity in the room without a contribution from me. I drifted through this happy hour as more alcohol took effect until finally Pattison raised his voice for the official welcome. He began a bit shakily, as if uncertain of their response, and some did react as he had assumed that they would, with the vulgarity so common to our old times together.

That was painful enough for him to speak hurriedly, and to direct much of what he had to say at his young assistant, Castellano, who had kept his distance from the rest. That was only fitting, for he did belong to another generation, and seemed to me to be thankful for it.

"I just want to welcome you on behalf of ETO Tours, which is happy to play a part in making these arrangements for you. But not officially because the 855th hasn't elected its officers yet. And I don't know if you want to do that now, because we are only a small part of the company here. I thought there would be more, but we had some cancellations because of sickness or the holiday.

"But that can be left for some future date and this is the time for some fun. We have only the one serious occasion, putting up our memorial tablet on Saturday.

"All the arrangements on the agenda are suggestions and we are flexible on everything. If you'd rather be on your own, go right ahead with anything that suits you.

"I would like to make one suggestion, that we give John Kowalski the chair at the head of the table here. John has worked very hard and contributed a lot to this event."

There was a scattering of applause, and unanimous agreement. He was so installed although he protested that he didn't deserve the honor. This brought a measure of legitimacy to the affair, for Kowalski was a solid and serious man who had served our vacuous assignment faithfully.

Insignificant as it was, the act certified us as an organization for charter and official listing in the veterans' magazines. Having accomplished so much, and fuddled to some degree after happy hour, we fell to and made our way through generous portions of the house specialties. After a tureen of lentil soup with sausages came schnitzels that overhung the dinner plates, fried potatoes, sauerkraut, and turnips. There were loaves of rye bread, mounds of butter, and our favorite condiments, a jar of mayonnaise and bottles of ketchup. The waiter sweated profusely in our service, filling and refilling pitchers of beer and pouring Alsatian wine for a subgroup of discriminants.

Replete, we considered the evening's attractions, a boat trip on the Seine or a tour of four nightclubs, one drink free at each. Paris By Night.

I joined the group headed for the *Bateau-Mouche.* Ten or twelve other tourists were already on board when we arrived at the Alexander Bridge. A taciturn deckhand, well bundled against a chill westerly breeze, took our tickets and the *Stella Polaris* edged out into the current. She yawed heavily in the chop; by the time we had reached the Ile de la Cité most of the seafarers had complexions of an eerie gray. The loudspeakers grated away in three languages offering a mélange of dubious information about a legendary city, Ys.

There were further squawkings of flying buttresses and floods, famine and famed citizens. The contemporaries seemed to have retired early. The quais were dark, and the leafless chestnuts clashed their bare limbs as we labored upstream. The channel between Cité and Saint-Louis was a confused millrace; the massive splayed supporting masonry of the Notre Dame apse appeared and vanished in sheets of spray.

Along the right bank we came astern of a barge edging downriver, and in the relative calm of its wake we returned to the Concorde Bridge, our journey having been shortened in both directions. No one complained.

Arquette, Wersba, and Scharfie shared a taxi to Saint-Germain. I suggested a comradely nightcap, but all declined. Understandably, for we were now feeling the effects of the time en route from New Orleans, Toledo, San Francisco, and the last long overseas leg— merely to appear at this ingathering that to this point might just as well have been mounted in Kansas City.

No one thought it odd that we were in different hotels. Arquette felt that Pattison had been considerate in putting distance between Wersba and himself, and certain others with whom they had nothing in common ever, and Scharf was delighted to have a garret by himself near the Sorbonne. He was working on a doctorate in linguistics, and had an appointment with a renowned authority on the Russian language.

I didn't mention Berdichevsky's theories to them. They had no suspicion of a devious purpose in assembling them here. There were no queries, certainly. They all seemed to consider this junket simply a piece of luck and a corollary to their original assignment. It was a cut-rate trip to a pleasure dome with only a few drawbacks.

At the Marinier, the lobby lighted at this hour by a single low-wattage bulb, our key was not at the desk. An aged porter rode up with me and unlocked the door. There were some companionable snores from the inner chamber and a heavy scent of cognac.

I fell asleep instantly. At some late hour the light between the beds went on briefly, and the cistern above the toilet emptied with a roar, but I did not awaken fully until I became aware of an icy draft in the room.

Proudfoot stood grinning before the open french window. Next to me in the other twin bed, Berdichevsky stirred, sat up, and, finally focusing, leaped out to shake his hand.

I showered first, and by the time I had finished, breakfast was on our table—a very large brioche, croissants, butter and jam, and three big bowls for our coffee and milk. Proudfoot and I sat down, Berdichevsky in and out of the room endlessly, half-shaved and then dripping wet, as though to reassure himself that Shotgun had not vanished.

From their first days in the company, disparate as their backgrounds and experience of life had been, they had established their bond. In many ways they had demonstrated their liking and appreciation, defending the other's opinions, adopting expressions and phrases, commiserating when necessary, sensitive to mood and viewpoint. Together once more, it was obvious that the time apart had not weakened the relationship. On the contrary, the years had elevated each man in the view of the other to some sort of an epitome of what a friend should be. An ideal for idealists or naives, I thought, but I was not so deeply involved.

Still, it was heartening for Berdichevsky for it renewed his confidence in his own theories and his commitment. For a brief period it relieved Proudfoot of the need to make a difficult decision about his future. Whether or not to resign from the army. He had a wife and two children, all of them in the United States for a month with her family in Vermont.

He was a major now; toward the end of his service in Korea, he had commanded a battalion. This was fine but he thought that he would not rise much farther. Not enough education, no associations on higher levels, no staff assignments. He didn't look forward to spending ten years training infantry or serving in it.

I didn't envy them their relationship, although it was affecting to a degree. I sensed some self-interest in both, and that was warranted. I could also see that such alliances as these are better tested in extraordinary circumstances. They would not flourish for long in adjoining offices or neighboring apartments.

Too much of a strain on the fellowship when it's under detailed scrutiny by those who did not share the past. Who would understand the hold this unkempt, rotund, opinionated, and discursive fellow had on anyone.

Nor, for that matter, this sardonic, rigid, disciplined believer in order and principle. That perception had softened to an extent, probably at the moment because he was not in uniform, and his civilian clothes were almost elegant—a houndstooth jacket, gray flannels, chukka boots. His wife picked out his clothes these days, and they had been tailored in Hong Kong.

"I think she was after a Brit and had to settle for less," he said.

We did not report for either the cultural program at the Louvre or the shopping expedition scheduled for this morning. We spent much of it in our room while Berdichevsky brought Shotgun up to date on his labors in his own spare vineyard. Much of it he had written to him, and a fair percentage Shotgun claimed was indecipherable, something like his conversation.

When he mentioned the Hamplemann sightings, Proudfoot fingered the scar just above his right eye. "Hasn't been much help to me in my career. Makes me look like I'm either scared or horrified.

"You ever try to dig anything out of Pattison?"

Berdie shook his head. "I tried to speak to him last night. He put me off. Arrangements to make. And he's busy today all day. And there is no way I can see to pressure him. Whatever he's done isn't illegal."

"Not at all. Just slimy. But you got a choice to make again, same as the one you had to make back then when you took matters into your own hands, Berdie." He looked at him quizzically. "And you're ten years older," he added softly, very much aware of what he was touching upon in the way of a scar that, like his own, would not disappear.

"Put it in words."

"Five people died that time for no good reason that I could ever see, and I have seen a lot of that. Too much.

"Now you're in the same position, Berdie. There's even the same people involved on both sides—your statement, not mine. You have a choice to make right now. Today. Sometime before all the onetime warriors assemble to go over to the Lido and get traditionally drunk and horny, and chase around looking for ass that they aren't going to get much of anyhow except in their minds, you ought to tell them what you believe they're going to be involved in. If you really do."

"I do believe it."

"Then you owe them that much. They aren't here for any high purpose. That's a position of privilege. You don't even have anyone to look out for—children, a wife, anyone. Do you? Do you have the right to say, 'Follow me, it's right and proper,' when you know damn well they couldn't understand your commitment, and even if they did would tell you straight out that it ain't theirs?"

"Maybe they'd surprise both of us. Maybe if they had the experience of serving a greater good they'd find it more rewarding."

"Transcendental, huh, Berdie? I read them but it didn't change my character. Not so's you'd notice. We always give each other the benefit of the doubt, though. Whatever happens, keep it in mind that I suggested the option to you. If it's rejected, so be it. My commitment's to you. Personally."

Berdichevsky went to the armoire, removed the ammo box, and set it on the table between us.

"Relics," he said, opening it. "I wrote to Earley's wife when I knew I was coming. I would rather have gone to see her and explain, but that was impossible.

"She's married again, and I was worried about the content— that it might seem that I was the one who was serving memory the more faithfully. The mental gyrations of the true weird, eh?

"Well, I gave some explanation of why, if it was at all possible, I was asking her for the items that had been forwarded to her that were 'personal and professional only.' Great phrase. Very comforting. What I meant, I finally spelled out—the ordnance maps of the sector where he was headed with the detail, his pocket diary that he based the company reports on, keys, and whatever else of that kind that she would choose to send me."

He took out the original Hamplemann inventory, an Elgin wristwatch with a radium dial that was scarred and blackened; the hands indicated 6:48. The pocket diary was scorched and stained. There was a requisition folded down and tucked inside the back cover, a number of German ordnance maps, portions of them burned away, and several heavy steel keys with crudely cut shanks. Shotgun picked one up.

"Last time I saw one of these it was in a blockhouse in Colmar." Berdichevsky thumbed over the last pages in the diary. "Twenty-eight November, 1410 hours," he read aloud.

This isn't peace. Lull between offenses and offensives. World full of thieves and plunderers. Am I one too? Only the blurred line between us.

Drives like I shit. Got the shakes. Like me. Shld keep his eyes on the ruts. Thinks I'm making a note to take away his pfc stripe. All things cnsidered I'd rather be in Leominster. Or the Pacific. Whole goddam frontier's full of hate and fear and enfilade. Only a gt mind could design a killing ground like this. Method. Forethought. Money. And a useful life of six months. Less. Wsn't it so? Only seemed like two years. Figures. How many rounds and pounds required to kill one man? As much and as many as you have on hand.

Finally. Would have been smarter to post two squads to guard it right in the magazin. Whoever said I was that smart? Got the family instinct. Hide the valuables. Or what passes for same. Worse if I had to ride in the back.

Make the gd decision. Only difference is 3000yds for C's
sake!

"That's great, Berdie. Like a ride in a tumbril," Shotgun said.

Proudfoot unfolded the requisition; a poorly mimeographed
form it had been even when first received at the company. Proof
every time, however, that all matériel and equipment had been
transferred at such a time and on such a date to the officer
who signed for it. There was his serial number too; another af-
firmation.

"Thought I remembered that. Case of grenades. I okayed that.
And a reel of phone wire."

The ordnance maps had been reinforced with tape along the
folds. Proudfoot spread them out upon my bed and peered at them,
sizing up route markings done by other hands.

"You been over the plot, I suppose?"

Berdichevsky nodded. One of them covered the sector of our
first station. The others were contiguous, and they moved them into
proper orientation, just as Earley must have done in the hours before
he left on his last mission. There was no subjectivity evident, it was
simply map reading. That it had ended in disaster was not a consideration. They read it off, noting the terrain features—marsh or
swamp, stream, road classifications, declivities—along a stretch of the
upper Rhine behind which was a spur of the Siegfried Line, the
West Wall. Even on this bright day, Earley's considered movement
of his little group, these few of his possessions given over to us, that
destination he had chosen intensified the memory of him, for me
and certainly for Berdichevsky.

"It seems that whichever direction you approach that line from,
it's the way to dusty death."

"Could've been worse, Berdie," Shotgun said, grinning. "Could
have been you on his orders."

"Never. He didn't trust me. With reason, the way I was behaving. More like a hysteric than a responsible officer."

"One thing's sure. You got a remarkable capacity for guilt. It may get to be too much for you someday."

"Someday this week?"

"Possible, I guess. But you can depend on me to see you don't add to it. And now that we know where we're going and that we'll have an escort, let's try to enjoy the time we have left."

We went out and we mingled, following Pattison's unimaginative agenda dutifully. We paid our respects to the Eiffel Tower, to Napoleon's tomb, to Notre Dame; we visited a necktie manufacturer where John Kowalski selected four dozen to be given to the workers at his plating factory in Waterbury; we went to a perfume and cosmetic wholesaler who offered the lowest prices in Paris, and sniffed as though to distinguish which ones might be suitable for a mother and which would arouse anyone else.

Along these well-trod paths there was always time for a drink or a couple of beers or a glass of wine in a bistro or a café, a halt for pastry, coffee, and only temporary sobriety. For most of the seventy-two hectic hours there was a haze of sharp recollection, and periods that were almost a blank. Arrival, amusement, dissatisfaction, argument, and finally sleep. Any thread of plan or purpose faded. There was no meeting with Pattison, although Berdichevsky and Proudfoot stopped at the Hôtel Saint James and Albany three or four times to seek him out.

On Friday evening we assembled like a delegation of the privileged to savor a rare experience—a visit to the erotic Paris that had existed between two world wars, when a revolution as far-reaching as its preceding one had supposedly occurred, this in the realm of cohabitation and sexual indulgence. We had reservations at André Temesvari's Cave, in a district between Montmartre and the Gare du Nord that to me was unique in the city; it resembled nothing so much as some blighted area on the fringes of a midsized American town not quite ready for the wrecker's ball.

The *cave* itself looked like a down-at-heel meeting place for a fraternal order that had lost both point and purpose. There was a narrow corridor that led to a large, high-ceilinged room with a dusty dance floor around which were two levels of tables that would accommodate four or six. Those on the upper level were in alcoves hung with drapes that could be closed off for the sake of privacy if the revelers wished. A pianist and three other musicians had a station, and we passed a service bar stocked with what was evidently the house specialty, champagne bottles with remarkable coiffures—bright gold foil, ribbons, garish seals, and labels that misspelled the names of every distinguished bottler.

Perhaps because it was still early in the evening, the energy level of both the staff and a scatter of patrons was low. When we entered, however, the musicians did strike up a lively tune. "My Blue Heaven" blared out in the tempo favored in the thirties, possibly. We seated ourselves, and a muscular waiter who looked like a veteran of the foreign legion appeared, brushed at the splintered tops of our tables with a towel that had seen service in other tasks, and we ordered up our drinks. The wine was twelve dollars a bottle; the only alternative was eight-year-old bourbon whiskey at two dollars a shot, and another fifty cents for soda and ice splinters. There were some expressions of discontent. They ended quickly as we became not part of an audience, but a group of extras associated in a performance, and our remarks, our whoops, laughter, and comments, additional dialogue.

The lighting changed from what had come from bare bulbs in the ceiling to a subtler play that cast deeper shadows, the band, behind the trumpeter, began "Stardust" softly and slowly, and a couple moved out upon the floor to dance. The woman wore a beige knitted dress that clung to her fine figure; she responded gracefully to his lead, not as a professional, but as a long-term partner, unsmiling, concentrating. Three times they circled the floor. Scibetta watched fascinated, and then he rose and went out himself and tapped her partner gently and formally on the shoulder to cut in. She came into his arms as though rehearsed, not missing a beat, and followed him through his intricate improvisations for some minutes before he relinquished her to her partner once more. We applauded loudly for our own as he came back to his table.

There were others on the floor now, an odd assortment, a brutish-looking fellow in a business suit with a very young girl in black velvet and flat-heeled shoes; an aging woman with a teenage boy in a belted Norfolk jacket; a heavyset man in breeches and boots wearing a Sam Browne belt. His partner was a slim fellow in black trousers and a loosely fitted white silk shirt. There was a pair of transvestites, thick with makeup, the one in a black suit with drooping peg-top trousers, the other in a bedraggled green satin floor-length gown. There were two couples miming wealth, the men in dinner jackets, the women in low-cut dresses and much paste jewelry. There was even an apache and his masochist.

I had not been aware of their entrances; they simply appeared on the steps between the alcoves, from beside the bar or the bandstand. The tempo changed; the trumpeter attacked some versions he had heard of "And the Angels Sing," "Blue Skies," "The Sunny Side of the Street" with little talent but much enthusiasm, and no concern for accuracy.

We emptied our glasses and called for more. The place was hazy with tobacco smoke; sharper, brighter spots blazed into it and down upon the gyrations on the dance floor. The music built to frenzied, high-pitched cacophony. The woman in beige and her partner were in the center of the floor, facing each other, a foot apart, their bodies in ceaseless and meaningful motion. In a single sinuous action, she was out of her dress, stark naked, and either offering herself or challenging him to take her. We cheered him on as, frenzied, he ripped at his own clothes. Jacket, trousers, shirt, and tie came away instantly and wound up in a heap on the floor, and he went for her. The lights went out, the music ended in a harsh shriek. For some moments there was silence, then suddenly the curtains over the alcoves parted in one sweep, and the cast reappeared in a series of brilliantly lit tableaux, all poised over or upon each other, half-clothed, unclothed, half a dozen different presentations of orgy seconds away.

There was only enough time for all to register some details of these variants. I could not tell whether seconds or minutes passed before it ended. The curtains closed; the room reverted to what it had been when we entered. The musicians lit cigarettes; the waiter eyed us expectantly. No one among us had any accurate comprehension of what we had seen—what portions of it were imagined and what was real. What was only suggestion, sequence, consummated by ourselves. We were as spent a detachment as I had ever seen on a return from furlough, and not disposed as yet to discuss this happening, or to compare it with the most impressive episodes witnessed in the past. The fabled dens of eroticism in Panama City or Hong Kong, outside Fort Bragg or in Phenix City.

We paid our bill, even adding a small heap of francs to it, and filed out, edging our way through the corridor to the entrance. A new group had arrived, couples, most of them, some having second thoughts about staying. We offered no assurances, instead eyeing them as though to calculate the eventual effect. Some of that had to do with what we had drunk; milling about on the street one or two were almost immediately nauseous, others slightly hallucinatory. I thought the evening a fitting end to this three-day japery, this excursion into a shadowy place where imagination and reality were not clearly defined. Dwelling on it that night, as the others must surely have done, I thought of it as an interlude seized and painted in hurried brushstrokes by one or another of those artists whose works were part of the Hamplemann inventory.

8.

We have some volunteers and they aren't "you, you and you" (Smile) working up a Company History. I have read what they have done so far and it's really good and accurate. More Details are needed! So bring your Recollections along with you, especially about where You were and what you were doing the day Our Buddies wound up in the Minefield. Or other stories you tell. Not too much BS, if you please (Smile).

        B. Pattison, Recorder

One hundred and some hours of prodding, pushing, scheduled and unscheduled debauchery, or what some had claimed to have been, had ended and had taken its toll. At six in the morning on Saturday, no one was very cheerful. It was much like the last day of any previous military leave or furlough all of the group had experienced. As if the date on the agenda still meant remand into official power. We were preoccupied, sunk in thought of the future, reentry, now twenty-four hours away.

Paris itself loured in the dull beginning of the day, shops shuttered in gray or green steel, dreary cafés, deserted street markets, empty barrows as our detail raced across the city in a caravan of three battered taxis to the Gare de l'Est, as if to catch the last train ever.

There was a pointless argument with the drivers, no two of whom agreed on the fare for the ride from the same district. That settled, nastily, we lined up at the station for coffee and stale croissants. I had a cognac against the chill and the previous night's indulgence. Others did too, for we had a forty-minute wait before we could board. Our train had three third-class coaches with wooden seats, decrepit enough to have hauled reinforcements to the Marne; there was a string of freight cars coupled to them that dated from the same era, with rusted half-round steel roofs. The equipage was well suited to the journey.

We coalesced into groups much as we had in our earlier time together, as though the years between had left the pattern unchanged. Berdichevsky was quite composed, as if he had made these arrangements and chosen the participants himself. Perhaps he saw something more substantial than a ball of Saint Elmo's fire dancing about before him, or merely sensed an end to his self-generated thrashings over the years that had served him with unequal amounts of progress and frustration. As we rattled on across northeastern France, I saw him staring as much into the reflection of himself in the streaked window as out upon that unlovely countryside. There was an expression about the mouth—hardly a smile—that indicated success or satisfaction. That, or a glint of madness. Having caught my eye, he shook his head, as though embarrassed.

"Well. After all, it's been a long time."

Behind us, Merolla, Silberglitt, Scibetta, and Scharf spread a coat over their knees, pulled out a deck of cards and wads of francs, and began to deal blackjack. None seemed to have any interest in the route, although most had passed this way before in units that had regrouped or rested and refitted at Châlons-sur-Marne, Sainte-Menehould, Thionville. This train halted at all of them and many others to pick up small shipments or a handful of passengers, elderly for the most part and giving less hint or reason for their journeyings than we did ourselves. At Metz we changed trains, this time to two coaches that were a kind of French compromise between train and tramcar. This crept along from one narrow-gauge spur to another as though picking its way around a sector that was still a contested battleground.

"We're an hour and half late already," Proudfoot said, "and I'm getting damn hungry. See what's available at the next stop. Probably C rations."

Berdichevsky spoke to the conductor, a young man in a uniform that looked sized to fit him over the next twenty years of service.

"We have half an hour in Saint-Dié. On account of equipment exhaustion, I imagine."

We organized several parties for the shopping, and returned in good time with half a dozen long loaves, cheeses, ham, salami, several pâtés, an assortment of salads, red and white wine, and a selection of pastries, some tart, crisp apples, and two liters of cognac. Traditionally openhanded, we shared it with our fellow travelers, and the conductor as well. He closed his lunch box and helped himself liberally, finishing up with a toast to us before he took a generous nip from the brandy bottle.

"In case of snow," he said with a grin.

That promised. The weak sun vanished in low cloud; the day grayed; the fields in the valley we were descending to were sere, with only a hint of green in a hedgerow or along a deserted dirt track.

At ten minutes of three we crept slowly into Marckolsheim. The conductor waved a farewell, and we filed off across several lines of unused trackage to the tiny station, unpainted and identified only by a barely decipherable metal signboard over the locked doors. We queued at the pissoir at the end of the platform, and went around that to a half circle of coarse gravel. Two vehicles were drawn up there, one a sleek Mercedes bus painted gray and red and brightly chromed. Berdichevsky waved and advanced on it. Its lights blinked on, the brakes chuffed, and it purred away, leaving a more familiar transport behind—an olive-drab two-and-half-ton truck, standard since 1940, this had side curtains instead of doors, and all of its accessory equipment in place: pioneer tools, jerry-cans, toolbox, and bumper-mounted winch.

It was unmistakably ours. Freshly stenciled in white on its bumpers I read 855TH SERVICE CO., SEVENTH U.S. ARMY. Hanging from the knob of the choke was a strip map of the route that would take us to the casern where we had reported for our first company formation, and above on the dashboard a packet of envelopes. Our return tickets from Orly to Idlewild.

"I'll take mine right now," Merolla said, grimly. "And I'll stop off in New York just long enough to beat the shit out of that bastard Pattison. Some fucking joke."

Berdichevsky had been studying the train schedule posted in a glass case at the door to the station.

"Then you'll be spending the night outside," he said quietly. "Next train back is tomorrow morning at seven. Whatever anyone wants to do is fine with me. I'm going on."

He climbed into the cab and started the engine. It promptly stalled.

"Flooded it," Scibetta said. "Move over." In two tries it caught for him. He ran it up with a roar in the stillness and settled it finally into a smooth idle. "Somebody tuned it right. Or maybe it's one of the good ones."

There was common indecisiveness among the others. Proudfoot and I were committed; we unhooked the tailgate and let it down. To make so unpleasing a choice took time, but there was no persuasion from any quarter.

They were peevish and annoyed rather than angry; so much had their lives changed in a decade and a half. They were, like me, the children of another era when they had had little experience of a comfortable present and a reasonably secure future. Scrimping, saving, making do were the commonplaces for them in the late thirties, and real security was a matter of chance. They belonged, the majority, to a class that had walked a narrow road skirting disaster.

Kowalski had spent two years in the CCC's. Scharf, on his way finally to a graduate degree, had only been able to afford two courses a semester in night school. Universities were for the privileged and not for the rank and file.

I knew something of their histories; there were similarities wherever they came from—a farm in Iowa, a steel town in Pennsylvania, a factory in Michigan, a furniture store in Illinois. City or town or village, they had all had a meeting or two with privation and worse.

Those days turned up in conversations over time together, and often they were quite revealing of principle or lack of it, resourcefulness, kindness, and courage. They spoke freely in darkness and the silence of the listeners. Some did, and if others did not, I was aware that they were responding nevertheless. All were veterans not only of that war we were concerned with, but of the previous wrenching upheaval.

Survivors they were and a fair proportion had never been in action. Like most of the millions involved. Still, none had been able to influence his assignment. The fates fixed that. In any case they had served, and they had found in the years afterward that their fellow citizens, now more enlightened than they had been after the First World War, were going to offer them a range of opportunities that they had not had in the past.

They, we, accepted them as our due. Support, stipend, vocational training, education, even the means to buy a house and give them a foothold in the middle class. They had become people of at least some consequence, and they objected to the sudden loss of status. The uncomfortable train ride they could ascribe to a nation still recovering from devastation or lacking the ability to design and build a decent rail system. The truck they considered a kind of personal insult, a reminder of their real rank in times past. This transport was a return to that and to the slights and the indignities as well.

They weren't properly outfitted for the ride either. Thin shoes, topcoats, fedoras, instead of warm wool and good sound boots. I had to smile, for now as then there had never been a rational alternative to obedience or acceptance of one's lot. Just the repetitive objections that tailed off quickly to a mumbled "Fuck this noise." We boarded, some not very nimbly, and moved off toward the east, the truck shuddering and lurching as Scibetta familiarized himself with it once more.

There was a delay at the bridge indicated on our strip map. It was new, and one of its two lanes had been blocked off for paving. There were no formalities; we were simply waved on after three or four westbound trucks had passed, duplicates of ours. With the Rhine behind us we entered into another country and, almost tangibly, another time. This was not immediately evident, and it did not become so until we had ascended to higher country some three-quarters of an hour later and arrived at our first headquarters.

Very little of it remained intact; nothing, in fact, but the walls and outer works, and the wide stone archway that opened out to the assembly ground before the casern itself.

Now it was only a shell, this building that had quartered historic battalions for more than a century. It had never been attacked, no complement had ever been required to defend it. That indeed was the reason we had been installed there in our own time. A good sweeping and hosing down and it had been as ready for inspection as it was in Bismarck's day. A squat block of closely fitted beveled stonework three stories high, it had been an outpost that demonstrated the presence of a new centralized power throughout the land.

In a decade, it had been picked apart piecemeal, from the copper-sheathed roof to the iron grilles that had guarded the cellars where arms had once been stored. Some remnants of rusted concertina hung in ragged festoons over the unframed windows.

No one passed the portico; it was enough to peer inside at the heap of rubble just beyond. There was no need to enter. I could see myself and the others quite clearly at this very hour when our day was ending, a little knot of claimants shepherded gently out into the gathering dusk to make their way down to the village. Where they sheltered for the night was not our responsibility.

Ourselves grouped in our sections to file papers and reports of progress in our onerous task. Plural pronouns, passive voice, figures only slightly inflated. There was a great amount of activity in the scene recalled; comings and goings throughout the station, conferrings, telephoning, much of it superficial and purposeless, no matter how praiseworthy this assignment. All of us had done better since then, serving our own ends.

Still there had occasionally been brief interludes when concept and sentiment coalesced and we could believe that there was something praiseworthy about our assignment. That was very rare, but it had occurred. It did now as we stood together in the twilight where Earley had first spoken to us.

Berdichevsky did not mount the steps; he could not adopt Earley's manner any more than he could have assumed his height. Still, when he held the bronze plaque above his head for us to see, there was an odd sense of the biblical about him. The stance was patriarchal, despite his dumpy figure, brush-cut hair, and the shapeless black raincoat.

"He's got the Tablets with him," Silberglitt said.

Hardly, but it served mood, clime, and self-esteem.

We commemorate the mission carried out by Alpheus L. Earley, Captain, AUS; Louis Stadle, Cpl, AUS; Robert S. Wise, Pfc, AUS; Kenneth Loody, Pvt, AUS; William Blankenship, Pvt, AUS; Royal M. Woods, Pvt, AUS.

To preserve the rights of others and the cause of justice.

Presented by their comrades, the officers and men of the 855th Service Company.

Stadel's name was misspelled, but there was no point in calling attention to it. He and Blankenship were the ones I had known best, and they warranted remembrance. They were two of Earley's ponderables, his partisans, two trusting instruments of what they knew was a worthy secular power.

I didn't know the others as well, but it was necessary to be generous to them also, and not only because they had shared this capricious outcome. We could see what had become of us, classified and consigned to our places that were as firmly strictured as any plan an army could design. We were all that we would ever be. Not so the dead. They still had a claim to what might have been. Deep or shallow, there were emotions aroused.

"This is not the place for this," Berdichevsky said. "It isn't suitable. If it ever did have any importance, it doesn't any longer.

"The captain's wife sent me the maps he had with him when they left. It's about thirty miles away, I think, and Frank Merolla can show us the exact place where they stopped. We should make the effort. We owe them."

Merolla paled, but he did not protest, nor did any of the others. There was a proper contrast at this point with the shallow entertainments of the last few days. Some may have seen Berdichevsky's suggestion as a reasonable penance. In any case, there was no opposition, and we boarded once more.

En route we passed through the town where we had discovered the Hamplemann inventory. Perhaps because it had suffered little damage, the town had grown in a decade. There were even a few tentative movements toward suburban development on its outskirts, and the magazin near the town hall was now a school for the building trades. There was still much work to be done, and much more planned. The future had arrived swiftly.

We went on in pale, cold, and windless twilight, silent on our benches in the truck bed under our heavy canvas hood, and seeing over the tailgate only that ground that we had covered. There was no sense of what lay ahead. The hidden prospect inched us further still toward the past when we had moved on the orders of others, and we sat and smoked companionably enough. The taillights went on and blinked often as we pitched along, less and less oriented to direction or even time itself.

We were climbing once again, and Scibetta downshifted often, then we were driving along a vast curving escarpment like those I had traveled on trains in the United States; when seated in the center I could see both engine and observation car. Below us along the declination of the great bowl were stands of trees, planted and cultivated over generations. A historic commitment to managing one of the national resources. This heightened the unreality of the journey, for the whole sector often appeared as a panorama constructed for this passage.

Farther down from these separated groves and aligned along the common elevation of the contours of the land were multiple rows of dentoid concrete antitank and vehicle obstacles. Dragon's teeth, so called, as if a term out of myth could make them more ominous to a force on the attack anywhere from twenty miles south of us to the border of Luxembourg, a hundred and sixty miles away.

They had been set deep in the earth, when originally put down, but now they were no longer precisely sited. Numbers had been shattered by shellfire or uprooted by bombs or demolition teams. Now there were channels that snaked through the whole defensive belt, unconnected to each other and wide enough for the passage of even the largest and heaviest vehicles.

Beyond the end of these approaches was another line—pillboxes or strongpoints meant to support each other mutually in defense. This system was in sight all the way to the military crest above us. Most of those nearby gaped emptily, some fire blackened, some pitted, holed, or smashed into heaps of scattered debris.

Our progress slowed, we halted briefly then moved ahead once more, only to halt again, as though the truck itself were in the throes of indecision. We went into reverse, Scibetta standing with a foot on the running board and the cab door open, peering backward into the gloom. That show of bravado was unnerving enough to arouse the second-class passengers. Kowalski leaned out from the tailgate and bellowed at him.

"For Christ's sake, you can't back this thing out of here. Find a turnaround someplace. Let me out and I'll do it for you, you dumb bastard!"

That touched off a shouting match with four or five participants until one of the conservatives in the cab set the handbrake hard and we came to a shuddering stop. There was a colloquy up front. Berdichevsky spread his detail map below the headlights, and he and Merolla studied it. Proudfoot climbed down and walked forward to survey the road ahead.

"You went too far," Merolla said. "We should have turned on the other side of the hill. That's the service road behind this where we were. We didn't come over to here."

Thirty yards away, Shotgun was out of sight. The seconds tracked past. A light fall of snow began, at first hardly enough to dampen the dead grass at the side of the track, but it persisted. When Proudfoot returned there was a dusting on hat and shoulders.

"Can't go up much further anyhow," he told us. "But there's a wide enough spot up there to turn if we're careful. Better put it in four-wheel drive."

There was a majority vote of no confidence in Scibetta; all but the two in the cab chose to dismount and follow on foot and then to form a ragged line inside which he maneuvered with care. Then we picked our way back, reached an intersection, turned left, and climbed once more. The bank at the sides of this track rose higher and higher—to engine level, to the top of the canvas hood, and then twenty feet above that—before we began a slow descent. Just beyond the crest we had passed two mounds of rubble and heavy timbers. On the left was the hull of a tank lying on its side, all but one bogie wheel hidden by brush and debris.

We bumped downward. Behind us the path of our tires was black upon the snow cover, and already, not far beyond, beginning to be obscured.

"Even the weather's the same," Arquette said. "We could have done without this."

We halted at a battered wooden gate swagged with remnants of barbed wire that had to be dragged open, and entered the access road that had served as supply track for this sector of the whole defensive system, all of it carved and excavated through the crest that overlooked the toothed contours below.

Proudfoot had rolled a foot of canvas back and stood peering ahead. I joined him there to stare before us at the darkness just beyond the two dim yellow cones from our headlights. To the right were scattered humps and depressions, some half buried in brush, indications of middens. To the left at distances that varied from a few hundred yards to half a mile were a series of splayed revetments thirty or forty yards deep. These led to bunkers the width of the revetments and twenty feet high. Above each was another brow of earth to the height of the hill line itself.

We passed them crawling in first gear, like a party of desecrators prospecting, for these entry areas looked like so many mausoleums, built to the standards of an awesome authority stricken not long before. All of these major strongpoints were fitted with heavy steel doors, some unhinged, some flung at erratic distances. Once they had been painted a uniform forest green; now they were pitted or gouged and scabrous with patches of rust.

"That's it!" Merolla shouted suddenly. "That's the son-of-a-bitch. There're the two mushrooms, and the little railroad track."

Scibetta braked sharply, turned into the apron, and stopped. This looked intact, still impervious as if built as exemplar that defied time and assault. We climbed down stiffly. Scibetta joined us, leaving the motor running.

"Okay," he said, "we made it. Put up the sign and let's get the fuck out of here."

Berdichevsky approached the door, fished in the pocket of his raincoat, pulled out the steel key that was part of Earley's bequest, and tried it in the door. It turned quite easily. He winked at us, smiled delightedly, and set his feet firmly to haul on the handle.

Proudfoot seized his arm.

"Not yet," he said. He had the spade from the truck in one hand and one of the hand lanterns in the other. He gave that to me. "Keep the light on it." Carefully, he set the spade between the edge of the door and its frame, levered gently, and inched it apart so slowly that there was hardly a squeak of hinge. He peered around its edge, slid his hand into the crevice as high as he could reach, and ran his hand down to the saddle.

"I make it three wires," he said to me quietly. "Somebody see if there's a cutting pliers in that toolbox."

There was, quite serviceable, like all of the other equipment supplied by someone who had considered all needs. Shotgun severed three trip wires—one to the interior door handle, the others to lifting eyes welded above and below it.

"Okay, Berd," he said. "You want to see if I got them all? Everybody else back."

Berdichevsky nodded. "Thank you," he said, formally, as if some rare protocol were involved. There proved to be oversights.

The door opened upon a cement slab, a railed balcony that overlooked the center of the casemate. A steel staircase led downward to the main floor of the vault. From this a series of corridors branched off to lesser dark mouths that linked it to other support and service enclosures.

Earley had also booby-trapped the balcony across its width and the staircase as well. The trip wires were fastened to the pins of the grenades he had requisitioned, and these in turn had been wired tightly to interior props and projections. Proudfoot clipped the leads at a distance from the grenades and let them fall free.

This place and the lethal devices that Earley had placed to protect it were subjects for introspection. On the role of chance in survival and the like, but not now. Still, I did dwell, however briefly, on what Proudfoot had said about Berdichevsky and his responsibilities to all of us here. It was he who had embellished Pattison's agenda—that done at someone else's bidding, and certainly bought and paid for.

Our presence in this cold man-made cavern was his doing. The elements, the imagination, the memory of what had happened to the preceding detachment roused unease, and properly anger at him and his persistence. If he sensed this attitude directed at his back, it did not weigh on him. He charged in, and down the steel stair as soon as Proudfoot had clipped the last wire.

Except for Scibetta, we crowded into the entry; he remained

in the truck cab, trusting no one but himself to keep the engine turning over.

The lights from the truck fell upon the doorway and reflected from the flaking whitewash of all the surfaces inside. There below, sequestered once according to plan in the magazin, and finally by Earley quite by chance in this place, were the cases of paintings from the inventory. Close to these was another selection, evidently chosen at random—other, smaller boxes. One that I remembered held an ornate silver service, and another contained a collection of porcelain. Over this whole cache and the other wrack that lay strewn about the main embrasure was a powdery layer of white dust. That sifting made Berdichevsky below look like someone bereaved considering a choice in a tombstone shop. We descended and joined him there.

If he thought this a triumph, he did not show it. He was aware of the past, when further difficulty followed every small success. He put his hand gently on one of the cases, as if to assure himself that it was real.

"We should open one anyhow," he said. "Just to be sure." He looked to his audience for agreement. None was voiced. Above and outside, the truck engine muttered, gasped, and went silent, and on the instant, all light vanished. There was a sudden shuffle of feet up there, and a sharp cone of light from a powerful hand lamp fell hard upon us so that we stood as figures in a frieze.

There was a bellow of command in a commingling of German and English and a burst of firing from an automatic weapon aimed over our heads and into the embrasure behind us. We scattered in panic into the galleries that flanked the chamber. Silence again and a roar of laughter from up there.

"Attention to orders! Your company is disbanded effective immediately! Assemble now and you leave unharmed. This minute. Otherwise you stay longer. Much longer."

He punctuated his instruction with another burst that echoed and reechoed through this warren of galleries. There was a sharp, unforgotten smell of powder fumes. I was safe, for the moment at least, in the cover of the tunnel to his left with several of the others, all of us flattened in the angle between floor and wall. Some seconds passed, and so did that other reaction, that shaking and trembling with a momentary palsy before realizing that there is no hurt. I inched forward on my stomach to peer out, to discover how many he had shot. As yet, none. He sounded off again, cock of the walk, master with the only working weapon. He reveled.

"What treatment is this when a man comes to file a claim, eh? Not at all what your notices state so clearly."

He quoted them from long memory. A dialogue, first in a stentorian tone of authority, then the pretended wheedling of a claimant.

" 'All persons deprived of property under the previous regime should file claims for restoration of such properties and possessions at the designated military offices.'

"Oh, sir, I swear on the heads of my children that things were taken from me worth a hundred thousand dollars U.S. Here is my proof that I was never a national socialist but only a God-fearing person who did no harm and I have also an uncle in Detroit city. Uncle Hans. Do you know him, sir?"

Another roar of laughter, and another five rounds, this time at the walls near the dark mouths of the arcades where we lay. I heard him change ammunition clips.

"No? A pity. Such a nice man. A real American, too, just like you.

"Vermin! Come out and process this claim. Now!"

Peering out, I caught a glimpse of him, the muzzle of the machine pistol in constant movement as he scanned the level below. There was another figure in the deep shadow beneath his position at the top of the stairway. Proudfoot. Unseen, he reached out stealthily for the free end of the trip wire to the grenade that Earley had set to cover the entry. There was activity near the doorway now. The engine of our truck turned over, and the sound lessened as it reversed out of the revetment. Then came the ticking of a diesel; the bus we had seen drew up close, and its lights flooded the interior. There was a conferring at the door.

Behind me Kowalski and Silberglitt cursed fervently, repetitively, in whispers like incantations, as though rage and hate might have the power to influence survival.

Hamplemann addressed us once again, restrained this time, controlled, in a change of mood. There was awareness on his part that some instability existed here. Some precautions were necessary. He wanted discussion only because he had not managed absolute freedom of action. He had not come away from the last meeting unscathed either.

"We proceed now to remove these cases. You have no official standing here. You represent no one but yourselves, and are here in your own interests to take away what is not yours in a corrupt and immoral seizure. If you try to interfere, you suffer the consequences. Understood? Then answer. You had much to say last time we met. You had many spokesmen then."

Berdichevsky walked out of the tunnel opposite and peered up at him, standing to attention, hands along the seams of his stained and powdered raincoat. To Hamplemann, he must have appeared as much the victim as any that had crossed his path in the years of conquest. This one made no pleas, however.

"You have no more right to this property now than you did before. There is no argument about that."

From beneath the stair, Proudfoot gestured with fingers and thumb to keep him talking.

"And there is no reason to threaten us. We can go together to the authorities, and let them decide on the disposition."

"I think not. We will agree on the terms without other parties under your influence. Imitating your idiotic methods and denying the rights of their own countrymen. Who served them faithfully. Better than they deserved. Such a government has no power here.

"I offer you a choice. Collect yourselves and depart unharmed. You have transport, your truck is there. Board it and leave. Otherwise, I withdraw. I close up this place and you can all lie here together until the day of judgment.

"If I wished, I could hunt you down as you hunted me down, unarmed and alone, but I would not be so contemptible."

"Your memory isn't altogether accurate," Berdichevsky told him. "You overlooked some details. But that is of no concern just now. What is the condition of our driver? The man in the truck?"

"A bump on the head. A temporary loss of consciousness only. Go and see for yourself. Or send your assistant, Stolzfuss. The sharpshooter. The one who wished to beat me with his pistol. I see he is not shoulder to shoulder with you just now. Have you had a falling-out? Or was it a weakness in his bowel?"

This exchange had never been a parley to either man. To Berdichevsky, the didact, the fact-gatherer and analyst of action and attitude, it fulfilled that desire, and there was the chance that no other injury would be inflicted on his party of innocents. But speciousness and disparagement, the offer of departure unharmed, must have conjured up in him all of those experiences that had set him on his path. He stared up at Hamplemann, and the other shadow figures just behind him. Even as only listeners and observers, these unknowns reinforced a presence that uprooted and destroyed according to its own power and purpose.

"You haven't brought me here," he said quietly. "I brought you. You're here because of my weakness. That's why I have been faced with you again. You should have been obliterated years ago by anyone with advantage or opportunity. I had mine and didn't take it."

I saw the gleam of light on the barrel, heard the action of the bolt, as Hamplemann made certain that there was no blank round in the chamber. Proudfoot had wrapped the trip wire around his hand; he did not jerk it, quite well aware even in this moment that the pin in the grenade was the more easily drawn so. I heard the pop that meant that it was armed and operative, as Hamplemann must have as well, and even saw a glint as the thin steel handle arced away from it.

In that confined space the blast deafened; there was a rattle of splinters against ceiling and far wall, and as though from a greater distance seconds later, a continuing shrieking.

From behind me, Merolla raced forward to the opposite side of the stair; I saw one foot hit the wall as he flung himself upward to grasp and pull the opposite trip wire and explode a second grenade. Landing and stair trembled, and all of us charged up it, leaping and scrambling over the humped and prostrate and out of there into the night.

A confusion of men with one or another objective, the first the bus, a massive dark shape, all lights extinguished, the engine shut down, nothing to be seen on board. Scharf was at the doors, the shovel in both hands. He swung it like a baseball bat. Silberglitt had a length of cable with a heavy junction box attached. He whirled it around his head and struck at the windshield. Kowalski passed that side on the dead run in some pointless pursuit, stumbling on breathless. Released from tension and fear they sought any objective, animate or no, to smash at. That too passed in moments. There was nothing but night and silence on the snow-covered apron, and a gleam of starlight above.

We formed a ragged picket line about the. bus, breathing heavily, like some tribe of nomads girding for a final assault. Berdichevsky and Proudfoot appeared last upon the scene; Shotgun had picked up Hamplemann's machine pistol, and he came forward with it and tapped almost deferentially upon the bus door.

"All over," he said. "Come out now. You won't be hurt." Scharf repeated it harshly, with embellishments in German, and there was movement low in the aisle, the door opened, and the driver descended, palms outspread before him, edging away from any incidental contact. Kowalski and Silberglitt seized him by the collar of his uniform and flung him against the side of the coach; Scharf threatened him with the shovel, and instantly Proudfoot interceded.

"What the goddam hell are you, a rabble?" he shouted. "Let him alone. The war's over and so's the entertainment."

In moments he established order and discipline. What had once been a unit became one again, however briefly. Two went to look after Scibetta. Scharf and I boarded the bus with the driver while he restarted the engine and turned on its lights again. Berdichevsky and Shotgun returned to the casemate, and the carnage.

Direction and organization, labor and assignment were the common need. We worked in our isolation like survivors after an action, without question or argument or emotion. Arquette had some first-aid experience; he took charge of the wounded. Scibetta was unconscious still from a blow on the head. Arquette thought it more than a concussion, most probably a skull fracture. His pulse was fair, and there was little bleeding, but this was a severe injury.

"Like what that bastard did to Elrod, Berdie. Remember? He never did come out of it."

Hamplemann was one of two dead inside the entry, he badly mangled by the first grenade. There was another semiconscious. Shotgun put the contents of Hamplemann's pockets and a partly shredded money belt into the crown of the velour hat he had affected over time. Ever the distinctive individual, whatever his purpose, from chicanery and thievery to transcontinental assassination. Another of his party was under our truck, wounded in the buttocks by shrapnel.

"Serves the fucker right," Merolla said. "Let him see what it feels like awhile. I still got to go to the VA hospital twice a year to have pieces removed. Last time it was a piece of seat spring. Really."

The fourth man had vanished, some thought up the service road we had followed here. We wasted no time looking for him.

The bus driver made every effort to help. He rooted out a stack of blankets from one baggage compartment, and a large first-aid kit for Arquette, folded down rows of seats for Scibetta and the other wounded, and showed us where Hamplemann had been seated and what he had brought aboard. Still, Proudfoot assigned Scharf to watch him. Their bus was our only way out, we learned. Despite Hamplemann's offer to let us depart in peace and friendship, Kowalski reported that the truck's distributor and its wiring had been ripped out.

"Don't let him in the driver's seat, and stay alert. Or we'll all wind up chasing the taillights, hear?"

Scharf sat down in the seat just behind the driver, his shovel across his knees, and whiled away the time in interrogation, his task years before. The rest of us prepared for departure, and some of the arrangements were unpleasant. Still, we could settle the responsibility for their end on the victims, the best possible place for it. History proved that; then too, we were following orders, another valid defense.

Also, we had no time to review an action that could only be seen as reaction. We did not think that any higher echelon would take up the matter, and no one demurred as we took steps to see that evidence of it would not surface anytime soon.

There were, of course, other factors to consider, but the location itself was not one of them. There were plenty of cryptlike spaces for the interment of Hamplemann and his follower. Theirs was the floor of one that had served an engineer detachment. It had remained untouched for years. There were rolls of white tape that had marked paths through the minefields beyond the casemate; there was a collection of sketch maps upon which tiny death's-heads had been pasted to indicate where antipersonnel and antitank mines had been set. If Earley or anyone in his detachment had seen these, they might have returned safely.

Also, I might have picked up the sheaf and mailed them with a covering letter to some official office somewhere that might use the information to advantage. When the time came to change this sector back into a harmless pastoral. A proper gesture to consider for this and the thousands of other hectares that required this effort. I wondered how the priorities were set, and returned to the casemate.

There, Berdichevsky, amateur geometer, had rigged the ammunition hoist with a sling made of pieces of electrical cable. His work party was hauling the first of the cases of paintings to the entry above. From there they were manhandled into the baggage compartments of the bus.

It was after seven before we were ready to leave. Berdichevsky wired our bronze plaque to the steel rail of the stairwell and read it over once more in silence.

"Anyone else want to?" he asked, gesturing at it. No one. Kowalski blessed himself, and four of us then heaved and shoved the door until only a small aperture remained. That was all that could be done.

We boarded and took seats, and the driver, Heik Deterling, backed the coach carefully out of the revetment. The last sight of it I had was the gleam of light on the key in that massive steel door. On the coach there were no expressions of satisfaction, or even relief.

Whatever remained in other corners of that complex of defensive works, an adaptation of developments that had begun in this country many centuries before, was of no concern either. Berdichevsky fixed on it too, as the coach moved forward on the track to the gate:

> "But what good came of it at last?"
> Quoth little Peterkin.
> "Why, that I cannot tell," said he;
> "But 'twas a famous victory."

9.

Your Committee has one last request to make for your cooperation!
Fill out the Form Enclosed with your agenda and give us your
opinion on everything from the Food to the Arrangements. Check the
box marked Poor, Fair, Good or make your own comments under
Remarks. No Profanity Please. (Smile) Help us make Future Re-
unions even Better!
  Bill Pattison

For the few hours we remained together at this time, we were at our best. We were comrades, and not as we had been before. This time we had shared an experience, all of us. This was no impersonal arrangement, a unit in a line of battle that faced an equally impersonal threat of extinction by cannon firing from twelve miles away. Chosen by chance ten years ago, all present had continued to be targets in the Hamplemann mind. This many, marked for obliteration when the opportunity arrived. Having survived, we were occupied with thankfulness and consideration for one another, and above all for Scibetta, the damaged one.

Three hovered over him; the rest concentrated on hurrying him to a hospital, preferably a world-renowned medical center. The only guidance available came from the driver. It was he who chose the route to what he had heard was the best one in the area, in Strasbourg. We took the autobahn to the bridge at Colmar. The customs and immigration posts had recently been turned over to the Bonn government, but this one seemed still to be in French hands; the German passport control officers deferred silently to them. Neither group was much interested in our passage. We were waved on with hardly a pause. We did the thirty-odd miles in as many minutes, halted on the outskirts at a police station while the driver asked directions, and, having mentioned an accident en route, were given an escort on a motorcycle to the Hôpital Val de Grâce. He left us in the middle of a dim square in the Vieille Ville with a wave of his gauntlet.

On three sides the square was surrounded by a skewed agglomeration of houses three and four stories high, variously half timbered, and sturdily shuttered at the windows, the doors with lintels of stone a foot thick and steps twice that, worn into hollows over the years. Ahead of us was a great oaken gate. Deterling cut the engine and dimmed the lights as though revering silence and times past.

There was a night bell that jangled at length and without response for minutes. At Val de Grâce misadventure or accident seemed to be suspended between vespers and matins. Finally there was a shuffling of feet at a measured pace, a squeal of drawn bolts, and half the door swung inward. An aged porter thrust his face out and surveyed the scene. No cases could be accepted here this night. If they were *"mort ou tot"* we must call the Transports de Corps, and he pointed to a call box across the square.

Once more Deterling took a hand, hoping to hurry circumstance so that he could be free of what had become the most outré of driving assignments. He harangued about a horrendous accident that was like a battlefield, we were only Samaritans, *Samaritains*, who had stopped to give first aid, departed from our route at great expense, and hastened to this place on orders of the police where we had been assured we would find help. He said we would use the telephone to speak to the authorities, the monsignor, or even the archbishop because we had been refused succor. In his own country no one refused succor.

I had no idea what points were effective, but the porter did listen in silence, mulled the matter over as though conning some formulary once given to him, and withdrew, leaving the gate ajar. Higher authority responded. A group appeared, two orderlies, still half-asleep, a young and energetic nun, and an elderly one who quickly took charge of our casualties, making her dispositions as though she had managed an aid station.

Since Silberglitt and Merolla were remaining with their close comrade, they served as stretcher-bearers for Scibetta; the orderlies, the porter, and the young nun handled the wounded from Hamplemann's group, and the whole party moved off across an expanse of cobbles toward a sudden glare of light at the building entry. Once admitted, the whole square reverted to what it had been before we arrived. The gate creaked closed, the bolts were driven home, and again, silence.

Down the narrow lane to the left there was a single light upon the pavement. There, opposite a stunted cenotaph, was a series of buildings clinging closely together as though for mutual support. The Auberge des Alliés.

At this late hour the fire was dying on the hearth, but the dining room was still warm and welcoming. There were trestle tables with benches attached, a small and well-stocked bar, its top sheathed in copper, and a proprietress who was all business, as if fifty customers were vying for attention instead of just the one aged local who lingered alone over a thimbleful of marc.

She brushed imagined crumbs from the spotless surface of the tables nearest the fire and seated the advance guard. When Scharf returned with Deterling, having parked the bus for the night, and Berdichevsky from the hospital where he collected Silberglitt and Merolla, we had a round of brandy to take the chill of the hillside out of our bones. There was a remarkable menu considering the hour—pot-au-feu, pork cutlet, chicken.

Having ordered, we listened to a somber report on Scibetta's condition. *"Très sérieux"*; an operation would no doubt be necessary. A neurosurgeon, "very skillful," would take charge in the morning. For now, he was stable. Instructions had been given. Hearing that we had done so well by him, we could eat with an appetite, some voraciously, all the way to a cheese platter, strong coffee, and liqueurs, as though in a rest and recreation area. There were rooms above, Berdichevsky learned; he booked us in and returned to the table.

None of us, including even Proudfoot, had been less disconcerted by this series of events than he. This, I thought, because of his original commitment that had oriented him almost completely to the past. That in its turn had drawn him to delve into minute details for facts or even bits of what may have been fictions to support his own theses. That was where he had lived, as no one else had. We had committed ourselves to the flow of the current in our time; he had not.

He had dwelled on a specific occurrence as a pure researcher in the sciences fixes on some subcategory of a discipline, or as a theologian worries away at the truth of a bit of apocrypha. What had been put in train, therefore, involving us was no more than the expression of what he was almost certain would appear. If some details did not quite correspond, enough did to prove his hypothesis.

I knew him best, but no one could ever take his proper measure. There were too many sides to him. We never knew at any point in time whether we were dealing with a moralist or a muddler, a philosopher with an understanding of the way to shape a society for the better or only a fool in cap and bells. Just now, he attracted and held our interest, having laid out on the table the items that Hamplemann had brought with him on his mission. Glancing at them, I found myself dwelling on what would have been found in my own pockets and luggage; nothing to impress or intrigue. Here was a difference.

Most of it had come from his heavy and well-worn leather haversack. It was what we, sitting like jurors, now knew to be the comparatively scanty equipment of an assassin.

It was as though the sheep on the way to the abattoir had suddenly been given the sense to understand intention. Simple enough, too. By way of Pattison, Hamplemann had had advance information about every movement that we would make, and it included every embarrassment, down to the falsehoods and euphemisms some had given in their correspondence with the "Committee," that fake organizer at the heart of our ingathering, that meretricious company that had brought us all here to participate in a fraudulent observance of a manufactured accomplishment.

A Walther pistol, a duplicate of the one that Proudfoot had taken away from him. Ammunition clips for it, and for the machine pistol he had fired at us in the casemate. Three passports from various countries, all with visas stamped and verified that indicated free access all over Europe and America as well. The equivalent of thirteen thousand dollars in different currencies in a money belt. Some of that now bloodstained and pinholed from the last exchange with him.

Worst of all was the picture of all of us taken at our first assembly in Paris. Grins, self-conscious expressions on our faces, as though most of us were undecided as to whether this was some momentous occasion or merely a preliminary to dances in the sheets or other joys not yet arranged. So many dupes and gulls, seen to be so by the worst possible audience—themselves. There was a palliative at hand, but Berdichevsky denied them that just yet.

"Getting drunk won't solve our problems. We have decisions to make right now. And that can't wait."

"Make them," Kowalski said. "I made mine. To get the fuck out of here and back to Orly and onto an airplane. I had all the fun I want."

"That's probably the best way," Berdichevsky agreed, "but what about Charlie—Scibetta. What about the cargo? What about Deterling here?"

"Pay him off," Scharf said. "Give him a bundle of whatever money suits him. Have him sign a confession. That'd be good for something sometime."

"Who gives a shit about the cargo," Merolla said. "Whoever wants those crappy pictures can have them. I wouldn't give one of 'em house room. None of those bastards could even draw. As for

Charlie, I and Jerry will stay till we see if he's going to make it. I owe him. Divide the cash and a share for him. That way we all made expenses. It'd be the first time I ever got paid right for blowing somebody away.

"As for him," he added, grinning wolfishly at Deterling, "one bus driver more or less don't bother me at all."

That was upsetting to Deterling; he may not have understood, but he comprehended, and he protested loudly that he had had no part in this beyond sitting at the wheel and going where he was bidden. More injustice at a time when there ought to be less. It took some minutes to ease his fears, for after every reassurance, he gave another instance of his helpfulness. He was not even a regular driver for "Tuchtig Reisen" but only a substitute trying to advance himself from his work as a steel hauler. These "river rats," as he called them, had appeared with Hamplemann in Bonn, and the journey, so he had been told, was on orders from the government to meet with another group coming from France to secure some lost materials.

None had been very pleasant to him either, and the one in the cloak, who looked like a gargoyle on a church roof, had treated everyone like a dog. Worse. He owed them no consideration. None. And the company had no right to expose him to such a scene. He might have been killed twice over. With a wife and two children left alone and penniless. One more righteous man among us. Berdichevsky pushed the cognac bottle to his hand. Comfort.

Then Arquette, with Wersba's tacit agreement as always between these two, for they had an attachment almost as physical as that between Chang and Eng, spoke out suddenly to address a specific concern, the shining window of opportunity that had attracted predecessors. It was a significant departure from his past behavior. That had been a drudging and trudging through orders and assignments, each and every one a burden. Since our arrival both had remained at a distance, aloof, civilly tolerant, a superior group of two. Few lapses escaped notice; they signaled their awareness with the slightest changes of expression. Subtle memoranda for discussion later. Alone.

Now, however, desire, if not need, impelled a whole new argument on a higher level of appreciation, but based, as all present understood, on the same common motive.

"We," Arquette said, shrilly and emotionally, "want to know about those pictures. We have a right to know what you plan to do with them."

"Who's we?" Berdichevsky asked quietly.

Arquette included all the savants present in a gesture, a sudden advancement for everyone.

"All of us. Just because some aren't knowledgeable about their value doesn't mean they don't have a stake in them."

Berdichevsky feigned an inability to understand.

"A stake? What stake? Do you mean you want to claim ownership? Is that it?"

"Why not? We found them. We recovered them. We own them. Together."

"Like musketeers, eh?"

"Not like musketeers and not like fools and followers either. You don't have any authority over us or any more of a say about those pictures than the rest of us do."

Berdichevsky rested his hand ever so lightly upon the pistol, covering it.

"Would you like to put it to a vote in the Republic of Arquette? Is that it?"

"Sure. Absolutely. Once they all know what's involved, that being more money than anybody here ever thought of having.

"This collection is worth thousands right now. In ten years, most of what's in those cases has quadrupled. Do you deny that?"

"No. I've heard it said before. I myself don't know. Also, I don't care."

"The point is the rest of us do care. I didn't come to share old times. I don't have any memories that were so enjoyable. I came for what I could get out of it. Now there's a lot more to get out of it than anybody thought, and I want it. We want it!"

Proudfoot and I at the foot of the table sipped away during

these exchanges. He the more amused, for he was not as familiar as I with Berdichevsky's weighty conception of Western man, elevated. Somehow Berdichevsky had created a stereotyped, rough-cast Everyman at the real center of this company, and enthroned him. That character was shaped by all that was best in the American imago. One needed only to point the way, and this paragon followed it, like the strongest swimmer breasting foul tide and adverse wave. A noble spirit was at the center of the concept, and in spite of every indication, Berdichevsky continued to believe like some humble priest, swayed, troubled, but never an apostate. Until now, gazing at the faces around him, he was aware of fallibility. Once and for all.

"Not that it matters," he told us, calmly, "but I am shaken. To the core. You had a better identity when you wore uniforms and dog tags. When the army and the government handed your principles down to you and tried to hold you to them. What's happened to you since does you no credit. But I won't argue about this. You were men, and now you want to turn yourselves into jackals like the original thief. Scavengers.

"You want to arrange a future on other men's lives and possessions. I don't believe in the common good, just individual guilt and individual responsibility."

The pistol now lay on the table before him, a distance from any other hand.

"I'm going to make a deal with you. You can take the crates of silver and the porcelain collection and ship them back. Turn that into cash and divide any way you want. The cash he had on him too. Except for a thousand dollars that I am holding for the moment, and you should set aside some for Scibetta's treatment and transport back. When he's able to go.

"Tomorrow I am taking the bus and the pictures to Lucerne, to the *Amt für Rückerstattung Beschlagnahmte Kunst*, that being the office for the return of confiscated art, where Hamplemann intended to deliver them.

"Tonight I am sleeping on board. With both sets of keys and this." He dropped the pistol in his raincoat pocket and left us.

"You always were a candidate for a Section Eight," Arquette shouted after him. "You were crazy then and you are now."

"Son-of-a-bitch," Merolla said, aghast. "Do you really think he'd use that thing? On us? After all we been through together?"

"You never know," Proudfoot said solemnly, "but I wouldn't want to fool with him. In the mood he's in and with all that's happened, I don't think he'd give a damn. Better leave it till morning."

We divided up for the night. Proudfoot and I took the driver with us into the room most easily secured up under the eaves. It came with feather beds and a square of starlit night through a high skylight. Shotgun locked the door and dropped the key into his pillow slip.

"If you have a piss call, wake me up," he said, and in moments he was asleep. Deterling too. He curled himself into a fetal position, took a good grip on the bedclothes, and soon relaxed it, like a child when the nightmare has ended. Not I.

Images rose and passed, sharp edged in blacks and grays, crowding, obtruding, without physical motion, caught and held only to vanish and then reappear in profile or full view. There was speech in remembered phrases and tones, the living and the dead, disjoined from each other but all linked to me. Garside, Marthia, Earley, Berdichevsky, Proudfoot, Hamplemann; even Willy Korn, Estes, Faulds. Finally, Deterling, at the door of his coach, in shock, both hands raised high.

These persons, real and wraith, interposed themselves and overcame exhaustion. The night crept ahead in the smallest increments. There was no order to the assemblage, no line or linkage save only my own association with them, and they persisted. They did not fade until after three, and no concentration upon brighter or better imaginings, not even the most satisfying erotic experiences, could dispel them.

Morning came sunny and soft, and so springlike that it seemed the trees should be in bud. Most of the snow had vanished, and at breakfast there was civility, if not reconciliation.

By ten o'clock the delegation returned from the hospital with good news. Scibetta had survived the operation, there was no paralysis or complication, and the surgeon was confident of a complete recovery. He might even be ready to leave for home in ten days.

"No charge. Imagine that," Silberglitt said. "They didn't even ask for a donation. So we all gave a pint of blood, and they thanked us."

I went to a bank and bought a draft for five hundred dollars made out to the hospital. Berdichevsky settled our bill at the inn and turned the money belt and contents over to Kowalski and the others.

"No paperwork," he said. Then we took Arquette and Wersba to the railroad station and off-loaded the cases of silverware and porcelain at the baggage room. The parting there was without warmth. They nodded their good-byes, and occupied themselves with a pot of black paint and a brush borrowed from the baggage master. One shipment was addressed to New Orleans, the other to Toledo.

"One more thing," Arquette said quietly, straightening up. "I expect to be informed about the final disposition of everything else. We do, that is."

"Sure," Berdie told him. "Absolutely. I'll send you a parchment with ribbons and a wax seal."

All of this rankled as we trundled slowly through the center of Strasbourg, he mumbling half to himself, mood upon mood change, like some half-demented tour guide.

"That bastard," he said at one point; "eventually they'll fight about the prices they got. Or lie about it."

The day was to Deterling's taste as much as it was to the three of us. We made good time on the two-lane macadam road on the French side, crossed into Germany at Colmar, and arrived on the outskirts of Basel in less than two hours. Sunday was a day for driving.

The previous day might never have occurred; no one referred to it. We made no plans for eventuality or difficulty. We toured,

Deterling humming to himself as we went along, as though forty vacationers were in company. The landscapes presented themselves, short views, far panoramas, until we reached the Swiss border. There the national police in field gray waved us into a concrete corral. Deterling opened his side window.

"The passports," he told us, "and forty Swiss francs. No dollars, marks, or French."

"What for? Twenty dollars just to cross their remarkable border. That's ridiculous!"

The border guard was equally angry, red to the wattles over his collar. "*Vierzig francs!*" he shouted. "*Nun!*"

"For Christ's sake pay him off," Proudfoot said impatiently. "Ain't as if it was your money. And don't forget what's in the luggage bin."

"The highway tax," Deterling said, placating. "For the use of the roads. All must pay."

"Sure. All but the Swiss." He worried out a hundred-franc Swiss note from his hoard. The guard did not deign to accept it himself. He folded his arms tightly and looked off in the distance at the chimneys of Basel. His subordinate took the note and passed the change. They had no more interest in coach or cargo or us.

We rolled on, toward Lucerne, across the valley and up into this interior isle, a land that looked like illustrations in a children's book. There is substance and comfort for all within these frontiers, symmetry, meticulous attention to houses, roads, rail stations, village surrounds, and the churches and public buildings gave an impression of a serene and powerful base for the national solidity.

Across the aisle from me, Berdichevsky sat hunched in his seat behind Deterling, the floor beneath his seat littered with flattened cigarette butts and ashes. He rubbed out yet another, closed his eyes, and finally relaxed. Just behind us, Proudfoot oriented himself with a map on his knees, checking one massif after another, together a far more effective defensive system than the ones behind us.

"Tell me, Berdie," I said, "you wouldn't have used the gun, would you?"

He did not open his eyes.

"Never. Were you convinced?"

"Don't know."

"Calling me crazy helped. What could they expect out of me anyhow? They remembered how I acted years ago, when the claimants first began to show up in numbers.

"Half mother hen, half partisan. As though I'd been part of their scene myself. Drunk regularly by six o'clock. My breath in the morning was enough to knock you down."

He smiled ruefully, remembering. "That's me with the warts, if anyone were to do a biography. Could be called *Nonentity* or *The Knight of Returned Possessions*.

"And here I am bearing my hard-earned prize and all my righteousness in the baggage compartment. I can't express my debt to you. And you," he told Shotgun over his shoulder. "But you both have your own peculiarities. How could you be so involved with me? I wonder about it."

"I have forever," I said. "It seems like that long."

"And my sympathies aren't with you at all. My instincts are with the others. Rationally. I identify with them more than I do with you. You are just an accident in place and time.

"I'm like them. I have never had the means of a good livelihood in my own hands. I may have just now, but that's uncertain. They all have the right to deal with their futures, protect them, especially when it doesn't hurt. There aren't many chances like this."

He looked at me owlishly, and turned to Proudfoot.

"You agree with him?"

"Hardly matters. You got your way, didn't you? Here you are on the high road. But the way you did it got me. You had to use a gun. Well, didn't you?"

"I would never have used it. You know that."

"Not on us. Sure.

"All I'm doing is making a point. In 1950 or so I spent a couple of weeks at Fort Knox. Had an old buddy in Oak Ridge, which was a kind of a peculiar place at the time. At any time, actually. He was a physicist. Smart, tough. Kind of character who would do whatever had to be done to uphold the right, if you'll permit that.

"Anyhow, they were integrating the elementary schools down there at the time. And it was peculiar because a lot of the families were not from there. Just like him. They came from up north or out west and they brought all their liberalism, all their concern for equality, with them. And they wound up in a real battle with the locals, the natives most of 'em rednecks, still holding on to their Confederate money and battle flags. And they had more children, and on top of everything else, they had complete charge of all the dirty jobs in the installation. Paid well, and on time, the housing, the hospital, recreation was all out of Washington. Also the schools.

"Which, like the army, the navy, the coast guard, the marines, and the coffeeshops, were going to be integrated. By God, Harry Truman said so, and he didn't lie. Not about that, anyhow.

"My friend was chairman of the school board. Everything went well enough with the locals. Got a little strained over the moment of prayer, and whether Young Kipper was a holiday and the Nativity, whatever you call it. Crèche. And there were some nasty jokes and some slights, all that shit. But they let 'em buy *Huckleberry Finn* and teach biology and such. Nice time, between wars. Until September when the little Negro kids showed up with their pencil boxes, all shined up and ready to go to the same schools as the others.

"I know small towns. An easy pace and a quiet time and then the shit hits the fan. As ever. Nobody knows how it happens, and people all of a sudden have something to defend or put right. Rumor, remark, lie, whatever. Nobody ever tracks it down afterward, when the time comes to clean up the whole mess.

"So there it was. School opened and closed the same day. Same hour. There was a mob in front of the school doors. And it kept on going all day. That night, the school board called a meeting to decide what to do. My friend didn't eat any supper. Too busy taking phone calls and trying to quiet things down in his own house, and he did not know at that point whether he had any allies or any support for what he was determined to do—open that school next morning for whoever was enrolled, black, white, or yellow.

"I was sitting there, finishing up my beef stew, and he comes downstairs finally, says good-bye to his wife and kids, and heads for the door. With his good old pistol in his armpit, and I got up and went along."

"What did it have to do with you?"

"I owed him," Proudfoot said. "I took his kid's baseball bat and came along. And we get there in front of the school and there's a crowd. Not a mob. A crowd. With four or five leaders that'd planted a Confederate flag on the lawn, and were cradling their shotguns like Daniel Boone, for Christ's sake, and the rest watching to see what would happen.

"So he walked up to them, and he reached out and grabbed the staff of the flag and said, 'You furl it or I will.' Didn't look around, didn't make any appeal to anybody's better nature. One hand on the flagstaff and the other on his pistol butt and damned if he didn't get away with it. He did.

"The point is, I didn't know what was in his mind, or if he had thought about it, walked around and considered what was to be done, and how to do it. But he had his convictions, and his position, and that was all that was necessary. And that's where it ended, right then and there.

"They had their meeting, they stated their position. Unanimously, and school opened next day. Period.

"It happens that way sometimes. Just like it did with you last night. Wasn't the pistol or the threat that stopped them. You know that. There are times when the group is better than anybody gives it credit for being, and does exactly what it should do."

"I couldn't take the chance," Berdie said. "Too much at stake for me.

"What do you see when you look at me? I ought to be a healthy, optimistic middle-aged fellow. A plump assistant history professor, something of a campus character as an eccentric. Benign, softly cynical, amusingly objective in comparing Hannibal's and Eisenhower's campaigns in Africa, or MacArthur with Genghis Khan.

"I'm not. Even of a good morning after a good night I look sixty. I don't know what I feed on half the time. I plod along fumbling and stumbling toward some conclusion that will be forgotten as quickly as yesterday's shallow victory. Which was none of my doing. If it hadn't been for you and the half-wit Merolla, it would have ended right then. I had no plan, no real preparation, even with some suspicion that there was a murderer in the vicinity. I ran along like a half-trained beagle with his nose to the ground, and a mental arrangement that ordered movement and the absence of thought.

"All I can say now is that I'm not the first to piss away a part of life in some hopeless pursuit. Now suddenly, it isn't hopeless anymore. My apologies to the 855th can wait a little."

We had arrived in Lucerne. The sun lowering in the west behind the great height of Mount Pilatus cast long rays upon the lake and the pine forests upon its shores. On a Sunday afternoon between the two profitable tourist seasons, there was little activity. The office of the *Amt* was in the Imperial Hotel, one of the many on the drive along the lake, all of them rambling nineteenth-century structures, sited for the sweeping views of the mountains in their majesty. Their architects and builders had decided that this was the style to attract the custom that all desired, that upper middle class that paid for the kind of lodging that confirmed their economic and social standing. This weighty and comfortable atmosphere had another attraction in that the guests were more closely associated with nature than in their usual habitats. They sometimes were not far removed from various phenomena—cold, avalanche, blizzard—and if these were rarely perilous, they did add another dimension to the stay. Danger at a safe distance in this land of fantasy, affected by, but never devastated in, the conflicts that had raged for centuries just beyond these mountains.

The staff at the Imperial was not overwhelmed at our arrival.

If anything, there was disappointment evident at seeing only three passengers in a coach that seated forty. It recovered quickly, and in a very few minutes all arrangements had been made for the transfer of our cargo to the substantial annex that was the headquarters of the *Amt*, and for our accommodation.

Deterling got a bonus—not large enough to ensure his silence, but that didn't matter, Berdichevsky told him. He could say what he pleased, and nothing would reflect badly on any party but the company. He drove off immediately, eager to put this whole sortie miles behind him.

We took a two-bedroom suite, and Berdichevsky signed for it grandly, recalling, no doubt, Proudfoot's comment that he was not spending his own money. We handled the transition easily, went up and refreshed ourselves, and came down eventually to a large and almost empty lounge for a drink before dinner. Beyond the double glass doors the dining room tables gleamed with white linen, but hardly half a dozen had been set.

Three guests settled in overstuffed green plush armchairs, drinks at hand. Before us, the fire on the hearth fed evenly, symmetrically, on four great logs.

Three chameleons, proof that our society could produce characters who could play any part on any stage. We could destroy with the most destructive, we could affect a high moral posture, we could dine with the most self-concerned.

We settled ourselves, not forty hours away from passion and death, to concentrate on a good dinner and a quiet evening. Even Berdichevsky became the most temperate of companions. We could admire the dignity of the maître d' who came to offer leather-bound menus and his recommendations, the livery of the waiter who served our drinks, and all of the other small attentions. Two more rounds before we considered our dinner orders, beatified, dwelling on a choice of several veal dishes, or perhaps liver with spaetzle.

A well-dressed man, whom I took to be a manager, introduced himself.

"Gessner," he said, "Jean. Do I intrude?"

"Not at all," Berdichevsky replied. "Very comfortable place."

"Yes, indeed it is. A bit old-fashioned, but high standards still."

We gave our names; before we could ask him if he would join us, he sat down, composed and assured.

"I think we have some business. If those cases at the *Amt* office are yours. I am the director, and I am much intrigued already. The crates alone are worth attention. So many Rembrandts inside?"

Berdichevsky shook his head.

"I'm afraid not Rembrandts. But worth attention nevertheless."

"Have you a manifest?"

"An inventory. Some years old."

"Provenance? For any of the works."

"Nor that either. It's a complicated story. How they arrived here."

Gessner smiled. "Many of the items brought to us have the same background. I have a suggestion. That I have my staff uncrate them this evening while you have your dinner. And afterward, come to the annex for coffee and cognac, and we will pursue the matter."

"Sunday evening? Your staff works odd hours."

"Dedicated. And concerned, and they live there as well. Come and see now if you prefer." He looked at us coolly. "Or is it simply that you want confirmation that I am who I say I am? In which case I can tell you that my father, Jacob Gessner, founded the *Amt für Rückerstattung Beschlagnahmte Kunst* in 1940. It has an unblemished reputation. And you did bring them here, did you not?"

"Sorry," Berdie said, "I'm a bit disoriented, and we have looked for these things for a long time. Years."

"Understood. I am not angry. You may accept or not as you wish. But no guards are posted here. And I assure you that we have taken the responsibility for many very important works, and are chartered by the Swiss government."

"Why not join us for dinner," Berdie said. "We accept your invitation and the arrangements."

Gessner nodded agreement and excused himself to make a phone call.

"Sound like a couple of plenipotentiaries," I said. "On to the feeding ground."

We went, joined in a few minutes by Jean Gessner, a most pleasant companion at dinner. Anecdotal, knowledgeable, but not in the least overbearing. When I ordered a dish of fried veal with rösti potatoes and an egg on top, he told us that it was what the "natives, the farmers, eat for breakfast. Keeps them going all day or at least until noon. A bit heavy, however." It was.

He chose the wine, light, white, and deceptive. Three bottles among the four of us. Very soon, all of us had an association, warm, clear for the moment, and compatible. It was as though we had come together according to plan with a common interest. Very rare it was, to me, certainly to Proudfoot, and remarkably, to Berdichevsky as well. Warmed, well fed, and with absolute assurance that we had entered into another system of activity with its own practices, far from what any of us had imagined.

Dinner over, we followed Gessner out into a clear cold night. There was hardly a breeze; the reflection of a crescent moon shimmered on the surface of the lake. Opposite, a line of tiny lights rose steeply toward the peak of Pilatus.

The annex had been designed as a gymnasium and a spa, Gessner told us. There had been a small spring on the site, and the flow, he said, "tasted so much of sulfur that it was presumed to be healthful." Fortunately or unfortunately, it had fallen to a trickle and finally stopped altogether. Not before the building had been completed, however. It had a stunted classical facade with awesome wooden pillars with striations that made them resemble barrels, and a deep porch across the whole width, very much out of proportion to the rest of the structure. By the end of the thirties there were fewer and fewer guests, and those who did come had little interest in the gymnasium. When Gessner's father was seeking accommodation for his *Amt*, the Imperial was delighted to lease it.

No space could have served his purpose better, Gessner said. This main room was a space two stories high, with vaulted ceilings and a clerestory above on three sides. He pointed out other features that his father had designed to his own plan. A light system mounted on a grid that could be raised and lowered as required, grooves in the floor surface to partition the area into large or small exhibition rooms, electrically powered hoists that could cover the whole range of the space, and an arrangement of soft, neutrally colored wall hangings that gave a choice of background for varied showings. Beyond were the staff workrooms, and above, behind a balcony, was a suite of offices.

He led us to his, functionally furnished with a long birch table for a desk, sturdy and simple armchairs, and bookshelves from floor to ceiling, filled to capacity. An overflow of volumes was stacked before them as well. There was a slide projector, a number of lamps with high-intensity bulbs, and a large light box in one corner.

"Good as my word, you see," he said, waving us to chairs, and poured coffee from an automatic urn on a small bar. He offered cognac, nodded to a cigar humidor and a cigarette box, and settled into a chair himself.

Berdie and I idled along the bookshelves, a jumble of titles, some of which had seen hard and long use. Publications current, publications from centuries past. Italian, French, German, Spanish, English. Journals, sale catalogs, monographs, folios, quartos, codices, commentaries.

"How many have you read?" Berdie asked.

"It seems never enough. Not all, by any means. But then again, many aren't worth reading. Some are fakes for the support of fakers and fakery. They do impress, however. Fortunately I was brought up on them, so I do know at least where to look for answers or corroboration.

"Are all of you laymen?"

I waited for the response. The cognac bottle had no dust on it, but neither during our reunion nor ever in the past had I ever had anything like it. I had heard of "nose" and other pronouncements on the character of such things, but I had never before experienced it. Perhaps a member of the Swiss guards had brought it back from Avignon and the cellar of a forgotten pope. But I was far gone by then. From Berdichevsky's reply, he was too.

"Pursuers," he said. "Trackers. Your cognac drinks like perfume. I had better switch."

"There is whiskey also."

"Fine. That's fine. The American one. We tracked whoever it is who assembled this collection. Who arranged to have these superb cases made and shipped them off to an obscure town for recovery at some indefinite time. When memory fades and history turns into a series of aberrations and fictions. It happened that we frustrated his first attempt, quite inadvertently. So he went on to another, more complex one. That ended the day before yesterday. And we then learned that the works were to be delivered here. To the *Amt*."

There was a single loud knock on the office door and a gnome wearing a blue-striped worker's apron entered.

"Ready," he said. Gessner nodded.

"So," he said, rising from his table, "let us go and see what is in your consignment. Mind the stair. It's steep." At that point, a caution was warranted.

The great space below was almost dark. Off to our right as we descended were two shadowy figures, the gnome and an assistant standing at the light panel. They had organized an extemporaneous exhibition this swiftly. The gnome indicated a starting point to us, moved the handle of a rheostat, and we viewed the Hamplemann inventory for the first time since we had seen it in our mess hall, ten years before.

"Unusual. That he should take such pains," Gessner said.

I thought he must be a dramaturge. In a few hours, he had arranged the discrete works in such a way as to make us all travelers in another time. Some of them I remembered in the smallest detail, some were only a vague impression, but presented here in harsh glare or half in shadows, and at varying heights, it could not be thought of as a collection.

It was a surveillance of recent history, a commentary that one might enter into while sensing the social, political, and psychological upheavals that had characterized the time. Associated on occasion yet apart, individuals, Poles, Germans, French, Italians, Russians, Spaniards, and Dutch, had tried to force a way to illustrate the common madness of an epoch. Gessner lingered, numbering each in a notebook according to some scheme of his own. Berdichevsky walked away to the foot of the stair within minutes, physically separating himself from the design, and Proudfoot and I joined him there, Shotgun having passed as though inspecting a guard and weighing the merits and capabilities of each on a personal scale of values.

The gnome switched off the lighting with the rheostat, and as his hand moved, the violence and strength of the images were obscured. But they never vanished. In almost complete darkness, they remained.

We climbed the stair once more to Gessner's office. The gnome and his helper followed, bidden wordlessly. Inside, Gessner served the gnome a tiny glass of mirabelle, and the assistant a large cognac, and clinked glasses with them before he introduced them to us.

"Wolf Reimers," nodding at the gnome, "and Emerich Hodl. Wolf has an encyclopedic and personal knowledge of the period," he said quietly. "He was at the Bauhaus for a time as a draftsman, framer, what-have-you. A believer. Emerich joined us more recently."

He sat down at his table and turned over the pages of his notebook.

"This is the second time these works have come here, the first being in 1939. I am quite sure that each was consigned for sale by the German government at that time. The catalog for that sale was compiled by my father."

He glanced through a shelf behind him, picked out a thick file folder, opened it, and spread the contents upon the table.

"This," he said, "gives all details of the matter. And this," taking down a handsome leather-bound volume, "is what one might call the commentary. My father's diary that relates his part in the affair. He considered it a very important event. It was in fact what influenced him to organize this *Amt*."

"A just man," the gnome said. "Upright."

Gessner nodded to him in appreciation.

"An irony. That is why he became involved. The German government sought him out because of his reputation for honesty and fairness.

"That is not to say he didn't know how to turn a profit. He did from the day he began as a dealer in 1898. I was, of course, born into it, and eventually we had our differences, but that had to do with taste. Not with principle."

I wished that I had had a recollection like this to call back. I had the sense that the others were making appraisals. A common sentiment. Disparate forebears weighed in their own balances.

"What is remarkable," Gessner said, "is that this is one of those meetings in which one finds an absolute. The action that set the affair in motion, and the exact basis of it. Here it is."

He took up his father's diary and began to read. Place and time faded, warped away. We listened like children to a storyteller. There was occasional interpretation from Gessner to explain a comment or reference.

"The first contact occurred in 1937. 'Today at his request I met with the president of the Reich Chamber of Art, one Ziegler, at his quarters in the Baur. I am flattered. He received me in a morning coat and striped trousers. Very distinguished dress that did not disguise the proletarian inside. A well-known artist in his own right. Another of whom I have never heard. He has come to offer me a very profitable commission. His government has now decided to cleanse the nation of numerous works by decadent artists. It places no value upon them, but if others wish to purchase them it has no objections. Hard currency only. Gold, Swiss francs, sterling, or dollars.

" 'The details are to be left to me. All sales are subject to the usual terms and commissions. Patent leather shoes and black silk hose. I am his personal choice for the task. I indicate some interest depending upon what is to be offered and further details.'

"'1938. President Ziegler returned this day. I am greeted as an old friend. Some changes in appearance. Quite military now. He wears something like an undress uniform. Tailored tunic and trousers with a gold stripe suited to a retired field marshal.

"'Much has been accomplished by an Appraisal Commission under his command. Many more works have been confiscated, some destroyed, the perpetrators invited to leave the country or forbidden to do others.

"'Presented me with a crudely hectographed list of hundreds of items. For so efficient a government a very poor compilation. At first glance I see that Matisse and Van Gogh works are included. Has drawn a contract to be signed immediately. It is very much in my favor so there is no reason to read it or to waste money on lawyers' gabble.

"'Had the sense that others were within earshot. He was performing. Reviewed the contract later, also the list. The document is totally arbitrary, which makes no difference except that it is disparaging and demeaning. The list is a sorrow, even to me, for I have no great respect for some of those included.

"'1939. Ziegler once more. Now it is a delegation in full fig. A whole floor of the hotel, and a supercargo as well. Secretaries and factotums, a legal expert to whom Ziegler hands over the contract I have drawn. He is a complete nonentity, a face and personality that has no structure or color to me. Another does, a hulk dressed like an Italian dandy who has just cashed a lottery ticket and spent it all on stylish clothes and flashy jewelry—the kind that is sold by weight. A foul mouth and arrogant. At one point literally pushed President Ziegler aside. Attempted to lecture me on my good fortune, and his country's noble purpose. They would not be cheated, however. I was to keep my profit at a reasonable level. Rubbed two fingers together and asked if I understood.' "

Gessner had been reading quickly in a monotone. Now he

paused to savor once more his father's reaction with a nod and a smile.

" 'I then gave all present to understand that I would end both the meeting and any association with them unless they changed their tone immediately. At this the dandy became so oily and ingratiating that it was almost worse than his previous attitude.

" 'It being necessary to instruct them in a law they had never heard of—supply and demand, I told them what they could hope for. Such a vast number of works presented at one time would depress the whole market for years to come, most particularly because of the present international situation.

" 'While one might form a consortium of well-endowed museums and well-capitalized dealers for a sale of old masters, they could not expect that response.

" 'Some things, the Lehmbruck and the Barlach sculptures, Kokoschka, Marc, Kirchner, Macke, Klee, and some others, might yield a decent price. The rest would be picked over like a jobber's stock and the offers would not be at all serious. A fact of the times and the trade.

" 'I then asked what form of payment they sought. Again. The dandy repeated what Ziegler had stated. Hard currency only. No swindler's pieces of paper. A proper irony, with thieves protecting what was not even theirs.

" 'That much established, I told them I would accept a first consignment of one hundred items that I had already selected. To be followed by others if the sale was successful. I wished to conclude the agreement at this point and told them so.

" 'Ziegler accepted at once and the nonentity also, deferring to my knowledge and experience. Whereupon the dandy erupted. At them. Vicious as he was, and villainous, no doubt, he had a commitment to and an understanding of the era we were all about to enter.

" 'He said they were worms who wanted only to lick the asses of those they were willing to acknowledge as their betters and to place themselves among them. To be like them. That they didn't want the change that was coming but acceptance by those who oppressed, until he and his comrades went into the streets and ripped that world apart. The first. The same thing would happen to others. Many others.

" 'He said that they had made a deal in the proper bourgeois manner with the gentleman who has conducted his business so since Franz Josef's time, and that those who sent them here would not thank them or appreciate it. They were here to rid the country of this pigshit. Of this madman's demented landscapes, that yellow bastard's fear of the future, the Yid's terror of the past.

" 'At that point, he kicked at the table with coffee and other refreshments on it, knocking it over, and stormed out. That relieved me of the obligation I may have felt to shake his hand on leaving. I then took my own departure, and told them that if they wished I might suggest some others to take my place in the affair.

" 'It proved unnecessary. They came to me that afternoon, still very troubled and shaken. I noted that President Ziegler had made himself president abdicate. The indistinct one managed the business. He said he had communicated the details to others in the hierarchy and was instructed not to waste any more time and to commit to the proposal. More important tasks awaited attention.' "

Berdichevsky rose a bit unsteadily to his feet and offered a toast.

"Jacob Gessner."

We arranged to meet again in the morning. When I looked out of our window long past midnight, the lights in the annex were still burning.

10.

Never in the years I had known him had Berdichevsky seemed so exhausted as he appeared on the next morning. Even in the early days of the 855th when the claimants had begun to appear in numbers, and he perforce had listened and tried to take unto himself part of the weight of their past.

A fall of snow in the night and on into early morning had ended; the sun struck deep-edged shadows everywhere with that clarity that one sees only in winter. We sat almost alone in the splendid dining room over the heartiest of breakfasts, Proudfoot and I, but Berdichevsky ate nothing. He concentrated on his coffee cup as though dregs were his lot forevermore.

"What's wrong?" Proudfoot asked. "After last night I thought you'd really be up. Old Gessner sounded a lot like you but more successful. Let that be a lesson to you. A man can be righteous and also rich."

He was much more responsive to Proudfoot than to me, usually. Ever responsive to the great difference in their backgrounds. As though a relationship with someone like Shotgun were proof that men with the most disparate histories could still be a peculiarly American amalgam, beyond any kind of antecedents. This time, he brooded away on a thought pattern of his own.

"I owe both of you a lot," he said, "but you can't enter my life. I don't want that. It isn't right for you. You shouldn't even be concerned with it any longer. The villain is dead, and wrapped in his Tuchtig Reisen blanket. He'll molder away until the Second Coming. Well and good."

He looked at Proudfoot and smiled momentarily.

"You did hit him, you know. When I went over him I saw where he'd been shot. Two star-shaped little rounds of scar tissue under his left arm. Inches to the right, and we never would have seen him again."

Proudfoot grinned. "That settles that. I won't have that memory anymore. That I missed him. It damaged my self-confidence for a long time. Maybe the third one went through his goddam coat."

"Finite," Berdie told him. "Not so for me. Now I'm like an old dray horse dragging along on a new route. There are no more familiar landmarks. This barn we are in is for another kind of animal.

"And worst of all is that the sense of enmity has vanished. There isn't that pall of evil that moved me for so long. No deep emotion." He looked at me.

"You said once you hoped that this would not wind up in a mush of legal sediment, or words to that effect. That's its present direction, I can tell. And what will I have left when it's over? A pale history that isn't history but a collection of footnotes and most of them illegible except to the three of us. My concept was too small.

"I would have been wiser to write an exhaustive biography of some princeling or hierarch. Schirach maybe, or Roland Friesler. Fritz Todt, his work I know at first hand. And all of its uses.

"Maybe I should eat. How was the sausage?"

We sat on with him and watched him eat like a couple of hospital visitors encouraging an afflicted relative. We met with Gessner again half an hour later. The exhibition was no longer lighted by the gnome's arrangements; much of it was in shadow, lost in the room. A cone of sunshine, however, fell upon an oil, a closed group of three clowns in costume. The central figure, Pierrot, was much troubled, downcast. There was a sense of failure about him, but his companions were supportive. The figure on the left, wearing a Napoleonic hat, was looking away, possibly toward those who had disliked their turn. The other, in a high rounded cap, commiserated.

Berdichevsky grunted acknowledgment. "My performance left something to be desired."

"If that's me," Proudfoot said, "it doesn't do me justice."

I agreed. "Nor mine. Too soft."

Gessner was animated and intense.

"Look here," he said, without preliminary. "Last night I took that corrected inventory of yours, sir. The one that you reworked after you removed the still lifes. You could not have had all the attributions right. Well and good. One would have had to be a specialist in these things, and even then some could have been mistaken.

"But all of them. Every one, I believe, was included in the consignment that my father requested. He chose a hundred and four by his count. The sixty-three items in your cases were sold in 1939. Thirty-seven remained unsold and were disposed of later. Four or five were returned. To A. Hamplemann. Transport supplied.

"From my father's records, I can now tell you where they went and the prices paid. For each."

Berdichevsky leaned toward him, staring at this well-organized worktable and the neat little gatherings laid out upon it. I could not help but smile, for he had brought with him his original ammo box, and in it that bundling up of relevant and irrelevant documentation that had moved him on so many journeys and too many byways.

Here was everything he had sought, well ordered, legible, detailed, and compiled by a single, authoritative source. Still, it could not be accepted without his own confirmings. Those he had assembled on the long march.

"A dealer in Rotterdam, Levi," he said hoarsely.

Gessner scanned a sheet.

"Confirmed. Eight acquisitions. Grosz, Nolde, Schmidt-Rottluff— Shall I go on?"

"No. Antwerp?"

"Beckmann. Kokoschka. Egon Schiele. Others—"

"Paris."

"Several houses." He handed him a page. "There is an addendum to this. Again by way of my father's notes. This time for 1944. Do you want to hear it?"

"Of course."

" 'Five March. A telephone call this day from S. the coin dealer. He had just received a man with a large assortment of bagged coinage to sell. The man said he had had business dealings with me in the past. Most of the coinage was in bank bags. Imperial State Bank of Hungary, Bank of Florence, State Bank of the Ukraine, Bank of Warsaw. S. considering a bid on U.S., British, and Danish coinage. Gold, since the old dies were so good. Most, he thought, was chaff, and he would need days to examine it. However there was little time; the fellow was here on official business and would have to leave tomorrow. What do I know of his *bona fides*?

" 'I told S. to follow his own instincts, which have served him so well in the past. This fellow came to me that afternoon and reminded me when we had last met. He was the assistant to Ziegler of the Arts Chamber, and made no more of an impression now than he did then. Indistinct. The presence of a factotum. President Ziegler has fallen by the wayside. No great loss.

" 'Insisted on engaging me in conversation. Unctuous. Some superior had commended them for their handling of the original consignment. That due to my efforts, of course.

" 'He went on *ad nauseam*. How meeting with me had changed

his life. He had experienced the spiritual and emotional satisfaction that works of art provide. Mental flatulence.

" 'Now a request. An approach like a mendicant's. Also false. Returning to Paris tomorrow, having just been transferred from an assignment in Italy. If I could give the names of dealers there who specialized in the expressionists. He had called on several in Holland and Belgium and had seen some striking ones. Not to buy, since government service was so poorly paid, but simply to see them would be an epiphany.

" 'I did so. With misgivings. The information from Paris is not good. Transports not only of workers, but of whole families. One or two I know of are out. Reif in North Africa, Sohn here. I mentioned Richard Mayer. Having misgivings immediately, but in such times, even the influence of so paltry a creature may be worth something. He is covetous and corruptible.

" 'I warned him in the next breath, telling him of our *Amt*, and how we had already assembled much information on confiscations and seizures and were receiving more.

" 'A most remarkable hypocrite. Thanked me profusely and added that he was sure our *Amt* was a very worthy undertaking in these times with upheaval and plundering and destruction everywhere. Losses of every sort and kind. He wished me luck and offered his hand. I could not bring myself to take it.' "

Gessner closed the book gently; he had handled it thus at both of our sessions. This was a legacy abiding.

"Well," he said quietly. "There is the one who assembled your shipment."

"And still without a name," Berdichevsky said. "Hamplemann was never mentioned."

Gessner shook his head. "John Smith. William Jones. I must ask you where specifically you found this shipment. You need not give details. I don't want to know them. But I have my own obligations. To the *Amt*. It has its responsibilities according to its bylaws. You must see that I will not waive my responsibility to the group."

However recent, it was carved in stone. Obligations that all of us must bear.

"What specifically applies here?" Berdie asked, as though he were inquiring about a procedure that had its roots in another century.

"The original agreement, concurrence, was that the site of the discovery gave authority over it to the country in which it was found. Where did you find your shipment?"

"Germany."

"Then it must be transferred to Freiburg, the *Amt*'s operative branch there."

"Never. We'll pack it up and leave. That, obviously, was the intention. That it go into other hands that are more susceptible to influence."

"Even if you could move it, organize it for shipping, it wouldn't go far," Gessner said. "Because of me. It would never cross the border. Any border." An indication that he had inherited some of the steeliness in his father's character. Still, he was sympathetic. He would have preferred another solution.

"All right," Berdie said, quietly. "Then let's look for a compromise."

"It's possible. I want to find one mainly because of the man my father mentioned. Richard Mayer. The majority of these works were in his possession, and I knew him. Well. We had parallel histories. His father started his business in Trouville in 1898, the same year that my father did. Both prospered. The Mayers moved to Paris, and when Richard's father died in 1907, he took over. Young as he was, he did well. He served in the French army for three years, and when he returned he did even better. A combination of good taste, learning, a fine manner, and sound judgment. A gentleman in the best sense. People trusted him, both artists that he dealt with and collectors. The latter paid for their education by him, but they were never victimized.

"He represented or sold to some of your most famous buyers—Carnegie, Eastman, Isabella Gardner, Frick, Rockefeller. Not Henry Ford, however.

"What fascinated me when we met, and we did frequently, were his conversations about the meetings he often had with Matisse, with Monet, Picasso, so many others. He had an eye for detail as perceptive as any master. He told about Renoir in the last year of his life, his fingers like fleshless claws but still hard at work at his vice—painting. His servant had to put the brushes in his hands and fasten them there with ribbons and string.

"He spoke about the way Proust lived. Never warm, never comfortable, never without the noises of the city that destroyed his concentration. An exquisite of a kind that we shall never see again.

"The point being that these personages—and that is what they seem to have been—are those who gave a shape to and a summation of their times.

"In any event, Mayer was an inheritor and a witness, and his observance had importance. He was not piling up a heap of canvases simply for his own profit, you see. There was more to him than that. He was a link, sometimes mistaken in his judgments, sometimes remarkably right. But always, he was serving an honest purpose.

"When he began in the business, if you had no provenance that was acceptable, you went about gathering letters and statements from various authorities who would give an opinion that this was absolutely a Masaccio, or a piece by Ghiberti, a Rembrandt, or even a Michelangelo. For a fee or a percentage, a commission. It was a time when even old copies could be passed off as genuine, no matter that they were reworked, restored, or retouched. Some such were bought at high prices not only by ignorant parvenus, but by respected museums. Your Metropolitan Museum had its bastards, and so did the Louvre. Fact. And such transactions still occur. Sometimes in a dusty attic a long-lost Dürer is discovered. Sometimes it is a Raphael shown in costly simplicity in a Paris gallery with a facade like the Parthenon.

"Mayer bent some principles, most certainly. But it did not

ever sit well with him. Finally he freed himself, gave up trading in altarpieces and aged tapestries, ancient stone figures with missing noses, and all pictures over fifty years old.

"He bought contemporary works and backed his opinions and expectations with his own money. He gave stipends to some of the artists and treated all of them fairly. He defended them in the press and wrote about them in the journals.

"He built up a surprisingly profitable business. For these works, the times were right. There always was and always will be an active market for academicians, landscapists, skilled portraitists, every age has them. But Mayer's was a time to throw off constraints and explore inner visions and interpretations. He still had his links to the past, but he was looking to the future and these were his investments. On behalf of his family, and other commitments."

"What commitments were those?"

"The artists themselves. To people he dealt with over the years who were having more and more difficulties simply in surviving. To his country also. It had been very good to him.

"I know nothing personally about the occupation. But someone as perceptive as Richard Mayer would have had an awareness that the grip was tightening. Registrations, laws, identity cards, various proscriptions that applied to him and his wife and sons.

"So it's very possible that he followed the suggestion that my father was making to him in dealing with this functionary. That he might wish to exchange works for well-being, however temporary. One has an intercessor, no matter what sort of character he is."

There were stronger alliances than one between greed and need, I thought. Gessner sensed the doubt.

"In the absence of alternatives, it was worth attempting," he said. "And there were none."

Berdichevsky's attitude had changed during this recitative. The lives and the affairs of Mayer and Gessner the elder were outside his purview. His own contact with their interests was far different. He called attention to this.

"I don't want to appear calloused or unsympathetic to an obviously extraordinary man, and, of course, to your father as well, but my—our—connection with their business and their possessions had appalling results. Death, injury, guilt, much of it planned. I want to put an end to it. Soon.

"Tell me, please, if you can certify that Richard Mayer, late of Paris, was the owner of the cargo, the works we have here."

Gessner considered his own past, sighed, and finally, reluctantly, replied.

"I can tell you that he bought a number of them. They were delivered to him, according to the records and the account books. So much is fact."

Berdichevsky reached into his ammunition box and brought out a square of placard, limp from handling, and put it on the table.

"What ought to be done is this. Before you ship the works back to Freiburg to your *Amt* there, exhibit them for a week or so here. Just as they are, just as the gnome—pardon, Reimers—has arranged them. Advertise it to the public and to dealers and collectors here and in Belgium, Holland, France. Germany too. They were out of anyone's hands for ten years—what difference does another couple of weeks make?

"And besides, it calls some attention to the work of your *Amt*. That's worthwhile too, isn't it?"

"What is to be gained if that's done? Do you expect your creature to come and file his claim?"

Intensely, Berdichevsky leaned toward him.

"Absolutely. Because these were his instructions to his hireling or associate or whatever term you like. Whom he will never hear from again, believe me. Two days have passed already, and there is no report for him. Nothing but silence. Until your announcement appears, he will have no idea whether Hamplemann, so called, set up on his own or not.

"He won't let the opportunity pass. Not he."

Gessner picked up the placard, the poorly done production of a mobile printing unit, one of the many posted all over our sector.

" 'It is forbidden to remove or deface this communication,' eh? And did they abide by the instruction?"

"Often enough. Well? What's your answer?"

"No need to put it to a vote of my board. These works have been out of the public eye too long. We shall welcome their reappearance with respect. That you can leave to me. Ten days is enough time."

We shook hands all around on the commitment. Even as we rose to leave, there was a bustle of activity. Reimers evidently had a sixth sense. An elderly white-haired secretary entered with a short-hand notebook and pencils. Miss Vermeulen. Before he began his dictation, Gessner looked up at us.

"I take it you will be staying on?"

"Me for certain," Berdichevsky told him. I would also, but not Proudfoot.

"Overstayed my leave. I'm past due in Vermont. I'll do some Christmas shopping and that's it."

Neither of us made an effort to persuade him to stay. That in itself was an indication, to me at least, that the matter had been raised to another level. Civil and sensible, in which ravin and spoli-ation were treated as common misdeed, and a proper subject for litigation. In the light of what had occurred, this was preposterous, but acceptable.

We drove him to Zurich in Gessner's Peugeot sedan and shopped away assiduously. Cuckoo clocks for the children, and some remarkable toys. A handsome little watch for his wife, a number of Liberty scarves, flacons of perfume, and a couple of bottles of cognac that he thought customs would permit him to bring in.

"They owe me that much," he said, and we went out for a heavy and drunken dinner afterward. We said our good-byes at the Zurich train station, and Berdichevsky became very watery.

"Fuck it," Proudfoot said, finally. "Just do me a favor and don't kill anybody. They might have the death penalty hereabouts and convict you on your own testimony."

Then he was gone, a tall and stalwart figure, dependable and resourceful in any situation, and we were alone.

The return trip took much time. Berdichevsky kept the right-hand wheels on the shoulder and rarely took the car out of second gear. From time to time, he snuffled and blinked tears away.

"His attitude is far better," he said finally, "goddam shallow sentiment."

Despite his small staff, Jean Gessner moved swiftly and efficiently. In three days, he showed us a proof of the catalog for the exhibition. Our placard was the cover design, legible, and overprinted: IMPORTANT EXPRESSIONIST WORKS RECENTLY RECOVERED. There were twenty-four pages illustrated with striking photographs of most of the pictures. Reimers had done the graphics, Gessner a commentary on each. He had scheduled advertising in newspapers in four cities reproducing the cover of the catalog.

We passed the time in still another anomalous circumstance, awaiting response. As ski conditions improved throughout the area, more guests began to appear. The staff became livelier and more attentive, the public rooms were brightened with lavish Christmas decorations. There were lights strung in the gardens and around the wide terraces overlooking the lake.

With little to do, we entered a vacationer's mode. Hesitantly, as if we might suddenly become lotus-eaters. Berdichevsky was the more wary, so he took to a regimen—exercise and self-denial. He clung to the former. Twice a day he skated on the lake in his city suit and black raincoat. The only concession he made to the temperatures and sometimes bitter gusts off the mountains was to wear black fur earmuffs and bright red mittens. Surprisingly, when he skated, he was an almost elegant figure, cutting tight patterns of interleaved circles and eights, and seeming to disdain any kind of theatrical flourish. The off foot was never raised high, nor did he bend low with arms flung wide. Just as well, there was little swanlike about him. The rest of his program was a prescribed number of circuits of the cleared area, hands behind his back, while, most probably, he considered the effect of pleasure.

I had seen too that a number of women had approached him to skate with them, but he had refused most politely, raising his battered hat.

I asked him where he had taken up this sport.

"Plattsburgh. When I was first drafted. There wasn't anything else to do all winter."

I tried skiing, myself, on smaller hills nearby. I learned quickly, and promised myself that one day I'd return. I overheard intriguing conversation in the bar about day trips on the higher peaks where one could actually travel from hamlet to hamlet.

Gessner reported progress. He lived in the town, we learned, and one evening he took us to dinner there for fondue, yodeling, and blasts from an alpenhorn.

"It ought to be heard once, like certain musical compositions. Actually, when one hears it on the mountain it has a fine effect. The yodeling also. Fortunately it's over early." All nightlife. When we went out into the crisp evening, a handful of tourists thought to offer an impromptu concert of their own and were halted in mid-bellow by a stern-faced policeman.

"Eleven o'clock. People are trying to sleep," he told them. "That's enough." Not another note heard. There were no late revels in Lucerne.

On the morning of the tenth day, we met with Gessner once more. The presentation of the works was unchanged. It was as stark and uncompromising a background as it had been from the first. There were, however, a few concessions to custom and the refreshment of the guests. A long bar set up beneath the stair to the offices. Buffet tables catered by the hotel staff, but even the arrangements of flowers seemed stark. Sharp-edged poinsettia plants with blossoms red as blood. Sheaves of long-needled evergreen boughs, earth-colored pinecones, bunches of holly.

"Naturally," Gessner told us, "a storm is predicted. Three or four inches. We'll hope for the best. But self-interested people are usually unstoppable.

"You have no formal clothes, I take it? That won't matter, however. Officially I am the host. You will want to mix."

"Observe."

"Whatever you wish. But observe the proprieties also. It is, after all, an exhibition, not a man-trap."

Having proprietary interests, we arrived early, just at twilight, the temperature having risen in the course of the day.

"Warming up to snow," Berdie said. A few people, guests at the Imperial, followed on, they having seen notice of the showing posted on a board in the lobby. For an hour, that was all. Reimers and Hodl stood by dressed in their Sunday best. Two waitresses and a bartender were at their posts. Gessner paced, glancing at his watch. The hotel guests, two couples, idled along impassively and, when they had paid their brief attentions to expressionism, advanced to the bar. I had a scotch myself and then another, and took one to Berdie. He swallowed a good half of it immediately.

"For Christ's sake," he said, "I could understand if it was my birthday party. I wouldn't expect anyone. Were we wrong?"

"We? Calm down. Jean has had telegrams, even a cable from London. Maybe they're delayed. Fashionably late. Snowed in some-place."

"Lights," he said suddenly, "look, headlights on the road."

Indeed, like a procession suddenly formed, and big cars most of them. They rolled heavily onward through the snowfall, wavered along up the incline to the hotel, and on to the portico.

Gessner took a moment for education and interpretation. He was, after all, an international ombudsman of a sort. Also, what he knew of us could hardly reassure him in the circumstance. One of the two was an utter outlander, and the other, I, certainly an un-known quantity. It must have relieved him very much when Proud-foot departed.

"I am not instructing," he told us, before this cavalcade arrived, "but you must understand that some of these people have a most peculiar attitude. It's not only money but passions, ambitions, desires. Their speculations, their judgments, all have a part in their behavior. Try not to let anything upset you. Try to regard it as an expression of our times. Whatever comments you hear, whatever opinions, control your reactions. To them, it only means that one day there will be an auction. A sale, no matter whose soul is going to be traded."

I accepted his comment as valid, for this was an oddly assorted company. There were successive crushes at the door, at the coatrack, at the bar, over the canapés and the cheeses, and as they trooped past Reimers's presentations. As it happened, I had stationed myself near a Grosz work that was half in shadow. He had drawn many of these very figures in his own time, and here they were once again, vivified, men in tuxedos and starched shirtfronts, bejeweled women already bored, others in turtlenecks and tweeds, in expensive business suits, black or banker's gray. There was a scattering of the less affluent, critics perhaps, or artists, and some of them set themselves to lecture on a specific canvas. As though opinions had to be stated, sometimes loudly. "Here you see" and "there you have" and "overrated endlessly" and "a determined bourgeois."

I drifted out to the portico to clear my head of fumes of cigarette and cigar smoke, wine, whiskey, and comment. In the parking area, the drivers of limousines brushed the still-falling snow from roofs and windows. The cars were of vintages and origins as disparate as the guests inside. Rolls-Royces from the thirties, new Jaguars, Citroëns, Peugeots, a Cadillac convertible with paired taillights set on airfoils, long Mercedes sedans. Hunched down among these were the insignificants, Panhards, Beetles, Fiats, already half obscured.

A late entry moved up from the Imperial's gates. This one looked like transport for royalty. A Daimler with fenders four feet high and a separate tonneau. A chauffeur descended and opened the passenger door. A group was leaving the building and a shaft of light from the interior fell upon it. A man walked toward the stair and halted, almost reverently, to glance upward at the undistinguished facade, as if his journey had been a very long one. As indeed it had. Dirk Bos.

I waited for minutes before I followed this presence, for that was what he was. Daimler, homburg, velvet-collared overcoat, white silk scarf, round pink face, stepping upward as though about to renew acquaintance with a treasured past.

So it was as I caught glimpses of him inside. There was an air of the proprietary as he peered about, reassuring himself that the rare harvest was all there. I looked about for Berdichevsky, and sighted him up above on the balcony as he entered Gessner's office.

"He's come, hasn't he?" I joined him.

I nodded. "Dirk Bos. Formerly my associate. Then my employer. Presently successful and secure. How did you know?"

"A sixth sense. He had an aura about him, a rare figure with a golden disk behind his head. He looked like a hysteric before he checked what was displayed against his mental inventory.

"And found it good. His creation."

Below on the main floor, the hubbub decreased. People were leaving, and Gessner was seeing some away. Bos had penetrated to the farthest corner of display. Only a few knots of guests remained, lingering at one or another of the works they favored most. Bos, the original curator, would have had much in common with them, but he paid them no attention.

Watching, more in curiosity than with Berdichevskyan emotion, I wondered what had moved him to his complex machinations. That had to do, no doubt, with my own indifference to seizing and holding possessions—the satisfactions, the sense of owning such a mass of abstract portrayal. Surely they could not be held like a pocketful of money. They might be traded, exchanged, bartered. But owned? For how long? Soon or late, as will and sense failed, they would be only that many blobs of paint, with less and less importance to the proprietor, when the keeping of anything ended.

"Render unto Kokoschka the things that are Kokoschka's," I

said to Berdie. He was as grim as the presiding officer of a kangaroo court.

From above we watched as Bos sought out Gessner, introduced himself, smiled widely, offered his hand. Congratulations, no doubt, further ingratiation, compliment, and that sensible, sensitive exposition of his involvement and his presence here.

There was Gessner paying polite attention, and finally frowning, as though in uncertainty. Bos was still in midsentence when Gessner escorted him into the office, the two of us having seated ourselves there hastily. A small panel of listeners.

"—a most remarkable coincidence, you will see, sir. My client had almost given up hope that he would ever see them again."

Nor that he would see me. He froze on the instant, lapsing into a momentary silence.

"You're acquainted, I take it," Gessner said.

"Briefly, some years ago. It was not a pleasant circumstance, and it ended badly." A slight and rueful shake of the well-barbered head.

"What is their part in this?"

Gessner offered a chair and he seated himself at a distance from us. That was to be Bos's choice. To set the two of them apart, and us away from contention and participation, and let a rehearsed flow of moderated speech settle the matter. In favor of his client.

Even to me it was effective. There was the confident assumption that he and Gessner shared a purpose and that we the ignored were only suspect interlopers.

At a pause, Gessner replied.

"You ought to understand that they brought these works here. They found them and delivered them to the *Amt für Rückerstattung Beschlagnahmte Kunst.*"

Bos glanced at us and nodded.

"Then eventually, we can take up the matter of a finder's fee or some such compensation. Otherwise I see no reason why they should remain or be a part of our discussion.

"This man, you should know, barely escaped a prison sentence for corruption while in the American army. The other spent months searching for hidden valuables as a civilian. He was seen throughout the occupied territories. Probably he was a member of the Red intelligence services. There is testimony to that effect. Witnesses. Official records."

The two malefactors remained silent. My condemnation was a trifle harsh, but Berdie's was far more offensive. He lit another cigarette and stared straight ahead, listening, as though fascinated.

"Very much beside the point here," Gessner told him. "Not at all germane. I take it you are claiming ownership of the works exhibited."

"Not I. Not at all. On behalf of my client. He has been such for more than ten years. I represent him and other such families. Or their heirs."

"What proof do you have of his ownership?"

"Detailed and incontrovertible proof. If you'll excuse me, I'll have my driver bring in my briefcase."

Gessner nodded him out and got up to pour himself a drink. He measured it and added another generous dollop. I had one with him. Medicinal. To ease the reminder of past transgressions. Berdichevsky refused.

"Don't you want to follow him? He may leave," Gessner said.

"Never."

I was in absolute agreement, although I said nothing. Berdie knew, as curiously as he had known in like circumstance in the past. Some kind of oracle, he was then, as if a second sight had been given him. A mystic who did not work wonders, but only knew behavior.

Reimers put his head in the door.

"All cleared out. Anything else?" he asked.

"Keep an eye out tonight," Gessner told him.

The gnome nodded. "Both of us. We will."

Bos returned with a new briefcase. From London no doubt. Much like the one Anthony Eden had carried. He would have been better advised to have used his immediate postwar model, the bulky satchel with its heavy straps. The top of this one sprang bolt upright when he opened it, the pounds of organized attestation it contained rising to his hand. This was the kind of product that Berdichevsky could never have compiled.

"All are certified true copies," he told Gessner, the proper and the only qualified participant; "the originals are in Zurich, and may be seen whenever you wish."

This was impressive. Heavy folders tied with ribbons. Folios and quartos and octavos, pendant with murky black duplicate seals. Bills of sale, receipts, liens, chattel filings, provisos, subordinate attachments, all of it assertion that such and such transaction had taken place according to the lawful procedures of the time. A thicket, so furcated that only a Dickensian chancery official could hope to follow it.

According to Bos, it had one point, that his client was the true and rightful owner of everything we had transported here.

All of us, Gessner included, had had some experience with such paperings; foxed and moldy or pristine and white, they had an intrinsic power to persuade and dominate. They could congeal thought, confound argument, stifle objection.

Bos pushed under Gessner's hand the file that dealt with his association with his client. Gessner glanced through that, pawed over several wills with codicils appended, thumbed thin bunches of provenances, put the batch aside, and rubbed his eyes wearily.

"You see there that my client, Alexander Hamplemann, assigned me the power some years ago to act for him in this and other matters."

"From his home in, where—Argentina?"

"Buenos Aires."

"And you are then claiming ownership of all items exhibited here. On his behalf."

"Correct. His right to them is clearly demonstrated by the information you now have. All that remains to be done is to arrange for their packing and shipping. Such expenses to be borne by my office, naturally."

"Notwithstanding the documents there are problems here," Gessner told him. "It's a very complex matter. You are aware of this, of course. All of the originals certainly will have to be examined by the proper authorities. The *Amt*'s, the Swiss government, perhaps others."

For Bos the remarks made the prospects even brighter; he saw a pure glint of success and realized, even as he spoke out boldly to exploit the opportunity, that he had erred.

"All of that could be avoided if you were simply to forward the pictures to the *Amt*'s Freiburg office. In the country where they were discovered.

"According to your charter and bylaws." The voice lost timbre and assurance. He did not lose his poise, but he actually reddened, either in embarrassment or chagrin. I thought it might have been due to a lack of practice in misrepresenting himself during these lengthy good times he had been enjoying.

"How could you possibly know this?" Gessner asked him calmly. A swift and even a reasonable reply. No groping necessary.

"I have extensive experience, as I said. Perhaps ninety percent of these discoveries are made there. As you too must know. I made the assumption. A valid one, no doubt."

Other strands followed, briskly, until he had spun a whole cable that led from the display below into Hamplemann's papers. There were many other items that had been traced to the original storage area—in the magazin we had come upon—that had vanished. He mentioned only a few, the "Steinweg, a truly rare instrument," other fine furniture, old silver, even a rare collection of children's toys, and another of phonograph records. Some, deplorably enough, removed by high-ranking officers in the occupying army.

"But these pictures, of course, cannot be regarded in the same light at all. They are a national asset, a heritage with importance in the rebuilding and restatement of new goals.

"I can also assure you that my client will, once his rights have been recognized, most probably donate them to an important museum. Or, of course, allow public access on reasonable terms."

He spoke as though reading subordinate clauses in a previously drawn last will and testament.

Gessner smiled.

"Closed Monday and national holidays. Very generous of you to make the disposition. But premature.

"Also the prices your client paid for some of this national asset are astonishing."

"How astonishing?" He was astonished himself at such a comment.

Gessner's demeanor had not changed during these exchanges. He had been as emotionless as a stenographer recording an affidavit. Now at last he was affronted.

"I've shown you every courtesy," he said, quietly, "but you are not to insult my intelligence. Do not do that!"

"I never intended to. The last thing I would wish to do."

"Here," Gessner said, shoving a fan of bills of sale at him. "Choose any one or all of them, and read it. Never mind. I will.

" 'Fourteen June, 1943. Franz Marc, *Tower of Blue Horses*, twenty thousand marks.' Not reichsmarks, occupation marks. You know what that paper was fit for in the time, do you not? It had no value at all unless backed by a rifle.

"That work was auctioned in Zurich in 1939 to Richard Mayer of Paris for over six thousand dollars, U.S. What do you think I am, a monk in an archive?"

Bos held up a hand, pained, but manfully bearing the responsibility to remind Gessner about the unsettled conditions then.

"My dear sir, it was the times. God alone knows what was in the man's mind when he accepted such an offer. But who has the right to say that he should not have agreed? Who knows what else was weighed in the scale? Not I. Not you. We would not make such judgments then. How can we now? What mattered was to survive. Perhaps some advantage was taken. But it is no crime to buy at the best price. As you must know."

That comparative ended patience and civility.

"I have nothing further to say to you," Gessner told him,

"except to tell you that I will oppose any and all attempts by you to claim this collection."

There had been a time, I well knew, when Bos had been quite sensitive to the character of others. He had known how to ingratiate himself, what to say, what approaches to make to place himself where he wanted to be. Once one has put that method behind him, once others have begun to curry his favor, once he settles himself as a consequential man in a stable society like some sturdy figure out of Ibsen, he locks away the very attributes that raised him to such a height. He remembers them too late. His tongue thickens when he tries to bring them into play. From disuse and self-approbation, he has forgotten his second language, idiom, accent, and tone.

At this point, it left him in Berdichevsky's hands. Who now grinned at him like some revolutionary set suddenly on a throne.

"This," Berdichevsky said, sweeping Bos's whole testament into a scattered heap on the floor, "is a bunch of crap. It's a fabrication like most of your life. I don't believe even you yourself can remember the details of it.

"If I wanted to, I could do it better. What neither of us could supply is a moral center to it."

Bos bent clumsily from his chair to gather his papers, a movement that was almost affecting. When he straightened up with the mismatched bundle in his hands, he was red-faced, distressed, even humiliated.

"I have nothing to say to you. Nothing."

"You are very fortunate in one way," Berdichevsky told him. "In that I came to know you so well over the years. So well that I can't now conjure up enough hatred and emotion to march you down to the lake, shoot you, and leave you in a snowbank to be discovered in the spring.

"With Mr. Hamplemann's sidearm. Another of his treasured possessions."

He leaned forward, his face taut and pale, the pistol in his hand. He clicked the safety off. And on.

"However, there are no guarantees. Because of you and your

history, I have become a little unstable, a little unpredictable. Like most murderers. There's something of that in all of us. Would you agree?"

"I am no murderer. In all of the time I never fired a weapon. Or even carried one. I am not involved in this matter, except as counsel."

"When did you speak to your client last?"

"Some time ago. As I said, he is now a resident of Argentina."

"Citizen or simply living there?"

"He never mentioned his status."

"How to account for this, then?" Berdichevsky produced the three passports. "Look here. A Dutch national. A Belgian. Even a Swiss.

"And the entry and exit stamps. Four months ago he was in Antwerp. Three weeks ago in Paris. Amsterdam. Bonn. He was a citizen of the world. And he was never in touch with you. Who had looked after his interests for so long. And so faithfully. Not a telephone call. Not even a postcard of the Eiffel Tower.

"Even if the photographs don't do him justice, you do recognize him, don't you? Alexander Hamplemann, connoisseur and collector?"

"They are not very clear. Any of them."

"It's not a face you forget. I had a meal with him only once, and I never forgot him."

"Three of us ate with him that night and none of us forgot him. He was an education. What I would like to know is how you, you, a completely different personality, ever became so involved, so entwined with him.

"You. Pitched on an absolutely different level. He gave us anecdotes, he argued with us, he told us not in so many words what he was. He actually inspired fear in me because he was so resolute, I would say. And no fanatic, either. How could a creature like you, with one foot in any camp that offered ease, comfort, profit, become his partner? That's what you were. You still are. Even now."

"Is he dead?"

"I wouldn't swear to it. Take a look outside. Maybe he walks the night. We can be sure of one thing, Manichaeans never die."

Even as he spoke, there was a sudden thumping at the door below, startling all of us. I peered over the balcony. Moments passed, and it was repeated. The gnome opened the door to Bos's shivering driver, a lap robe draped over his shoulders, left for hours outside. Reimers took him to his own quarters.

Bos picked up one after another of the documents he had brought, glancing at them as if he himself were now considering their validity, or as a bit of a personal history only recently recalled.

"A reassessment?" Berdichevsky asked him, genuinely interested.

"You can believe me or not," he said eventually, "but I have not looked at these for some time. When I drew up the first of them, it was no plot. I thought of it as a problem that I could solve. I put it aside. Not feasible." He smiled grimly.

"It was he, Hamplemann—of course not his name," Bos continued. "Who thought it was? We went back a long way together. We had some dealings with your father, you may or may not know."

Gessner nodded. "Under President Ziegler."

Bos nodded. "At least I had the sense not to strut."

"Moderation in all things," Berdichevsky said. "That's when you made your first five acquisitions."

"On the spur of the moment. I told the detail that was returning with the unsold pieces to ship them to one Hamplemann." A wan smile.

"That is when he was born, so to speak. At any rate they came to me eventually. I did feel they were worth something, and I knew that if I didn't take them, a foot would be put through them, and they simply would be burned."

He rose from his chair, walked to the door of the office, and peered into the semidarkness below, at the freestanding easels and the canvases hanging there, no longer unknown.

"They are also survivors. In 1939, I did not think I would have more of them.

"I must use your toilet. Since the session is going to continue."

We did in turn. A splash of cold water helped also. After this break we sat together once more, this time like conferees with interests in common. Looking to free the past from circumspection.

I remember it so. I knew the difference then between the shape in the bunker and this companion, for that was what he was. I believe that he was as much interested in an accounting of his life as Berdie was in his own. Or I in mine. Surely Gessner had this sense, and even Reimers belowstairs, comforting the half-frozen driver, another touched and discomfited by a slight contact with arcane events.

"How it spread," I said. There was no response from anyone, only a glance from each, as if there had been a hollow sound from outside.

"There was no plan, none," Bos said. "It was because of our assignment that we were thrown together once again. In a unit as far from any useful purpose as the one you two served in.

"Which I could see when I first saw it."

"Not so," Berdichevsky said curtly. "That was not so."

Bos shrugged. "Believe what you want to. None of you could know as much about your objective as I did. Or Hamplemann. You were going to put to rights a revolution. You could have rebuilt the Bastille with less difficulty. That wouldn't have been outside your resources. This was."

"Because of people like you and your ally," Berdichevsky told him angrily.

Bos too was aroused. He had a thesis to expound, explanations to make as much to himself as to any one of us. This was required of him, this proof that all of his responsibility for any occurrence was centered in one small area, far removed from any act of violence. That was no part of his plan or intention.

"What do you expect to get from your threats!" he said loudly. "Am I to raise my hands and confess to murder and theft and whatever crimes you accuse me of? That was never a part of my life. Never!"

I could see myself what was always evident—that falseness, misrepresentation, and most commonly self-delusion are so deeply embedded in all of us that we live and die by them. There is no way to remove these defenses. All we can do is to accept some as having a few particles of what we think is truth, provided that it satisfies preconception. I said so. Impatiently.

"For Christ's sake, Berdie, let him talk. Jesus! We all know what you are. Let's let him say what he is."

To be rewarded with an angry glare, but equally rewarding, his silence.

"What do we have here," Bos said, angry and impatient, "why do you place these obstacles endlessly? What are you, a bunch of Bible scholars? Or men. Common clay. That's what I can confess to, and nothing more. I had wants, needs, and I satisfied them. At bottom, what else matters? I'm part of a herd. You too. And after upheavals, all can sit down and discuss what was right and what was wrong.

"I went where I was told to go and did what I was told to do. I took and paid for—you needn't dismiss that—whatever there was in any sector that contributed to the greater good. That I didn't define. What in hell would I know about it?

"If a glove factory or a metal stamper produced what was needed, I bought it. And the rate of exchange, the value of my paper, was the currency of the time. Could you argue with it? Or he? Or any other functionary?

"As for my own possessions, I guarded them like a peasant who buried his bushels of wheat and hid the hams of the pigs that went to market. Canny. Shrewd. Is that criminal?"

Berdichevsky turned away from him, appealing to Gessner and me to react. He needed a larger panel, a wider audience. One that embraced idealists who were young and incisive, who could hang a placard spelling out the man's guilt around his neck. Neither of us made any comment, and the moment to do so passed.

"Just go on," Berdichevsky said, quietly, "and justify the rest of the campaign. Is that how Hamplemann thought of it? I know he had other motives. Hate and loyalty to his own dead heroes. And for my own information only, where did he serve? In Russia?"

Bos shook his head. "Briefly, and not in a combat unit. We were together from the time we first came here in 1939. That was a complicated assignment, there was approval for our handling of it, and having had the experience we were given other responsibilities. In other sectors, you see."

As he spoke, he moved to Gessner's bar and its stock of bottles and decanters, to the shelves mirrored at the back where ranks of polished crystal were arrayed. He deliberated, finally chose a small cut-glass pony, poured Goldwasser, and moistened his lips before he sat down once more.

He nodded as if to himself.

"It was my happiest time. Those years." He leaned back in his chair as though savoring them with a sip of his liqueur, before he spun a grand tour for us. Even with my own limited knowledge of the times, it had a wonderful attraction.

Here in this isolated circumstance he managed to establish a certain understanding. I could recognize it. Bos's desire lay within his reach, and to hell with what had brought him there, that being a small unit, an adjunct of their Office of Economic Warfare.

According to Bos, it was never very important; but still it represented this great and powerful state. There too it was similar to the 855th. It had absolute authority by that association.

Its assignment was the obverse of ours in that it contracted for goods and services, the output of small businesses. Brick works, china factories, printers, garment makers, canneries became part of a single economic system. They were guaranteed labor, power, and raw materials at a fixed price, they were assigned quotas, and a percentage of production was reserved for home consumption. The remainder was shipped to where it was needed, also at a fixed price. It was he, Bos, who drew the contracts. "Always mutually agreed upon. Always!"

That done, his unit was a part of the management in most cases, and acted jointly with it. The great majority were well satisfied with these arrangements; cooperation was almost 100 percent. No problems.

Still, and most unfortunate, some of the participating personnel, some workers and even owners and managers, were schemers, and a few were simply criminals out for themselves. They channeled raw materials, sugar, meats, gasoline, even coal into the black markets that existed everywhere. They adulterated, they stole, there was no low trick they wouldn't try.

Which of course resulted in punishments. Some were harsh, but none of his, Bos's, doing. That was Hamplemann's responsibility, security, quota enforcement, criminal activity. He could not count the number of times he had interceded on behalf of those Hamplemann had seized. And even pointed out to him the illegal nature of some of his procedures.

"Which were?" Berdichevsky asked as Bos paused during this solemnly reported train of fatuities.

"I was never fully informed. He reported independently."

"Make a guess. We deserve that, don't we?"

Bos shrugged. "One had to understand that the man had a peculiar personality. Power. Military bearing. His detachment was turned out like an honor guard, and had the newest equipment—weapons, transport, everything. He was always able to wangle them, even in a shortage."

"Where did you conduct these operations?"

"As ordered. Some areas offered more opportunities than others. In the east there was very little, for example. Poor-quality goods. No efficiency. Hand-to-mouth kinds of businesses.

"That improved, naturally, in the western sectors. But Italy was a disappointment to me. Holland was excellent but limited. Belgium good at some things, terrible in others."

He raised his glass to the light.

"France was the best. No equal anywhere. Civilized, once one was accepted. One could establish a relationship. Even a friendship. I am welcome in some houses in Paris to this day, I assure you."

He nodded at me.

"There was some of that between us, was there not? We respected each other. I recall that I offered to help you in any way that I could when you were having your difficulty."

"You wouldn't want someone with my character as a witness," I said. "If there should be a trial, of course. But why concern yourself with that? Maybe the whole thing can be put to rest right here. Tonight."

"This morning," Gessner said, looking at his watch. "Two-fifteen."

"Whose idea was the reunion?" Berdichevsky asked him.

"It simply came up in the course of a conversation with him. Hamplemann. He was quite hard up at the time. And he called on me for help, as he often did.

"We spoke about the past also. How much better off he might be if some of that inventory could be recovered. He told me he had had a go at it. He returned to your sector, but it was as if the unit had never existed. And the magazin was then being converted to another use. Whatever had remained there was long gone."

"Sad."

That roused the first honest emotion in hours.

"Yes," he said, loudly, "yes sad! Years wasted, and some of those things were honestly acquired. There were some beautiful things there."

"The reunion."

"His idea. He had no very high opinion of anyone. Not even me, I knew. He was very ribald. He said the thing to do was to hire your unit to recover the works for us. We could rely on your idiotic sentimentality, your greed and self-indulgence for the purpose.

"I didn't take him seriously, but he came back a few weeks later with a plan, first to involve your company clerk. He selected him because he knew him to be the most knowledgeable about the personnel, and that he was susceptible. That was his experience with him. I had no opinion. He then made his second—"

"Trip to the U.S."

A nod.

"Because there was another claimant. Not to the inventory, about which he knew nothing, but to official recognition of his name. And what might come of that but delay and possibly even disaster? Official disaster."

Berdichevsky rested his head between his clenched fists. "Everything I wanted to avoid," he said to me. "This man could create a court of law in a telephone booth.

"We knew the man as Hamplemann Two. Do you know what happened to him, by any chance? He must have told you something. He would never let his accomplishments pass without some appreciation. And who else was there but you?"

"He simply said there was nothing more to fear from that quarter. When he returned."

"Nothing more?"

"Some comments about the city. That he would rather live in a cellar here than a palace there."

"He got his wish. Part of it."

"I don't care to hear about that either."

"There was an art dealer, Faulds by name, who came here a year or so ago, from New York. Approached the collection from another angle. He was tracing those who specialized in them before the war. He started in Paris and worked from there. He was in Belgium next."

"I know. Again no details."

"Of course. One more. The former company clerk. William Pattison. Without his assistance you never would have managed.

"Actually, I don't care what happened to him. But what did?"

"My understanding was that he began to frequent certain meeting places in Paris that were known to victimize foreigners. He carried a lot of money, too, and talked about his resources."

"Yours?"

"I didn't ask for an accounting. That was our agreement. If it was required, I supplied it."

"This is stultifying," Berdichevsky said, rising. "Why don't we adjourn below."

True enough. Stale tobacco smoke and alcohol fumes. Any chill of fresh air would be welcome, to me at any rate, and Gessner agreed readily.

We descended the stair like so many prisoners in lockstep into the half-lit gloom that Reimers had left behind him. The remainder of an exhibition, of work completed long ago, a comment on the past, the uncertain present, and a future that no one would care to see in such terms.

We separated there, the four of us. No real respite at all, but only an interlude during which I need not listen to this recitative.

Bos had no real association with any vicious action, merely a tenuous linkage to a plan that needed capital. He had given no orders and had made no suggestions. It was obvious that he and Hamplemann had nothing in common excepting only the recovery of the collection. Even in the arrangements afterward they were poles apart. Hamplemann wanted a percentage of its market value. Bos wanted to own it in perpetuity.

I went out to the portico, leaving the door ajar. The snowfall had ended. The cover of cloud dissipated before a firm north wind, and a thin crescent of waning moon appeared. Bos's Daimler lay at the foot of the stairs like an undetailed snow sculpture.

When I went back inside, Berdichevsky was standing silently before a more complete work. This was of wood, by Ernst Barlach; there were three of them in our cases. Reimers had placed them together on a rough balk of timber fixed to the rear wall. *Sorrowing Woman, Man in Stocks,* and between them, *The Avenger.* Quite a small piece to have such strength.

It was this that he was contemplating, as much relief as sculpture, the figure placed aslant. Draped in a heavy cape, it was poised to strike, running at full tilt on bare feet. The powerful hands gripped the haft of a crudely finished blade, that carried over the shoulders along the level of the back. Very soon it would lash out and deliver a mortal blow. Mouth agape, eyes fixed, its intention was clear, and its prey almost within reach.

Berdichevsky beckoned to Bos, peremptorily.

"This is how I would like to put an end to you," he said, quietly, nodding at the Barlach work. "In an instant. I wish I could. But it's beyond me. Maybe if I had had personal experience with you and your dealings that you claim were legitimate. If I had had to negotiate with you—actually engage in one of those meetings in which you were agreeing on a price for a picture when you knew damn well what you were trading in was lives. Possibly.

"But all my contacts with you are through papers and talk. No blood. No dimension. Nothing animate here to overwhelm a very common shortcoming. The inability to kill without emotion. Bred out of me, I suppose. I regret it.

"Still, I don't want to hear any more of your history. I recognized you when I first saw your possessions.

"I also want to give you something to remember me by. If you had had the courage to come and claim them yourself instead of sending your murdering accomplice, you might have got them eventually. That ingratiating manner, that impression you made of wishing to carry a share of the common responsibility, the concern for the victims who had lost property might have passed you right by me, certainly.

"At the time I came to that office of ours every single day hoping to find a representative like you. I would have been swayed by that kind of testimony. I wanted to see it.

"But you chose Hamplemann. Who couldn't have passed muster before a blind man.

"So good-bye. Call your driver. You are leaving now. With what you had in 1938, and too much more. But not with these, and damn little of anything else you had. Also your life."

He went to the door, flung it open, and jerked a thumb over his shoulder, as though ejecting a beggar. Reimers appeared, escorting the driver. Gessner handed Bos his homburg and his velvet-collared coat. He struggled into it silently.

We remained in a group at the door while the driver hurriedly cleared enough snow from the windshield to see out of it. The engine ground and heaved and finally caught. Bos waded out to the car and turned to say a last word, lost in the roar of the Daimler's engine. The car bucked away, the few lamps at the Imperial casting only a dim glow along the track, the car sliding and veering as the driver tried to feel his way along to the road below.

From the edge of the stair we watched. There was a violent skid at the hotel gateposts and a crunch of steel on stone, a sudden whine of at least one wheel without traction, and it careened out toward the shore of the lake, straightened, and slid into a tree. The right-side headlight vanished, but it reversed, successfully, leaped back, and finally crept cautiously forward toward the town.

"Not enough," Berdichevsky grunted. "I was hoping to see it turn over. But it's done."

"Served a purpose," I told him. "You eliminated his future, and you still have yours."

EPILOGUE

I suppose that on every level of human endeavor there is the same sense of disappointment at the end. Having found and followed the tortuous path to the peak, considered to be one during the thrashing about in the thickets below, you find that it is no vantage point at all. Simply another boulder-strewn enclave, and hardly empyrean. If there had been bright bars of sunlight along the way, well and good, that was some satisfaction. But you are at a distance from triumph or ovation. You are plagued with the need to examine the effort, and even more distressing, to weigh the outcome.

So it was with Berdichevsky returning, picked up and flown in so few hours from admirable accomplishment to an empty and unpleasing future.

I told him that he had set a portion of injustice to rights, an action that very few would have even attempted. There was no question of convincing him. It wouldn't have mattered if a whole plenum had agreed unanimously. Also, I had other preoccupations. There was my own niche to reclaim, and that was a priority. I put him up again, he having made no other plans but to take himself with me, but he moved and behaved like an automaton. For me the clocks still ran and calendar pages moved. Not for him. For the two weeks before Christmas, there were only casual and brief contacts between us while I established myself once more at Scott's in the middle of the annual madness.

No one had time for more than a nod of recognition. I was a scrimshanker who had taken himself out of the line of fire when disasters were apparent on every hand. I, who was one of the architects of the castle. I managed it well, for nothing had changed. Tactics and solutions were forever the same. Longer hours, bellowing and pleading on the phone, promises, winning explanations, humility, and above all the knowledge of the system, the memory of whom to push and where to call for help and favors owed. The clamor diminished, the figures for the year met projections and even surpassed them in some categories. All was well, and by the middle of January there was time for consideration, reflection, and Berdichevsky.

He had kept his distance unbidden. To mark this he had organized separate supply shelves for himself in the refrigerator, the cupboards, and even the bar. He stocked his own quarter pound of butter and quart of milk, cans of beef stew, corned beef hash, spaghetti, some pints of whiskey. Seeing this, I thought I ought to address it; lightly, if possible.

"What are you doing," I asked him, "making a statement about the accommodations?"

"I owe enough already," he said. "It weighs on me. Like the other details."

"A pint of Four Roses doesn't make much of a dent. In your obligations, I mean."

"I'm aware of it. It's symbolic. For the moment that's the way it must be. Maybe I'll do more someday."

"You don't owe me anything. That's it. You owe something to the others, though. And yourself. You can start by making an accounting and moving on with your life."

"I've thought about it." Grimly. "I'm walking the floor over it."

I knew that much. I had heard him in the late hours, hectoring himself aloud as he paced.

"It's time you came to some conclusion. For better or worse, it is over."

"Exactly so," he said quietly. "Exactly so. And I don't see anything ahead of me that will ever have much meaning."

I shrugged.

"Then you will have to come down with the rest of us. To another level. Where most of us live. What you found after all those painful efforts was no monstrous evil, just a miscellany of commonplace sinners. Except for Hamplemann himself, you probably wouldn't find any of them lower than the Seventh Circle. I figure myself somewhere around the gate with the rest of the indifferent.

"How about joining me in a little gluttony tonight. Maybe your diet causes depression."

Heavy going. I took him to the Homestead, far to the west side on Fourteenth Street, a neighborhood dreary enough to match his mood and outlook, where the food was as heavy as the atmosphere all around. Shuttered warehouses, a scatter of decrepit hotels that had once provided small comfort to sailors whose ships were berthed at the ramshackle piers down here, far from the comparatively well maintained ones uptown where Cunard and the French Line docked.

Gloom, but no matter. He ate hugely. An end cut of roast beef that must have run three pounds, an aluminum warmer of O'Brien potatoes with the print of the waiter's thumb pressed into them.

I waxed philosophical, reasonable, since compared to him I was on an eminence and also my third martini. That is a necessity when offering advice or trying to move a personality like this one out of his own shadowed land.

"Listen," I said, "you have convictions and they aren't superficial ones. You don't have to be told what's worthwhile and what isn't. You'll find a place for yourself again."

Hopefully outside my ken.

"You've had some satisfactions, and there will be others. Have you been in touch with Gruenbaum at all?"

"What for?"

"He backed you. He and his wife, and their friends. You ought to tell him what happened. Some of it, anyhow. The good part. They deserve that much consideration.

"Also the 855th. You ought to give them a report. You could

even reopen that benighted office and help claimants. Make a commitment. There must be thousands who have no idea how to get compensated."

"That's over with since the Israeli government made the settlement. And there's another claims office right here. A real one, with a staff and procedures."

As adviser, I wasn't deterred.

"Why not work with them? They'd probably love to have you. You have all the practical knowledge."

A grunt. Then a strange smile. He settled back in his chair, replete certainly, and reflective.

"I could do with a brandy," he said. "For old times' sake.

"Don't think for a minute that I don't appreciate your efforts. Some self-interest there too, but I know you wish me well. Someplace else, no doubt, but well.

"I have an idea that the best view people can have of me is my back. Over time that seems to be proved out. It occurs to me that I am as much a displaced person here and now as those we saw ten years ago were then. At this point most of them have been absorbed somewhere or other. But not me.

"I wonder why that should be so since at best I am what is called a secondary source and no eyewitness, yet I am a casualty of those times. Another victim."

There was no indication of self-pity in what he was saying. He was stating fact, quite calmly and reasonably, as if noting the passing of an acquaintance.

"Not as important an event as I imagined it would be once."

He grinned, suddenly.

"You won't believe it, I know, but there was a time when I was a comparatively happy man. Didn't have much money or accomplishment, but I had won a place for myself. The day I got my appointment as instructor, I shook my own hand. And in my classes, I was very winning. I could establish that we were all in the process of learning together.

"An old method of instruction, but very effective for the most part. The best students make good use of that latitude, you see, so they are not overwhelmed by authority or position or experience, age. All to the good, but we know that the approach was at odds with the times. Probably at any time.

"Looking back, I don't think I was as secure as I thought I was. When I went into the army, my department head offered a handshake, but no promises. Another illusion, self-generated by the would-be-one-day Professor Berdichevsky. Just as well. Knowing what I did, having seen how feeble a hold principle has on behavior, the only history I could have taught with any zeal is the history of darkness. What a syllabus. Long, involved, bloody, and common. Unfortunately also fascinating. Far more than the lives of the saints."

"I don't think I'd take the course," I said. "In fact, it would be better to suppress it or restrict entry to iconoclasts and misfits. And I'm proof that it would have no lasting effect. It hasn't had on me, and you've been instructing me one-on-one for all these years."

He smiled, slyly.

"Don't be too sure. Some of what we've been through together was far beyond the dramas you're acting in nowadays. I'm as familiar with your scenes as you are with mine. However it happened, you were raised up from your negligible past where you were an apprentice in legal thievery. You came from your sleazy youthful adventures to a rare place. So did we all. We had an association with the greatness of others. Those artists were our betters. That will be increasingly important to you, believe it. I tell you this like a prophet who knows more than he can transfer into his own time. How sad it is that it had to come about in such an upheaval that cost so much in human life.

"That's what can't ever be reconciled, accident and circumstance. There's never a proper reckoning. Or for that matter a good time for a parting. Which is tomorrow. A good feed. Thanks."

As good as his word. When I came home the next night he was gone, having neatened up the last traces of his stay. Not so tidily as I do, but the effort was apparent. He left his battered ammo box and a copy of the Hamplemann inventory on the bureau in my bedroom.

Yet another trace of his passage, I realized, recalling the others: that battered bus, *Grauhund*; the corpses interred until Judgment Day in a classic of fortification; a memorial plaque to dead comrades who were casualties well beyond the day of battle; a consignment of artistic works to be celebrated or disparaged according to the authorities in later times.

Together with his comments about me. Deserved, but a bit more kindness would have been warranted. Still, at my age, I was not inclined to make any assessment of my own insignificance.

The box sat there. I did not dwell on it or its implications, but I did sit down at my desk one night and prepare a message to the men of the 855th. In the Pattison style.

Now hear this! Your Committee has decided that there will be no more reunions of the old 855th. Some of the Wives must feel that the first one was too many. Apologies for the shabby treatment they had in NY with no hotel rooms and no entertainment as promised. Thanks to Mrs. Eva Silberglitt and her uncle Al Deutsch for coming to the rescue. Your Committee has reimbursed them for their out-of-pocket expenses. It also gave a donation to the International Red Cross for their much-needed assistance after the untimely death of our former company clerk, William Pattison.

Your Committee wants to thank all participants for their Courage and cooperation in an unexpectedly difficult experience. Just like it says on your discharge papers, you gave "Honest and Faithful Service" once again.

Protean, I suppose, but perhaps Berdichevsky and Proudfoot, and a couple of the others, would be amused. Who among us fits his own image?